CONCLUSION OF
THE MEMOIRS OF
MISS SIDNEY BIDULPH

broadview editions
series editor: L.W. Conolly

CONCLUSION OF THE MEMOIRS OF MISS SIDNEY BIDULPH

Frances Sheridan

edited by
Nicole Garret and Heidi Hutner
with an Introduction by Nicole Garret

broadview editions

Library and Archives Canada Cataloguing in Publication

Sheridan, Frances Chamberlaine, 1724-1766, author
   Conclusion of the memoirs of Miss Sidney Bidulph / Frances Sheridan ; edited by Nicole Garret and Heidi Hutner.

Sequel to: The memoirs of Miss Sidney Bidulph.
Originally published: Dublin : Printed for G. Faulkner, 1767.
Includes bibliographical references.
ISBN 978-1-55481-026-0 (pbk.)

   I. Garret, Nicole, editor   II. Hutner, Heidi, editor   III. Title.

PR3679.S5C65 2013   823'.6   C2013-905360-3

Broadview Editions
The Broadview Editions series represents the ever-changing canon of literature in English by bringing together texts long regarded as classics with valuable lesser-known works.

Advisory editor for this volume: Juliet Sutcliffe

Broadview Press is an independent, international publishing house, incorporated in 1985.

We welcome comments and suggestions regarding any aspect of our publications—please feel free to contact us at the addresses below or at broadview@broadviewpress.com.

North America
Post Office Box 1243, Peterborough, Ontario, Canada K9J 7H5
2215 Kenmore Avenue, Buffalo, NY, USA 14207
Tel: (705) 743-8990; Fax: (705) 743-8353
email: customerservice@broadviewpress.com

UK, Europe, Central Asia, Middle East, Africa, India, and Southeast Asia
Eurospan Group, 3 Henrietta St., London WC2E 8LU, United Kingdom
Tel: 44 (0) 1767 604972; Fax: 44 (0) 1767 601640
email: eurospan@turpin-distribution.com

Australia and New Zealand
NewSouth Books
c/o TL Distribution, 15-23 Helles Ave., Moorebank, NSW, Australia 2170
Tel: (02) 8778 9999; Fax: (02) 8778 9944
email: orders@tldistribution.com.au

www.broadviewpress.com

This book is printed on paper containing 100% post-consumer fibre.

Typesetting and assembly: True to Type Inc., Claremont, Canada.

PRINTED IN CANADA

Contents

Acknowledgements

The editors would like to thank the people whose support and collaboration have made this edition possible, including all of the wonderful students and colleagues at Stony Brook who are working in the eighteenth century. Leanne Warshauer, Lisa Makros, and Elana Kurshan were of great help in typing and compiling the materials for the edition and Kimberly Cox and Margaret Kennedy were tireless with their assistance with the introduction. We are especially thankful to Ula Klein for her help at many stages of the project from start to finish. And, of course, we acknowledge our tremendous debt to Marjorie Mather, Leonard Conolly, and the editorial staff at Broadview Press, whose commitment to recovering the work of eighteenth-century women writers has opened new avenues to researchers and teachers working in the period. Finally, we are thankful for the support of our families, especially Olivia Sydney Hutner Fine, Keith Garret, and Michael Sidney Garret. Most devotedly, this edition is dedicated to Amelia J. Garret, beloved and deeply missed daughter and sister.

Introduction

Published five years after the first three volumes of the story of Sidney Bidulph, *Conclusion of The Memoirs of Miss Sidney Bidulph*[1] is a conclusive sequel: it concludes the title character's story, her life, and Frances Sheridan's response to her critics; as her last novel it concludes Sheridan's part in establishing the terms of the discourse in which she participated at an early, formative moment. The *Conclusion* engages in new and more poignant ways with many of the debates about marriage, filial duty, education, and poetic justice within which sentimental and epistolary fiction negotiates the role of women in the mid-eighteenth century.

Though it has not been published since the 1790s, the *Conclusion* is an important text for the study of Sheridan and her school, and in critical discussions of sentimental and epistolary fiction. In many ways it benefits from Sheridan's development as a novelist and a comedic playwright in the five years between *Memoirs* and the *Conclusion*: her characters are unique and more various, they are anchored more solidly in place and time, and their individual minds, especially those of the villains, more subtly revealed. With the *Conclusion*, Sheridan furthers and refines the ideology of her oeuvre by pursuing her fictional daughters[2] into motherhood, and by letting ancient struggles continue to unfold over generations. In this book about daughters, mothers, and grandmothers, Sheridan gives her "series of fatal events"[3] far-reaching consequences.

Frances Sheridan was born the youngest of four children to Philip Chamberlaine and Anastasia Whyte Chamberlaine in Dublin in 1724. Most of what is known of her comes from a biography by her granddaughter Alicia Lefanu,[4] published in 1824, but there have been numerous minor biographies over the centuries. Frances produced her earliest works despite the restric-

---

1 Hereafter I generally refer to the two novels as *Memoirs* and *Conclusion*.
2 Sheridan often referred to her writings as her "children" in her correspondence.
3 Sir George uses this phrase in *Memoirs*. See Frances Sheridan, *Memoirs of Miss Sidney Bidulph* (1761), ed. Heidi Hutner and Nicole Garret (Peterborough, ON: Broadview, 2011) 489.
4 Alicia Lefanu, *Memoirs of the Life and Writings of Mrs. Frances Sheridan: With Remarks Upon a Late Life of the Right Hon. R.B. Sheridan* (London: G. and W.B. Whittaker, 1824).

tions put on her by her father, an Anglo-Irish clergyman with the Episcopal Church of Ireland, who believed that writing was "superfluous in the education of a female."[1] As his housekeeper, Frances had access to paper meant for housekeeping accounts and, with her typical economy, used however much she could to write a romance, *Eugenia and Adelaide*, at the age of fifteen. Years later she showed the manuscript to Samuel Richardson, author of *Pamela* (1740) and *Clarissa* (1748), who encouraged her to publish it, and to write "a work of higher importance and greater length" (Lefanu 87); however, *Eugenia and Adelaide* was not published until 1791. According to Lefanu, Frances wrote poetry and several "successful" sermons. Of her poetry what remains is a later work, "Ode to Patience,"[2] and "The Owls," a poem in defense of her future husband in what is known as the Cato affair.[3] Thomas Sheridan, the young actor and theatre manager at the Theatre Royal, Smock Alley, Dublin, had refused to play the title role in Joseph Addison's *Cato* due to a missing costume, which he believed was purposely removed in furtherance of a personal vendetta. When Theophilus Cibber offered to play the role in Sheridan's stead, it sparked a public argument. Parts of this argument, and Frances' poem, appear in a pamphlet, *Cibber and Sheridan* (1743).[4]

It is most likely that Thomas Sheridan's sister introduced him to Frances after the publication of "The Owls," and the two married in 1747. By all accounts, the marriage was one of mutual love and respect. Thomas was "the choice of her youth" (Lefanu 74) and she was to him "a bosom friend, another self."[5] But their domestic harmony was besieged by the often-violent controversies that marked Thomas Sheridan's career. As an actor and

---

1 Alicia LeFanu, *Memoirs of the Life and Writings of Mrs. Frances Sheridan*, 2.

2 Printed in Samuel Whyte, *Miscellanea Nova* (London: R. Marchbank, for the editor E.A. Whyte, 1800) 114–16. The ode makes reference to the many difficulties and periods of sadness in the life of the poet.

3 See Robert Hogan and Jerry C. Beasley (eds.), *The Plays of Frances Sheridan* (Delaware: U of Delaware P, 1984) 15, and John Watkins, *Memoir of the Public and Private Life of ... Richard Brinsley Sheridan, with a Particular Account of His Family and Connexions* (London: John Watkins, 1818) 52.

4 See *Cibber and Sheridan: Or, The Dublin Miscellany* (Dublin: Peter Wilson, 1743).

5 These are the words of Thomas Sheridan in a letter to Samuel Whyte on the death of Frances Sheridan. See Whyte 37.

manager at the Theatre Royal, he was subject to the vicissitudes of the public taste and the political controversies that sometimes played themselves out on the stage. The Cato affair of 1743 was only the first of these trials; in 1747, the theatre sustained damages during the Kelly Riots, named after one man who objected to Sheridan's refusal to allow him to visit—and harass—actresses backstage. This was a class battle, with the gentlemen in question accusing Sheridan of denying them certain privileges of station, and Sheridan himself having to attest to his status as a gentleman, although an actor, himself.[1] The theatre was partially destroyed during the *Mahomet* riot in 1754. *Mahomet* is a play by Voltaire that resonated with the inflammatory politics of the age (Hogan and Beasley 16). Rioters attacked the theatre after the actor West Digges charged that Thomas Sheridan had forbidden him to repeat a speech that some of the audience wanted to hear read twice.[2] The *Mahomet* riot damaged the theatre, Thomas' Dublin career, and the family's financial stability for the rest of Frances' life, and also, according to Lefanu, brought on the death of Sackville Sheridan, the child she was carrying at the time who died of convulsions at three months old.[3]

After the *Mahomet* riot, Thomas quit the theatre; the Sheridans and their eldest son, Charles, moved to Henrietta Street in Covent Garden, London. The rest of the children stayed behind with their nurse, eventually to enroll in Samuel Whyte's academy. In England, Thomas acted on shares[4] at Drury Lane and began several writing projects while the Sheridans mixed with luminaries such as Samuel Richardson and Sarah Fielding,[5] and met Elizabeth Pennington, who would become her closest friend. Miss Pennington later died in the arms of Frances, who expressed her deep sadness at this event in "Ode

---

1 See Allardyce Nicoll, *The Garrick Stage: Theatres and Audience in the Eighteenth Century* (Athens, Georgia: U of Georgia P, 1980) 91.
2 See Lefanu 67 and Hogan and Beasley 15.
3 See Lefanu 67 and Hogan and Beasley 17. As the story goes, Frances was told, incorrectly, that the theatre had burnt to the ground. This shock traumatized her and put her pregnancy at risk.
4 Sheridan was paid a percentage of the profits, rather than per diem.
5 Sarah Fielding (1710–68) novelist and sister of Henry Fielding. Her works include *The Adventures of David Simple* (1744) and *The Governess, or The Little Female Academy* (1749). She also wrote a defense of Richardson's *Clarissa* (1749).

to Patience."[1] Over the next five years, the Sheridans moved several times between London, Windsor, and the Sheridan estate at Quilca, outside Dublin. Letters reveal Frances' fears of isolation and concern for the family's finances. In part to fight the isolation and idleness at Windsor, as well as to ameliorate the family's financial situation, Frances wrote *The Memoirs of Miss Sidney Bidulph*, concealing it for a time from Thomas and, once again, stealing moments from her domestic duties to produce the manuscript. The Sheridans returned to London in 1760, where Frances published *Memoirs* and wrote *The Discovery* and *The Dupe*.

By the time Frances Sheridan began writing the *Conclusion of the Memoirs of Miss Sidney Bidulph* in 1766, she had already known a wide range of the joys and ordeals unique to women who write for the public. Her first novel, of which the present text is the conclusion, was a tremendous success, loved even by those who doubted its exemplary power to teach or encourage virtuous conduct.[2] *Memoirs*, as its anonymous author seemed to be a lady, was judged even more skillfully executed and affecting than those sentimental novels by her "brother novelists"[3] and for that it was lauded by its readers, including Samuel Johnson and James Boswell.[4] Following its critical success, Sheridan wrote a comedy, *The Discovery*, which ran for seventeen nights in 1763 at the Drury Lane Theatre, Covent Garden, starring her husband, Thomas Sheridan, and David Garrick. Her second play, *The Dupe* (1763), was the last of her works to come out in her lifetime. It failed on the stage, but enjoyed a financial success, earning her a hundred pounds in addition to the copyright. As critics have shown, the possible reasons for the stage failure are numerous, including the apparent "talkiness" of the play, a disagreement with one of the actresses, Kitty Clive, who might have given a less than stellar

---

1 Elizabeth Pennington (1734–59) was a poet and friend of Sheridan and Richardson and is featured in a poem by John Duncombe (1729–86) called *The Feminiad, or Female Genius* (1757). Part of "Ode to Patience" laments Sheridan's loss of Miss Pennington: "When robb'd of what I held most dear, / My hands adorn'd the mournful bier / Of her I lov'd so well; / What, when mute sorrow chain'd my tongue, / As o'er the sable hearse I hung, / Forbade the tide to swell." For Sheridan's sadness at the death of Miss Pennington, see also Lefanu 91.
2 See the reviews in Appendix A in the Broadview edition of *Memoirs*.
3 See *The Monthly Review* (24) 1761 in the Broadview edition of *Memoirs*, 534.
4 See James Boswell, *Life of Johnson* (Oxford: Horace Hart, 1904) 259–60.

performance because of her dislike of Thomas Sheridan, and the subject matter being altogether too risqué for the stage, and, in particular, for a woman writer.[1] *The Dupe* presents characters whose romantic escapades fall outside the bounds of virtuous middle-class marriage, and they contrive to hide their affairs and embroil others in their misconduct. Regardless of whether *The Dupe* suffered from personal vendetta or from a subject matter unfit for a woman writer, what is certain is that criticism of the work was based in large part on who Frances Sheridan was rather than how well she wrote.[2] Her final three works were written at Blois, France, where the Sheridans moved to escape creditors in 1766 and where they both appear to have worked at a breakneck pace to raise money. Here she wrote the unproduced, unfinished comedy, *A Journey to Bath*; an oriental tale, *Nourjahad*; and the *Conclusion of the Memoirs of Miss Sidney Bidulph*. *Nourjahad* and *Conclusion* were both published posthumously in 1767. Beloved by all who knew her, and published and republished for decades after her death in 1766, Frances Sheridan, as a virtuous and industrious wife, as the matriarch of one of the most prolific literary families, as the mother of Richard Brinsley Sheridan,[3] and as a woman writer, has remained a subject of fascination for over two centuries.

The Memoirs of Miss Sidney Bidulph is typically read and critiqued without serious consideration of the final two volumes, the *Conclusion*, which are published here for the first time since the eighteenth century. One notable exception to this rule is John C. Traver's comprehensive study of both parts, wherein he notes that they were frequently published together until 1796.[4] Traver's work indicates that the *Conclusion* is indispensible to *Memoirs* in

---

1 For the critical response to *The Dupe*, see Hogan and Beasley 25. For a feminist analysis of Sheridan's critics of *The Dupe*, see Elizabeth Kuti, "Rewriting Frances Sheridan," *Eighteenth-Century Ireland/Iris an dá chultúr* (1996): 120–28, esp. 125. For the antagonism between Thomas Sheridan and Kitty Clive, see Lefanu 235–36. For the success of the printed play, see Whyte 118.
2 Reviews of the play criticized it for indelicacy and vulgarity unbecoming a woman. See Kuti 120–28.
3 Richard Brinsley Sheridan (1751–1816) was the eighteenth century's most celebrated playwright. His works include *The Rivals* (1775) and *The School for Scandal* (1777).
4 See John C. Traver, "The Inconclusive Memoirs of Miss Sidney Bidulph: Problems of Poetic Justice, Closure, and Gender," *Eighteenth Century Fiction*, 20.1 (Fall 2007): 35–60, esp. 36.

developing its main themes. To be sure, in its turn, the *Conclusion* may be enjoyed on its own as the masterwork of a writer who has clearly gained some ground as a stylist and a consummate purveyor of sentimentality.

In *Memoirs*, Sidney is engaged to Orlando Faulkland, a man whose personal merits join with family approval to endear him to her for the rest of the novel. When it is found that he has fathered a child with another woman, Miss Burchell, whom he refuses to marry, Sidney's mother, Lady Bidulph, breaks off Sidney's engagement and marries her hastily to a Mr. Arnold. Though she will not admit it, Sidney is heartbroken, and her brother, Sir George, estranges himself out of anger at his mother and sister. Mr. Arnold turns out to be a philanderer who wastes his fortune on a widow, Mrs. Gerrarde, who was also instrumental in Miss Burchell's seduction of Faulkland. Arnold ruins Sidney and her jointure[1] and separates her from her children on account of his suspecting that she is having an affair with Faulkland. By the time Arnold is disabused of this notion through the heroic contrivances of Faulkland, it is too late; Arnold repents but dies shortly after, as does Lady Bidulph. Rejecting again the advances of Faulkland, whom she enjoins to marry the false Miss Burchell, Sidney is left in very poor conditions until her cousin, Ned Warner, returns from the West Indies in search of an heir to his fortune. Warner dispenses his riches on Sidney, who reunites with her brother and lives happily bestowing charity on the poor until the arrival of Faulkland once again. Believing he has accidentally killed his cheating wife, Faulkland returns to England. Sir George and Ned Warner convince Sidney to marry Faulkland at last and abscond with him to Holland, hoping to avoid the murder charges that would inevitably find him if he remains in Britain. But it is not to be: Mrs. Faulkand, it turns out, is very much alive, and Faulkland, destroyed by this final blow, dies in misery.

The *Conclusion* takes up the story eight years later. Like *Memoirs*, the premise of the *Conclusion* is that an unnamed editor, a male persona and a "man of feeling" himself, has collected letters that illustrate the rapid deterioration of Sidney's familial bliss at her estate in Oxfordshire, called Woodberry. Sidney lives with her two daughters and her adopted son, Orlando Falkland[2]

---

1 Jointure is part of the marriage settlement in which property is held in tail for the wife in the event of her widowhood.

2 Sheridan changes the spelling of Faulkland to Falkland in the *Conclusion*. Here, Faulkland is used in discussion of *Memoirs* and Falkland in discussion of the *Conclusion*.

Jr., and plans are in the works to send Falkland to Oxford and the Miss Arnolds to London; thus a central concern of the novel is the effectiveness of their preparation for their first separation from parental guidance and oversight. Most of the letters that make up the *Conclusion* are written between the two villains, Sophia and Sir Edward Audley, who pose as friends of the Woodberry children, but who are actually conspiring to marry the dissolute Sir Edward to one of the Arnold sisters, each of whom is in possession of twenty thousand pounds. What ensues is a complex story of forbidden love triangles and betrayals.

Miss Sidney Bidulph as Sentimental Fiction

Memoirs and the *Conclusion* are both sentimental fiction and novels of conduct; they take seriously though not uncritically the obligations of filial piety, subordinate domesticity, and chaste virtue exacted by arbitrary codes of conduct that serve patriarchal power. The conduct tradition dictates that women are to be cheerful and complaisant even under the worst treatment from those who exact their obedience, to gain admiration through chastity, and affection through gratitude and self-denial. They are understood to be less faithful in love and weaker in mind than their male counterparts, yet as husbands these men demand constancy of affection and evenness of temper from wives. This is an often contradictory and oppressive code of behavior that is sometimes rewarded by marital bliss (according to conduct manual authors such as the Marquis of Halifax, Wetenhall Wilkes, and John Gregory) or ease of conscience, solace in the knowledge that one has done right in the eyes of God (as in the writings of Mary Astell and Mary Wollstonecraft). Sidney, as a sentimental heroine of conduct fiction, must experience personal catastrophes but not seem to feel them.

The aim of sentimental fiction is to exact pity from the reader, either by distressing a virtuous heroine, or by depicting her reaction to the distress of others.[1] *Sidney Bidulph* includes both,

---

1　See Patricia Meyer Spacks, *Novel Beginnings: Experiments in Eighteenth-Century English Fiction* (New Haven: Yale UP, 2006) 127. According to Spacks, women's novels differ from men's in that they typically posit the main character as the pathetic figure whereas men's novels, such as Henry Mackenzie's *The Man of Feeling* (1771), often depict the hero's response to others' suffering. See Patricia Meyer Spacks, "Oscillations of Sensibility," *New Literary History*, 25.3 (Summer 1994): 505–20, esp. 505.

engaging us to feel the misery that Sidney represses in herself, as well as featuring the suffering of other characters, less fortunate than Sidney, who are often unable to maintain their integrity in the eyes of the world. In *Memoirs*, Sidney's adherence to the system of self-repression, passivity, and unwavering obedience to parental or patriarchal power produces the affecting crises of the sentimental novel. As Patricia Meyer Spacks argues, Sidney is a paragon of conventional virtue, but the result of this virtue is a succession of negative consequences effected by Sidney's refusal to rely on her own judgement, always conceding to the hasty and often wrongheaded judgement of Lady Bidulph instead.[1] According to Spacks, "Sidney's compliant silence, the conspicuous sign of her refusal of overt agency, results mainly in unhappiness" (Spacks, "Oscillations" 509). Thus *Memoirs*, like the *Conclusion* after it, defies the claims of conduct literature to lead to any kind of worldly happiness besides a kind of self-satisfaction, a clear conscience that one has conformed as far as possible to standards that are not always accessible nor serviceable.

Of course, in the story of Sidney Bidulph Sheridan rejects this worldly serviceability, what we should call poetic justice, emphasizing over and over again that the reward for Sidney's flawless conduct will be heavenly, not worldly. As the editor says at the beginning of the *Conclusion*:

> [T]he only reflection that could enable him to pursue with any alacrity the thread of this affecting story, was, that the principal person concerned in it, is long since at peace, and in possession of the rewards which were denied to her virtue and her sufferings here (43).

Poetic justice had been a staple of narrative since Sir Philip Sidney's *Defense of Poesy* (1579) and Sheridan's eschewal of it speaks to contemporary debates about realism and the function of the novel to teach virtue. The suffering of the ideal woman is meant to inspire readers not only with sensitivity to humanity, but a love of virtue in themselves. But whether virtuous conduct was encouraged in a story in which it went unrewarded, and where the goodness of the heroine defies credibility, was a question of great import.[2] Samuel Richardson, being himself charged

---

1 Spacks, *Novel Beginnings* 152.
2 Another important question was whether there was more edification in a character drawn from nature, like Henry Fielding's Tom Jones, than in an idealized portrait like that of Sheridan's Sidney. For more on the

with an irresponsible neglect of poetic justice in *Clarissa* (1747), argued that he had in fact conformed to ideas of poetic justice by making it clear that his heroine had been redeemed and rewarded in the afterlife.[1] In his postscript to the novel, Richardson says,

> [the present age] seems to expect from the poets and dramatic writers (that is to say, from the authors of works of invention) that they should make it one of their principal rules, to propagate another sort of dispensation, under the name of *poetical justice*, than that with which God by Revelations teaches us he has thought fit to exercise mankind; whom, placing here only in a state of *probation*,[2] he hath so intermingled good and evil as to necessitate them to look forward for a more equal distribution of both.
>
> The history, or rather the dramatic narrative of Clarissa, is formed on this religious plan; and is therefore well justified in deferring to extricate suffering virtue till it meets with the completion of its reward (1495).

Sheridan thus follows the example of Richardson, to whom she dedicated the story of Sidney Bidulph, without, it should be noted, any mention of *Pamela: or, Virtue Rewarded* (1741), whose heroine *is* rewarded for her virtue.[3]

This peculiarly religious variety of poetic justice, which the *Conclusion* also adopts, is not without its problems. For starters, eighteenth-century critics doubted its ability to inspire virtuous conduct.[4] As John C. Traver argues, the miseries that befall Sidney as a result of her passive obedience to her mother seem to

---

terms of this debate, see Candace Ward's introduction to *The Governess; Or, The Little Female Academy* by Sarah Fielding (Peterborough, ON: Broadview, 2005) 7–36, esp. 17–19. For more on poetic justice, which refers to the rewarding of good characters and the punishment of villains, see also Clara Reeve, *The Progress of Romance*, vol. 2 (Colchester: Keymer, 1785).

1 See Samuel Richardson's Postscript to *Clarissa* (1747), ed. Angus Ross (New York: Penguin, 1985) 1494–99.

2 Italics original.

3 See also Richardson on poetic justice in *Clarissa* in *The Correspondence of Samuel Richardson* (1804), Volume 4 (New York: AMS Press, 1966) 187, 225.

4 See these reviews in the appendices in the Broadview edition of *Memoirs*.

validate the male perspective, expressed by Sir George, that providential activity, rather than resignation to the activities of Providence, is the one thing needful to achieve happiness.[1] In other words Sir George asserts that Sidney should be mistress of her own fate. It is easy to see how in *Memoirs* a speedy marriage to the elder Faulkland, rakish as he may well be, would have precluded the suffering inflicted on Sidney by jealousy and poverty. Secondly, as Patricia Meyer Spacks says, Sidney blames Providence for her suffering, but Sir George blames Sidney herself. Additionally, Sidney's implicit trust in Providence "gives [the reader] tacit permission to indulge in vicarious suffering without worrying about any need for change in the order of things" (Spacks, *Novel Beginnings* 150), inspiring a sort of complacence in and about the patriarchal order. The novel also raises serious questions about maternal authority: the altar upon which Sidney sacrifices herself and her love for Faulkland is not built of patriarchal but matriarchal authority. As Spacks points out, the two towering maternal figures in *Memoirs*, Lady Bidulph and her friend Lady Grimstead, are bad examples.[2] Their behavior renders the maternal perspective, which Sheridan is apt to privilege in her other works, very unreliable.[3]

Some of these problems are resolved in the *Conclusion*,[4] and some new ones are created. In the intervening years between *Memoirs* and its *Conclusion*, Sidney has adopted Faulkland's son, who has been disinherited by his father's family because of his illegitimate birth. Sidney raises Orlando and her daughters, Dorothea and Cecilia, as siblings, who are now young adults. Sheridan persists in her adherence to the Richardsonian brand of poetic justice, this time making sure to discredit the alternative possibility that Sidney's suffering is of her own creation. Eight years have passed since Faulkland's death. Sidney is now the mother in question, and she consciously avoids many of the mistakes that we lay at Lady Bidulph's feet, and all of the mistakes of Lady Grimstead. Our faith in mothers is somewhat restored.

---

1 See Traver 36–37.
2 See Spacks, *Novel Beginnings* 146.
3 Frances Sheridan's comedies feature maternal figures who evade patriarchal efforts to silence them and bring about equitable resolutions to her marriage plots. See, for example, *The Discovery* and *The Dupe*.
4 Traver argues that the *Conclusion* was written specifically with such resolution in mind.

Motherhood and Maternal Inheritance

In the 1760s women's novels were characterized by what Susan Greenfield and Ruth Perry have identified as a preoccupation with the role of mothers, the decline of maternal inheritance (Perry 7), and the "growing cultural obsession with motherly duty and influence"(Greenfield 13). The mother–daughter plot, or the plot at the center of which is an absent mother's legacy to her daughter, rises to prominence at mid-century, just around the time of the *Conclusion*. In Sheridan's Sidney, we have a mother who is not dead, but frequently absent; she is away consoling Lady V— on the death of Lord V—, and when she returns home to Woodberry, her daughters are in London. In her absence her daughters get into trouble, which dramatizes the effects of their absent mother's hereditary and educational influence upon them. Sidney's authority over them is a kind of cult of love that sustains them in their conduct, albeit only inconsistently. Her storied filial duty to her mother serves as a check to their behavior and, para-doxically, as a cautionary tale of what happens when such duty is taken too far.

As heredity and education work against each other for con-structive dominance, the central question in the novel is whether maternal or paternal traits will have more influence on the respective characters and destinies of her children. Both of Sidney's daughters have fallen in love with Orlando, a forbidden object[1] whose very existence pits true love against duty and belies the possibility of marital bliss as a reward for virtue that is prom-ised by conduct literature. As was the case for Sidney, it is not the fate of Dorothea or Cecilia to be able to reconcile duty with love. Dorothea says, "O fye, fye upon such a heart, that never gave me warning of my danger till it was past remedy" (67), feeling that she, very much like her father in his love for Mrs. Gerrarde, was insensibly led to misery. Although Dorothea is goaded to pursue this love by an interested party, Cecilia certainly is not, thus lending credibility to Sidney's belief "that there was a fatality attended all her [Sidney's] actions, and that her best designs have been perverted into evil" (89). In other words, Orlando is fated

---

1 Kathleen M. Oliver suggests that this is a further punishment for the elder Faulkland's initial sin: his son's eventual disgrace and partial redemption indicate that Faulkland's trials cannot end until after Sidney's death. See Kathleen M. Oliver, "Frances Sheridan's Faulkland, the Silenced, Emasculated, Ideal Male," *Studies in English Literature, 1500–1900*, 43.3 (Summer 2003): 464.

to be the undoing of Sidney's daughters, just as Sidney was the ruination of Faulkland. The fatalism at work in this new love triangle, and Sidney's conventionally passive yet ultimately effective responses to it, contradict conventional understanding of maternal failure, even as they inscribe other forms. Sidney's only mistake here is the charitable act of caring for young Orlando, an act that his father's dying wish compels.

Sidney is also, as was her mother, a terrible judge of character, embracing Lady Audley as an acquaintance and consenting to the friendship between their children. Sophia Audley, who plants the seeds of disobedience in Dorothea, says, "Is it not strange that Mrs. Arnold, so prudent, so cautious, and so penetrating as she seems to be, should so widely have mistaken the character and designs of a certain friend of ours?" (75-76). Indeed, Mrs. Arnold mistakes the characters of both Sophia and Lady Audley, though not of Sir Edward, whom she knows to be a rake.

Sidney thus partially fails to detect the true character of her children's friends, but the maternal "indulgence" with which she treats her daughters, and which is cursed in nearly every educational treatise of the period, is ultimately conducive to a gratitude that compels obedience. Motherhood was a particularly fraught concept in the eighteenth century,[1] as some sought to subordinate the duty of mother to that of wife, and others, like John Locke, and Lovelace, the villain of Richardson's *Clarissa*, blamed maternal indulgence for nearly every adult defect imaginable.[2] In his *Thoughts Concerning Education* (1693) Locke positions himself against indulgent mothers who, he expects, will balk at his prescriptions as being "too hard." He warns that "the little, almost insensible impressions on our tender infancies have very important and lasting consequences," (2) and since it is in infancy that mothers have the greatest influence over their children, he implicitly enjoins fathers to intervene lest their "children's constitutions are either spoiled, or at least harm'd, by cockering[3] and tender-

---

1 See Susan Greenfield, *Mothering Daughters: Novels and the Politics of Family Romance, Frances Burney to Jane Austen* (Detroit: Wayne State UP, 2002); Toni Bowers, *The Politics of Motherhood: British Writing and Culture, 1680–1760* (Cambridge: Cambridge UP, 1996).
2 See T.G.A. Nelson, *Children, Parents, and the Rise of the Novel* (Newark: U of Delaware P, 1995) 87. See also Stone 248 and Perry 23.
3 Indulging or pampering.

ness"(3).[1] Maternity and indulgence, in Lockean theory, are as inextricable as paternity and reason.

In *Memoirs*, Lady Bidulph's conduct is more in line with what Elizabeth Kowaleski-Wallace has termed "the new patriarchy": a program of guilt and manipulation, a sort of cult of love that comes to replace authoritarian patriarchy.[2] That Lady Bidulph assumes this paternal role, and that she also refuses a morality that absolves men of responsibility for their indiscretions, leaves her open to charges of unfeminine tyranny or, in the words of the novel, "rigidity." She necessarily is both female and father, caught between Scylla and Charybdis. In her turn, Sidney tries to avoid the trap her mother has fallen into, and maintain the appearance of leniency while at the same time compelling perfect obedience.

In keeping with the assumptions of educational literature, Sir George blames Sidney's motherly indulgence for Celia's refusal to marry Lord V—. Sheridan, however, shows Sir George, much like Richardson's Mr. Harlowe in *Clarissa*, to be too heavy-handed in his attempts to compel Cecilia, cultivating her disgust for the man he would have her marry. Sidney employs Sir George as a counterpoint, making him the foe whilst she continues to play the friend, and Sidney's indulgent goodness is what ultimately brings her daughters to capitulate to her will. She says,

> Advice from a mother was always considered by me as a command; yet I do not desire you to regard it in so severe a light. [...] You were always treated with the kindest indulgence, with all reasonable allowances made for the inadvertence of youth [...] I early had my neck bowed to obedience. (120)

Sheridan thus posits naturalized ideas of maternal indulgence and passivity as the distinguishing feature of Sidney's parental conduct. This allows Sidney to conform to conventional ideas of femininity even though she is, as a widow who is lucky enough to

---

1   See John Locke, *Some Thoughts Concerning Education: By John Locke, Esq.* (London: A. and J. Churchill, 1693), 3. See also *The Common Errors in the Education of Children* (London: M. Cooper, 1744). See also Stone 277.

2   See Elizabeth Kowaleski-Wallace, *Their Fathers' Daughters: Hannah More, Maria Edgeworth, and Patriarchal Complicity* (New York: Oxford UP, 1991) 110.

have guardianship over her children,[1] in the position of serving as both mother and father to her children. In the latter role she acts, as Sheridan's maternal figures often do, by proxy:

> I am under a promise to both my children never to urge their acceptance of a man whom they did not like, but my punctilio does not bind you. You are therefore at liberty to use every means (absolute force excepted) to prevail on Cecilia to receive as she ought so advantageous an offer (127).

These lines, written to Sir George, but extending to nearly every other friend and relation of her daughter's, enforce the parental will as far as any father could do. Because this preserves for Sidney both conventional maternity and the love and allegiance of her daughters, it is a maternal success that presents an interesting counterpoint to those arguably "failed" mothers in *Memoirs* and *Clarissa*.

Sheridan's construction of maternity along these lines presents problems for the maternal perspective, however, that are not present in her plays. The mothers in Sheridan's drama succeed by recruiting agents to act for them in the public sphere while they act behind closed doors against male-centered codes of behavior, and succeed in reconstructing the terms of the domestic scheme.[2] By contrast, we can read Sidney as too passive a mother, and while her passivity does not necessarily cause her children's pain, it does finally succeed in obliterating the maternal voice. Sidney works diligently at nothing, relying instead on a passive goodness that, though effective, manages to erase the maternal perspective. The *Conclusion of the Memoirs of Miss Sidney Bidulph* contains relatively few letters from its eponymous heroine. The only way Sidney's authority as a mother can bind her children to obedience is in the form of a sentimental deathbed wish for their happiness and protection: "Will you, my dear Cecilia, will you give your dying mother the consolation to think that she leaves her child under the protection of that worthy lord?" (293). Thus Sidney achieves by expiring helplessly what

---

1 Stone 222.

2 Spacks argues similarly in "Oscillations of Sensibility": "If Sidney causes her own suffering, she does so by being too good, in the most orthodox female fashion. Unlike Lady Medway [in *The Discovery*], her goodness carries no obvious undertones of rage. (On the other hand, as we shall see, Sidney resembles her dramatic successor in finally establishing virtue as power.)" (509).

could not be done by force or harassment, but, to be sure, it is not much comfort to the reader.

Nature v. Nurture

The concept of heredity figures in other interesting ways as well. Ned Warner has left each of Sidney's daughters enough money to let her make her own choice in a husband. Therefore the plot of *Conclusion* does not hinge on making an eligible match or fending off the threats of poverty, as it did to a large extent in *Memoirs*. Instead, the central question in the novel is whom each of the children will turn out to be most like, whether mother or father. Each child has at least one parent with a passionate or vicious nature and heredity of character is a system of inheritance in which mothers and fathers take an equal part. Describing the character of Orlando to his sister, Sir Edward explains,

> I have studied Falkland minutely since I have been acquainted with him, and find he is of a very mixed character. The father and the mother pretty equally blended in his composition; but I hope the latter may predominate, else even under *my* prudent guidance and example, he may sneak out of the world without *doing* any thing worthy of remembrance. (83)

Sir Edward describes a character, as he says, "pretty equally blended," which yet shows no sign of his future conduct. His father was honorable, heroic, and steadfast in love; his mother was fickle, scheming, and ingratiating. Because Audley's intentions are dishonorable, he is hoping to manipulate Orlando's nature to make him more like his mother. Orlando, young and inexperienced, is an equal mixture of his "good" and "bad" parent, pulling him in opposite directions and producing a kind of equilibrium in his character that leaves him eminently tractable.[1]

---

1 Orlando might be said to objectify the warning Locke gives in *Thoughts Concerning Education* (1693): "A young Man before he leaves the Shelter of his Father's House, and the Guard of a Tutor, should be fortify'd with Resolution, and made acquainted with Men, to secure his Vertues, lest he should be led into some ruinous Course, or fatal Precipice, before he is sufficiently acquainted with the Dangers of Conversation, and has Steadiness enough not to yield to every Temptation." See Appendix A1, 312-13.

This preoccupation with predicting the behavior of young men has continued from *Memoirs*: in that text Sidney speculates on the elder Faulkland's quick temper and "turn to ridicule" (55) in considering him for a husband, but it is impossible for her to tell that the seemingly retired gentleman musician, Mr. Arnold, would have a penchant for expensive mistresses. In a time when marriage lasts until death, this is much more than idle speculation. What is new in the *Conclusion* is how fully Sheridan embraces theoretical debates of nature versus nurture in the education of young people. According to Lawrence Stone, there were four theories on the nature of the newborn child: the first, based on original sin, was that all children are born wicked and need strict discipline; the second was the Lockean environmentalist view that a child is a *tabula rasa*, whose character is a product of education (and the quality of its "company"); the third view was that a child's character was biologically determined at conception and there is little that subsequent education can do; the fourth, which he calls the utopian view, was that a child is born good and then corrupted by society.[1] Sidney insists on having her children "educated differently [from herself], with all reasonable allowances made for the inadvertence of youth," whereas Sidney has had her "neck bowed early to obedience" (120). Like the Arnold sisters, Falkland has been educated at home under the direction of the Reverend Mr. Price, who has been as solicitous in teaching him virtuous conduct as he has been in preparing him for Oxford. We are thus reintroduced to the family at Woodberry at the moment when we can begin to see whether nature or nurture has had the most impact on them.

For the Woodberry children, this question produces a great deal of anxiety. Orlando's education under Mr. Price does not seem to be enough to counteract the residue of his mother's ill nature. He is, as she was, easily led to vice and proves to be inconstant in his amorous affairs, in action if not in heart. His nature and his education war within him, as Sir Edward says, in the way good and evil conflict Satan in book four of *Paradise Lost*.[2] The Arnold sisters each seem to have assumed the characters of one of their parents, Cecilia showing herself to be more like Sidney in character and in their shared history of true love lost; Dorothea, like the father who favored her, is passionate, melancholy, and possessed of an unregulated heart that leads her insensibly into

---

1 Stone 255.
2 *Conclusion* (213).

unhappiness. Sheridan's emphasis on inherited characteristics furthers the novel's sense of fatality; if they are simply copies of their parents whose natures are determined at birth, Sidney's success or failure as a mother is a moot point, and I do not think that is what we are meant to take from it.

Despite strong evidence that hereditary nature is a powerful indicator of future behavior, the influence of peers is the greatest threat to good nature and well-taught conduct in the *Conclusion*.[1] Sir Edward and Sophia Audley lead the Woodberry children to their crises by suggesting and manipulating their feelings for each other. They begin by bringing to the surface feelings that Orlando and Dorothea have rightly and obediently repressed. As critics have shown, sentimental and amatory fiction calls for the repression of desire and emotion as necessary to domestic serenity.[2] It is what Sidney endeavors to do throughout *Memoirs*, telling herself that she does not love Faulkland and that she wishes only to be obedient to her mother, even after Lady Bidulph's death.[3] As Ruth Perry says, *Memoirs* is "a monument of self-abnegation" (100). The Arnold sisters do not aspire to such lofty heights of self-repression, although Cecilia comes close to suffering as much as her mother has.

In the *Conclusion*, the Audley villains begin by unearthing the forbidden desires of their victims, and finish them off by convincing them of the propriety of indulging repressed feelings, whatever the means and whatever the cost. Though he has good intentions, Orlando is the tool with which Sir Edward manipulates the Arnold sisters. Sophia, whose name evokes thoughts of a worldly wisdom at odds with filial piety, persuades Dorothea that it is right to consider as a lover one who has been treated as

---

1   Indeed, Sheridan seems to subscribe to Locke's view that "company" or the influence of peers could eclipse all in the determination of behavior. Locke says, "Having nam'd *Company*, I am almost ready to throw away my Pen, and trouble you no farther on this Subject: For since that does more than all Precepts, Rules, and Instructions, methinks 'tis almost wholly in vain to make a long Discourse of other Things, and to talk of that almost to no Purpose." See Appendix A1, 311.

2   See Rosalind Ballaster, *Seductive Forms: Women's Amatory Fiction from 1684–1740* (New York: Oxford UP, 1992), and Nancy Armstrong, *Desire and Domestic Fiction: A Political History of the Novel* (New York: Oxford UP, 1987).

3   See Ruth Perry, *Novel Relations: The Transformation of Kinship in English Literature and Culture, 1748–1818* (Cambridge: Cambridge UP, 2004) 100.

a brother, and that disobedience to a parent is no crime compared to disobedience to one's own heart. Dorothea knows better, even as she is led to reveal her most intimate secrets, first to Sophia and then to Orlando: Dorothea says, "but to *me* 'tis the crime of our first parents, 'tis the sin of disobedience" (77). Disobedience, then, is the worst of all sins because it opens the way for all other sins, yet the desire to disobey when once expressed is impossible to recall. This is a strong argument for the corrupting influence of the world on the development of young people.

Indeed, Sheridan makes clear that the Audleys are improperly educated, and thereby dishonorable:

> Miss Audley's education had been ill calculated to inspire her with the principles of virtue. Her early childhood had, by the indolence of a mother, too fond of pleasure, turned over to the care of an ignorant governess of a boarding school. (300)

Sophia Audley's boarding-school education, then, is the antithesis to the at-home education of the Woodberry children and the prescriptions of parental conduct literature, which emphasize close parental involvement. We can extrapolate that Sir Edward was brought up under a similarly ignorant tutor; in defense of his dishonorable conduct, he perverts the meaning of moral stories, which a young man should be taught to interpret in ways that incline him to virtue. Following Locke and others, an anonymous parents' guide called *The Common Errors in the Education of Children and their Consequences* (1744) describes a conventional method of moral education:

> Whenever they read of the lives and Actions of great Men, they should be ask'd their Opinion of such an Action or Saying, and why they take it to be good or bad. The Youth should be taught to descant upon their Actions, and shew wherein they were excelling, and where defective. This will soon give him early Seasonings of Morality.[1]

Instead of seasonings of morality, Sir Edward, much like Richardson's Lovelace, has a tendency to descant wrongly on such moral stories; he is proud to espouse the cause of Satan in

---

1 See *The Common Errors in the Education of Children and Their Consequences* (London: M. Cooper, 1744) 70. See also Eustace Budgell, letter in *The Spectator* (27 March 1712).

Paradise Lost, associates himself with Shakespearean characters at their most debased and desperate moments, and quotes sections of poems that seem to celebrate inconstancy and libertinism. He has an impressionable, if often hesitant, pupil in young Orlando Falkland.

The Woodberry children, at least Orlando and Dorothea, are pulled every which way by nature, education, and corrupting influence. These forces combine to doom Sidney and her children to a continuance of suffering. While the *Conclusion* appears on the surface to espouse the third theory of the child, that education and learned duty are paramount, she shows the influence of friends to be the greatest variable. The difference between the teacher or parent and the acquaintance, in the *Conclusion*, is the latter's capacity to play upon the repressed feelings of the child, thus rendering both nature and nurture almost entirely unpredictable. The warning, found in so many conduct books, to take care in choosing friends resounds in this text.[1]

Marriage and the family

The target of the Audleys scheme is the Arnold fortune, which is actually the fortune Ned Warner bequeathed to Sidney's daughters before the book begins. Thus the maternal inheritance, though also delivered by proxy, takes precedence by compensating for the missing paternal inheritance. The terms of Ned Warner's will are in harmony with Sidney's promise never to impose husbands on unwilling daughters:

> And forasmuch as parents, guardians, and relations, do sometimes from mere caprice, or a greediness of wealth, withhold their consents to marriages on which the happiness of their childrens [sic] lives depends; I do hereby give and bequeath to my two kinswomen Dorathea [sic] and Cecilia Arnold, the sum of twenty thousand pounds each, to be at their own full and free disposal at the age of eighteen years, relying on their prudence and the goodness of their dispositions; to the end that they may not (as their mother was) be compelled through fear to accept of a man they do not like. (200)

The editor cites this provision as an example of Warner's "whimsical" nature, indicating that at the time in which this was set, the

---

1 Some of these conduct books are excerpted in Appendix A of this volume.

concept of a woman pleasing herself in her choice of a husband (or to remain single) was something of a novel concept, but Warner's will looks forward to trends in marital arrangements. Historians of the family show that as the theories of governmental power shifted from patriarchal to contractual, the family, which was ever the central metaphor for government, evolved as well.[1] A social contract theory of marriage in some ways allowed the affectionate and companionate marriage to supersede the patriarchal model, which emphasized the economic, wealth-creating role of marriage. Lawrence Stone identifies a rise in what he calls "affective individualism," which was signaled by radical shifts in the way marriages were contracted, from parents having total power in marriage arrangements to children contracting their own matches, leaving parents the right of veto only.[2] Similarly, Ruth S. Perry identifies a transformation in kinship relations from a consanguineal to conjugal model. Marriage, if it is to accommodate broader notions of individualism, must allow for greater freedom of choice.[3] On the other hand, if not well regulated by external authority and accompanied by financial security, affection alone can lead to great unhappiness, as it does with Mrs. Vere in *Memoirs*.[4]

Before and after 1754, unhappiness in marriage was common, particularly for women, who had no legal rights to property or their children even in widowhood unless appointed guardians by their husbands' wills.[5] Conduct literature legitimizes this subordination as both natural and biblical. Conduct books by the Marquis of Halifax, Wetenhall Wilkes, and John Gregory encouraged women to submit cheerfully to the authority of their husbands, telling them that they were by nature better inclined to be agreeable and subordinate, and that their husbands ruled them with the greater portion of reason endowed to them by God. This

---

1 See Janet Todd, *The Sign of Angellica: Women, Writing and Fiction, 1660–1800* (New York: Columbia UP, 1989); see also Nancy Armstrong, *Desire and Domestic Fiction* (New York: Oxford UP, 1987) 37–39; see also Christine Roulston *Narrating Marriage in Eighteenth-Century England and France* (Burlington, VT: Ashgate Publishing, Ltd., 2010) 15–20.

2 See Stone 183.

3 Mary Astell was the first to point out the hypocrisy in a social contract theory of government that did not extend itself to domestic governance in her treatise. See *Some Reflections upon Marriage* (1700).

4 Mrs. Vere is the daughter of Lady Grimston, who marries without her mother's approval; Lady Grimston's re-appropriation of her daughter's fortune proves disastrous for the young married couple.

5 Stone 222.

was a "harshly oppressive regime offered in the explicit interests of both family and commonwealth" (Jones 60). Birthing children was presented as an explicit duty to the state as well as the family, and women often found themselves torn between their duties as wives and as mothers, neither able to control their own fertility nor make decisions for their offspring. Breastfeeding, for instance, was lauded as the natural right and duty of a mother, but many husbands forbade it, desiring full possession over their wives' bodies and procreative abilities.[1] In *Memoirs*, Sidney herself is separated from her children when her husband suspects her of adultery; upon his death, Mr. Arnold gives Sidney complete authority over her children, but this comes only after she suffers under the yoke of marriage without affection.

The Memoirs of Miss Sidney Bidulph and its *Conclusion*, beginning early in the reign of Queen Anne[2] in 1703 and ending sometime before 1738,[3] looks back on a time before individual choice in marriage was the norm, when clandestine, mercenary marriages of the type Sir Edward attempts to make led many women into marital misery, and before the terms of legal marriage were given clear definition. We see several types of marriage in the *Conclusion*: there is the binding engagement between Orlando and Dorothea; there is the "sham marriage" of Sir Edward and the unfortunate Theodora Williams; there is the attempt to coerce Dorothea into marriage by forced cohabitation with Sir Edward; and then there is the parentally sanctioned wedding between Cecilia and Orlando, which is interrupted with the revelation that he has already pledged himself to her sister. Before 1754, any of these could constitute a legal, lifelong commitment.

Hardwicke's Marriage Act[4] of 1753, named for Phillip Yorke, Earl Hardwicke, was designed to standardize the marriage con-

---

1   Stone 248, 261, 270. See Richardson's *Pamela, Part Two* (1741) wherein Mr. B prohibits Pamela from breastfeeding and orders her to hire a wet nurse instead. This ignores the prescriptions of medical texts that urged women to nurse their own infants. According to some, the refusal to breastfeed was a practice peculiar to the aristocracy (Stone 270).
2   Anne's reign lasted from 1702 to 1714.
3   This is the date that the editor gives for Mrs. Askham's contribution to the story at the end of Volume V. *Memoirs* is set during the reign of Queen Anne.
4   For more on Hardwicke's Marriage Act, see David Lemmings, "Marriage and the Law in the Eighteenth Century: Hardwicke's Marriage Act of 1753," *The Historical Journal* 39.2 (June 1996): 339–60, esp. 343. See also Stone 32–4, 165, 213, 397.

tract. It was ostensibly to protect women from the schemes of libertines, but also very much meant to preserve for the parents their right of veto.[1] Before 1754, when the law was enacted, "clandestine marriages"—marriages without parental consent—were legally binding. Any exchange of vows that was followed by cohabitation or consummation was considered a legal marriage. Only after 1754 were public weddings necessary for the marriage to be legal. Therefore, in the *Conclusion*, Theodora's sham marriage to Sir Edward is legal, even though they had neither license, nor clergyman, nor a church wedding. Theodora, knowing that such marriages are binding, trusts in the honesty of the only witness, who is later revealed to be Sir Edward's dishonest servant.[2] She is legally married, yet unable to claim her title because Sir Edward and his servant regard her as simply a kept mistress. Whereas after the 1753 act against clandestine marriages Theodora would simply have been the ruined woman that Sir Edward considers her to be, in the *Conclusion*, she is a jilted wife. Significantly, Theodora is an anagram of Dorothea: though in different ways and at different times, they are both led by imprudent love to filial disobedience, both find themselves at the mercy of a man who uses his power under the law to act in any way he chooses. Theodora acts legally on her passion; Dorothea, although she remains chaste, acts unlawfully on hers; yet as victims of the machinations of Edward Audley, both of their lives are ruined.

It is precisely because of this uncertainty in the law, and the latitude it provides for manipulation, that emotional restraint is of such great importance. The marriage vows that Dorothea and Orlando utter to one another, because legally binding, signify their permanent, joint unhappiness. But even before the exchange of vows, Dorothea is unhappy from the moment she

---

1   According to David Lemmings, the debates in the House of Commons during 1753 and the passage of the bill signaled "continuing patriarchal and materialist instincts" at odds with the theory of affective individualism propounded by Stone and others (343). Opponents of the bill argued that it was unfair to women because it tightened their tether to parental authority; proponents argued that the bill would protect women from bigamy and the bride-napping that we see in so much literature of this period, including *The Memoirs of Miss Sidney Bidulph*. But ultimately, Lemmings argues, debates about the bill surrounded male power and the privilege men had in being able to make their fortunes by taking rich wives (341).

2   See *Conclusion*, 141.

confesses to herself, and to her untrustworthy friend Sophia, that she has romantic feelings for Orlando, who in his turn acts on jealousy that follows from acknowledging his feelings for Cecilia. Thus, while the cult of suppression and withholding of emotion is ambivalently treated in *Memoirs*,[1] in its *Conclusion*, it is decisively sanctioned.

If Frances Sheridan is making a comment on the recent changes in what constitutes legal marriage, it is that the new law is unfair to people like Theodora, who is without powerful family to protect her from Audley's imposition. Whereas she is given the chance to claim Sir Edward's title by the end of the book, in 1754 she might have had no legal recourse whatsoever. Sidney tells Theodora, who saves Dorothea from a very probable rape at the hands of Audley, that her "virtue" will be "rewarded" (262). This judgement defies the court of public opinion, which often doomed such duped women to infamy on account of their own alleged stupidity. Sheridan seems to assert, like Richardson, that women disgraced by men deserve the pity and charity of their luckier counterparts, and wished for their rehabilitation into society.[2] By doubling Dorothea and Theodora, Sheridan emphasizes that the only thing separating the fallen from the virtuous is the minutiae of the law, and other conspiracies of men. The doubling of Sidney and Miss Burchell in *Memoirs* is similar in that both Sidney and her mother advocate Burchell's restoration to honor and Faulkland's making restitution, taking the fallen woman's side over the man's. But *Memoirs* fails to make clear the point that the difference between the virtuous and corrupted women is circumstantial, because Miss Burchell is, in fact, a villain.

Conclusion

Sidney Bidulph is epistolary fiction, and it is perhaps in this genre that Sheridan has made her most indelible mark. In *Memoirs*, and in the much earlier *Eugenia and Adelaide*, the letters are passed

---

1   About *Memoirs*, Spacks says, "Sheridan both exploits and challenges a commonplace convention of sentimentality. Not all feeling is positive feeling, she reminds us, and not all verbal withholding enforces community"(*Novel* 4). In *Memoirs*, Sidney's silence about her love for Faulkland is arguably the cause of her misery.

2   For Richardson's opinion on this, see for example letters between himself and Lady Bradslaigh in *The Correspondence of Samuel Richardson* (1804), Volume IV (New York: AMS Press, 1966) 212, 236.

between female friends, confidants whose pledge of honesty and full disclosure serves to establish both the premise and the ideal audience for their recorded histories. Epistolary fiction is often psychologically complex and dialogic; it imparts a sense of immediacy to the narrative. But in the *Conclusion*, Sidney and her confidant Cecilia B— receive information second hand, and in turn write about events that they have heard from others after the fact. The letters of the Woodberry children serve rather to occlude or corrupt, than to facilitate communication: they lie, obfuscate, and hide their feelings; they find themselves in situations where no one but their enemies knows the true state of their hearts. The greater portion of the letters is between the Audleys, providing a unique glimpse into the psychology of villainy of the same caliber or greater than Richardson's portrait of Lovelace, and with a concentration that prefigures the construction of villainy in *Les Liaisons Dangereuses*.[1] Sheridan, as I have suggested, was a consummate painter of profligate villains, a talent that did not go unpunished in the reception of her plays.

As I note above (9), the *Conclusion* stopped being published along with *Memoirs* in the late eighteenth century. There are several possible reasons for that. Ruth Perry calls *Memoirs* "a triumph of consanguinity" (403), a triumph of filial piety over love. In both novels, the only stable entity is the family. Love falls apart; friendship disintegrates, but sisterhood and maternal love win out. Whereas in *Memoirs* we are brought to pity for the love lost, in the *Conclusion* there is no such pity, only a crisis averted, a bullet dodged. The younger Falkland, inasmuch as he is beloved by the Arnold sisters, is not the hero his father was, and the reader's vicarious feelings do not stir for him with quite the same passion. We are never tempted to wish him married to one of the Miss Arnolds. Therefore, in *Conclusion*, the victory of the consanguineal family is more complete. This puts Sheridan's novel at odds with a trend that is moving more and more in the direction of rewarding virtuous heroines with true love. Additionally, Sheridan's tenacious embrace of Richardsonian, Christian poetic justice, extended to its logical end in the *Conclusion*, militates against the more popular secular mode of poetic justice advocated by Clara Reeve at the end of the century.[2]

Ultimately, however, it might be Frances Sheridan's legacy that has prevented too much attention being paid to her *Conclu-*

---

1 Choderlos de Laclos, *Les Liaisons Dangereuses* (1782).
2 See Appendix B in the Broadview edition of *Memoirs*.

sion. In her correspondence and in her many celebratory biographies, she is fashioned as a mother and a wife, whose devotion to her family encouraged her to write in order to rescue them from poverty. She has therefore been lauded as a virtuous heroine herself, a defender of female innocence and a model woman writer who produced a model character to serve as example to her sex. The *Conclusion* takes risks that *Memoirs* does not, jeopardizing this picture by showing that Sheridan knew and could represent the most private thoughts of depraved characters, and the grievous failings of decent ones. Therefore, those who want to see her as pure and selfless only will find plenty to recommend her in *Memoirs*, but those who want to know her mind cannot do better than to read her *Conclusion*, too.

Frances Chamberlaine Sheridan: A Brief Chronology

1724 Frances Chamberlaine is born in Dublin, the youngest of
five children. Her mother, Anastasia Whyte Chamberlaine, who was English, dies shortly after Frances is born.
Her father, Phillip Chamberlaine, was a Dublin cleric in
the Church of Ireland and held various titles, including
prebend of Rathmichael in the Diocese of Dublin,
Archdeacon of Glendalough, and Rector of St. Nicholas
Without in Dublin.

1739 Writes *Eugenia and Adelaide*.

1743 Defends Thomas Sheridan (1719–88) for his role in the
Cato affair in a poem, "The Owls." Sheridan is a leading
actor and manager at the Theatre Royal, Smock Alley,
Dublin. His refusal to play the role of Cato because of a
missing costume led to a press battle with Theophilus
Cibber. Frances Chamberlaine's poem appears in a pamphlet called *Cibber and Sheridan*. Frances Chamberlaine is
introduced to Sheridan by his sister.

1747 The Sheridans marry. Frances's brother, Walter Chamberlaine, officiates. The couple divide their time between
Dorset Street in Dublin and Thomas's estate at Quilca.
The theatre sustains damages during the Kelly riots,
named for one of the "Galway gentlemen" who claims
that Thomas Sheridan assaulted him backstage at the
Theatre Royal.

1747 The Sheridans' first child, Thomas, is born. He dies in
1750.

1750 Charles Francis Sheridan is born in July.

1751 Richard Brinsley Sheridan, one the century's most brilliant playwrights, is born in October.

1753 Alicia Sheridan is born in January.

1754 Riots over a politically charged speech in *Mahomet the
Imposter* destroy the interior of the Smock Alley Theatre
in March. Frances Sheridan is told that the theatre has
burnt to the ground, but this is false. During Frances
Sheridan's lifetime, the family never recovers from the
financial losses sustained during the riot. Thomas Sheridan quits the theatre and Dublin, and moves his family to

London in November 1754. They live in Henrietta Street, Covent Garden, and Thomas Sheridan acts at Drury Lane. While in England, the Sheridans become part of a literary circle that includes James Boswell, Samuel Richardson, Catherine Macaulay, Sarah Fielding, and others.

The child Frances is carrying, Sackville, dies from convulsions three months after he is born. This is attributed to Frances's shock during the *Mahomet* riots.

1756 The Sheridans return to Ireland. Letters to Samuel Richardson in 1757 reveal concerns about finances and Frances' isolation at Quilca.

1758 Anne Elizabeth (Betsey) Sheridan is born. The Sheridans return to London. *Eugenia and Adelaide*, which Frances had turned over to Richardson, is rejected for publication, and remains unpublished until 1791, when it is printed without attribution.

1759 The Sheridans move to Windsor, where Frances Sheridan begins writing *The Memoirs of Miss Sidney Bidulph*.

1760 The Sheridans return to London.

1761 *The Memoirs of Miss Sidney Bidulph* is published in two volumes. A three-volume edition comes out later in the year.

1762 Writes *The Discovery*, a comedy, which runs for seventeen nights in February 1763 at Drury Lane. The Abbé Prévost translates *Miss Sidney Bidulph* into French.

1763 Writes *The Dupe*, also a comedy, which runs for only three nights at Drury Lane in December.

1764 The Sheridans travel to Bristol, Bath, London, and Scotland, where Thomas Sheridan gives lectures on oratory and performs at the Edinburgh Theatre. Unfortunately, they are unable to stave off creditors and the Sheridans flee to Blois, France. While at Blois, Frances Sheridan writes a third comedy, *A Journey to Bath*. David Garrick rejects the script, even after her vehement defense of it. *A Journey to Bath* will later influence Richard Brinsley Sheridan's famous play, *The Rivals* (1775). While at Blois, she also writes two more novels, *The History of Nourjahad* and *Conclusion of the Memoirs of Miss Sidney Bidulph*.

1766 Frances Sheridan dies at Blois in August or September. The Sheridan Banshee is heard wailing at Quilca.

1767 *Nourjahad* and *Conclusions* are published posthumously. *Nourjahad* is translated into Russian, French, and Polish.

A Note on the Text

The two-volume *Conclusion of the Memoirs of Miss Sidney Bidulph* was published in two posthumous editions in 1767, one by J. Dodsley in Pall Mall, London, and one by G. Faulkner in Parliament Street, Dublin. The London edition labels the volume numbers IV and V; the Dublin edition, following the first, uncorrected, 1761 edition of *Memoirs*, which was published in two volumes, labels the volumes III and IV. We chose to follow the second, author-corrected, three-volume London edition in our Broadview edition of *Memoirs* (2011) and so have chosen the London edition of *Conclusion* to maintain volume numbering. We have standardized possessives to prevent confusion, but retained the original spelling. We have made capitalization in terms of address conform to modern standard, such as, for instance, in "Miss Audley" and "Miss Arnold" wherein Frances Sheridan's capitalization is very often inconsistent, but in places where she maintains a consistent standard, such as in the case of "lord V—" and "lady Sarah" we have retained the original capitalization. Long Ss, of course, have been converted, and we have silently corrected any obvious typographical errors, of which there were very few.

CONCLUSION OF THE MEMOIRS
OF MISS SIDNEY BIDULPH

CONCLUSION

OF THE

MEMOIRS

OF

Miſs SIDNEY BIDULPH,

As prepared for the Preſs

By the LATE EDITOR of the
FORMER PART.

VOLUME IV.

LONDON:

Printed for J. DODSLEY, in Pall-mall,
MDCCLXVII.

Introduction
to the
Continuation
of the
Memoirs
Of
Miss Sidney Bidulph

The editor[1] of the former part of these memoirs having been extremely sollicited by many people, to procure, if possible, a further account of Mrs. Arnold and her family, would gladly have gratified the curiosity of his readers if after having left so melancholy an impression on the minds of the tender and humane, he[2] could, in the succeeding part of the history, have thrown in some rays of sunshine, to brighten the prospect, before he dropt the curtain over so gloomy a scene; but as that satisfaction is not permitted him, the only reflection that could enable him to pursue with any alacrity the thread of this affecting story, was, that the principal person concerned in it, is long since at peace, and in possession of the rewards which were denied to her virtue and her sufferings here.[3]

The gentleman by whose means I was favoured with the first part of this history, told me upon my re-urging my enquiries after some farther lights into it, that as all the events which occurred even after the close of his mother's narrative had happened when he was in his early infancy, he could give me very little information about them: he only knew in general that some very distressful incidents had succeeded in Mrs. Arnold's life after that period: he added that his mother never cared to speak on the subject, which had prevented his asking her any particulars; but that he recollected to have heard her say, that she believed Patty

---

1 Sheridan employs the familiar eighteenth-century trope of the editor of letters for her novels in order to maintain the illusion that the letters are real. The editor claims to have compiled and redacted the story from actual documents, the former part of which is contained the *The Memoirs of Miss Sidney Bidulph* (1761), volumes I–III. The reference on the title page to the "late editor of the former part" indicates that this novel was published after Sheridan's death.

2 The editor; Sheridan assumes a male persona.

3 Here, as in the beginning of the first three volumes of *Sidney Bidulph*, Sheridan indicates her rejection of poetic justice in favor of a divine justice. Sidney's reward for her virtuous suffering is not expected to be in worldly currency, but is awaiting her in the next life.

Main, the young woman who formerly waited on Mrs. Arnold, was in possession of some papers which contained the whole story. I asked him if this gentlewoman were still living, and where she was to be found; he told me she had married a gentleman of the name of Askham, who had an estate in Oxfordshire; but whether she, or any of her family, were now in being he could not inform me.

Upon so slender a hope as this of recovering the remainder of so interesting a story, I took a journey into Oxfordshire: where I soon learnt that Mrs. Askham and her husband had both been dead many years; but that they had left three daughters, amongst whom (as they had no son) their father's estate of about six hundred pounds a year, had been equally divided. The two eldest were settled in a different part of the country; but the youngest who was her mother's favourite, having married unhappily a man who squandered her little fortune, was now a widow, and residing in the city of Oxford. The persons from whom I had this account, added, that she kept a haberdasher's shop, and as she had two or three children, they believed she was in streightened circumstances.

To this person therefore I applied, and easily introduced myself by buying some of the goods in which she dealt. I found her a modest sensible woman, who seemed with great industry to apply herself to a little calling for the subsistance of her family; at the same time I could easily discover that her education had qualified her to appear in a much better sphere.

After I had, by two or three visits, made myself a little acquainted with her, I took occasion one day to ask her, whether she had ever heard her mother talk of Mrs. Arnold? She seemed startled at the question: Be not alarm'd, Madam, said I, at my enquiry, the part that Mrs. Askham bore in the history of that unfortunate lady will always do honour to her memory. I am surprized, Sir, replied she, how Mrs. Arnold's story came to be published; for tho' the names are all changed, I was too well acquainted with the characters of every person concerned in it, not to know for whom they were intended. I then told her without reserve that I myself had been the editor, and the means by which I had got possession of the manuscript; acquainting her at the same time that I had learnt from the son of Mrs. Cecilia B— that Mrs. Askham had had some papers containing very interesting particulars; and that if they still remained in the family, I should look upon it as a singular favour if she would procure me a sight of them. She told me she had them herself;

but that as she should be very unwilling to part with them, she hoped I would excuse her not giving them out of her hands; but that to oblige me I should be very welcome to peruse them at her house, which she said I could do in two or three mornings, if I would take the trouble to call.

I thanked her for this permission, and accordingly waited on her the next morning; when I found her busied in ranging[1] the papers in order on a table in her dining room. Here, Sir, said she on my entering, you will find your curiosity fully gratified. These are copies of letters which passed between the several persons concerned in the story they contain; they are all in my mother's hand-writing, who as she was in Mrs. Arnold's confidence to her last hour, wrote them out with the permission of the family, in order, as she has often told me, to preserve from oblivion the memory of so many uncommon events crowded into one life, and to leave the whole as a useful lesson to her children. I was the child she most loved, and she left these papers to me at her death. You will find in this parcel, continued she (pointing to a large packet which lay by itself) the former part of Mrs. Arnold's history, carried down to that period at which she retired from London on the news of Mr. Falkland's[2] death; 'tis drawn up in a concise manner by my mother herself; if you are desirous to re-peruse this part of her story, I will leave it with you. I told her as I was already acquainted with Mrs. Arnold's history down to that æra, I had no curiosity to examine that packet; upon which she locked it up in a scrutoire[3] which stood in the room, and left me to the perusal of the others.

In three mornings I accomplished my task; and having expressed my acknowledgements to the owner for the entertainment these letters had afforded me, I frankly proposed the purchasing them from her, as I thought her situation in life would prevent her taking offence at such a proposal. She seemed at first very unwilling to part with them; but after urging a good many arguments, together with the offer of a very handsome gratuity, she at last consented; and I had the satisfaction to carry away with me the remaining part of Mrs. Arnold's history, which the following sheets contain.

---

1 Arranging.

2 Sheridan changes the spelling of Faukland to Falkland for the *Conclusion of the Memoirs of Miss Sidney Bidulph.*

3 Variant of escritoire, a writing desk.

The letters which passed between Mrs. Arnold and her friend Mrs. Cecilia B— for the first eight or nine years after the final departure of the former from London, contain nothing material to the ensuing story. The melancholy state of Mrs. Arnold's mind gave a gloomy cast to most of those which were written by her in the first two or three years of this period: her patience and her fortitude seemed at length in a great measure to have subdued her grief, at least they taught her to suppress any expression of it in her letters to her friend; and as the sad cause became less and less recent, she appears by degrees to wear off in some measure the impressions of her sorrow. The only events that the editor could gather from a series of letters during this interval, was the marriage of Patty Main to Mr. Askham; the death of Mr. Warner; who after having purchased a considerable estate in Oxfordshire (with a handsome house which he called Woodberry) left it to Mrs. Arnold, and appears to have died two years before the date of the first letter in this collection: and it seems to be much about the same time that Mrs. Arnold removed from her former dwelling in Buckinghamshire and came to settle in this near Oxford, with a view to be near young Falkland, whom she purposed to enter in that university. He learn'd also from these letters that lady V— had undertaken a journey from Lancashire on purpose to visit Mrs. Arnold, and had passed a whole summer with her; and it appears that Mrs. Cecilia B— had generally paid her friend a visit once a year.

In order therefore to take up the narrative as near as possible to the æra where Cecilia breaks off hers, he has suppressed all the preceding letters, and commences this collection with that which seems, if not immediately necessary, at least most pertinent to the following story, as it gives occasion to Cecilia's reply, which throws considerable lights on it. The editor has here and there only given extracts from letters, the remainder of which were foreign to his purpose; and has sometimes even ventured to throw in little narratives, the circumstances of which he collected from a variety of letters, containing several other things, and therefore too long and too immaterial to be inserted here.

Thank you, thank you, my dear, for delivering me so speedily
from my fears. And so this frightful alarm has ended at last in a
friendly fit of the gout! I congratulate Mr. B. upon it; yet I wish
the disorder had been so complaisant as to have settled in his
foot, before it attacked his stomach; and the good man now truly
can't part with his nurse, but tell him I shall think him a very
tyrant, if he does not let you down to me again, as soon as he
grows a little better. Here it was *two* years since your last visit to
me, you were but twelve hours in my house, (seven of which you
were asleep) when slap comes down an express to hurry you away
to Mr. B—, who took into his head forsooth that he was dying!
Oh these men, Cecilia, are so pusillanimous when anything ails
them!—then it is (tho' perhaps they never discovered it before)
that they find the comfort of a good wife. Pray ask him, my dear,
who but yourself would sit whole days stifling in a room like a
hot-house, to hear him snarling in his elbow-chair? He must
think me very sawcy for talking thus of one with whom I am so
little acquainted; but is not that his own fault? How often have I
pressed him to come into Oxfordshire? No, *the constant business of
his employment could never suffer him to pay visits in the country.*—
And you one would imagine had an employment at court too, for
it was almost as difficult to draw you from London (to which
place you *know* I have bid an eternal adieu) as it is your husband;
but that I know is his fault, for which I am really angry with him;
for let me tell him I love you, I am almost tempted to say as well
as he does.

Remember in this last hasty visit we had neither time nor
opportunity for half an hour's private chat. The presence of my
little family prevented my asking you your opinion of them; and
you are so full of Mr. B— and his gout, in your letter, that you
speak of nothing else.—I expect that you will make amends for
this in your next.—But to be serious, for after all 'tis nothing but
the joy I feel on being delivered from a painful suspense of your
account, which has occasioned my spirits to flow into imperti-
nence, I do most sincerely felicitate you on Mr. B—'s disorder's
having taken so favourable a turn. According to the common
opinion it may give you hope of a much longer continuance of so
valuable a life. That you may for many many years continue a
blessing to each other is the prayer of your affectionate, &c.

Mrs. Cecilia B— to Mrs. Arnold
London, March 12th.

If you knew all, my dear Sidney, you have less reason to reproach Mr. B— than you have to thank him for his indulgence to us both. You know I told you I had taken lady Mapletost in my way down to you, and spent a week with her. The truth is, this was a thought which occurred to me on the road, merely suggested by seeing her house at the distance only of a mile out of my route; and as I had leave of absence for a month, I thought of stealing two or three days out of it, in order to dedicate them to this old friend; but I could not refuse her pressing entreaties to stay the week out. Now you must know that during that whole week poor Mr. B— had been labouring under his painful disorder, for he was attacked with it the day after I left town, and his physicians could not tell what to make of it; yet he, supposing I was with you, would not send for me till the danger was apparently encreased: see therefore, ungrateful as you are, how much you are indebted to his good nature, so let me have no more complaints; but make up by your correspondence, the loss I must submit to in being deprived of seeing you; for I certainly shan't have it in my power to repeat my visit to you till next year.

You wanted to ask my opinion of your young family, you say.— Sidney, you, who when a girl, with more reason to be vain than any woman living, had less vanity than any woman living, are I am afraid now you are come to years of discretion, (for we are neither of us old, you know) beginning to grow proud of your children. What should my opinion of them be? The girls are well enough, I think, for little things bred in the country; and your son Falkland, as you call him, is a good tolerable sort of a youth.

I have a great mind to stop here; Mr. B—, by whose bed-side I write, bids me do so; and to be revenged on you for talking of his snarling, leave you with this mortifying reply; but I have too much christian charity to bear malice in my heart, therefore take my real sentiments, which are, that I do from my soul think I never saw two such perfect creatures as your two daughters. I could scarce think it possible that a little more than two years could have produced such an alteration; they appear'd but children when I was last in Buckinghamshire, and I believe they now want but very little of your own fine stature. I think I never saw any thing equal to the exquisite delicacy of Miss Arnold's figure; and for my name-sake, *such* a complexion and *such* eyes! Oh,

Sidney, that girl would do a world of mischief if she were in London; the men would tack her name to sword, pestilence and famine. Yet I imagine, that tho' her beauty might *surprize* more, it would *captivate* less than that of her sister; there is an expression in the softer charms of the elder, that would steal into the heart without one's perceiving it; and she has one of those faces that a man would fall in love with, without having first discover'd that she was a beauty. The endowments of their minds I think are answerable to those of their persons. How sensible, how polite, how modest is their whole deportment! As for the lesser accomplishments in which the common run of parents fancy the whole of a girl's education consists, which indeed are no more than a little garniture to it, they had made so considerable a progress in all those when I last saw them, that I suppose they are now complete. Indeed, Sidney, they wanted not the addition of twenty thousand pounds apiece, to enhance their worth; and I can't help thinking it was a strange caprice in that whimsical old cousin Warner of yours, to leave them such a fortune independent of you. Yet he lived long enough to judge that their dutiful and sweet dispositions would not make an improper use of such an advantage.

How happy is your present situation, my dear, if you can forget the past, and look forward to the delightful prospect that is before you! May your prudence, your virtue, your piety be revived and flourish, as well as your beauty does, in the persons of those two lovely girls. Yet I thought at the time I saw her, and with a sigh have since recollected, that Miss Arnold's health does not seem so perfect as I could wish. I observed a sort of languor in her countenance; perhaps it was only my fancy; or it may be the natural cast of her visage. I had not time to mention this when I was with you, yet I beg you will get the advice of some able physician; if a decay[1]——I won't finish the sentence——God preserve the dear creature to you! But pray consult some one about her health; the slightest attack would shatter so delicate a frame.

Well now I have done with your daughters, a word or two for your son. That same Falkland is a charming pretty young man! You say he is not so handsome as his father was: as I never saw his father, I can't contradict you; but in my mind he is agreeable enough to be a very dangerous object in the same house with two young girls. I know you don't design him for either of them, don't you therefore think it time to separate them? Falkland must be

---

1 In Miss Arnold's health.

near eighteen; were I to judge from his person only I should think him more. —I was pleased with his whole carriage, his filial respect towards you, and the tender innocent appellation of sister to the two girls, delighted me, and checked the fears, which would otherwise have arisen, that he might possibly have considered them in another light. I think him very happy in having so worthy a conductor as Mr. Price, who seems well to have discharged his duty in the care of this youth's education. With what pleasure the good old man regards his hopeful pupil!—I could say a thousand things more to you; but Mr. B— cries out, Have not you done yet? Yes, my dear, for I am come to the bottom of my paper. So adieu, my Sidney, God bless you and your amiable family.

   I am, &c.

Letter III.
Extract from Mrs. Arnold's answer to Mrs. Cecilia B—
Woodberry, March 16th.

————With regard to Miss Arnold, 'tis only your tender fears, my dear, that have suggested to you the thought of her being in an ill state of health, I never had any reason to be of that opinion; yet as I know young people are apt to conceal slight indispositions, I have questioned her strictly on the subject, and she assures me that nothing ails her. Yet in consequence of the deference I pay to your judgment, I have consulted the ablest physician in this country. I suppose he thought it necessary to advise something, and therefore delivered it as his opinion, that tho' at *present* no symptoms of a disorder appeared, yet it was not impossible but that the young lady might be *tending towards* a consumptive habit,[1] on which account he recommended by way of prevention only, that she should drink asses milk; and accordingly she is to take it every morning.

I am very glad my little Falkland has your approbation. I know you look with a scrutinous eye into the manners and behaviour of youth. I love this boy almost equally with my daughters; for is he not, my Cecilia, the son of him who was once so dear to me, and whose memory must ever be precious to my heart? A hundred times a day does he recall his father's image fresh to my remem-

---

1 Characterized by lung disease, coughing and wheezing, or of the appearance of wasting away associated with consumption (tuberculosis).

brance; the same agreeable vivacity, the same insinuating address, the same tender regard to every one with whom he is connected. His tutor perfectly adores him. My two children have always considered and loved him as a brother; and I make them call him by that affectionate name. This idea I inculcated early amongst them; for having taken the dear unhappy orphan into my protection, with a design to have him educated under my own eye, I thought that precaution would sufficiently guard the young people from ever entertaining a thought, much less a wish, that any other tie should ever take place; and indeed it has succeeded to my expectations; fraternal affection there is between them, and so I would have it; but nothing like a particular preference. To say the truth, I believe it seldom happens that persons brought up together from childhood, conceive a passion for each other. The eyes thro' which the hearts of most young people are reached, are first struck by novelty; and persons educated together almost from infancy, not having this advantage with regard to each other, by the time they come to an age susceptible of love, would much sooner be caught by an object less amiable than that to which they have been accustomed, merely because it was new. I mean to provide very handsomely for Falkland, and have always told him so; yet deserving as he is, I would not carry my partiality so far as to bestow on him either of my daughters. The unhappy circumstance of his birth forbids such a thought, had he even a fortune which would intitle to so considerable a match, as each of my daughters will be. Yet after all, my Cecilia, I think with you, that Orlando is now arrived at an age, which requires more precaution on my part, than has hitherto been necessary. I left it to his own election to make choice of any liberal profession to which his inclination most led him, for his patrimony is but a trifle.—His tutor, who you know is piety itself, would have persuaded him to the gown, for with his abilities, he says, he would be an ornament to the church; but my son, whose genius seems to incline him more to the military life, modestly excused himself to the good old man, and said he should prefer the army. To which poor Mr. Price unwillingly assented; but as he could not bear the thoughts of his pupil's launching out into the world so extremely young, (for this proposal was made before we left Buckinghamshire) he beg'd to retain him a year or two longer under his care; and afterwards pleaded hard that he might enter the university, where he said he would learn to set a proper value on his literary acquisition, a thing which the old gentleman himself rates very highly. This step therefore having been long determined, Falkland is to enter as a gentleman commoner of Exeter College the week after next. Thus you see, my dear, are your wishes anticipated, as Orlando will of course remove immediately from my house; and as you know we are five miles from Oxford, we probably shall seldom see him but in the vacations, and at the same time be near enough to have an eye to his conduct. Mr. Price is to continue with me, my chaplain in effect, tho' my rank in life does not qualify me to confer on him so formal a title.

All under my roof kiss your hands a thousand times. Mrs. Askham, who dined with me yesterday, presents her best respects to you; she was inconsolable on hearing that you had been in this part of the country, and had left it before she knew of your arrival. She says, had she been informed of it, she would have flown to Woodberry, if it were only to get one look at you. Adieu, my love.

I am, &c.

Letter IV.
Mrs. Cecilia B— to Mrs. Arnold
London, March 18th.

Rejoiced as I always am to hear from you, I never was better pleas'd at the receipt of any letter from you than at that of your last, which came into my hands at a most happy juncture. You must know we have had a visit from Sir George Bidulph to-day; he was coming from court, and step'd in just to ask Mr. B— how he did. He seem'd surprised at seeing me, as he knew not I was come to town, having been inform'd the last time he was here, that I was gone down to Oxfordshire, with a design of passing a month with you.

After the first how-do-ye's were over, and Mr. B— had sworn two or three oaths at him, for hurting his toe with the point of his sword, as he brushed by his elbow-chair, Sir George addressed himself to me with Well, Madam, how does my sister do, for I have not had a line from her these two months. Sidney is too methodical a correspondent for me, for if I don't answer her letters punctually, I am sure not to hear a word from her; and faith 'tis impossible for a man to find time to write, when he is so perpetually engaged as I am;—and then he strutted up to the glass, again hurt Mr. B—'s toe, and received two or three more curses. I told him I had left you and your family perfectly well, and that you had been complaining to me of his silence. When are those two girls to take the vail?[1] Said he, turning round to me with a sarcastical smile: Or does their mother intend to marry one of them to young Falkland, and the other to old Price; for I don't know any other choice they can have, in that d—m'd place where she keeps them buried alive. I was provoked at his gibe, not having such an answer ready as I could have wish'd. Mr. B— laugh'd, and Sir George went on; I declare, Mrs. B—, you ladies of the *first* rate understandings, are the most unfit people upon earth to conduct the *common* affairs of life. Would any woman in the world, but Mrs. Arnold, keep two young ladies like my nieces, mew'd up in such a retched obscure corner, where it is impossible they can *learn* any thing? You forget, I replied, how accomplish'd your sister herself was, who was bred up in the same manner. I don't mean, said he, the common accomplishments that are to be bought by paying a master;[2] the learning I would have them acquire is a little knowledge of the world; which I'm sure my sister with all her wisdom, nor Price with all his philosophy, will never be able to teach them: that is a Science to be learnt only by mixing *with* the world. Three years ago, continued he, you may remember, when lady Sarah was in Buckinghamshire, she press'd my sister to let the two Miss Arnolds pass the winter with her in London, and Sidney's refusal of this request, though gloss'd over with a thousand fine excuses, is to tell you the truth, the reason of our never having paid her a visit since. They were too young at that time, I replied, and (for want of something else to say) added, for which perhaps you won't thank me,——I dare say were lady Sarah *now* to make the same proposal, Mrs. Arnold would readily embrace it. I don't know that, answered Sir George; I am afraid that Sidney is in some respects but too like——he stopped short: but I know what he *would* have said, and that your dear good mother was then in his thoughts. For heaven's sake, pursued he (in his impatient way) do you know what she intends to do with that boy? To marry him to her eldest dau—ghter, cried Mr. B— lengthening out the last word from a twitch of the gout which at that minute seized him. By my soul may be so, said Sir George; that would be tipping the spire, and

---

1 Take the veil: join a convent.
2 A tutor in music, art, or languages.

winding up her bottoms with a witness.[1] Mr. B— who only spoke in jest, laughed and grunted at Sir George's taking it so seriously. I will venture to say, replied I, such a wild thought never entered into Mrs. Arnold's head. I should suppose so too, said Sir George; your husband has only a mind to be pleasant. No, Mrs. B—, continued he very solemnly, well as I loved that noble fellow his father, whose fate to this hour I deplore, I would not consent that my niece should marry the *illegitimate* offspring of the best man in the kingdom.—But in the present case, nothing but frenzy could suggest such a thought; a poor young fellow who has no prospect in the world but from my sister's bounty! I own I could never have a very cordial regard for that youth, on his vile mother's account; it is an unwarrantable prejudice I grant; but as my mother used to say of hers, (which by the way she would never allow to *be* prejudices) it is *unconquerable*.

Just at this word my maid entered the room, and gave me your letter: having read it over to myself, and found there was nothing in it but what your brother might see, I presented it to Sir George, who having kept a profound silence during the time I took to read it, I concluded had been waiting in expectation of at least hearing part of it. I requested him to read it aloud, that Mr. B— might participate with us.

I saw Sir George's countenance brighten, for I watched his looks, when he came to that part of it where you mention your designs with regard to Orlando. In returning me the letter, your brother said, Sidney is more *rational* than I expected (a high compliment you'll say) you see in *this* particular, laying his finger on the paragraph which related to young Falkland's birth, she judges pretty much as I do; (a sufficient reason, my dear, for allowing you to think *rationally*): and yet, pursued he smiling, I perceive, from some part of my sister's letter, that *you* Mrs. B— were not without your fears, ridiculous as the idea appeared to us all just now; for my part I shall be always ready to *serve* the young man, and as far as my interest goes will push him forward in life when

---

1 "Tipping the spire" means to crown, top off, or complete. "Winding up the bottom" is a weaving metaphor, the "bottom" being the cocoon of a silk worm. "With a witness" means with authority, beyond doubt, or with a vengeance (*OED*). Marrying young Falkland to one of the Miss Arnolds would crown all, and bring things to a conclusion with a vengeance. He is referring, sardonically, to bringing to a fitting conclusion the unfortunate and unusual events detailed in the first three volumes of *Sidney Bidulph*.

he enters into the profession of which he has made choice; poor fellow, he is not accountable for the iniquities of his mother. I found that Sir George, so soon as he had lost his apprehensions, suffered his humanity to return. These men of the world learn, I believe, to accommodate their feelings as well as their language to exteriour circumstances. As for my nieces, continued he, there is no doubt of their being intitled to marry into some of the best families in the kingdom; but unless my sister supposes that on bare *fame* of their perfections, she will have them demanded of her like princesses, I don't see how this is very likely to be effected. 'Tis a pity you don't get them to town, said Mr. B—; I know no one so fit as lady Sarah to introduce them into life. I bit my lips at this: Ah, thought I, my Sidney *has* a friend, whom I dare believe she thinks as well qualified as her ladyship for this task; but unfortunately *that friend* is not enough mistress of her own actions to make the offer. Lady Sarah would like it extremely, said Sir George, and if Mrs. Arnold is disposed to let them, I shall be as ready to receive them as I was before; but the season is now too far advanced for such a proposal, as we shall go into Somersetshire early in the summer, so that this design can't possibly take place till next winter; I shall however, when I write next to my sister, again make her the offer.

I have given you the substance of Sir George's conversation, and shall now throw in as my own opinion, as well as that of others, that it is really time for young ladies of your daughters' fortunes and condition in life, to see a little of the beau monde.— Their situations in the world will probably be very conspicuous (at least Sir George's endeavours will not be wanting to make them so) and one would not chuse that young creatures should emerge at once from solitude, and appear as *principals* in the glare and bustle of the gay world; for fine as are their understandings, and charmingly elegant as is their whole behaviour, there is a certain ease of deportment, which you know characterizes real good breeding, and which can be attained in no other way but by being familiarized to the modes of the great world; and your *very* fine people, who do not give modesty the first place in their catalogue of virtues, would be apt to call the sweet timidity of Miss Arnold, country bashfulness. Now I want this to be a *leetle* overcome, before she is set down perhaps under the necessity of keeping visiting days for half the coxcombs and flaunting women of quality in town to assemble at her house. Sir George really keeps the best company, and lady Sarah, poor as her intellects are, is an adept in all the fashionable fopperies of the times, and even *passes* for a sensible woman: besides, what situation can be more eligible (your own maternal care out of the question) than an uncle's house, under the guidance of his lady, both of them people in considerable estimation?

I have urged this point the more, as I know you have so mean an opinion of lady Sarah, that I am still apprehensive of your unwillingness to venture so precious a charge as your two daughters with her: and I have been the speedier in writing to you, that as I am certain your brother means to repeat his offer, I may be beforehand as well in preparing you for it, as in begging of you to accept it. Pray, my dear, *descend* a little, and think more, like one of *us*.

I embrace you, and the dear girls, and salute the fine old man and the fine young man; and pray tell Mrs. Askham that I regret as much as she does our not having met.

Letter V.
Mrs. Arnold to Mrs. Cecilia B—
Woodberry, March 29th.

Cecilia, with all my faults, I was never accounted inflexible; you needed not therefore have united your force, with that of my brother, to persuade me to a thing which in itself I think reasonable, and against which, whatever little collateral objections I have to it in my own private thoughts, I can offer none to Sir George, because they relate altogether, as you very well know to lady Sarah. Poor woman! She was herself spoil'd when a girl by the weak indulgence of her mother. She has never had any children of her own, to call forth those little maternal attentions, so necessary in conducting young people; and she is besides (notwithstanding the world's kind opinion) not overburdened with discretion, so that, upon the whole, I do indeed think her but a sorry pilot to guide a young lady through the stormy pleasures of your great town. I rely however on my brother's care, and *have* consented to let both my girls be with him next winter: now are you satisfied?

I received a very obliging letter from my brother three days ago, in which he kindly repeated his invitation to my daughters; but at the same time threw out a hint that vexed me, viz. that having no children of his own to provide for, his nieces' fortunes might not be *impaired* by making themselves agreeable to him and lady Sarah. —This very item, Cecilia, almost tempted me to write him a refusal; for won't it look, to one of Sir George's cast, (you, my dear, know him as well as I do) as if it had its weight in inducing me to comply with a proposal which I had before declined. Yet *you* must be convinced such a motive could have no influence on me at any time, if balanced with more material objections to the offer; how much less then in my present afflu-ent flow of fortune? The truth is, I have yielded to Sir George's request merely for my daughters' sake; for I agree with you in every argument, that you have urged in favour of this step; and at the same time I acknowledge that I should be very unwilling to disoblige a brother with whom I have now lived for so many years upon the best terms. And upon reflection, I am pleased that matters are settled as they are; for to tell you a secret, I had resolved to send my daughters to town early next winter under the care of lady Audley, to whom, next to yourself, I would sooner commit that important charge than to any one I know. For she has united in her, qualities which do not *constantly* meet in the same person, that is to say, she is an excellent good woman, besides being, in the *best*, not the most *modish* acceptation of the word, a *real* fine lady. I believe I formerly mentioned her to you as one of the first acquaintances that I have made on my coming to settle in this country. She has an elegant little house at Oxford, just without the town, where she generally passes half the year; and were she to follow her own inclinations, would prefer living entirely in the country; but in complaisance to her daughter, she always spends her winters in London. She is to an extravagant degree partial to my two girls; and as there is a great intimacy between them and Miss Audley, I thought they could not be more agreeably situated. I am sure lady Audley will be very sorry for the disappointment. She had pressed me most earnestly, and I made her a half promise that my daughters should be with her; but if this intention were to have taken place, I know Sir George would never have forgiven me, so I think 'tis better as it is. My son took his leave of us yesterday, and repaired to Oxford to enter on his academic course of life. You can't imagine how awkward we all felt after his departure. My two girls cried all the morning: and when we sat down to dinner, the footman having thro' inad-vertence placed a chair for him, disconcerted us again, when on his removing it, he said, I forgot that Mr. Falkland was gone. What do you mean by *gone*? Said Mr. Price, with as angry a look as his complaisant countenance could assume; is not he just by us here in the neighborhood? He look'd at me and then at my two children. The good man himself was affected at parting with him, and saw that we were so too: but this little passing cloud soon blew over, and we are all sunshine again.

Letter VI.
Mrs. Arnold to Mrs. Cecilia B—
Woodberry, May 26th.

Poor lady V—, how I am grieved for her! I have just received a letter from Miss Darnley, her youngest niece, who tells me they are all in the deepest affliction. I believe I have told you that lord V—'s undutiful behaviour had so disobliged his mother, that she had never seen him since his father's death. He was always her favourite son, and this disappointment of her hopes it was, which first disgusted her with the world, and occasioned her retiring from it. Lord V—, it seems, whether from a compunction, or the overflowings of a heart naturally good, and perverted only by evil habits, had lately by letter sollicited a reconciliation with his mother. Lady V— received this overture from her son with joy; and having expressed a desire to see him, he immediately set out for Lancashire, and about a month ago arrived at Mrs. Darnley's house; where he was received by his tender mother with as much pleasure (so Miss Darnley expresses herself) as his first entrance into life had given her; but her joy was of a very short duration. Lord V— was invited to an election-dinner, where having drank too freely, he was seized with a fever which in six days carried him to his grave. He died in his mother's arms, with the strongest expressions of regret for his past ill conduct towards her. What a blow to so affectionate a parent! How I feel for this excellent woman! Her tenderness had revived towards him with redoubled ardour in this melancholy moment of eternal separation; and he was snatched from her at a time, when his returning duty and filial affection had opened to her a source of happiness, which she thought had been for ever shut up. Miss Darnley says she is inconsolable; and adds, that neither she nor her mother are at present in a condition to comfort her, being themselves too deeply affected at both so unexpected and melancholy an event. Miss Darnley concludes her letter with the most pressing instances for me to go down to Burnly. "Your conversation, Madam," says she, "I know would have a better effect on my aunt than any thing we can say to her. Can you then refuse this consolation to poor lady V—? If you do favour us with your company, I believe I need not tell you how happy it will make me, if you bring with you the two Miss Arnolds. Remember you have long owed us a visit."

Miss Darnley tells me in a postscript, that the younger brother, now lord V——, is at present with his regiment in Flanders; but that they expect him home at the end of the campaign. —— I think, my Cecilia, this event must unroot me. I had as good as resolved never to have stirred from hence, and began to consider myself like one of the trees in my grove, which are doomed to drop unnoticed in the solitude where they grew. I am really become so in love with my retirement, that it is a pain to me to think of quitting it, for ever so short a space; yet I am afraid this is being too selfish; I will not therefore indulge the habit which I find every day growing stronger upon me. How I should hate myself, how you would despise your Sidney, if she should prefer her own satisfaction to that of the friend she loved!

I have written a letter of condolence to poor lady V——, and have told her I mean immediately to follow it myself, and intend to bring my two daughters with me to kiss her hands; adding, that I shall pass the summer at Burnly, if Mrs. Darnley will suffer me and my little household to incommode her so long.——

Letter VII.
Mrs. Arnold to Mrs. Cecilia B—
Woodbery, June 2d.

Our little plan of operations has been partly disconcerted by an accident, which however I hope will be attended with no other disagreeable consequences than that of obliging me to leave one of my girls at home.

A cold which Dolly had got by walking too late by the river side, occasioned my deferring my journey into Lancashire for some days; but as she is now better, we were all in readiness and intended to have set off to-morrow morning, when to-day, just as we sat down to dinner, I perceived a chariot, the horses upon full gallop, driving up the avenue. It stopped at the door, and Miss Audley sprung out of it, with a precipitation that alarmed me, as I thought that something extraordinary was the case; and so indeed there was; for what can occasion greater consternation to a fine girl than the fear of losing her beauty? The case in short was this; Master Audley, a boy of about nine years old, and the darling of the family, was taken ill of the small-pox. Miss, who is about eighteen, has never had it, and the doctor no sooner announced the distemper, than poor lady Audley, in the utmost terror, ordered the chariot and hurried her daughter out of the house, who you may imagine was not less frightened than herself. Miss Audley told me her mama's extreme apprehensions had obliged her to intrude upon my good nature, in begging that I would suffer miss to stay with me till the danger was over. I told the young lady I was extremely obliged to lady Audley for honouring me with such a preference; and that I should have thought myself but too happy in her company, if an indispensible engagement had not for the present rendered it impossible for me to enjoy it. I then told her of the absolute promise I was under of going into Lancashire; but without mentioning my design of taking my daughters with me; said if she would dispense with *my* absence, the two Miss Arnolds and Mr. Price (whom I looked upon as the father of the family) would endeavour to make her stay as agreeable as possible. I know, Madam, said she, you never go any where without the Miss Arnolds; I am certain you meant to take them with you, and 'tis your politeness only which prevents you from saying so. I see I am come unseasonably; Lord what shall I do! My dear, answered I, 'tis paying you but a very slight compliment to leave my daughters with you, and I assure you if it were not for breaking thro' the laws of faith and friendship, as well as good manners, I would not stir from home myself. As I had not in this reply denied my intention of taking my girls with me, Miss Audley answered, I would not for the world be the means of hindering the young ladies from going with you, I am sure lady V— and Miss Darnley would hate me. Dear Mrs. Arnold, continued she, you can't imagine how I am distressed; for besides the opinion my mama has of you and the Miss Arnolds, she really has not an acquaintance with whom she would take the same liberty, whose house she thinks at a sufficient distance from the infection, for there is nothing in nature I so much dread. I know she would be very unhappy to be obliged to send me to London, neither should I be easy to be so far out of the reach of hearing from my poor little brother, yet that must be my choice, for positively I won't consent to have the Miss Arnolds left at home. Well, my dear Miss Audley, said I, to make you easy at once, I'll compound the matter with you; I will take one of my daughters with me, and leave the other to keep house with you. That settles the matter at once, cried out both my girls in a breath. Miss Audley made a few civil objections to this proposal; but they were easily got over, and in the end I agreed to leave Dolly to bear her company; tho' by the way I thought Cecilia would have been as well pleased to have staid as she; but I made choice of her sister for together, Oh, Sophy, I am not a match for that reflection; I do not wish to be beloved; but indeed I could not bear to be despised.

Just as she spoke this we heard some one tap at the door, (we were in the garden parlour) May I come in, ladies? Said Falkland, for it was he. Miss Arnold was too much discomposed to see him; she ran into the adjoining room, and I bid him come in.

I thought Miss Arnold had been with you, Madam, said he, and I came to bid you both good-bye.—You are not going away now, Sir? Yes, he replied, Mr. Price dines at Oxford to-day, and he thinks I may as well take the opportunity of going in the chariot with him, as defer it till evening when I purposed to have gone.

My zeal for your interests, Edward, made me cruel in that instant; I did an ill natured thing, for without giving poor Dolly time to re-compose herself, I called her out of the other room, from whence, as the door stood on the jar, she had heard what was said. She entered; I pitied her from my heart, for she looked as pale as death. Orlando took her kindly by the hand, What's the matter, my dear Arney? (For so he sometimes calls her) no ill news from Burnly, I hope! (he knew she had received a letter) how does your mama and Cecilia do? They are very well, she replied, but I am myself a little indisposed to-day. Poor Dolly, said Falkland, and slightly kissed one of her cheeks; this easy familiar action soon chased away the paleness from them. He looked earnestly at her, 'Tis your too close attendance on me, said he; that has made you ill; it were better a hundred such worthless fellows as I am should die, than that you should lose an hour's health. 'Tis only her want of sleep, said I; she will be well again in a day or two. I hope so, replied Falkland; I shall call on you again soon. Adieu, and pray be well against I see you next. Good morning to you, Miss Audley, have you any commands to Sir Edward? He made to each of us a graceful bow and retired, and we saw the chariot drive away with him and Mr. Price in it presently after.

Poor Miss Arnold! Lord! Edward, it is a sad thing to be in love without being sure of a return, but that is at present our case: not that I can have the least doubt of Falkland's catching the flame if it be communicated by a skillful hand; but to tell you the truth, I have not observed any thing in him which gives me room to believe he loves her; yet I may be mistaken, and he may have art enough to conceal his inclinations, where there appears so little probability of their succeeding. She seems now glad that he is gone, and has besought me not to talk of him. In this I must conform to her desires, or perhaps forfeit her good opinion, without which nothing can be effected. It now rests upon you to make Falkland speak for himself, and I think I can answer for the consequences.

We are at present most intolerably humdrumish; and if I were not the best sister in the universe, I should leave Dolly to read Homilies to old Price, and return home, though, by the way, my mama has *permitted* me (for we writ to her) to stay here till Mrs. Arnold's return.

Letter XIII.
Sir Edward Audley to Miss Audley.

Oxford, July 20th.

Very near sinking, by Jupiter! If I had not been a skillful seaman, and cried *'bout ship* in an instant, we had gone souce to the bottom! You have an excellent nose, Sophy, to use a sportsman's phrase, and can scent out a little lurking Cupid as well as my Basto can a hare. You were right with regard to Miss Arnold, you are right with regard to Falkland, for he not only does *not* love Dorothy; but as fortune in her spite would have it, he *loves* Cecilia! Thanks be to my better stars I am not dying for either of the puppits, yet I *will* have one of them; and since my heart has been so amenable to me as to turn out Dolly to make room for Cecilia, why should not Falkland's be the same, and turn out Cecilia to make room for her elder sister? Ay, it must be so, the change is easy, and it will be so extremely convenient to us all, that I will have it so; but Falkland must not yet know my design, for on that depends its success, though I had like to have betrayed it, which would have blown us all up.

Have you ever seen two children at play, Sophy, delighted with the sports in which they were engaged, and galloping in full career round the room on hobby horses? One of them, tired perhaps of his pastime, spies some toy that was put up on a shelf, probably to be out of both their reaches; he climbs to get possession of it, which the other brat no sooner perceives than he immediately dismounts, and nothing will serve him but the identical bauble of his companion; he squalls for it directly, Waugh, Sir, it was mine first, and they fall instantly to scratching. Thus would it have fared between Falkland and me, had he discovered that I had any views with regard to Cecilia; for though he never yet entertained the most distant thought of possessing either of those girls, and considered them, like the toy on the shelf, as things our letter; Poor Falkland! Dear Orlando! Broke involuntarily from her lips. Sir Edward blames my mama here, continued she, but how could she foresee that in her pious care of an unhappy orphan, she was laying up misery for him, and her weak imprudent daughter? Yet I have heard her say, that there was a fatality attended all her actions, and that her best designs had been perverted into evil. It will be her own fault, said I, if this should be rendered so. She only shook her head; when coming to the conclusion of your letter, she smiled, and said, she loved you for your spirit in resolving to think no more of her; adding, that she was very sure you would not find it difficult to keep your resolution. I replied, My brother has a very vulnerable heart; at the same time he is so volatile, that I should not be surprized if I were to see him in love with some one else in month or two; (I said this by way of a little preparatory step for your attack on Cecilia) yet, continued I, were he to meet a kind return, I know it would fix him; and the plains of Arcadia never saw a tenderer or more constant swain than Sir Edward might then be made. There was a pretty speech for you! I hope, replied Miss Arnold, he may then soon meet with a lady who will deserve and return his affection. But let me now ask you one question, Sophy; Have you written to your brother since you received this letter? I saw the tendency of her question, and was prepared with an answer; yet I hesitated as if I were not. Have you written to Sir Edward? She repeated——I have—Sophy, I fear, I fear you put too much confidence in that brother of yours; yet, if you have betrayed my secret!——I clasped my arms suddenly about her neck—Dolly, I can't deceive you, yet I *must* be forgiven; I will not let loose my hold, till you promise me your pardon. What have you done? Cried she eagerly; tell me quickly. I have trusted my brother, said I, with a secret which I myself discovered. I am lost then! Cried she, flinging from me, and throwing herself into another chair; Falkland by this time knows it all! 'Twas barbarous in you, Sophy; would I have used you so? My brother will not mention it, said I; I charged him strictly on that head. Oh, ridiculous supposition! Cried she; do you think that *men* have more virtue than *we* have? Don't you see that your friendship for me got the better of your fidelity to your brother, and you communicated to me what he charged you to conceal! I seemed to be struck dumb with this reproach, and the truth of the observation—but recovering myself; he has not the same reasons to excuse a breach of trust, nor the same motives for committing it. I was overcome by your importunities; and had you not found and pressed to see my brother's letter, I should never have mentioned Falkland to you more. The same accident cannot befall Sir Edward; what inducement then can he have to betray me? This flimsy apology was (as I meant it should be) very easily answered. Friendship for Falkland, replied she: he loves him, and will be very glad of an opportunity of telling him what he thinks will make him happy—Again I stood in amaze at her sagacity! But still willing to excuse my fault, I am extremely sorry, said I, that I should have been so imprudent; but I don't know how it is, I never *could* keep anything from my brother—And I spoke it in the tone of one who is ashamed of their own absurdity.

To what have you exposed me! cried she, clasping her hands together; how shall I bear to look Falkland in the face, after such an indiscreet, such an *unsollicited* confession? Had he remained ignorant of my weakness, time and my own endeavours, joined to a belief of *his* indifference, would have enabled me to overcome it; but now what hope have I left? If Falkland, encouraged by what I am sure he knows too well, should venture to declare himself, I am undone! Sophy, you know not what thorns you have planted here—and she laid her hands on her bosom. Accept of my penitence, my dear Miss Arnold, said I, and hope for the best. I was really affected with the account my brother gave me of poor Falkland's situation: I thought *he* was so too; and (as he had no hopes for himself) that the knowledge of this secret would, far from creating any jealousy in him, rather be a consolation, when he reflected that it was not an *unworthy* rival to whom you gave the preference. Come, prithee, my dear, dry your eyes (for I perceived tears in them) you are the first woman, I believe, that ever cried for finding herself adored by the man she loved. I don't weep for *that*, said she, but to think how unhappy we must *both* be. Had I suffered alone; but poor Orlando – must be your husband after all, Dolly. She smiled through her tears, and sobbed out, A——h, Sophy, that's impossible! A good deal more of pretty girlish chit-chat passed between us, to the same purpose, till we were called down to supper, where Mr. Price's presence was a check to any farther conversation on the subject.

The family are all, long since, retired to bed; and here am I, like a witch, scrawling dire characters at midnight. My chamber joins that where Miss Arnold sleeps; but where she *sleeps* not at present, for I hear her sighing. These very reserved girls, I have observed, when they *do* love, love unmercifully. We lively ones, with a little dash of the coquet in us, are mere babies to them. Another sigh! Oh, Edward, the position operates rarely!

Well, but all this while Falkland steps not forward to meet us. We are prepared for him here; and I shall have but a poor opinion of your abilities, if I do not very soon see a pair of *mutual* lovers. If you can once bring him to unfold his heart a little, Dolly's will expand of itself, and we may trust to sympathy to do the rest; but it will be absolutely necessary to engage him in the pursuit of this amour before Cecilia's return. Once entered, he cannot retract; and the reception he will be sure to meet with, must infallibly fix him: for after all (putting romance out of the question) I believe he would bless his stars to get either of these girls.

I take it for granted he has not the least suspicion that you ever made any overtures to Miss Arnold; on which account, nothing will appear more natural than that you should urge *him,* already so much favoured, to lay hold on his good fortune; besides, the indifference you expressed towards Cecilia, will put him off his guard there too; so that it will be impossible for doubts of any kind to awaken his jealousy: and once there comes to be a reciprocation of vows between him and his love, (for that, I expect, will soon be the case) he cannot be such a snarling cur as to stand between you and a good to which he has given up all pretensions. Dolly, on the other hand, very probably, will not be sorry to see her sister in the same predicament with herself. We are all Eves, brother, and are ready to stretch out the apple to our friends of which we ourselves have tasted. You know Mrs. Arnold thinks her daughters as safe with my mama as with herself; we shall, therefore, have many opportunities, after they return from Burnly, of making little parties at our own house, till the time appointed for the young ladies going to London; and as you mean to quit the university at Christmas, you may pursue your mistress the whole winter in town; for I count upon your having secured her heart before she leaves Woodberry. I am quite tired with writing so long a letter; yet I will not go to bed till I have scribbled a short one for Falkland to see. It will require no management in the world to shew it to him, but all the skill of which you are master to make it produce proper effects. You will have it inclosed; so adieu————

P.S. The servant who brings you this attends Mrs. Nelson to town; who having ten thousand things to buy, it will take her up almost the whole morning; so that you may order him to call on you before he returns home; and by that time, perhaps you may be able to tell me how my billet worked.

Letter XVI.
(Which was inclosed in the preceding.)

'Tis almost a fortnight since I have seen you, and yet you are within five short miles of me. Indeed, brother, you are very unkind, and I almost begin to think you have no affection for me. You ought to consider the melancholy life I lead here: I see no body but a few primitive people, whom Mrs. Arnold has selected for her acquaintance. As for poor Dolly, she is become such a mope, that she is really fit company for no one but herself; and if I did not love her dearly, I would not sacrifice my hours to her. Poor dear creature! I pity her from my heart.

Upon my word, Edward, I begin to be seriously alarmed for her; for I think her health is daily impairing. Would to God, she had never known a certain friend of yours, or that he was in a situation that would take off all objections to him; but as that is never likely to be the case, if you have any regard to the peace of the family in which I now am, or set any value on my friendship, take care never to let drop the smallest hint of what I intrusted to your confidence; for if any improper consequences should ensue (as no doubt there would) I should certainly be suspected by Mrs. Arnold as an abettor in her daughter's imprudence; for I know not to what lengths Dolly's unconquerable attachment might carry her, if Falkland were to know and avail himself of it.

Her mama talks of sending for her to Burnly, as she knows not when she shall be able to disengage herself from lady V—. I wish she would, as it would at the same time help to divert *her* mind, and deliver me from a confinement of which I am quite tired. Dolly does not seem to relish the thoughts of going; but I have a great inclination to get my mama to write to Mrs. Arnold to send for her. She need only be told of that melancholy which is preying on her mind to hurry her away directly. She will attribute it, no doubt, to her being, for the first time, absent from her friends. How much does poor Miss Arnold envy that little sprightly gipsey Cecilia! Mrs. Arnold says she is the life of the whole family at Burnly; and that her constant flow of spirits supports those of her mama, as well as of Mrs. And Miss Darnley. Happy girl! She is a stranger to that tyrant who commits such ravages in the bosom of her poor sister.

For Heaven's sake, Edward, send me some books, and some news. Tell me who and who's together at Oxford: pick up all the anecdotes you can get, both good and bad, cram them into your budget, and empty the contents of it at Woodberry within these

eight and forty hours, or thou art no brother of mine; though, for the present, I will subscribe myself
Your affectionate sister,
S.A.

Letter XVII.
Sir Edward Audley to Miss Audley.
Oxford, July 25th.

Now, by Saint Paul, the work goes bravely on—I was in bed when I received your packet; and having read the great letter and the little letter, (the precious engine of our designs) I bethought me of a curious expedient, which I instantly put in practice. I bounded out of bed, threw on my nice night-gown and slippers, and having nicely picked off the seal from your inclosed billet, I as nicely clapped on a fresh one; then giving it to David, I bid him follow me in a quarter of an hour to Mr. Falkland's chambers, and give it to me there. Have not you it already, Sir, said David, what occasion is there for my bringing it to you again? Do as I bid you, you dog, and ask no questions. I then sauntered into Falkland's room, whom I found just up. Give me some coffee, quoth I, and threw myself into his easy chair. Just as we began our breakfast, David entered, and with a very grave face, and a low bow, presented me your letter; but thinking himself in a plot, he could not refrain from tipping me a sly wink, which it was happy for the repose of his bones that Falkland did not observe. Having read it, I tossed it down carelessly on the table. *An Indian scrawl*,[1] said Falkland, looking at the lines backwards; *which* of them is it from? (for I have other ladies who write to me besides you, Sophy.) If you have any curiosity, said I, you may read it; for the mischief is done already, and cannot be made worse by a farther communication. He took the letter up, and I could observe by the rogue's face as he read, that his vanity was not a little flattered. He rose from his chair without speaking, and walked up as it were mechanically to the glass, where having taken a survey of his own dear irresistible figure; You can't imagine, said he, turning round with a very solemn face, how much I am affected with this account which your sister gives of poor Miss Arnold. I wish indeed, as Miss Audley says, that we had never known each other. It would have been happy for *her*, said I, tossing off my dish of

---

1 Ornately delicate handwriting.

coffee; but I hope her mother will send for her into Lancashire, and by way of curing her melancholy, clap up some hasty match for her, as old lady Bidulph did for Mrs. Arnold. How I should laugh at you, Falkland, if we were to see her return a bride! Poh, cried he, how can you jest upon so serious an occasion? I would not for the world that any constraint should be laid on poor Miss Arnold's inclinations; but I am sure her mama is too fond of her, and has besides too much humanity to be capable of exercising any tyranny towards her children. I would not trust to that, said I, if her mama were to know how *wisely* her daughter has bestowed her heart; and if my mother should pick the secret out of Sophy, (who by the bye has not the gift of retention) she would think herself bound in duty to tell it. Then the old gray noddles at Burnly (lady V—'s and Mrs. Darnley's I mean) would be laid together to prevent the *mischief*, as they would call it, and they would be for giving their musty advice to Mrs. Arnold, who, good woman as she is, would, I believe, as you observe, were she left to herself, be far from acting tyrannically. Then we should have Sir George Bidulph, with his overbearing insolence, blustering all the poor women into a state of putrefaction; and lady Sarah, screwing up her mouth, would be *astonished* how a young person *allied* as her niece is, could forget herself so far as to condescend—, Hold, Sir Edward, cried Falkland, stop where you are. Fortune has indeed cast me beneath Miss Arnold, in depriving me of the inheritance of my ancestors, else where's the mighty difference? I believe the name of Falkland is at least as respectable as that of Arnold, and perhaps Bidulph into the bargain. Doubtless, said I; I was not speaking my own sentiments, but those of lady Sarah, who you know is one of the proudest women in England. Curse her pride! Cried he. With all my heart, said I, (glad to hear the lad utter so sensible a sentence.) I despise it, continued he, as much as I do the arrogance of her husband, who always affected, even in my childhood, to treat me as a wretch whom his sister's charity preserved from perishing; but there may come a day of retaliation. I wish, said I, for I hate Sir George most cordially, that both the girls would run away with two such idle fellows as you and I; I think that would mortify him completely, for I know he will be for clapping a coronet on each of them, merely for the pleasure of saying, My niece lady such-a-thing, though the title were lady Beezlebub.

I saw Falkland was full of indignation; he walked backwards and forwards two or three times, then taking up your letter again, which still lay on the table, and running it over a second time,

And so, said he, *Miss* Cecilia is the life of the family at Burnly. I wish she would spare a little of her vivacity to her poor sister. The *miss* was emphatical, and I perceived he was nettled at the judicious hint which you threw in with regard to Cecilia's happy indifference.

But what is the meaning, Sir Edward, said he, that you don't go and see Miss Audley? I think she really has reason to complain of you. Why truly, Falkland, answered I, I don't think a *sister* an inducement quite strong enough to turn a man from more agreeable engagements. If I had the same motives for visiting there that you have, probably she would have less cause to complain. Ay, but compassion, Sir Edward; suppose we were to go to Woodberry this afternoon, just to ask the ladies how they do? With all my heart, said I, yawning and stretching myself out almost at full length in the arm-chair.—What time shall we go? Said he. Oh, when you will; about five o'clock I suppose.—Falkland, will you lend me this book? Pointing to a collection of poems that stood on the chimney-piece.

I left him here; and now, Sophy, you may expect to see Falkland at the above-mentioned hour; but not your humble servant you may depend on it. Your messenger has just this minute called on me, so I hurry him off with a heap of trumpery pamphlets for a blind; but remember I expect a good account of this same visit.

Letter XVIII.
Miss Audley to Sir Edward Audley.
Woodberry, July 25th.

Edward, I am not amorous enough to enter into the spirit of a love scene, and had any eclaircissement been brought about, I should have laid down my pen in despair, for I would not attempt to describe the sublime folly of a pair of happy lovers met together. I shall however, I think, be able to paint the moderately silly scene that passed here this evening. Trust not to Falkland's representation, but take it from my faithful hand.

He arrived here a little before six. Miss Arnold and I were sitting at work in her dressing-room. Mr. Price, according to custom, gone to take his evening's nap. We heard Orlando coming upstairs, talking to, and caressing Miss Arnold's little lap-dog, who had ran to meet him. There's Mr. Falkland, said I; Dolly turned pale, and instantly took out her smelling-bottle, which I believe prevented her from fainting. The footman threw open the door, and in darted the triumphant varlet,[1] blooming as a cherub; the wind as he rid had heightened his colour and blown his auburn hair about his cheeks; he really looked insufferably handsome. Poor Dolly made him a very low curtsie, unable to speak. He addressed me first, then advancing to her with something in his air that I never observed before, I hope, ma'am, you are perfectly recovered from your indisposition since I saw you last? *Madam* was a new expression. She answered in the same strain, I am much better, Sir, only to-day I have had a little return of the head-ach. Falkland looked earnestly at her; her conscious eyes, unable to meet his, were cast down to the ground. He took the work she was doing out of her hand; (it was a purse which she intended for him) Extremely pretty, he said it was, so well fancied! But would not working make her head worse? And he held it behind his back. It is for you, said I, that she is so busily employed. For me, my dear creature! Then I insist on your laying it by, at least that you do not more of it whilst I am here. Miss Arnold blushed excessively; but suffered him to put her work into a little basket that lay on the window. He did this with that sort of authority which a man assumes even in trifles where he knows he has power. Dolly looked exceedingly silly, having nothing now to take off her attention from Falkland. He said he should be obliged to her for a dish of tea, and she flew to ring the bell with an alacrity which shewed her readiness to prevent, if possible, his smallest wish.

I enquired after you: He is a sad lazy fellow, said Falkland; I proposed to him that we should both wait on you together this evening, and he promised to come with me; but when the appointed hour arrived, no Sir Edward was to be found. I suppose some vagary came across him, which made him forget his engagement.

The tea was brought up, which a little relieved Miss Arnold from the awkwardness of her situation, as it afforded her something to do; but how different was this from our former little parties! Nothing entertaining, nothing instructive, nothing even lively was said of either side; in short, neither of them spoke a word of common sense, a visible constraint chained both their tongues; and Falkland who has as much vivacity, and Dolly who has as good an understanding as any one, appeared each under greater disadvantages than ever I saw them. Yet I could perceive that Falkland was not inattentive to his deportment; (what

---

1 A knave or a rogue.

designing wretches you men are!) the creature contrived to be amiable in every attitude into which he threw himself, and when their eyes happened to encounter, he had the impudence to blush; ay, the *impudence*, for it was not modesty; while, on the contrary, the answering vermillion that mantled in the cheeks of Miss Arnold, was laid on by the innocent hand of bashfulness. He asked, was there any hopes of Mrs. Arnold's speedy return? No, Dolly replied, she can't leave poor lady V—; my mama is to be pitied in so melancholy a situation. Your sister must have but a dull time of it, said the sly toad, over-doing the thing from a conscious knowledge of what I had written to you on that head. I should have thought so too, said Dolly; but my mama writes me word that Cecilia's constant chearfulness is the only resource which supports my mama's own spirits. This was a most fortunately reply. Falkland was silent for a little while, then with an expression in his looks, which said in plain English, *I know you love me, and I am almost inclined to return it*, he answered, Some people are happy through insensibility; I wish I could change hearts with Cecilia. A sort of a half sigh which he blew away, conveyed even more than he spoke. Whether this was drawn from him at the thoughts of Cecilia's indifference, or through compassion for her sister, I can't pretend to say.

Dolly's confusion was too apparent to be concealed; she leaned her head on one of her hands, resting her fine turned arm on the tea-table, her eyes half closed; and I thought that Falkland gazed at her with a mixture of tenderness, gratitude, and pity. This seemed a lucky crisis, and I thought might be productive of something, if a third person were not present, I rose from my chair. Where are you going? Cried Miss Arnold, starting from her reverie. Only for some thread to finish my work, said I, (for I had pretended to be fiddling at it all the time we were at tea). Pray, my dear, work no more this evening, said she, let us go and take a turn in the garden. I must go for my hat then, I replied. She looked embarrassed, as if afraid of being left alone with Falkland; and rising up, said she also would go for hers, and accordingly followed me out of the room.

What's your opinion, said she, taking me by the arm as we entered my chamber, has your brother been faithful to you or not? I know not, I replied; but of thus much I am sure, that Falkland has betrayed the lover more than once this evening. I thought so too, answered she; Oh, Sophy, where, where will this end? In your mutual happiness I hope, my dear. Oh, no, which ever way I cast my eyes, Sophy, I charge you never leave me when

Falkland comes to visit us, for I tell you once more, I have no security but in his silence. I wish my mama would return, or send for me to Burnly; 'twere better I were in my grave than that I should overturn the hopes and the peace of my whole family.

When we went back to the room where we had left Falkland, we found Mr. Price with him. They had entered upon some literary subject, in which the pupil seemed to acquit himself very much to the satisfaction of his tutor. The old man joined us in our walk into the garden, so that nothing more to the purpose passed for the rest of the afternoon; only I could observe that Falkland in bidding Miss Arnold adieu, looked—I don't know how; but not as he used to do.

Old Price entertained us with his praises all supper-time, and Dolly seemed so delighted, I thought two or three times she would have kissed the old man.

Edward, if this affair should turn out unfortunately, I should never forgive myself for the part I have acted in it; for next to your happiness I really wish that of poor Miss Arnold. Yet at worst, I cannot see any great harm that can ensue, but a little *fracas*[1] in the Arnold family; and if they should be so obstinate as never to take her into grace again, she has a fortune in her own power sufficient to make her happy with the man she loves.

As for Cecilia, if you can win her affections, which I am partial enough to you to think very probable, I believe you would not find it difficult to obtain her. She loves gaiety, and by the bye, is a little weary of restraint; and one thing I am sure of, as she has more spirit than her sister, she will not have a choice imposed on her by her friends, of which she herself does not approve. I remember once when we girls were talking over Mrs. Arnold's unfortunate story, Cecilia blamed her grand-mama Bidulph's scruples with regard to Mr. Falkland, the father of your friend, and went so far as to say that she thought her mother had made too great a sacrifice to duty, in giving him up so easily. This makes for you, Edward; she is not so much terrified at the thoughts of a giddy fellow as her sister is; besides, really I think your family and rank in life might fairly entitle you to either of them, so that (abstractedly from the absolute necessity you are under of getting twenty thousand pounds *some* where, and which is not to be found under every stone) I am far from looking upon our alliance as an injury to the family, not even to Sir George Bidulph's saucy looks, and lady Sarah's pinched nose.

---

1 A disturbance, row, or quarrel.

I have left Dolly reading politicks to the old dryad, whose eyes begin to fail him, and have stole upstairs to scribble. I shall dispatch this to you early in the morning by my flying-post, as I call Jerry, and you may return me a line by him to inform me how Falkland's pulse beats, if you have seen him since his visit here.

P.S. I had almost forgot to tell you that Dolly and I had half an hour's chat by ourselves after Falkland was gone, for I am now no longer *forbid* to speak of him; the case is altered, our fears of his indifference are at an end. The poor girl finds herself plunged in deeper than before, and wonders at the cause; *for she is affected beyond measure at the thoughts of his being as wretched as herself;* the pleasure of being beloved again, more than counterbalances her fears for the consequences, and I believe at this minute she does not well know whether she is sorry or glad.

Letter XIX.
Sir Edward Audley to Miss Audley.

Oxford, July 26th.

A few words, Sophy, and no more. Falkland supped with me last night, and after having railed at me for breaking my engagement, which I excused my own way, he told me what passed in yesterday's interview pretty nearly as you related it; only with a few additions suggested, I suppose, by his own vanity: for he said Miss Arnold looked so pale and languishing that it grieved him to the heart and he could *kill* himself for being the cause. Coxcomb, muttered I to myself, what pity it is thou canst boast of such a conquest! The thing was now so apparent, he said, that a man must be blind not to see it; and the lady must think him very stupid or very ungrateful, if he did not at least appear sensible of the honour she did him. Very true, Falkland, undoubtedly, the laws of humanity, the laws of civility demand so much from you. For though it is the farthest in the world from my thoughts, said he, to take any advantage of her tenderness, yet surely I may make her a return of friendship and esteem, though I mean to go no farther. By all means, said I; or suppose you were to throw in a little *Platonic* love, there can be no harm in that either; two seraphims[1] might entertain *that* for each other; and Miss Arnold seems of a turn to relish those aetherial ardors, much better than

---

1 Seraphim are angels who hover near the throne of God. Platonic love is a spiritual love or friendship in contrast to sexual or physical love.

a vulgar passion. I said this with so grave a countenance and tone of voice, that he did not find me out. I am much of your mind, replied he; and if I thought it would contribute to her happiness, I would pay her my Platonic adorations with all my soul, for I have absolutely no designs upon her person, though I think her very handsome, but Cecilia has been beforehand with her in my heart. Well, prithee, said I, take compassion on the poor girl; you may make love to her in blank verse; (for a man is never serious but in prose) and if she allows you the privilege of kissing the tip of her little finger, (though I believe even that is beyond the bounds of Platonism) you must seem in raptures with the favour, and speak of it as the ultimate of your wishes. This will sooth her and divert you, and no harm can come of it; and so here's Dolly Arnold's health. We both drank it, and he seems pleased with the conceit. Yet 'tis such a sly varlet, that even my plummet, which is not a short one, cannot fathom him to the bottom; for whether he really means to pursue this hint, or pretended to adopt it merely to save his credit with me, after his former declarations, I am at a loss to determine; but be it which way it will, the success is equally sure, for I never knew a pair of seraphic lovers who did not bring matters to a very earthly conclusion in the end, no matter what their designs were, at setting out. I think it only now remains to contrive opportunities for Falkland to express his *disinterested friendship*, and *exalted esteem* for Miss Arnold, without any witnesses. I wish the venerable Price would take a nap for the remainder of the summer, for he is very much in our way; yet he sometimes dines abroad; can't you give me notice of those days, and I'll engage for Falkland's attending you on them? depend upon it he will not want much spurring; I shall turn his vanity to good account. And then you know, Sophy, you must sometimes pay your duty to your mama, why not *that* day as well as another? You had absolutely promised before, and your mama will take it ill if you disappoint her. As for my part, I have so many whimsical engagements, that I can never be at loss to excuse myself for not going with Falkland, if he should ask me; I don't know whether I shan't even tell him, that having had myself a little *penchant* for Miss Arnold, it would not afford me the least entertainment to be an humble spectator of his triumphs. There will be nothing amiss in this, I think; yet I shall either venture it or not, as occasion serves.—

Here follows a series of letters between Miss Audley and her brother, by which it appears that Mr. Falkland daily gained a stronger ascendancy over the heart of Miss Arnold; and if he did not altogether adopt the Platonic system, he at least had not made any declarations of another nature. The lady gives her brother a circumstantial account of what passed in every visit, some of which were contrived (though without Miss Arnold's knowledge) in Mr. Price's absence; Miss Audley herself sometimes forming pretences to be out of the way, on which occasion her friend always told her the substance of those conversations she held with Falkland.

Sir Edward Audley, on the other hand, relates to his sister what discoveries he had made in the *investigation*, as he calls it, of Falkland's heart, and wherein he hints that he still thought him devoted to Cecilia. During the course of this whole correspondence, there is manifested a surprizing deal of art, practised by this intriguing brother and sister, in order to pervert the minds of the two young persons, on whom they had their separate influence; in which attempt, Sir Edward seems to have in some measure succeeded. It appears that Miss Audley and her brother but seldom met, which in one of her letters she accounts for in these words, "It will not now be in my power to see you, for as my mama is going to the Farm with Harry, (who I think continues very puny) I shall have no pretence for going to Oxford, as Miss Arnold knows I have no acquaintance amongst the townspeople, and she is with me in every other visit I make."

As the above-mentioned series of letters contain a very minute detail, which tho' not unentertaining, does nevertheless not very considerably advance the story; the editor has, to avoid swelling this collection to too great a bulk, omitted them; and in this place presents the reader with one from Mrs. Arnold, which he has selected from some others as that which more immediately carries on the narrative.

Letter XX.
Mrs. Arnold to Miss Arnold.
Burnly, Sept. 3d.

I thought to have embraced my dearest Dolly as on this day, and am as much mortified at the disappointment, as I am sure she will be; but an unlooked for accident has occurred, which will detain me here a week or ten days longer.

You know, I told you in my last, that lady V— had been ordered to the Bath by her physicians. Poor woman, she has not only lost all appetite, but now complains of such a constant and violent pain in her stomach, that if the waters don't relieve her, we are apprehensive of the worst consequences. The very day on which this journey was determined, and fixed for the first of September, I received a letter from lady Sarah, in which she informed me that she was going immediately to Bath to spend a couple of months there; that Sir George was to call on her in his way to London, and that they should come to town together, she *hoped* before Christmas. She complains of not being well; but the truth I believe is, she was tired of Sidney Castle, for, you know, she hates the country. A thought unluckily came into lady V—'s head, which has been productive of something that has vexed me extremely. She begged I would write to lady Sarah, and intreat the favour of her to hire a house for lady V— and her family. As Mrs. and Miss Darnley go with her, they do not choose to be in lodgings, and they wished to have a place ready for their reception against they went down.

I writ immediately to lady Sarah agreeably to this request, and was favoured directly with an answer, wherein she tells me she has engaged a house for lady V—, beseeching me at the same time to let Miss Cecilia come with her to Bath, as she (lady Sarah) was quite alone, and I should make her wonderfully happy by indulging her with her niece's company. Inconsiderate woman! She values not the repose of any one but herself. Is she not to have you both with her next winter? And next winter may perhaps open to you new prospects, such as probably may separate you from your mother's arms; why then am I to be deprived of my Cecilia's chearful society sooner than there is a necessity for it? Why are you to be robbed of your sister's company after an absence already too long? For she adds in her letter, "*I shall bring Cecilia to London with me directly from hence, and Sir George himself shall go down to Oxfordshire for Miss Arnold on our return to town.*"

You cannot imagine, my dear, how this unseasonable demand has distressed me, because I cannot well tell how to refuse it. You are no stranger to the captious temper of lady Sarah, nor to the influence she has over your uncle. I know I should utterly disoblige both by a denial, and perhaps deprive you of the advantage of being with Sir George next winter, as my brother's actions are altogether regulated by her ladyship's pleasure. Lady V—, who looks upon this as an agreeable jaunt for my daughter, is very pressing that I should let her go; so are the other two ladies, but the child herself wishes to return to her sister. I cannot, however, excuse myself; Lady Sarah's instances are so pressing, the opportunity so convenient, and the company with whom she is to go, so eligible, that I have had an unwilling consent wrung from me already.

The house which lady Sarah has taken cannot be ready, it seems, this week, which has postponed lady V—'s journey, and in consequence of that my return home; as I would fain enjoy as much of my daughter's company as I can. She embraces you, my love, with all her heart. Tell my Orlando I am delighted with the account Mr. Price gives me of the progress he is making in his studies; he shares my heart equally with you and your sister. I hope the good old man approves as much of you in your capacity of mistress of a family, as he does in every thing else; and that you have supplied my place on more important occasions than merely that of presiding at my table. Assure Miss Audley I am highly sensible of the obligation I have to her and good lady Audley, for thus prolonging the happiness you have received from your young friend's amiable conversation. Adieu, my beloved; my next greeting to you, I hope, will be face to face in my own peaceful dwelling.———

Letter XXI.
Miss Audley to Sir Edward Audley
Woodberry, Sept. 6th.

[Miss Audley having in the beginning of her letter given her brother the substance of the above, proceeds:]

———What's more to be done now, Edward? How provoking it is thus to have this little lively eel slip through our fingers! She will have all the flutterers in the place about her, for the jackanapes[1] loves to be admired. Had she received her first impressions *here*, I should not be half so much alarmed; for constancy is accounted a prime virtue; and abiding by a first love, is a tenet held in great veneration amongst your young maidens bred up in the country; and you cannot conceive the advantage it gives a man to have made a *first* impression in a solitude; he will for a long time maintain the superiority he *then* appeared to have over the rest of mankind, and the same vows which perhaps would be rejected with scorn in a brilliant drawingroom, would probably be received with transport in a sequestered bower.

---

1 A monkey or a mischievous or impudent person.

This untoward accident has really damped my spirits so, that I cannot conjure up a single idea that affords me a gleam of comfort. I wish that narrow faced and narrow hearted vixen, lady Sarah, were bed-ridden at Sidney Castle. What's to be done, Edward? I repeat it once more.—

Letter XXII.
Sir Edward Audley to Miss Audley.
Oxford, September 6th.

I'll tell you what's to be done, Sophy; I set out to-morrow morning post for Bath, where, getting the start of the Burnly snails, I shall be on the spot to receive my little divinity, and shall take care to anticipate every puppy that dares approach her. I'll dance *with* her, sing *to* her, write verses *on* her, and shoot any man through the head that looks at her. My access to her will be easy, as Sir George Bidulph is not there; for I shall bribe all the servants, make love to lady Sarah's monkey, and swear she herself is the best bred woman in Christendom: and if the Lancashire family should be for putting in their *whys* and their *wherefores*, I'll accommodate myself to them too. I'll moralize with lady V—, lecture on housewifery with Mrs. Darnley, and bespatter reputations with the middle-aged maiden the daughter. Why, lord, child, 'tis the luckiest thing that could have happened; I look to be the idol of the whole set, and think it not at all unlikely that I shall trundle off Cecilia in a coach and six before the end of November—Ay, say you; but what pretence have you for taking this journey? What will Falkland say to such a flight? Bless me, Sophy! Have you not heard that our uncle Howel in Wales, who has been dying for these ten years, is now going to die in good earnest? And that, forgetting all old animosities, he is going to make his last will, and has sent for me, his heir apparent, to see me before his departure, and commit to my hands the pious care of closing his eyes? You have not heard a syllable of the matter? Heark ye, Sophy, a word in your ear; nor I neither. I would I could. Yet the thing must be just so; and I shall have, in ten minutes, the letter from his steward, commanding my personal attendances, ready written in my pocket. The short cut is from Gloucestershire across the Severn; and then, what so natural (the old gentleman having grown somewhat better, his mind being relieved by this his prudent disposition of his worldly affairs) what is so natural, I say, as for me, poor young man, wearied with my constant attendance on a sick bed, in my return to take a little trip to Bath by way of relaxation. For the story shall pass current there too—Ay; but then Cecilia will write home word that you are not only at Bath, but that you make love to *her*. She tells this to Dolly, Dolly tells it to Falkland, and then—Prithee stop. Sophy, don't be so rapid in thy conclusions; for not a tittle of this will come to pass. Cecilia is good-humour itself, and I need only say, My dear ma'am, pressing her hand gently (at a ball perhaps) when you write into Oxfordshire, if *I* am ever honoured with having a single thought bestowed on me, be so good as not to mention my being here; because I know if it should by any means come to my mother's ears, she would be much displeased at it, as she supposes I am still with my uncle, though I have absolutely his permission for returning home; but you know, ma'am, that ladies of a *certain* age do not always make proper allowances for young people. I am mistaken in my girl if she tell after this. The letter from Burnly, you say, was received this day, just after Falkland had taken his leave. He will not then know the contents of it till his next visit, which probably will not be these three or four days; and the deuce is in it if he can suspect against all likelihood, that I was before-hand with him: so that I mean tonight (for I have not yet seen him to-day) to shew him the letter that I received from my uncle's steward (he himself, poor soul, is not able to write) and I leave it to my mother to apprize you of this my sudden journey, as I have not a minute's time to write you a single line. So pluck up your spirits, chit, for our vessel skims before the wind.

Thus far in rhodomontade,[1] by way of answering your querulous demand of, *What's to be done, Edward?* But now to be serious; you and I consider this circumstance of Cecilia's visit to Bath in very different lights. Had Falkland had either love enough, or courage enough, (for I know not in which of the two he is most wanting) to have brought matters to a conclusion with Miss Arnold, Cecilia's return to Woodberry would then have been a desirable thing, as I might, in that case, agreeably to your ideas, have safely ventured to offer up my incense to her in some *sequestered bower*, without fear of having my devotion interrupted by any competitor for her favour. But unsteady as Falkland is in all his purposes, and particularly so with regard to Miss Arnold, I think his having her sister before his eyes (to whom I know him attached) was a thing rather to be dreaded; and though he has no

---

1   "A vainglorious brag or boast" (*OED*).

hopes of her himself, he would certainly be a bar to my pretensions. On the contrary, cut off as he now is from the expectation of seeing her (as she is to go from Bath directly to London)) I think he will, in all human probability, be wise enough not to lose a substance for a shadow, but, laying hold of Miss Arnold's favourable prepossession for him, he will, in some soft minute, determine, and declare himself. Once fixed, he is no longer to be feared; and I may, without reproach, pursue my fortune. I shall spend all the coming winter in London, an advantage which will be out of *his* power; and as I intend studiously to cultivate lady Sarah's acquaintance, I shall at least be always sure of a reception in town, whilst poor Falkland perhaps will be glad to use my intervention with his love; for I do not suppose the little dastard will venture at once to run away with him. This, you see, will make me a person of importance with Dolly; consequently get her on my side, and engage her to promote my interests with her sister: so that though things have taken a turn in some respects different from what we expected, our main purpose remains unchanged; and I hold it expedient that Falkland's amour should be advanced with your best skill. Fail not to let me know how the quicksilver rises and falls in that variable machine—

P.S. our mama is in the secret, and you will be *properly* apprized of my departure for Wales—

Letter XXIII.
Sir Edward Audley to Miss Audley.
Bath, Sept. 20th.

Every thing hitherto has happened precisely as I foresaw it would—And where do you think I am lodged? Even under the very roof with my Cecilia; for I took care, the moment I got hither, to secure lodgings in the same house with lady Sarah Bidulph, who perfectly *doats* on me. What do you think of that, Sophy? I would not change my knack of dissembling for an estate of five thousand a year: and I am wise in the preference; for I should squander the one in a year or two, and the other is an inexhaustible treasure.

Lady Sarah (to whom I early paid my court) told me by way of news (for I was but just arrived from Wales) that she expected her niece in a day or two. 'Tis very kind in your ladyship, said I, to take the poor young creature under your own conduct; for to say the truth, Mrs. Arnold (though she is an extremely *good* woman) is not *quite* the pattern that one would choose for young persons to form their manners by, who may probably one day make a figure in the polite world—Why that's the very thing, Sir Edward; the poor creatures are absolutely rusticated—Oh, ma'am, they will be totally undone, if you don't take them into your own hands; for all the world knows your ladyship's knowledge in the science of good *breeding* is superior to that of almost every woman of quality in England—Oh, Sir, your humble servant—I believe, indeed, (with as pleased a look as the little crabbed countenance could assume) I have been rather more conversant in those matters than poor Mrs. Arnold. How do you pass your time, lady Sarah? Are there any people of fashion here at present? Lord, I don't know; I am but just come myself; though I fancy there are but few here as yet that one can converse with. If your ladyship has any services to command me, I am intirely at your devotion.

We walked out together. She fell in love with a set of china that stood in a shop window as we passed by; but upon enquiry, finding them, as she thought, too dear, her avarice got the better of her person, and she went home without buying them; but I took care to send them to her, and was invited to drink tea out of them the same evening.

When the family of Burnly arrived, having already dedicated myself to lady Sarah, I was determined not to lose ground by the approach of Cecilia. On the contrary, I have made myself absolutely necessary to them all. I go to church with lady V—, and to market with Mrs. Darnley; for she is too notable to trust this office to a servant. I *shop* it, as the ladies call it, with lady Sarah, and bespeak caps at the milliner's for the girls. In short, they all allow me to be a *very modest pretty kind of young man*; and if my *state* were answerable, lady Sarah should not *much* dislike me for one of her nieces. This she whispered to Miss Darnley, who dropped it to her waiting-maid, who told it to David, who communicates every thing to his master. But all these serve but as a chorus to a dramatic piece: they may help to carry on the business of the scene, but are none of them in themselves objects of attention. The principal personage, the heroine of the story, the Cecilia, I have not yet been able sufficiently to draw out from amongst this group of supernumerary figures. 'Tis such a little flash of lightening, there is no knowing where to have her; and if I were to be hanged for it, I cannot at this minute divine whether she likes me or not; but I rather suspect she does. I have been playing my batteries on her for several days, and am always received with good humour. I make love to her sometimes, even before lady Sarah's face, who, looking upon it (for that very reason) as pleasantry, does not discourage it; but if I grow serious, as I now and then do, when I get Cecilia in a corner, the urchin always calls Miss Darnley to her assistance, and then the two wasps fasten on me, and sting me to death with their flippant tongues. This is, Sophy, but the opening of the campaign; yet I hope to return to you crowned with laurels; and then, I think, with the help of Falkland's myrtles, we may twine a pretty garland.[1]

Letter XXIV.
Miss Audley to Sir Edward Audley.
Oxford, Sept. 25th.

What an idle creature are you, brother, not to have given me a line sooner! When you might be very certain, that irregular as I know you to be in your motions, I would not venture to write to you till I was sure you were fixed. I believe I must allow, after all, that though we women have livelier imaginations, you men have deeper judgments, and know better how to deduce consequences; for our affairs here are beginning to fall into the very track which you foresaw and foretold. Falkland seems nettled at Cecilia's going to Bath, instead of returning home with her mama, as if he thought himself neglected by it; and by way of being revenged on her for slighting a passion of which she is ignorant, and which probably were she to know she would contemn, he is become more assiduous, than ever with regard to Dolly. How ridiculous is this! Yet 'tis human nature, at least 'tis the nature of you striplings. It is matter of astonishment to me, that he has not yet assumed courage enough to declare himself; for that he has not done so I am convinced, and Miss Arnold begins to lull her fears asleep with a pretty idea which she has lately taken up, viz., that there is a *most perfect friendship* subsisting between them, which, if it were not for considerations of duty, *might*, she owns, possibly rise to a real passion on *both* sides; but checked as they now are, they content themselves with confining their ardor within the bounds of *esteem*, and desire no greater felicity than seeing and conversing with each other. I indulge her

---

1 Sir Edward refers to the traditional association of laurel with victory and myrtle with love.

in this romantic folly, relying on your sagacity for what the conclusion of this fancy will be, when opportunity serves.

I returned home, overwhelmed with thanks and acknowledgement, the day after Mrs. Arnold arrived at her own house; and since that, Falkland's visits to Woodberry have not been so frequent, for the good lady does not approve of such repeated excursions from *our* studies; but you may be sure I do not suffer a harmless and disinterested friendship to languish for want of the means to keep it up: therefore whenever Dolly pays me a visit without her mama, which is often the case, Falkland is always of the party; for what is more natural than to ask him, who is next door to us in a manner, to come and drink tea with his *sister* Arnold? But the worst of it is, I cannot, upon those occasions, contrive, with any colour of decorum, to leave them to a *tete a tete*; and I don't take it to be the mode now-a-days, as it was in times of old, for lovers to breathe out their amorous wishes in the presence of a confident. I have, however, given a little stroke, on which I pique myself, and from which I expect wonderful effects.

I was yesterday to pay Miss Arnold a morning visit. Whilst I was with her, a letter arrived from Bath: it was from Cecilia. Dolly opened it with impatience, and I observed smiled as she read. What entertains you so much? Said I. Cecilia is in high spirits, said she, and extremely pleasant in her little narratives. And why won't you let me partake of the pleasure? She read part of the first page of the letter to me, in which Cecilia, in her sprightly way, gives an account of the company, amusements, &c. when coming towards the bottom, she stopped short, skipped over some lines, and began a paragraph at the other side. What's that you boggle so at, Dolly? There is a secret here, said she, which I must not divulge—Tell it me this minute; you do nothing if you don't give me the secret. Would *I* keep one from you? Ah, fy, Miss Arnold!—She smiled again, and giving me the letter, There, said she, there seems to be very little in it, nor can I conceive why my sister should enjoin me secrecy; but since she *has* done so, I desire, Sophy, you won't speak of it to any one. My mama is so indulgent, she never desires to see the correspondence which passes between my sister and me. Cecilia, after having, by way of raillery, talked of some conquests she had made, says these words: "All these are but flutterers, and I believe only *pretend* to like me, because I am the fashion; but I *have* a lover here, who is one in sober sadness: for when a man tries to win the good opinion of one's friends, we may be sure he means something more than mere compliment. You would be surprized were I to name him, but that I shan't do till we meet. Mean while I have particular reasons that even thus much should not be known: therefore, I beg, my dear, you will not mention it to any one whatsoever."

I returned the letter to Dolly, telling her I thought her sister had instructed just *nothing* to her confidence. I concluded, Cecilia meant no other than *you* by this nameless lover, and thought her very faithful in keeping your counsel; but I resolved at the same time to make a proper use of the hint she had given her sister. I engaged Dolly, with her mama's permission, to spend the next day with me. She came accordingly this morning; Falkland was with us; we three were in the garden together. He asked Miss Arnold when she had heard from her sister? Yesterday, she replied. He hoped Miss Cecilia was well? Very well, was all Dolly's answer. But I, who was determined he should know a little more, blurted out, Ay, but you don't tell him of the lover that Cecilia—Dolly looked at me. I clapped my hand upon my mouth, as if conscious of having done wrong. What a blab am I! Cried I. A blab, indeed! Said Dolly, a little gravely; upon my word, Miss Audley, I will never trust you again. Falkland coloured up to the eyes; but affecting to laugh, Prithee, who is this lover? Said he. 'Tis nothing but a joke, answered Miss Arnold, yet I love fidelity even in trifles.—I winked at Falkland, as much as to say, Ask no more questions. He took my meaning, and turned the conversation; but, as I expected, failed not to demand an explanation after Miss Arnold was gone. *I* affected mystery at first; but after much pressing was at last *prevailed* on to tell him, that Cecilia had written her sister word that she was addressed by a gentleman of whom she spoke very handsomely, and who had made himself very acceptable to lady Sarah Bidulph; but that till her mama was properly apprized of it, either by her ladyship or Sir George, she desired the affair might not be mentioned at all. Falkland asked the name of this lover; I told him, that either Cecilia had not named him, or if she had, Dolly had not thought proper to trust me with it; and I begg'd of him never to speak of the thing to Miss Arnold, as it would only serve to make her reproach me with my indiscretion. He looked mortified; but said I might depend on it he should not give himself the *trouble* to make enquiries about a subject in which he was *no way concerned.* Good, said I to myself. If I be not mistaken, young man, you will become a lover in good earnest out of pure spite—Call you not this advancing his amour, Edward?

[Here follows another series of letters between Sir Edward and Miss Audley, which, for the same reasons before offered, are omitted, as they contain nothing more than reciprocal accounts of the progress of their schemes. Sir Edward maintains in several of them that he had hopes of succeeding with Cecilia, as lady Sarah not only admitted but encouraged his visits. Miss Audley informs her brother that her young friend, without knowing it, was every day more and more in love, and she thought that Falkland himself was become more tender. The following letter the Editor thinks the only one of this number materially necessary to the carrying on of the story.]

Letter XXV.

Miss Audley to Sir Edward Audley

Oxford, Nov. 2d.

Io, Io, triumph! Oh, Edward, I wish thy vows and Cecilia's were reciprocated with the same solemnity, as those of Falkland and Miss Arnold were last night. I knew it would, I knew it *must* come to that; and the lovers, without absolutely being married, are hampered in the very ties we wished them.

Miss Arnold came to us yesterday about five o'clock; she had got leave to go with my mama and me to an assembly, and consequently was to lie at our house that night, for Mrs. Arnold has indulged her in greater liberties than usual on account of her sister's absence. My mama (as was preconcerted) had gone out immediately after dinner. *She was sent for in a violent hurry to a lady, a particular friend of hers who was in labour; there was no refusing such a summons; but she would, if possible, return time enough to go with us to the assembly.* Falkland was with us by appointment, and was to have attended us thither.

Dolly was dressed with the utmost elegance, and looked like an angel; but I saw by her informed countenance the minute she entered the room that something disturbed her. I made my mama's excuses to her, telling her, if she could not disengage herself time enough from her friend, that I would, if Miss Arnold chose it, endeavour to get some other married lady to go with us. Suppose, said Falkland, we were to change the scheme of this evening's entertainment, and instead of going to the stupid assembly, pass the evening where we are? With all my heart, answered I; And mine, cried Miss Arnold, for I do not find myself at present much disposed for the amusements of such a place.

Falkland now approached her, and sitting down by her, took her hand respectfully; Something has disconcerted you, my dear Miss Arnold, said he, I have seen it in your looks ever since you came in; *tell* me?—What's the matter?—There are certain persuasive tones (of which Falkland is a perfect master) that are not to be resisted; he can, when he pleases, assume a sweet plaintiveness in his voice, that I have often considered as a dangerous advantage. Dolly, I believe, felt the force of it in that instant. She withdrew her hand gently from his, and, not daring to confess the true cause of her uneasiness; she replied, I am the most unfit person in the world for a life of hurry; you cannot imagine how much my spirits have been fluttered to-day, to think of what a scene of tumult and dissipation I am going to plunge into at my uncle Bidulph's for lady Sarah is never happy but in a crowd. You do not as yet think of going to London? Cried Falkland. I apprehended Sir George purposed not to return till after Christmas. He has changed his mind, answered Dolly, or rather lady Sarah has changed it for him; for they purpose setting out together from Bath next Sunday, and the following week my uncle comes himself to fetch me to town. I believe, added she, Sir George has a husband in his thoughts for my sister, for he informs my mama that my lord V— is now at Bath. He bestows great encomiums on him, and says that lady V— and he have already given him to Cecilia, with whom my lord is quite charmed; and this I suppose was the lover that Cecilia hinted at.

I saw the blood mount into Falkland's cheeks; he seemed mortified,—but whether at the thoughts of Cecilia's marriage, or at those of losing his conquest by Dolly's removing to London, I can't say; for I know not whether love or vanity was in that moment most predominant. They were both silent for a little while; Falkland's eyes were fixed on Miss Arnold, hers were bent to the ground: and I perceived it was with difficulty she restrained her tears. He saw it too; this was the time to speak. You are going, madam, said he, to receive the homage of all the world; this obscure corner will be no longer in your thoughts, and you will forget perhaps even the *friendship* with which you have honoured me.—No!—was all Dolly could reply; she dared not to trust the steadiness of her voice with any more; even this poor little monosyllable, though uttered emphatically, was not raised above her breath. Again they were both silent, and I waited with that kind of expectation, I believe, in my face that tame fowls appear to have when they expect a shower. What would I then have given for a decent pretence to have left the room! The juncture seemed so critical, if let slip perhaps it was irrecoverable. In short, I was just going to rise and leave them without any pretence at all, when a loud rap at the door offered me a very fair one; up I bounced from my chair, and flew out of the parlour to order myself to be denied, as I told them, having forgot to use this precaution before; but one of the servants, happening to be in the hall, had already opened the door, and in rustled Miss Leatham. I led her into the little drawing-room, called for lights, and we both sat down. Right glad was I of her company, insipid as it is, as it afforded me a very good excuse for absenting myself a while from the two friends, who, I had reason to believe, would in that interval discover the fallacy of the Platonic system.

Miss Leatham was going to the assembly; but as she is one of those who affects coming in late to a public place, she chose to oblige me with her company for half an hour before she went. Having exhausted her whole stock of ideas, she asked me (observing I was dressed out) whether I did not mean to go to the assembly? I told her it had been my intention, but that a young lady who was to have gone with me, and who was then in the house, having been taken ill had prevented my design. This was a sufficient hint, and she went away directly.

I returned to the parlour, and was very soon convinced that Falkland had not made a foolish use of his time. Dolly had but just time to withdraw her hand from his lips, as I entered the room. You and I, Edward, who can read faces, would have wanted no other information of what had passed, than what we could have learnt from both of theirs. On his, sat an air of triumph, mingled with pleasure and gratitude: On hers complacency and redoubled tenderness, chastened by fear. He now assumed the conversations with the utmost freedom, and rattled away on the subject of my visitor (whom he knows very well) with that kind of ease which a person discovers, who having happily dispatched some important concern that hung on their mind, descends into the common affairs of life with a disposition to be pleased with everything. Dolly, on the other hand, was silent, and even appeared embarrassed; yet through this I could discover an inward satisfaction that proved to me her *heart* was more at ease than before. *She* seemed *more* relieved than usual; Falkland, much *less*. He more than once ventured to take her hand; she constantly withdrew it, yet her looks reprimanded not the freedom. Lord, how prettily foolish was all this! I would have given six-pence for a lover myself; and had Cecilia and you been present, all the world to nothing she would have been your own; for, as I told you before, Edward, we girls hate to be like cyphers.

My mama returned to supper (she could not possibly get away from her friend sooner.) We were all infinitely good humoured, but rather sillyish; for every one was full of themselves, though each asked questions of the other, about which they did not care a pinch of snuff to be informed. Falkland took his leave at a very decent hour, and Miss Arnold and I retired to my chamber, for she chose to sleep with me. When we were alone, Well, my dear? Said I. Oh, Sophy, (both her hands held up) what have I done? *What* have you done, Dolly? No harm, I am sure.—I have given myself away! An irrevocable vow has passed my lips never to be the wife of any man but Falkland! Bravo! Said I. Good God, cried she, clasping her hands together, are you not startled at the phrenzy of this action? I am frightened when I look back; how little ought we to be trusted with ourselves? Oh, Miss Audley, you left me in a fatal minute. Had I escaped to-night, I was determined never to have given Mr. Falkland another opportunity, for *till* to-night he never explained himself. And what said he to-night, Miss Arnold? For hitherto, as far as I understand, (whatever his secret wishes might have been) he seemed not to *claim* more than friendship and esteem from you. Sophy, said she, whilst you live never contract a friendship with a *man*; 'twas that deceitful word which has ensnared me, and led me at last to burst the bonds of filial duty, of confidence, of gratitude to the best of mothers!—Cecilia, too, what will *she* say to find her sister castaway? A flood of tears now burst from her eyes. Have you not, my dear, said I, received the vows of Falkland in return? Oh yes, answered she, yet I know not how it came to pass. My mind was all a chaos, I forgot every thing, I existed but to him; and he obtained my promise before I was sensible that he had demanded it. The moment you left the room, conscious of my own weakness and terrified at my situation, I burst into tears; Falkland wept at the same time. I could not bear this; I started up from my chair and would have ran out. I believe I should have flown to you, my eyes all red as they were; but he catched me by the hand,—You are going, my dear Miss Arnold, said he, you are going to be the idol of a thousand hearts, and I shall be forgotten. Impossible, I cried; Oh, Falkland! You know too well that that is impossible!— Say then, said he, that I shall never lose the place that I have now the happiness to possess in your heart.—Sinking almost into the earth with confusion, I scarcely articulated the word, Never! Will you then be mine? He demanded.—I know not what answer I returned; an assent no doubt it was, for he instantly (for the first time) took the liberty of saluting me, and then in the strongest expressions swore he would live only for me.—Awaked as it were from a dream, I cried out, What have I said? What has made me the happiest of men, he replied, you have promised to be mine only. See, Sophy, continued she, into what an irretrievable error a few short minutes may betray us! He talked afterwards of a private marriage, hopeless as he is of getting my friends' consent; but I conjured him not to speak of that.—Why, what do you then mean to do, my dear? Interrupted I: surely you purpose to fulfill your engagements to Falkland? Doubtless, said she, I wed him or my grave; yet how is it possible for me all at once to determine on a step so rash, and but a few hours ago, so unforeseen? We are both very young, we may wait a while—Time, with the interposition of a few compassionate friends, may do something in our favour. I know my uncle has ambitious views both for my sister and me; but perhaps he may be satisfied with disposing of Cecilia to a titled husband, and leave me free to make an humbler choice. If my sister should marry lord V— I stopped her short here, thinking it very expedient to throw in a seasonable word for you; A propos, Dolly, said I, you imagine that lord V— was the nameless lover whom Cecilia hinted at in a former letter to you; but I am of a quite different opinion, and rather suspect 'tis my mad-cap of a brother. Though I affected to say this very jocosely, Miss Arnold seemed surprized, and asked me why I thought so; Because, said I, I have had a letter from him very lately, wherein he tells me he has been at Bath for some time; but charges me not to let my mama know it, as she would be very angry with him for absenting himself from my uncle Howel. Well? Said Miss Arnold. Well, said I, and he says, that in order to drive you from his thoughts, and be revenged of you at the same time, he makes love to your sister. This is so like Sir Edward! Continued I, laughing; but I can tell you, he adds that Cecilia receives him kindly, and that he is a great favourite of lady Sarah's; and really your sister's keeping his secret, which I suppose he begg'd of her to do, *does* carry with it an air of kindness. 'Tis very true, said Miss Arnold, smiling, and I am very glad to find that the slight wound he received from me is so soon healed. My brother, said I, is not so romantic as to love on without the hopes of a return; but if Cecilia be disposed to make him one, I insist on it, Dolly, that you do not endeavour to divert her inclinations from him, by telling her what has passed, with regard to yourself. Ah, Miss Audley! Replied she, I have *now* no right to prescribe to my sister; I am too much humbled in my own eyes, to presume to be a monitor. There was something indignant in her manner, like one who felt themselves under the mortifying necessity of conforming (however repugnant to their own sentiments) to the will of those in whose power they have put themselves. This, Edward, is not the least of those ourselves, when we deviate a little from the very narrow and thorny paths of rectitude; but let Miss Arnold consider it thus if she will, it makes for our purpose; and one sometimes obtains from fear, what even friendship would deny, and gratitude itself would refuse. If Sir Edward, said I, is so happy as to succeed with Cecilia, it will pave the way for Falkland. The disparity between *them* is not so great as between your lover, and lord V—, and your choice would not throw you at such a distance from your sister; that single consideration should induce you to countenance my brother's pretensions; besides, the strict friendship between them will enable you to hear from, and perhaps oftner to see Falkland than you could otherwise expect.—No, Sophy, said she, my sister shall never have *my* example as an excuse for disobedience. If Sir Edward wins her heart, I shall not interpose between them, (though I do not think 'tis likely he should ever obtain the suffrage of my family) but Cecilia shall not have the frailty of her elder sister to plead in her excuse for an imprudent choice; therefore be assured I shall conceal my engagements with Mr. Falkland as carefully from her, as I would from the rest of my friends, till the more favourable opportunity shall offer of divulging them. What a perverse determination is this, Edward! It has unhinged the principal movement in our machine; yet my hope is, that Dolly will not be able to keep her resolution.

But if after all the pains with which I have been labouring for your interests, my lord V— should step in and snatch away the reward of our toil! The thought is not to be borne; *Have I for Banquo's issue*, &c.[1] Oh, Edward, it rests upon the single point of a young girl's liking a sprightly young fellow of twenty-three, better than an exceedingly grave man (the very reverse of her own

---

1   Miss Audley cites the following lines from Shakespeare's *Macbeth* 3.1: "He chid the sisters / When first they put the name of king upon me, / And bade them speak to him; then prophet-like / They hail'd him father to a line of kings: / Upon my head they placed a fruitless crown /And put a barren sceptre in my gripe, / Thence to be wrench'd with an unlineal hand, / No son of mine succeeding. If 't be so, / For Banquo's issue have I filed my mind" (lines 56–64).

temper) with the comfortable addition of, I believe, ten years more added to his age. That's something yet;—but I like not his pretensions, and wish he had staid in Germany.

My mama purposes going to London in about a fortnight. I suppose you will soon join us there, and as you stand so well with lady Sarah, the way is open to you, at least as far as access to Cecilia will carry you. When Falkland comes to town, I take it for granted, you will fix him at our house. Our acquaintance (my mama's and mine I mean) is but slight with lady Sarah Bidulph, yet we mean to cultivate it; the two girls, of course, will be often with us. Cecilia must then necessarily discover (spite of her sister) how matters stand between her and Falkland. What then will become of Dolly's wise precautions? And who knows but the path may look so flowery to the younger, as may tempt her steps to wander as far as we are disposed to lead her?—Adieu, my dear Edward; what a plotter am I become for thy service!

Letter XXVI.
Sir Edward Audley to Miss Audley.
Bath, Nov. 8th.

And so Miss Arnold has given herself to Falkland; an irrevocable vow has passed her lips, is't not so? Oh, those ruby lips! Well, let him take her; and now to other business, for I am in a horrid ill humour. The Bidulphs set off this morning for London, and have taken my little girl with them. I have lost since I came to this scurvy place—more than I'll tell you; for though none of the sober ones knew of my playing, I fell in with a set here who used to meet every night in a private room, and curse them, they have stripped me. Another thousand deep since I left Oxford. But this is not the worst, the rival I have got is a devilish formidable one. That same lord V—, who came down hither to pay his duty (as the old bel-dames call it) to his mother, dares to eye my Cecilia; but thank heaven she seems utterly regardless of him; yet is he one of those plausible curs, that all your mothers, and aunts, and cousins would be for hampering directly in lawful wedlock with any young thing of whom they had to dispose. Besides, he is an earl, Sophy, and I being but a simple baronet, he consequently mounts three steps higher on the ladder of lady Sarah's good graces. Sir George (with a vengeance to him!) invited his visits in town. Oh, to be sure his lordship does not *mean* to drop the acquaintance. Now could I drink hot blood! And utter such imprecations on them all!

I tell you, Sophy, I am desperate, and if a change is not wrought and that suddenly in my fortune, I know not to what extremities I may be driven. If I find this interloper is likely to snatch away the fruits of our long laboured process, by my soul, I'll snap up Cecilia at the first short turn I meet her, and leave it to her own good nature, and Mrs. Arnold's *christianity* to work out my pardon. Falkland, at the same time, may carry off *his* legal prize. What a glorious triumph would this be over the insolent blood of the Bidulphs! I shall leave Bath directly, and make straight to London, without returning to Oxford, as I at first proposed.

[Here, in the order of the manuscript, follow some letters which passed between Mr. Falkland and Miss Arnold after the latter had gone to London, those to her being directed under cover to Miss Audley, but as these contain nothing more than mutual expressions of affection, they are omitted. Miss Arnold says in one of them, "The Audley family are our constant visitors, which is the chief pleasure of my life; for Sophy and I talk whole hours of you. Sir Edward pretends to be an admirer of my sister, but she likes him not; and indeed he is so volatile there is no knowing whether he is in jest or earnest.]

Letter XXVII.
Miss Cecilia Arnold to Mrs. Arnold.
London, Dec. 18th.

"One of the best girls in the world," you say I am. My dear mama, those are the kind words with which your last letter was closed. I wish I may continue to deserve that character, for indeed I am so flattered and so caressed that I am in great danger of being spoiled. I am the darling of lady Sarah; and only my uncle Bidulph is fonder of my sister than he is of me, my vanity would carry me away for want of a little ballast.

I have now no less than *four* lovers. Dolly is so exceedingly retired (for she hates company) that she has not one, at least not one who has ventured to declare himself. Lady Sarah calls her a prude, and says she freezes the men with her cold looks. My uncle swears she is handsomer than I am, to which opinion I very readily subscribe.—Well, but about these four lovers—besides the three I mentioned to you before, lord V—'s name now graces my list. He is come to town, has been several times to visit us, and has said such fine things to me! Dear mama, you can't imagine what a fool they make of me. My spirits hurry me away, and I

know you love my idle prattle, yet I am disposed to be very grave at this minute, for I suspect there are serious designs going forward. My three first lovers I laughed at, but my fourth, I am afraid, will vex me. Both Sir George and lady Sarah speak of him as of a desirable alliance; but remember I tell you, mama, I do not like lord V—, and I am sure you will never constrain your own poor Cecilia. My sister approves mightily of him. I think he would make an excellent husband for her, for he is as sober as she, and she would have no objection to his being twelve or fourteen years older than herself.—She looks over my shoulder and says, "No, indeed, I should not."—Well, then take him, Dolly, for I can spare him. Here, my dear mama, let us both subscribe our names with the tenderest affection and duty. I have written the letter, Miss Arnold, and therefore my name shall be signed first. C.A.
D.A.
P.S. Our respects attend Mr. Price. Our loves to Orlando. Pray, mama, why does he not come to town to see us?

Letter XXVIII.
Mrs. Arnold to Miss Cecilia Arnold.
Woodberry, Dec. 22nd.

Continue, my dear, continue to cherish those charming spirits that make you so agreeable to all your friends, and which were the support of my life during my melancholy visit at Burly. But beware, Cecilia, of letting them run away with you. I am not afraid of your vanity; your good sense will be a sufficient counterbalance to that, though your uncle were even as partial to you as he is to your sister. I am not therefore afraid of your vanity, I say, but I am afraid of your caprice; for is there not something of that, child, in a resolution so suddenly formed not to like lord V—? For so I must construe your words; and sure I am 'tis impossible you can have any *rational* objection to him.

I remember him a boy when he first went into the army. He was then remarkably handsome, and time cannot have wrought such a change in a man not much over thirty, —but that he must still retain at least a very agreeable person. And for his character, 'tis such as must recommend him to every one of understanding and virtue. I would not constrain you, Cecilia; no, far be it from your affectionate parent's heart to constrain so obedient a child; but I would *advise* you, my dear, advise you for your good.

Advice from a mother was always considered by *me* as a *command*: yet I do not desire you to regard it in so severe a light. We have been educated differently. You were always treated with the kindest indulgence, with all reasonable allowances made for the inadvertence of youth, and the overboiling spirits which your natural vivacity has given you. I, on the other hand, though tenderly beloved by my ever honoured mother, had, nevertheless, my neck early bowed to obedience; and this it was which constrained me to yield up my nearest wishes, and as it were, mold my heart to the will of her to whom I thought I owed all duty. Perhaps your grand-mama exacted too much of me; for at the time Mr. Arnold was proposed to me as a husband, she knew I entertained more than a bare inclination for another object; but this is not your case, Cecilia; your young heart has not, it cannot have had the opportunity of engaging itself.

Why then reject an offer so honourable, so advantageous, so desirable in the eyes of all your friends? I am the more serious on this occasion, my dear, because I have very lately received a letter from lady V— herself on the same subject. She tells me her son was (to use her own words) smitten by you the moment he saw you; the account he received of your fortune and your education, probably, did not damp his growing inclination. Lady V— says in her letter, "If you will trust to the judgment of a parent not extremely partial to lord V— he is a very valuable young man, and in every respect worthy of being my dear Mrs. Arnold's son." These were her affectionate expressions; and she added, "how delighted should I be to call you a sister!" See, then, my love, what a prospect is opened before you of making yourself, of making your whole family happy! Yet *remember*, Cecilia, (I retort your own words back on you) I do not constrain you. I repeat it once more, I never will; though I should be sorry my daughter could not give a more substantial reason than mere whim, for refusing a man so unobjectionable as lord V—. Tell my dear Dolly, I do not think she has the less merit for not having so many *admirers* as her little lively sister. I am sure she has as many *lovers*, and perhaps Cecilia ought to be more mortified than proud, that she has so many *declared* ones.

My brother and lady Sarah have my warmest wishes. Mr. Price kisses both your hands, and my Orlando, who was here when I received your last letter, and to whom I read it, says he hopes soon, in person, to do the same. Receive both of you, my dear children, the tenderest love, as well as ardent prayers for your happiness poured from the heart of your affectionate, &c.

Letter XXIX.
Mr. Falkland to Sir Edward Audley.
Oxford, December 20th.

How I curse my stars for what is past! How curse my own folly,
my own vanity, my own childish pity, and weak resentment! But
above all, how I curse you! Yes, *you,* whose blind officious med-
dling friendship combined with them all to undo me. Did I not
tell you in the beginning that I loved Cecilia, that I adored her,
and that I felt nothing for her sister beyond the warmth of friendship? Why do you awaken my compassion, by discovering to me
that she loved me? Why did you encourage me to feed a flame
that I never thought of kindling, that I never wished, that I never
meant to return? This, this is what I accuse you of; but the charge
I have against myself is still more flagrant. I acknowledge myself
coxcomb enough to have been pleased with the conquest of a
heart on which I set not the least value; I acknowledge myself fool
enough to have in some moments mistaken mere compassion for
love; and I own myself traitor enough to have suffered the simple
effusions of gratitude to pass upon an innocent creature for the
genuine expressions of passion. My pride urged me on against
inclination, and I felt a secret pleasure at the thoughts of hum-
bling Sir George Bidulph, by triumphing in the affection of her
whom he calls the *boast* of his family. See here the source of all
my actions, despicable sot that I was, thus to let such paltry passions wind me about like a machine! That fatal letter, written by
the arrogant and ill-boding pen of Bidulph, put the finishing
hand to my destruction. *He had already given my Cecilia to lord V—,*
he said. Cecilia herself tells her sister she had a lover; cruel and
thoughtless as she was, why did she not then say that she hated
him? What a load of remorse would that declaration have spared
me! I thought *her* irretrievably lost to *me,* her sister's tenderness
affected me; jealousy and indignation, mingling with gratitude
and pity, lit up a momentary fire in my heart. I offered bows to
Miss Arnold, which that heart, treacherous to its master as well
as her, forced me in the instant to think sincere. I received hers
in return, too, too sincere, I am afraid they are, for such a villain!
For will you not think me one? Will you not even call me one,
when I tell you, that the next day all my indifference for her
returned, and I found nothing in my heart but rancour against
the happier lord V—?

The letters I have constantly received from her since, filled
with tenderness and faith, reproach me in every line. How diffi-

cult do I find it to frame my answers! For I am not yet hardened enough in deceit not to be shocked at professing a love which I do not feel; for, spite of all my efforts, I find that Cecilia holds her first place in my heart. I have oftentimes been half distracted with this thought; but something occurred yesterday which has made me desperate. I happened to be with Mrs. Arnold when she received a letter from Cecilia, wherein she tells her mother positively that she *cannot like lord V—*. How delighted was I with this declaration, till I recollected my own fatal engagements! But this is not all; she mentioned other lovers. I demanded of Mrs. Arnold who they were. She named, as one of them, Sir *Edward Audley*. Sir Edward Audley, the lover of Cecilia! The baby-face, whose beauty was not to be compared to that of her sister! I could stab you for daring to think of her; and nothing saves you from my vengeance, but Cecilia's indifference for you.

I am half mad, Sir Edward; so take nothing ill that I say. I dread the sight of Miss Arnold; but I a thousand times more dread the invincible Cecilia, whose heart, perhaps, is still at liberty. What a storm has this thought raised in my bosom! I shall come to town in a few days, and woe be to him I find a successful rival! For I tell you, I would rather see Cecilia dead than in the arms of another.

Letter XXX.
Sir Edward Audley to Mr. Falkland.
London, December 23d.

Ha, ha, ha, ha, poor Falkland! And so it is visited with compunction and remorse! All the bugbears that old Price used to conjure up, in order to frighten you in the nursery, have followed you, I find, to the university. Oh, fy, fy, Orlando! I am quite ashamed of you. I thought I had left you pretty well fortified against these sort of fopperies when I went to Wales; but I see there is no trusting such a half-fledged sinner to himself for no sooner is my back turned, than whip you take your conscience out from between the leaves of your Bible, where you keep it like your band,[1] for fear of being rumpled, and *like* that, after a game of romps, you clap it on again, to visit your grave acquaintance; but why put it on to me, boy, who like you so much better in dishabille? I do

---

1   Sir Edward might be referring to a clerical collar or another type of
    band meant to hold or decorate clothing at the waist, neck, or wrists.

think thou art the most whimsical fellow that ever I met with in my life; the dog in the manger[1] was thy prototype. Why what a snarling cur art thou, to begrudge lord V—and me a little snap at what thou canst not touch thyself? But your great consolation is, that this dainty morsel is out of the reach of us both; for, by her own confession, she does not care a farthing for either of us. I do firmly believe it, Falkland; and so things are just as they were before we set out: for as for your vows, and your gratitude, and your villainy, and your sensibility, and your perfidy, and your repentance, 'tis all such a bead-roll of Arnoldian nonsense, that I blush to hear a fellow of your spirit talk thus like a 'prentice-boy making his last speech at Tyburn,[2] and bidding the good people beware of evil company, which had caused his downfall, and brought him unto that shameful end. You accuse *me* first, and then yourself; exactly the malefactor's cant. But pray, my penitent youth, what have either of us done to deserve condemnation? Thus the affair stands between us; I find out by chance that a fine girl is in love with you (by the way I liked her myself, and would have given a limb to have been in your place); but jealousy and rivalship giving way to friendship, I acquaint you with your good fortune, and advise you, as I would have done my own brother, to make the most of it. Was there any harm in this, pray? You tell me, you love the sister of the lady. I ask you, did you ever receive any encouragement from her? Ever make any addresses to her? Or, in short, have you any hopes of obtaining her? No, no, no, was the answer to these three questions. I bid you quit the shadow, and pursue the substance. Was not that the advice of a friend? Yet this it is for which I am to be cursed by bell, book, and candle!

As for your own part, what has passed between you and Miss Arnold, you know best. If matters have been brought to a conclusion, why I have no more to say, but if, on the contrary, the nymph is in status quo, and you make all this fuss and self-condemnation about a few silly oaths, and lover's protestations, you are even below pity, and fit for nothing but to scribble miserable ballads, "shewing how a young maiden's ghost came and tore out the eyes of her false sweetheart."[3] Why, thou silly gentleman, dost let a vow stick in thy throat? What the plague *is* a vow? For hang

---

1 One of Aesop's fables featuring a dog that occupies the manger of a bull and prevents the bull's access to its straw.
2 Audley infantilizes Falkland by comparing him to a "prentice boy"—a young apprentice. Tyburn was a place of public execution until 1783.
3 Sir Edward is parodying gothic romance.

me if I know. I know what it is to sweat roundly, in order to make a woman believe that I shall love *her*, and *only* her, as long as I live; and I have made many a damsel (by way of carrying on the farce) swear as many to me in return; but it never once entered into my imagination that she expected I should *keep* those oaths, no more than I expected she should keep hers, longer than we liked each other. If these be what you call *vows*, I have made and broke as many of them as most private gentlemen in England; but I don't remember that ever even my slumbers were haunted by the injured nymphs.—Ay, but the case is different: *My* nymph is immaculate! Diana herself was but a flirt to her. I make this answer for *you*, Falkland, because I take it for granted your courage never carried you farther than the back of her white hand.[1] If that be so, then pray what is the worse for your *vows*? You squandered away a little breath on her, and got nothing but breath in return. Oh, but to break one's promise! One's oath! Suckling, who ever thought that an oath made to a woman was binding? The creatures themselves don't expect it. Is not the most solemn of all oaths, the matrimonial oath, violated every day? Is the husband thought the worse for infidelities to his wife? And would not the wife be laughed at who complained of them? I am amazed that you, who judge so well in other things, still retain some very false notion of honour. I flattered myself that I had taught you pretty well how to distinguish; but I see how difficult it is totally to erase early wrong impressions.

As for Sir Edward Audley's being the lover of Cecilia (which you mark with a point of admiration as long as the Monument) what is there so very extraordinary in it? Sir Edward Audley is the lover of every pretty woman he sees. 'Tis true, I liked her sister better; but finding you had stepped into her heart before me, I gave up the thoughts of her; and supposing your *interest* might fix you where you were, I looked upon Cecilia as a right of commonage, and that I was free to nibble on the borders, without encroaching on any body's ground; but I'll tell you fairly, I have not now any prospect of success. I say not this, Falkland, to deprecate your threatened vengeance. Had I hopes of winning the fair, I would use thee and thy vengeance for my sport, yea, for my laughter. But the truth is, I want you to join me in a noble enterprize I have conceived, no less than the carrying off, by force or strategem, those two mischievous beauties; and when we have them in our power, you may take your choice of them; for I am

---

1 Falkland's vows, he supposes, are unconsummated.

humble enough to be content with which ever of them shall fall to my lot.

This lord V— is the mignion of the odious Bidulph pair, and all their adherents, and notwithstanding Cecilia likes him not, she may be borne down by persuasions to accept of him. Think of her being lady V—, lost to your hopes for ever! And her poor sister either condemned to virginity, or thrown away upon a fellow who takes her for mere pity. In this case, we must *all* be discontented; Cecilia must be discontented in being married to a man she does not like; my lord V—, who sets up to have what the ladies call delicacy, to be sure must be discontented, without the heart of his wife. There, you see, is one couple miserable. It will be the same with regard to you and Miss Arnold. *You* will sigh for Cecilia in the arms of her sister; and she, poor tender soul, will break her heart, at finding she is not beloved by her husband; so there is another couple for you unhappy. And for myself, I shall be ready to knock my brains out at my own disappointment. Now in the other way, at least *half* the mischief will be saved. The possession of Cecilia makes *you* as happy as a god. I shall be sufficiently contented, for a mortal, with her sister; and I'll be sacrificed, if both the girls, in time, won't grow very fond of us; or at worst, if they should be perverse enough to continue indifferent, the indifference would be of the best side; for the poor dears, tramelled as they have always been with the notions of duty, would never once take it into their heads that there were any consolatory wanderings beyond the matrimonial pale.

Thus, I think, I have made it appear as clear as the sun, that no one would suffer materially but lord V—; for which, I fancy, neither you nor I should have very deep regrets. But the glory of our triumph would be in the discomfiture of the Bidulphs; when if, like a brace of towering falcons, we could souce upon our prey, and bear away, like trembling doves, the two young Arnolds in our strong pounces! The very idea lifts me above the clouds! Dost not thou, Falkland, kindle at the thought? Hasten to town then, thou dreamer, and do not sit sighing and moping in the chimney-corner, and raving of what you call the *past*. What is the past, but an idle rhodomontade, never to be thought of more? Think of the present, think of what's to come, think of Cecilia, think of our friend, and that one bold stroke makes us both happy.

Sir George Bidulph to Mrs. Arnold.

London, Dec. 26th.

Dear Sister,

The many avocations in which I am perpetually engaged, prevent me from being so punctual a correspondent as I otherwise should be. Indeed I can scarce prevail upon myself to take up a pen, but upon important occasions, such as I consider this on which I am now going to write.

Your daughter Cecilia, I suppose, may have informed you that my lord V— makes his addresses to her, under my sanction, which I concluded I might venture to give him, without previously consulting you, who, I am sure, cannot possibly have any objection to him. I am very willing to allow a young lady all the indulgence which the levity of youth requires, and all the homage which beauty exacts; but this must not be carried too far, and a man of lord V—'s rank, and unquestionable merit, is not to be treated on the footing of a Sir Edward Audley. I am sorry Cecilia knows so little how to distinguish, and that she has hitherto paid no more regard to the real passion of a worthy as well as very amiable man, than she does to the fluttering pretensions of that very insignificant boy. Sidney, this is not an offer to be trifled with; and the very noble proposals which lord V—makes, are such as may not fall in our way every day. I should be very unwilling to interpose parental authority on this occasion; but where a giddy girl does not know how to chuse for herself, 'tis the duty of her friends to chuse for her. Cecilia can have no previous engagements; at least her sister knows of none in Oxfordshire, and lady Sarah is certain she could have contracted none at Bath, as she was never from under her own eye; and she professes the utmost indifference for every man with whom she has become acquainted since she came to town. What is it then but vanity, and a love of admiration, that can make her averse to the thoughts of marrying? Lord V—is past the age of dangling; yet is he so much in love with this mad-cap, that he admires even her faults. I would not here be understood to mean that she has any thing really blameable in her conduct; on the contrary, I think her an admirably good girl, and when she comes to be a little more serious, will make any man happy who has the good fortune to please her.

Lord V— had thoughts of going to pay you a visit; in which design I prevented him, as I imagine his lordship has a much longer journey to take to Miss Cecilia's heart. I told him, there was no doubt of obtaining your consent, if he could win that of your daughter. I must, therefore, request it of you, Sidney, that you will write to her *strongly* on the subject. I find she has one subterfuge, to which she always flies whenever I urge her on this point. My mama, she cries, would not press me to what I dislike. I am afraid this indulgence of yours may be productive of consequences as disagreeable in their effects as the too ready submission of her mama was upon another occasion.

Lady Sarah is very much yours. Neither of my nieces know of my writing to you; but I am sure they both love and honour you.

I am, &c.

Letter XXXII.
Mrs. Arnold to Sir George Bidulph.

Woodberry, Dec. 28th.

Dear Brother,

You did but justice to lord V—'s worth, in supposing I *could* have no objection to him. I *have* none; on the contrary, I should look upon his alliance as an honour both to my daughter and me. I love his excellent mother, and revere the memory of his good father, to whom I had obligations never to be forgotten. I have but little personal knowledge of my lord himself; but know enough of his character to make me wish to see him united to us by the closest ties. It is with equal suprize and concern I hear Cecilia is averse to him. A *reasonable* cause of dislike she cannot have; I therefore am in hopes that time and a little perseverance on my lord's side will overcome her reluctance. I have written to her on the subject in such a manner as, I believe, you will approve. The *authority* of a parent I never will exert; too dearly have I myself experienced the consequences of such a proceeding; but as far as remonstrance, advice, and admonition goes, I have not been sparing. I am under a promise to both my children never to urge their acceptance of a man whom they did not like; but *my* punctilio does not bind *you*. You are therefore at liberty to use every means (absolute force excepted) to prevail on Cecilia to receive as she ought so advantageous an offer. I own I could have wished that Dolly had been lord V—'s choice, as I think her sedate temper would have suited him better; and I am sure her gentle and complying disposition would have yielded, without repugnance, to the will of her friends; but as we cannot direct the heart where to make an election, and my lord V— has already fixed his, we have nothing more in our power than to endeavour, by every warrantable method, to procure for him such a return as he deserves.

I salute lady Sarah with my best regards, and am, &c.

[The letter to Miss Cecilia, which Mrs. Arnold mentions in the above, does not appear.]

Letter XXXIII.
Mrs. Cecilia B— to Mrs. Arnold.
[The letter to which this is an answer is omitted, as the substance of it may be gathered from the following.]

London, Jan. 3d.

I know not what to do with this negotiation in which you have employed me, my dear Sidney. I find Cecilia strangely averse to lord V—, yet I cannot get from her any satisfactory reasons for her dislike. Both your daughters were with me on Monday, by invitation, and I entered heartily into the subject. Is he not, said I, (speaking of lord V—) a very handsome man? (the first consideration, you know, with most girls): yes, certainly, the man's not amiss as to person. A very accomplished man? No doubt of it; he speaks several living languages, and, for aught I know, may be an excellent scholar, and a rare musician. Extremely well bred, and perfectly good tempered? The man's civil, and I never saw him angry. The monkey would give her own flippant answers. Of unexceptionable morals? She turned her eyes at me with so arch a look, that I could scarce refrain from laughing. I know nothing to the contrary, madam. Has not he a fine estate? I do not want money, Mrs. B—. Of a considerable family, and noble rank? I desire not titles either. What then *do* you desire, Cecilia? Only to please my self; and she shook her little head so, that all the powder and the curls in her hair fell about her face, and I never beheld such a pretty wild figure in my life. Miss Arnold reproved her; Cecilia, you are too giddy. Dolly, you are too grave, the other replied. I have nothing but my spirits to support my courage; for indeed, my dear Mrs. B—, I am sadly teized by my uncle about this same Lord V—. I wish he had staid where he was, or that he had made choice of my sister instead of me; she is the *very* thing for him. She then flew to my harpsichord, rattled away a tune on it, then turning round, she began a minuet, singing to herself, and danced two or three turns round the room with inimitable spirit and grace. In short, there is no being angry with this girl for any thing; for 'tis such a bewitching little gipsey, that I believe she could persuade any one to be of her way of thinking. I made two or three more efforts to renew the conversation, but could not get her to be serious. Sir George sent his coach for them at eight o'clock. When she was going away, You think me very wild, said she; but I have my hours of address. For what, my dear? Oh, you'll know all in time in a low voice, as she curtsied to take her leave; and down she flew like a lapwing.

I find I did not know this girl, from what I saw of her in your presence. Restrained, perhaps, a little by that circumstance, she gave not such full scope to her vivacity; yet how charming is that vivacity, when joined to so much innocence and sweetness of temper as she possesses! I do not wonder that she attracts more than Dolly, though (in my eye) she is a more captivating beauty; yet the other is the little ignis fatuus[1] for the men to follow. But now I speak of Dolly, indeed, my dear, I am afraid that poor young creature has some secret malady lurking about her, though she herself is not sensible of it. Her dejection of spirits seems increased, and her looks considerably altered for the worse, since I last saw her at Woodberry. She says, the late hours she is obliged to keep at your brother's, do not at all agree with her. There may be something in this; yet shall I give lady Sarah the same advice that I once before gave you, viz. gave to consult with some physician about her. Mr. B— and I are to dine with her to-day, and I will keep this letter open till my return in the evening. Perhaps I may have something worth adding, as what I have said above is so little satisfactory.

Thursday, Jan. 4th.

I have indeed something to add, my dear, which, I am afraid, will not be very pleasing to you, yet such as it is, you must have it. We dined yesterday (as I told you we intended) at Sir George's. An intolerable crowd there was. Lord V—, Lady Audley, and Miss, were part of the company, and seven or eight more with whom I had scarce any acquaintance. After dinner we adjourned to the drawing-room, where the card-tables were placed, for lady Sarah said we were a snug little party. We had not yet sat down to

---

1   A Latin phrase meaning "foolish fire"; the term generally alludes to a misguided hope or delusion.

cards, but were still sipping our tea; every one had got into separate parties; Cecilia, aimed at all points, sat like a little divinity dealing her shafts about her; a lover on each hand, lord V— on this, Sir Edward Audley (who had dropped in after dinner) on the other; on each of whom she seemed to bestow an equal share of her attention, her good humour, and her wit. Lady Sarah with some other ladies had entered into a dissertation on a new Persian carpet, which had for the first time been that very day spread on the floor. My sovereign lord, who had engaged in a political dispute at dinner, had brought the argument up stairs with him, and was re-tracing it to a little auditory of his own. Miss Arnold and I were sitting together, and Sir George, playing with my fan, was standing before us talking to us both. Such was the disposition of things, which I know you love to have, as it were, brought before your eyes, when a loud rap at the door warned us of the approach of some visitor. Lady Sarah, always present to herself on those *little* occasions, turned her eyes mechanically towards the candles to see how they burnt, then on her two nieces to observe if any thing in their dress required to be adjusted, and lastly on herself for the same purpose. Miss Arnold, who complained of having a cold, was obliged to wear a cap under her chin, which, as it hid her fine profile, made her appear rather to disadvantage. As for Cecilia, I never saw the little hussy look so handsome in my life. The servant who introduced the visitor pronounced the name of Mr. Falkland, and in walked your son Orlando. All the company who were not already standing, rose of course. Lady Sarah just cast her eyes at him, and averted them immediately with a look as one should say, Ah, is it nobody but *you*! Falkland made his bows with a good grace, though without being well able to distinguish who and who were together, and a little abashed, I believe, at seeing so large a company. He advanced, however, towards lady Sarah, Your servant, Sir, said she, turning immediately (in her forbidding way) to stir the fire, which by the bye did not want stirring. Servant, Mr. Falkland, cried Sir George, bowing low enough; but raising himself again with that quick and careless motion which a man never uses but to those with whom he is either very free, or whom he considers as his inferiors. The servant had placed a chair for him; Sit down, Mr. Falkland, said Sir George, in an imperative tone, which implied, *Young man, don't keep the company standing.* It was rather coarse in Sir George, it lessened Falkland, and made him appear as if he were not worth the attention of any one present. He seemed to feel it in this light, for he coloured extremely; however, as he is not a stranger to good breeding, he quickly took his place, every one re-assuming theirs except Cecilia, who removing from her two admirers, came and placed herself between her sister and me.

Falkland now discovered several faces that he knew; he addressed himself severally to lady Audley, and her daughter, to me, to the two Miss Arnolds, and, lastly, to Sir Edward Audley. Your two poor girls, who had reddened with joy at the sight of him, had their eyes wishfully fixed upon him from the moment he came in; but not having had an opportunity of speaking till he paid his compliments round, seemed impatient for him to take notice of them.

The conversation, which he had interrupted, now appeared to flag altogether, every one seemed as if retired into themselves, and poor Orlando looked embarrassed. Sir George humm'd a tune, When did you come from Oxford, Mr. Falkland? This morning, Sir George. You left my sister well, I hope. Cards, cards, cried lady Sarah, and up bounced the women with that alacrity which girls do at the first scrape of a fiddle for a country dance. I beckoned Falkland over to me, whilst lady Sarah was adjusting the maneuvre of her tables. He came to me, and standing before me in a bowing posture, each of the girls in the same instant presented him her hand; he took one in each of his affectionately enquiring after their health. Miss Arnold asked many tender questions about you. Cecilia put forty to him in a breath, and without waiting for an answer to the first, proceeded to another. I found that Falkland, though he seemed not a welcome guest at your brother's, was not an unexpected one; for your daughters said they thought he would have been in town as yesterday, you having said to that effect in your last letter.

Lady Sarah always makes her nieces play, and she now summoned them and me to our several parties. The two sisters were partners, lord V— was mine, we were all at the same table. Falkland leaned over the back of my chair: lady Sarah had slightly asked him if he chose to play, but he declined it. I could observe that lord V—, as he sate opposite to him, examined him with a most inquisitive eye; no doubt he remembers his poor father well. I think I have heard you say they were related, but this is not a relationship that will be acknowledged. The suit commenced by the heirs of that unhappy gentleman, made the proofs of this poor youth's illegitimacy too notorious; and I have even heard lady Sarah say, that she thought it would be prudent in the young man not to assume the name of a family who would not own him. You can't imagine, my dear Sidney, how mortified I felt myself on account of his situation. I wish I could stop here, but you had better receive the account of what followed from me, than perhaps an aggravated relation from your brother.

I thought Dolly seemed not at all well. She complained her cold was heavy on her, her colour went and came several times, and I was afraid she would have fainted. The room, she said, was too warm; You had better step out, my dear, said I, the air will relieve you; give Mr. Falkland your cards. She did so, and Falkland took her place. Miss Audley, who was only a looker-on, followed her out of the room. Lady Audley having finished her rubber,[1] now got up; she said she was engaged just to *shew* herself at Mrs. L——'s assembly; she summoned her away. You must know that Mrs. L—— is the great rival of lady Sarah; they contrive to have their nights, as they call them, precisely at the same time, and their great delight is to draw away the company from each other. Three or four more of the ladies were under the same *absolute* necessity with lady Audley, and lady Sarah had the mortification to see herself deserted by almost all her female visitors; but she had the comfort to reflect that this was not one of *her* nights. The company now seem'd broke up, excepting our table, which still held together, and lady Sarah looked very much out of humour. The men began to saunter about the room, as if they did not know what to do with themselves; when my Mr. B——, who clearly loves a game of whist,[2] proposed that they should make a party amongst themselves. Then we will leave you together, said lady Sarah, as soon as Mrs. B—— is out. We had done our game presently after, and Mr. B—— obliging all the gentlemen to cut in, fortune allotted lord V—— to him for a partner; Sir Edward Audley and Mr. Falkland were together, all four at the same table. Lady Sarah whispered Mr. B——, "You sup with me to-night." With all *my* heart, said Mr. B——; "And you, my lord," in a whisper to lord V——. Thank your ladyship; but I am engaged, answered lord V——. We then left them, lady Sarah, Cecilia, and I, retiring to Miss Arnold's chamber to enquire how she did. I have

---

1 In card play, the term refers to either a set of three games played as best out of three, or to the third game itself.

2 "A game of cards played (ordinarily) by four persons, of whom each two sitting opposite each other are partners, with a pack of 52 cards, which are dealt face downwards to the players in rotation, so that each has a hand of 13 cards" (*OED*).

been minute about trifles; but trifling as these preliminaries are, they led to very serious consequences.

We found Dolly a little feverish, and we made her undress and go into bed. Indeed, Sidney, I am afraid this irregular life will not do with her tender constitution; yet be not alarmed, my dear, she is now much better. I called on her this morning, she was up, and her complaint, she said, quite removed. We sat chatting by her till we were told supper was on the table; we went down to the parlour, and found no one there but Sir George and Mr. B—, all the other gentlemen were gone. I observed Sir George looked extremely ruffled. I am sorry lord V— could not stay to sup with us, said lady Sarah. I would have asked Sir Edward, but I could not get to speak to him without Mr. Falkland's hearing me; and I did not think it necessary to invite *him*. I am very glad you did *not* ask Sir Edward, said Sir George, in a gruffer tone than I ever heard him use to lady Sarah. Lord, why so, Sir George? Because, answered he, he is an impertinent jackanapes, his friend Falkland is no better, and from this time forward my door shall be *shut* against them both. Cecilia, added he, your sister seems very fond of Miss Audley; but to tell you the truth, I don't think either she or her mother very desirable acquaintances, and I should be much better pleased if you dropped them both. Lady Sarah is her own mistress, but, I suppose, I may have influence enough upon you two young ladies to comply with this. Sir Edward is not a *favourite* of yours niece, is he? He asked this with a provokingly ill-natured smile. Not in the least, Sir, answered Cecilia. Bless me, Sir George, I don't understand you! What can be the meaning of all this? Cried lady Sarah. Well, well, Sir George, said Mr. B—, let's have done with it; I think Sir Edward was drunk this evening. (By the bye, I myself had suspected he was not quite sober.) A pleasant apology, answered your brother. My dear (to lady Sarah) I'll tell you the affair another time. The presence of the servants prevented lady Sarah from asking any more questions; but she pouted all supper-time, and poor Cecilia look'd frightened out of her wits.

When the cloth was removed, Sir George not re-assuming the subject, and Mr. B— warding it off by other conversation, we took our leave without hearing any farther mention made of it; but the account I had from Mr. B—, is this.

It seems some little inadvertence had been committed by lord V— during their play, which turned the game at a very critical juncture, and Falkland and Sir Edward Audley lost. It was at the very conclusion of their play, the thing was taken no notice of at the time, and lord V— went away directly; but Mr. B—, who loves to fight his battles over again, in talking with some triumph of his victory, Sir Edward told him he might thank the *dexterity* of his partner for his having won; he said the word *dexterity* with an emphasis which implied something more than mere skill at the game, (of which, to say the truth, lord V— has very little). Falkland was imprudent enough to join him, and said, lord V— had let a card drop very *opportunely*. Sir George immediately took fire, and defended his lordship (Mr. B— says) with unnecessary warmth. Sir Edward, jealous, I suppose, of lord V—, said some tart things of him; and Falkland, nettled perhaps at Lord V—'s having taken no notice of him, declared himself of Sir Edward's opinion. Sir George told them they were a couple of *boys*, and they replied, they were men enough to maintain what they had said. Do you choose, gentlemen, that lord V— should be informed of this? Just as you please, Sir George, was their answer. Mr. B— says he interposed here, not thinking Sir Edward quite sober, and telling your brother he was convinced that lord V— had made an unintentional mistake, (which was certainly the case) that the whole ought to be passed by without any farther notice. The young men seemed full of resentment, and Sir George said, Young gentlemen, you had better *cool* yourselves; upon which they snatched up their hats, and went away without the ceremony of a good night.

Sir George declared, after they were gone, that though he did not think it worth while to engage lord V— in a quarrel with them, yet he would never let either of them into his house again. Sir Edward, he added, upon the strength of lady Sarah's indulgence, has had the assurance to flirt with my niece; but as I would as soon give her to Satan (that was his expression) I am very glad of this opportunity of being rid of him.

Whilst I was with Dolly this morning, Miss Audley called to enquire how she did; but she was refused admittance; *both the Miss Arnolds were gone out*, that was the answer she received at the door. The poor girls are mortified to the last degree at this affair, as it not only robs them of an acquaintance they like, but deprives them of the sight of Falkland too, for he lives at lady Audley's and all communication is now cut off there.

You cannot think how this little event has disconcerted me; for though I am sure your brother's friendship would be of very little consequence to Falkland, yet one would not wish a young man in his setting out in life should create to himself enemies. You, my Sidney, who have been used to much rougher incidents, will not, I hope, let this affect you.—

I wanted not this, my dear Sophy, I wanted not this last blow to weight down my heart already but too much depressed. Your brother has told you, I suppose, what passed last night between him and Sir George; but he little knows how miserable the consequence of his indiscretion has made me. Oh, my dear, I was not abroad when you call'd on me this morning; but my uncle is so full of resentment against Sir Edward, that he insists that my sister and I should break off our acquaintance with your family, more especially as he knows your brother has some designs on Cecilia. How could Mr. Falkland be so thoughtless, why would he be so cruel to me, as to cut off, by his imprudence, the only hope that can sustain my life, that of sometimes seeing him; for might he not easily have guessed the consequence of offending my uncle Bidulph? They are the worst that can be conceived, he *shuts his doors against him forever.* Dear Miss Audley, tell Falkland, if he has any regard for my happiness, he will endeavour to retrieve his error, (for he certainly committed one) by making the best apology he can to Sir George; else think what I must suffer, nay, what he himself must feel on our being deprived of the sight of each other. 'Tis impossible I can see him any where but either here or at your house; at present both are interdicted by my uncle, and at the only third place where there might be possibility of our meeting, I cannot take the liberty of proposing it. This is at Mrs. B—'s; but Mr. B— was himself so much offended at the behaviour of both the gentlemen, that I doubt whether he would permit Mr. Falkland's visits at his house.

I have not closed my eyes the whole night. Cecilia is exceedingly concerned at what has happened; but what is *her* cause of uneasiness to mine? I beseech you, my dear, do not let the part which Mr. Falkland takes in your brother's resentment influence him to refuse the request I have now made. Tell him I conjure him to write to my uncle before it be too late; for it is not with the customs of the world as it is in matters of conscience; and man to *man*, though not to his Creator, may too late acknowledge himself in a fault.

How my mama would be shocked to hear of this! I hardly know what I am writing. No one that I dare trust with my thoughts, and *you* are taken from me too! Indeed, Sophy, that is too much, indeed it is very hard.

If Mr. Falkland should write me a line, let the servant who brings it enquire for Helen; I must be obliged to trust her with receiving, and delivering it to me privately. Lord, to what shifts am I already driven!

Letter XXXV.
Mr. Falkland to Miss Arnold.
[This came inclosed in one from Miss Audley, which is omitted.]
Friday evening.

I am sorry to refuse you, my dear Miss Arnold, the first request you ever made me. Indeed I have so sincere a regard for you, that if I did not think my own honour at stake upon the present occasion, I should certainly comply with your desires. A man should be much more ashamed to defend than to acknowledge an error, and no one would be more candid than myself on such an occasion; but in the present case there are no measures to be observed. When I took Sir Edward Audley's part, I thought him in the right; I do so still; and your uncle may (as he gave us to understand he would) inform lord V— when he pleases of our sentiments. As for Sir George Bidulph, 'tis plain he was glad to lay hold on any pretence to rid himself of a man whom he has always treated with unbecoming arrogance. Ask yourself, therefore, if you would wish to see me subjected to any farther insults from him. I think you, who are so extremely delicate yourself, would be sorry to see less so the friend whom you honour with your esteem.

I hope the time will come when I shall be at liberty to shew you, without *his* permission, how much I am
Your most devoted, &c.
O.F.

Letter XXXVI.
Miss Arnold to Miss Audley.
[In which she inclosed the above letter from Mr. Falkland.]
January 5th.

Sophy, *read* the inclosed letter, and then tell me if you really think it was written by Falkland? *You* sent it to me as from him; 'tis his hand-writing; but good God, what is become of the heart that used to speak to me! Let him refuse my request; let him, if he pleases, prefer his imaginary notion of honour to my substantial happiness; let him even absent himself from my sight; but why, why with such coldness return an answer that has almost chilled me? The *regard* he has for me—The *esteem* with which I *honour* him! Oh, were it *but* esteem, I should not feel as I do, his indifference. Give him the within letter; I have not reproached him in it, perhaps he was out of temper when he writ to me and I would not aggravate his resentment by ill-timed complaints, of what I *hope* is but the effects of a mind, irritated by passion. Yet sure he cannot be angry with *me*! If my relations behave haughtily towards him, it is not *my* fault. Ah, Sophy, see what it is to give away our affections without being authorized to do so.

[The letter which Miss Arnold writ to Falkland, and which she mentions in the above, does not appear.]

Here follow several letters which passed reciprocally between this gentleman and lady. Those of Miss Arnold are filled with tender complaints of Mr. Falkland's growing indifference. In his, he defends himself from the charge with much art and gallantry; but little shews the lover in any of them. In this place also are some detached sheets of paper, wherein Mrs. Askham herself gives some particulars of the conduct of Mr. Falkland and Sir Edward Audley whilst they were together in London, very little to the credit of either of them, and by which it appears that Sir Edward has but too unhappily succeeded in debauching the morals of his companion. All this the editor omits to avoid prolixity, excepting a little narrative extracted from some letters written by Mr. Main* to his sister Askham, which he inserts as it has a material connection with the story.

Mr. Main in his first letter acquaints his sister that a very beautiful young woman, whom he calls Theodora Williams, having lost her parents, (people well born) who left a numerous family of children all unprovided for, was by her relations in the country sent to London, and recommended to Mrs. Main's care, in order to place her either in some genteel family, or to procure for her plain work, as she was very excellent at her needle. That Mrs. Main not having it immediately in her power to fix her agreeably in the former way, had put her in a lodging near her own house,

---

* Mr. Main is mentioned in the former part of these Memoirs. He was brother to Mrs. Askham, and married to the daughter of Mr. Price. He was a linen-draper, and had been settled many years in London. [Frances Sheridan's note.]

and constantly furnished her with work. That having employed her to make up some linen for Sir Edward Audley, he had accidentally seen her *at their shop*, Mrs. Main having sent for her to take the linen home whilst Sir Edward, who had just bought it of them, was there. In consequence of this unlucky interview, the young woman in about a fortnight afterwards disappeared from her lodgings, and no one could give any account of her. Mr. Main in this letter, which is long and circumstantial, hints his strong suspicions of Sir Edward Audley's being the person who had decoyed her away, and expresses the utmost regret at this accident, as the girl was the daughter of an old friend of his for whom he had the utmost regard.

In his next letter, he informs his sister that after a fruitless search of nine or ten days, he had at length, by accident discovered the place of her retreat. That passing through a court in Bedford Street one night, he had seen Sir Edward Audley go into a house of no very reputable appearance; and judging that this was the place where the unhappy girl was concealed, he had resolved, in the warmth of honest zeal, to go to her next morning, in order, if possible, to prevail with her to go home with him; or in case she refused, (to use his own expressions) to overwhelm her with reproaches.

He, with difficulty, was admitted up stairs to the dining-room, where he found the poor Theodora alone, her eyes red and swollen with tears. It was about nine o'clock in the morning, and Sir Edward Audley, who was then in the house, was not yet up.

The young woman related to him the particulars of her story, which I shall endeavour to compress in as narrow a compass as possible.

Sir Edward Audley, said she, after having called on me two or three times under pretence of hastening me with his linen, at last writ me a passionate love-letter, in which he begg'd I would give him an opportunity of seeing me alone the next evening, not having had it in his power to speak his sentiments to me, as I always had with me a person whom I had taken in to help me at my work. Convinced that Sir Edward could have no warrantable designs, I shewed his letter to this woman, expressing, at the same time, my indignation at his request; but she only laughed at my fears, telling me I was not the first young person of obscure condition whose fortune had been made by her beauty; that I might, without any danger, hear what the gentleman had to say, and that it would be time enough to reject his proposals if I found them dishonest. Seduced by the arguments of this person, and dazzled by the appearance of Sir Edward Audley, I suffered myself to be prevailed on to grant him the interview he desired, without the presence of a third person. In this visit, he explained his designs at full; and after making use of all the persuasions in his power, he concluded with the offer of a handsome settlement. I hope you will believe me, Sir, when I tell you I rejected this offer, with the contempt it deserved; assuring Sir Edward I would give directions to the people with whom I lodged never to admit him into their house again.

He retired upon this, bestowing high encomiums on my virtue, and declaring he loved me more than ever.

I received a letter from him the next day, in which he told me, that finding it impossible for him to live without me, he had taken a resolution to marry me; and that, as in consequence of this it was necessary he should have some farther conversation with me, he requested I would once more permit him to see me alone. I will own, Sir, my vanity was not proof against the flattering prospects that now opened before me. I saw him that evening, and he renewed to me the same protestations that he had made in his letter; but telling me it was of the utmost importance to him to conceal (at least during his mother's life) a marriage so disproportionate, I must consent to have it performed with the utmost secrecy, and in a private house, as he would not hazard the having it solemnized in a church. I readily enough agreed to this, desiring only permission to acquaint you and Mrs. Main with my good fortune. But this Sir Edward positively forbid, telling me you would not fail to acquaint his mother with the design, which would be the sure means to overthrow it; and this it was, Sir, which made me guilty of so much ingratitude as to conceal the whole affair from you. I then told Sir Edward, I would desire nothing more than the liberty of having a friend of mine present as a witness. He reproached me with my distrust of him; but asked me in whom it was that I intended to repose this confidence. I named the person he had seen two or three times with me, as the only acquaintance I had in London, your family excepted. He said, people in that low condition were seldom to be trusted; but having asked several particulars relative to her, he at last consented that she should be present at our marriage.

He then appointed as our place of meeting, this very house, and telling me he should have a clergyman ready at ten o'clock the next morning, desired me to bring my friend with me at that hour; after which he took his leave with all the respect due to a woman he intended to make his wife.

I failed not to inform my acquaintance the same night with this happy turn in my affairs, requesting she should be in readiness the next morning to go with me to the appointed place, where I thought my good fortune was to be ensured for life.

I had agreed to call on her at her lodgings, and you may be sure, I was punctual to my time; but I was not a little surprized and mortified to find she was gone out. She had, however, left a note for me with the maid of the house, wherein she told me, that, "having been sent for in a violent hurry by a relation who was dying, she had been obliged to obey the summons; but as she was certain she should not be detained long, she desired me to proceed on my way, and that she would infallibly meet me by the hour agreed upon at the appointed place, as it lay in her way in returning home." It was now ten o'clock; I made no doubt but she would keep her word, and unsuspicious of any design, I got into a chair and ordered myself to be carried to this fatal house. Sir Edward Audley met me at the bottom of the stairs, and led me directly up to the dining-room, where I found a clergyman sitting in his canonical habit. Sir Edward asked me where was my friend? I answered him by putting her note into his hand: I suppose, said he, she will be here presently. Half an hour however passed away without any appearance of her coming; Sir Edward grew uneasy and impatient, telling me if I could have confided in *him*, he would have provided a witness who would have been more punctual. The clergyman now took out his watch, and saying he was under an indispensible necessity of going at eleven o'clock to read prayer at the church where he served, told us if the ceremony was retarded he could not possibly stay. I looked fearfully at Sir Edward, and ventured to ask him if it would not do as well another day? Resolving, if he consented to it, to take the opportunity of going away with the clergyman. But he replied with an oath, If it is not done now, Madam, it *never* shall; I cannot bear to be treated with so much distrust. The clergyman then said, that though it was more regular to have a witness, yet as the marriage would be equally good without one, he would make no scruple of joining us, if I would consent to it. Sir Edward said nothing; but walked about the room seemingly very much displeased. What could I do, Sir, in such a situation? I was afraid of losing a good establishment by being over scrupulous; and depending on what the clergyman said, I turned to Sir Edward and told him, if the marriage was lawful, I had no objection. In short, Sir, we were married, and immediately after the ceremony was over, the clergy man slipp'd into the other room, where having staid a few minutes he returned again into the dining-room for his hat, which having hastily taken up, he went away. I observed that he was without his gown, and that even the hat that he took up was that of a layman. I asked Sir Edward the meaning of this: he told me, that to avoid observation he had himself desired him to come in that dress, that he had sent his robes before him, which he had put on for decency sake; but that he had pulled them off in going away for the same reason that he had come without them. As this seemed likely enough, it raised no doubts in my mind.

Sir Edward said, that if I approved of those lodgings, he would recommend it to me to stay in them, as he believed I could not find any others more private; but that I must consent to go by a different name from that I had a right to bear, as he himself was not known to the people of the house by his real name. I consented to every thing he proposed; and though I own I did not think these lodgings handsome enough for *his* wife, I thought them full good enough for me. He added, that he would pass as many of his hours with me as he possibly could; but that his mother, with whom he lived, being very old and extremely captious, he was obliged to dedicate much of his time to her.

As Sir Edward likes to lie very long in bed, he had given orders that he should never be disturbed in a morning till he rang his bell. I rose the next morning about eight o'clock, and leaving Sir Edward asleep, came softly into this room.

A maid who had been hired to wait on me, came up stairs soon after, and said there was a person below who wanted to speak to Mr. Edwards, (the name Sir Edward had assumed). She said she had informed the man that she dared not disturb her master; but he told her his business was very urgent, and he must see him. I ventured upon this to go in to tell him, that such a person attended to speak with him. He desired that I would order the maid to send him up, and requested I would withdraw into the dining-room. I did as he directed me. Sir Edward rose immediately, and coming into the room where I was, said his servant had brought him a letter which he must answer directly; he called for pen, ink, and paper, and returned again into his own chamber.

I stepped down stairs in the interval to give some directions to my maid, and came up again in the instant that the men came out of Sir Edward's room, with the letter in his hand which his master had just written. But, Sir, what was my surprize, when in the person of this pretended servant, I saw the very clergyman who had married me the day before. His dress indeed was different, for though he was not in a livery, he had not on the grave cloaths that the clergy usually wear. He bowed to me as he passed me on the stairs, but did not speak. I was struck at the sight, and could not tell what to make of it. I was certain it was the very man, for I had sat so long in his company that I was sure I could not be mistaken; yet it appeared so unlikely, that I thought it best not to mention it to Sir Edward, for fear of offending him by my suspicions.

I entered the dining-room at the same time that Sir Edward came out from the bed-chamber. He asked me in a sudden manner where I had been? And having told him, he answered, My dear, I should wish for the present you would not let yourself be seen by strangers. I replied, no-body had seen me but his servant. Did he speak to you? Said he, (with some confusion in his looks). I answered, he had not. 'Tis a wonder, said Sir Edward, for he is a forward fellow, and as I have been obliged to trust him, I concluded he might be disposed to let you see he was in our secrets. He kept his eyes fixed on me while he spoke; I made no reply; and he presently after went out, telling me he had business which he was afraid would detain him the whole day, but that he would be with me early in the evening.

When I found myself alone, I could not get the thoughts of this clergyman out of my head. The more I considered, the more I was convinced that he and Sir Edward's man were one and the same person; but I thought it much more probable that he should have imposed his servant on me for a parson, than that he should disguise this visit of this clergyman to him under colour of being his servant. Yet what could I do? I had no witness to my marriage, and I thought it vain to speak of it.

I passed the day very unquietly. About ten o'clock Sir Edward came in, and, to my great astonishment, another young gentleman with him, whom he said he had brought to sup with me. He introduced him to me by the name of Falkland; but did not introduce me to him, nor call me otherwise than by my christian name all the evening. I was sadly out of countenance and vexed; for I thought Mr. Falkland, though a good-humoured and civil young gentleman, behaved to me with less respect than was due to Sir Edward's wife, if he had believed me to be such. The two gentlemen were in high spirits, and as they seemed inclined to sit to their bottle, I thought it proper to retire, and went into my own room.

I had scarce time to shut the door after me, when I heard Sir Edward ask his companion how he liked me? you may be sure,

Sir, I had the curiosity to listen to his answer, and putting my ear close to the door, I heard Mr. Falkland say, "She is very pretty, and looks very innocent too; I should not take her to be one of that stamp." What do you mean by *stamp*? Said Sir Edward. I'd have you know she is as modest a girl as any in England. Mr. Falkland laughed, and answered, I suppose you have taken the poor girl in by the old bait, a promise of marriage? Sir Edward made some reply, which I could not hear, and they quickly changed the discourse; but as my curiosity was so rouzed by what I had already heard, that it took away from me all inclination to sleep, so I could not leave the spot where I stood, in expectation of discovering from their discourse something farther of my own miserable situation; for it was very plain to me that Sir Edward had passed me on this gentleman for his kept mistress. I could learn, however, nothing more, than that Sir Edward and his friend were both very loose men.

I went to bed in great affliction, considering myself, though very innocent in my intention, as living in an unlawful state. Sir Edward observed my melancholy next morning, and with his usual kindness asked me the reason of it. I told him that I suspected the man whom I had seen the day before was the very person who had married us. Who, my man David? Said Sir Edward, laughing: By my soul, child, he can make as good a marriage as e'er a parson in Europe.—I interrupted him, Oh, Sir, if you had the barbarity to use me thus after all your promises! He took me up short, and still in merriment, If you *fancy* yourself married, said he, your virtue is as safe as if an archbishop had joined us: all those things are in the imagination; but don't turn *wife*, my dear Dora, by beginning to grumble. Consider we are in our honey-moon. He then patted me on the cheek, and bidding me good-bye, ran down stairs.

I won't trouble you, Sir, with my sorrowful reflections; I shall only say that I was now convinced that I was undone; and had great reason to believe that Sir Edward, as soon as he grew weary of me, would abandon me, and that it was not in my power to redress myself.

In the midst of my uneasiness, my acquaintance, who had so shamefully broke her promise to me, came in to see me. She made some excuses for it not worth repeating. Then looking about her, smiling, Indeed, Miss Williams, said she, I am very glad to see you so well settled. I hope Sir Edward's love may last; but at the worst, to be sure, he will take care to provide handsomely for you. I was provoked, and almost confounded to hear her talk in this manner. I have not forgot myself, said I, nor do I want to take the airs of a lady upon me; but I should be glad you would remember that I am Sir Edward Audley's wife. She burst out a laughing, You don't want to persuade me to that sure? Said she. Not persuade you! Answered I; why, what reason have you to doubt it? Lord, child, said she, I only thought you wanted a handsome excuse for putting yourself into Sir Edward's hands, when you told me he intended to marry you; for do you fancy any gentleman would bring his wife into such a place as *this*? I know nothing of the place, answered I; but 'tis very certain we were married here the day before yesterday. Be it so, said she, (With a sneer, as if she did not credit what I said); I am glad, however, I was out of the scrape. I was so shocked at this woman's behaviour, that I knew not what to say. I told her, as I found she was determined either not to believe, or *pretend* not to believe me, that her company was far from being agreeable to me. She said, if I was grown so proud since I had changed my lodgings, she knew as well as I how to keep her distance; and adding, she was sorry that she had given herself the trouble to call on me, she walked down stairs.

I was almost distracted with vexation and shame. I concluded immediately that this vile woman had been tampered with by Sir Edward. I recollected how particularly he had enquired about her when I first mentioned her to him: and as she was in low circumstances, I made no doubt but he had given her money to act in the wicked manner she had done; knowing very well, to be sure, that though the marriage ceremony had been performed by his own servant, yet (I being ignorant of the cheat) had a witness been present, it would have been lawful; for I remember to have heard of such a thing happening in my own neighbourhood in the country.[1]

You may judge, Sir, how miserably I spent the rest of the day. I saw not Sir Edward till the next night. He came in about nine o'clock, and was very much fuddled; but as he was in a good humour, I thought I could get the truth out of him. I asked him,

---

1 Before the institution of Lord Hardwicke's Marriage Act in 1754, a formal promise to marry was legally binding, and a marriage was legal if done in the presence of a witness and followed by cohabitation (Stone 30). Since the novel is set sometime before 1738, the main impediment to Theodora asserting her marital rights, therefore, is not the lack of a clergyman, but that the only witness of their marriage is Sir Edward's dishonest servant, David.

smiling, as we sat together, whether it was really his man David who had married us? Why, ay, said he; and I'll answer for it, you never were better married in your life: that's a very clever fellow, let me tell you. I believe it, Sir, said I, but still I am afraid the marriage won't hold. It will hold as long as any other marriage would with *me*, said he; that is as long as I shall like my wife.

He was not in a condition to be talked to seriously at that time, therefore I forebore saying any thing farther on the subject; but when I would have renewed it next morning, he either had or pretended to have forgotten what had passed the night before. He endeavoured to laugh me out of my apprehension; but without giving me any assurance that they were ill-founded. In short, he told me at last, that he should always expect to pass those hours agreeably that he spent with me, otherwise I must not hope for much of his company. I was afraid to urge him farther; what resource had I? I had thrown myself from under the protection of my only friends, and knew not whither to go. I saw too well that Sir Edward did not consider me his wife, yet I was sensible I did not deserve a worse name. I have passed every day since in the same unquiet state; Sir Edward turns my scruples into ridicule. I pressed him yesterday, if he really meant me fair, that, in order to make my mind easy, he would consent that we should be married over again, in presence of a witness, even of that servant who I found was already in our secret. He resented the proposal extremely, and told me, I had taken a very wrong way to secure his affections. I cried almost the whole night; for I am determined rather to submit to the lowest station, than to live with him upon these terms.

This, Sir, is my unfortunate story; and though I dreaded of all things to see either you or Mrs. Main, yet I am now rejoiced at our meeting, that you may advise me what to do.

I told the poor creature (proceeds Mr. Main) that I was afraid her case was without remedy; for that if Sir Edward resolved not to acknowledge her as his wife, I did not see how it was in her power to oblige him to do it; for that having no witness, the man who performed the marriage ceremony would undoubtedly, if he was (as she believed) the servant of Sir Edward, deny the matter as well as his master. I shall, however, said I, speak to him before I leave the house; and after I heard what he has to say, shall be the better enabled to advise you. She seemed terrified at the thoughts of what might result from my questioning Sir Edward; but I bid her not make herself uneasy, telling her, that in a just cause I was not afraid of any man living.

Sir Edward rose soon after, and entered the dining-room with the utmost carelessness, little expecting to find anyone there but the poor deluded girl. He stopped short, when he saw me, and reddened up to the eyes. Your servant, Mr. Main, said he. Your humble servant, Sir Edward. Have you any business with me, Mr. Main? Sir, I should ask you would permit me to speak a few words to you. You know where I live, Sir; what is the reason that you come to find seek me here? I did not expect to find you here, Sir Edward; my business was with this poor young gentlewoman. But since I *have* met with you—He interrupted me, turning peevishly to the poor girl, who hung down her head, I suppose, madam, said he, 'tis you who have sent for your friend Main? I thought I had warned you sufficiently on that head. Sir Edward, she did not send for me, answered I; but as she was put by her friends under mine and my wife's care, I thought it my duty to search her out—Well, Sir, now you have found her, what then? Sir Edward, you must pardon me for asking you a free question; Is this young woman your wife? For she tells me, she is married to you. Prithee, honest Main, said he, do not ask impertinent questions; for you may take it for granted I shall not answer any of them. This lady is my property; and I don't know that you have any thing to do either with her or me. Sir Edward, I don't pretend to have any thing to do with *you*, but I think myself accountable for the actions of a young person whose conduct I was desired to watch over. The girl is discontented with her situation. If she be *not* your wife, and is willing to leave you, I think the laws of both God and man will authorize me to take her from infamy. On the other hand, if she *be* married to you, though I must acknowledge, that as well as for your family's sake, I would have prevented it, had been in my power; yet as that is now too late, I will give you my oath, if you require it, to keep your secret, provided you will let me see the clergyman who married you, and permit me to get a certificate from him of his having done so. I told you before, said he, that I would answer none of your questions; and as for your part, madam, since you have been so impudent as to betray your own interests, I shall give you no farther satisfaction on the subject; only I shall take care to remove you to a place where it will not be in your power to expose either yourself or me. By what authority, Sir Edward, will you remove her? By my own, Sir; she belongs to me. Mrs. Dora, said I, are you Sir Edward's wife? We were married, answered the poor thing, the tears running down her face. You hear what she says, Sir Edward? Why, what the deuce would you *have* her say? Answered he. Nothing, Sir, I *will* say nothing; but take her from me at your peril! Sir, if she be your wife, you will have the laws on your side; but as she looks upon it only to have been a mock marriage, performed by your own servant, and in all likelihood, the intended witness suborned[1] to be out of the way, she does not consider you as having any authority to detain her; therefore, if she is willing to go with me, I think myself bound to receive and protect her.

He seemed confounded at what I said; and I believed the firm manner in which I spoke, convinced him that I was neither to be trifled with nor frightened.

You know very well, answered he, that I am under such restraints with regard to my family, that I cannot do myself public justice in an affair of this kind; otherwise you would not dare to behave thus. But assure yourself, if you attempt, either by contrivance or force, to take this girl from me, I shall treat you as I would a robber. I hope, Sir Edward, said I, you have more honour than to assault an unarmed man, who is under the shelter of your roof; I, therefore, am not, at present, alarmed at your threats. As for what may happen hereafter, I shall only say, that I will always defend myself against violence; but as I do not think myself obliged to fight, you may depend upon it, Sir Edward, I shall have resource to a legal reparation for any injury you may attempt against me; and I must take the liberty to tell you, that I look upon this young woman as under *my* protection, not *yours*, unless you convince me that she is your wife, which, I again repeat to you, that I will keep secret. He swore a great oath, and asked me what reason I had to doubt her being so. Her own account, answered I; she believes herself deceived, and I own I am one of the same opinion. She is a fool, and you are another, answered he. Sir Edward, you shall not provoke me by using hard names. Do you insist, madam, (turning to the young woman) upon the proof which I have required of Sir Edward? Or are you satisfied to live with him without it? She took courage at seeing me so resolute in her defence. I will not live with him without it, answered she; and if he refuses it, I shall look upon it as disowning me. I shall be as unwilling as you, Sir, added she, applying herself to Sir Edward, to draw on you the resentment of your friends; nor have I any desire of being known for your wife, till you shall think proper to acknowledge me; but I will not be passed upon your acquaintance for a kept woman; for such, I am sure, Mr. Falkland thinks me. If we were legally married, it cannot hurt you to put

---

1 Cheated or induced to stay away.

me in possession of a proof of it, and, in that case, I am ready to retire wherever you shall command me, and shall willingly, if you desire it, hide myself from every body but yourself. As for Mr. Main, as I have already told him every circumstance that has passed, he may as well be trusted with the proof of our marriage as myself, more especially as he has offered to you his oath, if you require it, to keep the secret as long as it shall be thought necessary.

The spirit with which the girl made this fair proposal, put Sir Edward with his back to the wall; he affected an air of indifference, and, swinging himself back and forward in his chair, Upon my soul, madam, I did not think you had been so knowing in the ways of the world. I thought I had got an inexperienced girl; but I find—She interrupted him briskly, Sir, you have got an honest girl, and, if the expression became me, I would say, a girl of honour—Mighty fine, ma'am! Were you ever play'd any trick before? Or is this your first adventure? The poor girl burst into tears. 'Tis unmanly of you, Sir, to add insult to deceit. By Jupiter, said he, I believe the girl has been on the stage! That is so theatrically pretty! But come, Mr. Main, added he, rising, I must desire the favour of you to walk down stairs. I will offer you no violence; only I advise you, as a friend, to go home quietly, and mind your shop; otherwise, without doing you the least injury, I will shew you the way to the streetdoor.

The poor girl now clung to my arm, and declared she would go with me, as she was determined not to stay another night under the same roof with Sir Edward. He pulled her roughly from me, calling her an ungrateful little fool, who would sacrifice both her duty and her interest to a ridiculous whim. I was about to make him a reply, when we heard someone tap at the dining room door, and, without waiting to be answered, Mr. Falkland walked into the room. He seemed surprized at seeing me there; but without saying any more than civilly asking me how I did, he desired to speak with Sir Edward in the next room. They both retired. I heard Sir Edward (who, you know, speaks loud and vehemently) swear to or three oaths, and, by an imperfect bit of a sentence that now and then reached our ears, it seemed as if Mr. Falkland had come to warn him of some danger; and I judged it to be that of an impatient and very urgent creditor; for I heard Sir Edward say, I wrote the scoundrel word yesterday of my difficulties, though he is so pressing.

As I wished for nothing more than to bring to a conclusion, with as little noise as possible, the unlucky affair in which I was engaged, I intended waiting till Mr. Falkland should be gone, in order to receive, if possible, Sir Edward Audley's final determination with regard to the unfortunate girl; but she, who had her thoughts only bent upon quitting him, took it into her head that this would be a fair opportunity of doing so, as it would save me from any further indignity, and herself from the terrors of any thing that might ensue, in case he should forcibly oppose her going away. She proposed making her escape directly, with an eagerness which shewed how much her heart was set upon it. For my part, I thought it the best course we could take; and therefore, without hesitating, I took her under the arm, and, just as she was, without either hood or cloak, I led her softly down stairs, out at the street door, and, hastening our steps, we were in a minute out of the court. I popped her into a hackney-coach, on the stand in Bedford-street, and getting in after her, we drove directly to my house; where having told my wife, in a few words, her unhappy story, she received her very cordially.

This is the substance of Mr. Main's second letter to Mrs. Askham. And in a third (dated a few days after) he tells her, that his wife and he, not thinking it advisable that the young gentlewoman should continue in London, lest she should fall a second time into the hands of Sir Edward Audley, they had immediately come to a resolution to send her out of town, an opportunity just then very luckily offering. A lady, who was their customer, and who used to lodge at their house whenever she came to London, which was but very rarely, had, a few days before, written to Mrs. Main, to request she would look out for a genteel servant for her to wait upon herself. It was to this lady, therefore, they determined to send her; but before she went, they thought it proper that she should write a few lines to Sir Edward Audley; which she did, in the following words, Mrs. Main having dictated them to her.

Sir,
As I should be as unwilling to be suspected of infidelity, or even levity, as I should be to be guilty of a breach of duty, I think myself bound to declare, in the most solemn manner, that no other motive has induced me to take the step I have done, but a belief next to conviction that you have deceived me, and that I cannot live with you, without considering myself in a state of infamy. Your conduct to Mr. Main, as it has left me no room to doubt of my misfortune, so it has almost deprived me of hope; for

your love, Sir, if you should still have any for me, can never be of any value to me, so long as you think me unworthy of your esteem. I was highly sensible of the honour you did me, in condescending to make me your wife: had you thought me worthy of the title, I should have endeavoured, by my gratitude and humility, to have in time, perhaps, appeared not undeserving of it.

By the time this letter comes to your hands I shall be out of your reach; but if you should ever wish to recall from poverty, grief, and shame, the poor wretch, who but for you would have lived contented in the former, and perhaps had never known the latter, my friend Mr. Main will know where to find me. I shall only beg the favour of you, Sir, to give orders that the few things left behind me at the lodgings may be sent to that gentleman's house. You will know, without my signing a name, which I dare not assume, from whom this comes.

Though my wife (continues Mr. Main) thought it advisable to tell Sir Edward that the poor girl would be out of his reach before he should receive her letter, she yet judged it necessary to keep her in town till she should recover her cloaths, as she had nothing in the world but what she had then on her. We sent the letter to lady Audley's house, and the same night all the young woman's cloaths were brought to mine by a porter; but no message from Sir Edward. Concluding from thence that he meant the affair should drop quietly, and seeing no possibility of the unhappy girl's being able to do herself justice, I thought she had no part to take but to retire into the country as soon as possible.

The following day I received a visit from Mr. Falkland. I am come to you, Mr. Main, said he, from Sir Edward Audley, who has received a very extraordinary letter from the young person whom you took the other day from her lodgings. She talks in that letter of a marriage, and accuses Sir Edward of having betrayed her. I will not pretend to justify him for having seduced a girl to quit an honest livelihood in order to live with him upon an improper footing; but I am to assure you from him, that the story of a marriage ceremony having been performed, is all an invention of hers, contrived to save her credit with you and Mrs. Main, after you had discovered where she was.

My wife interrupted Mr. Falkland here. Sir, said she, I should be very unwilling to believe that you are any way privy to Sir Edward's wicked designs; on the contrary, I am inclined to think that he has really imposed on you, as he would now endeavour to do on us; but pray, Mr. Falkland, let me ask you, if this poor young creature had voluntarily consented to live with Sir Edward as a mistress, what should induce her to quit him so suddenly? For she complains of no ill treatment from him. So far otherwise, she acknowledges he was very fond of her; and had she meant nothing more than to have saved her credit with us, she needed only to have told Mr. Main she was married, and that it was necessary to keep the affair secret, Sir Edward, I dare say, would not have scrupled to have confirmed this, if his base assertion would have been taken without any further proof; and in that case, it would not have been Mr. Main's business to have interposed any further.

My good Madam, said Mr. Falkland, (whose words you know are as smooth as oil) what you say is very true, and it was the very question I myself put to Sir Edward when he shewed me the young person's letter, and requested I would come to you to explain matters; but Sir Edward's answer to me was, that in the warmth of his pursuit of this girl, he had made her some promises of marriage. I reproached him for this; but Sir Edward, you know, is a very gay man, and too much devoted to his pleasures; he only laughed at me, said he had made the same promises twenty times before, and that she was the first who had ever claimed the performance of them. That it was a thing of course, and meant no more than to give a girl a pretence for yielding to her own inclinations with a better grace, and that he thought the person in question had experience enough to know how far men were to be trusted on those occasions.

Mrs. Main lifted up her hands and eyes at this. Mr. Falkland inveighed against the profligacy of the present times, and said he was very sorry his intimate connections with Sir Edward Audley (which it was not in his power to break) had led him to the knowledge of so much of it. He then proceeded to tell us that the girl, in consequence of Sir Edward's foolish protestations, had pressed him earnestly to marry her; that he had endeavoured at first only to evade her instances, and thought in a little time she would have dropt them; but as he now found her an artful creature who had consented to a union with him only from motives of interest, and that she had vanity enough to suppose he would come into any terms rather than part with her, he was determined not to give himself any farther trouble about her: but that she might not reproach him with having lost her time to no purpose, he had sent her fifty guineas: which Mr. Falkland at the same time presenting to me in a purse, begg'd I would take the trouble of remitting to her where ever she was, and that the affair might not be mentioned any more, as he was sure it would give lady Audley great uneasiness.

I told Mr. Falkland I desired to be excused from taking a sum of money which I was certain the young gentlewoman herself would reject with scorn. That as I saw she had nothing to expect from Sir Edward's justice, she should not be obliged for his charity.

Mr. Falkland put up the purse again into his pocket, saying he had no more to do in the affair, but added, he hope our prepossessions in favour of the young person, would not lead us to believe every thing she had said to the prejudice of a gentleman, who, though wild and extravagant, was not capable, he was sure, of so base an action as that with which she charged him. He then took his leave, telling us he was sorry, very sorry on our account for what had happened, and again begged that it might not be mentioned at Woodberry, lest by that means it should come round to lady Audley's ears; for which reason I request, dear sister, that you will keep the whole affair to yourself, as perhaps it might draw on Mr. Falkland some displeasure from his best friend.

We informed poor Theodora of what had passed; her grief is not to be expressed. She declared with the most solemn attestations that could be framed, that she had spoken nothing but the truth; and said she was the more affected at his baseness as she acknowledged she loved him.

There was nothing now to be done but to remove her from the scene of her misfortune, and accordingly we yesterday sent her down to the country to the house of the lady whom she is to serve, where the poor creature may pine away the rest of her life in sorrow, while the base man who had doubly betrayed her triumphs in the success of his wickedness.

Letter XXXVII.
Mrs. Cecilia B— to Mrs. Arnold.
London, Feb. 1st.

I am so vexed, my dear Sidney, I hardly know how to collect my thoughts, and still less to arrange my words in such a manner as to convey those thoughts to you, without giving you more pain than, I hope, the occasion demands; but to say the worst at once, matters are in a very disagreeable situation at your brother's.—Sir George, I am afraid, carries the authority with which you have invested him too far. He urges Cecilia without ceasing, to accept of lord V—. Lady Sarah is violent in her instances;[1] my lord himself is extremely assiduous in his courtship. Miss Arnold, influenced by her uncle, tenderly presses her sister to make lord V— happy, and to oblige all her friends. Mr. B— and I, at yours as well as Sir George's request, have joined our entreaties, but all to no purpose. Cecilia remains inflexible, and has begg'd her uncle's permission to return to Oxfordshire; which he has refused, unless *you* should absolutely *command* her return, which, to use his own words, "he supposes you will have a little more prudence than to do." I own I am at a loss to account for this unconquerable obstinancy in a young creature bred up as your daughter has been. Sidney, I am afraid there is some prepossession in the case, of which you are ignorant. Perhaps Sir Edward Audley,—yet I do not think 'tis he either; she assured Sir George in my presence, with an indifference that carried not the least mark of affectation in it, that she had not for him the smallest attachment. She had two other lovers, both agreeable men, who knows—

I am interrupted; Miss Cecilia Arnold, the servant tells me, is in the drawing-room. She is without her sister; an odd visit enough, my dear, for you must know this is a good Sunday morning on which I am scribbling to you, and it is now churchtime; but I am not yet well enough to go out. I go to attend your daughter; you shall know the result of our conference.

An odd visit I said it was, before I had seen Cecilia; I now think it much more so. I found her alone, her pretty little face full of embarrassment. She made an apology for coming at so improper an hour; but said it was the only time which she could command. Lady Sarah, said she, *now* never suffers me to stir abroad without her, except to church; as her ladyship seldom rises early enough for the morning service. And I omitted attending that duty to-day in order to get the opportunity of speaking to you alone, as I concluded your indisposition still confined you. Indeed, madam, I am made exceedingly uneasy, they drive me to extremes, I am quite miserable, I can't bear it; and I am come to beseech you, madam, to write to my mama and to beg of her to recall me home. You know my uncle declared he would not suffer me to return without my mama desired it; I am sure she will do any thing that you shall recommend to her. Do, dear madam, (pressing eagerly my hand) conjure my mama to send for me.

---

1 Entreaties, urgencies.

She spoke so rapidly, and with so much earnestness, that I could not interrupt her before; but now assuming a very grave countenance, You know, Miss Cecilia, said I, that there is nothing I would not do to promote your real interests; but you will pardon me, if I tell you that I do not think the step you would have me take could in any wise contribute to them; neither do I imagine that it would be at all becoming in me to interfere in the manner you would have me. I have already taken my party; Sir George and lady Sarah have both made use of the influence they supposed I had over you, in order to induce you to yield to the desires of all your family. I *have* used my best endeavour, and though they have not succeeded, I cannot think of giving up the interests of all those who have a right to your obedience, in order to assist you to avoid their importunities.

She seemed abashed at my rebuke, and after a short silence was about to reply, when we were interrupted by the sudden appearance of a very unexpected visitor.

Your son, Falkland, was shewn into the room where we were sitting. Cecilia started at his entrance—I absolutely *stared*, for I was astonished at seeing him. He made his compliments to me with politeness, though with a certain degree of even something more than *ease*, which convinced me he had mixed much with the gay world since his arrival in London. He asked pardon for the liberty he had taken in just stepping in as he passed by, which he acknowledged he had been induced to do from seeing Sir George Bidulph's chariot at the door; and concluding that one or both of the Miss Arnolds were with me, (for he knew that neither lady Sarah nor Sir George made such early visits) he relied on my goodness to forgive his impatience to ask his sisters how they did, as he was denied the means of seeing them anywhere else; he added, with an air both of sincerity and respect, that exclusive of any other motive than the pleasure of seeing *me*, he should long since have done himself that honour, if he had not thought his visit would have been unacceptable to one so much the friend of lord V— and Sir George Bidulph as was Mr. B—. He reddened as he spoke these last words, which shewed me the resentment he still had in his heart again them both. As I knew Mr. B—'s mind on the occasion, I could make no other reply than a civil compliment at large, which was by no means an encouragement to his visits.

Sidney, this boy has an infinity of address, and something so captivating in his manner, that however mal apropos his company appeared at this juncture, I could not help being pleased with it.

Mr. B— was not at home; and to say the truth, I was not sorry for the interruption, as I did not chuse to be pressed any farther on the subject of Cecilia's visit to me, and I imagined that after the repulse I had already given her, she would not be fond of renewing the conversation; but I was mistaken, she was too full of it to let it drop so easily. After a few speeches had passed between Falkland and me, he addressed himself to Cecilia, and asked her coldly, *When am I to wish you joy, Madam?* Cecilia answered with quickness, "When you see me delivered from persecution, if ever that will be." Persecution! Repeated Falkland. Yes, replied your daughter, all my friends have combined to make me unhappy; they would force me to marry lord V—. I *never* will. And she pronounced the word *never* with a most decisive energy.

You wrong your friends, my dear, said I, when you accuse them of using force; they have hitherto only endeavoured to persuade, and, I dare say, never mean to carry their authority farther. She shook her head, Ah, Madam, you don't know what *sort* of persuaders my uncle and aunt are. Their requests are commands, and their persuasions are threats, and I dread even downright violence from their authority. If I were at home, I am sure I could depend upon the tenderness of the best of mothers. She knows not what I suffer.

She could say no more, and seemed ready to burst into tears.

Why do you not write to your mama, said Falkland, and entreat her permission to return to Woodberry? It was in order to prevail on Mrs. B— to do this for me, answered Cecilia, that I have waited on her to-day. And will you, Madam? Cried Falkland, briskly. I answered him pretty much in the same terms I had before done your daughter; then added, And now, Mr. Falkland, let me appeal to your own good sense (all little prejudices apart that you may have conceived against lord V—) is he not in every respect a desirable match for Miss Cecilia, and one to which she cannot have any reasonable objection? I then enumerated all the personal merits, and every other advantage which lord V— possessed, and desired he would give me his opinion freely. I believe every thing you say of him to be true, Madam, was his answer. Ought he then to be rejected, Mr. Falkland? Cecilia's *heart* alone can answer that question, Madam. Cecilia was silent, and seemed as if in expectation of hearing what we should say farther on the subject. I wish, said I, my lord V—had made Miss Arnold his choice instead of her sister. I wish so too, interrupted Falkland. If he had, continued I, I am inclined to think we should have met with less opposition. Cecilia presently catched my words; I wish, said she, my sister were married to lord V—, and then we might *all* be happy. Does Miss Arnold like him? Demanded Falkland. No; replied Cecilia; but I believe she likes no one else. These words apparently slipped from her; she blushed extremely after she had spoken them, as if conscious of what they implied. Perhaps, my dear, that is not *your* case, said I; she smiled in endeavouring to turn it off; Dear Mrs. B—, can't a young woman *dis*like one man without *liking* another? Very possibly, Cecilia; but how do you know that Miss Arnold's heart is in such a state of indifference as you say it is? She never dropp'd to me the least hint to the contrary. That may be, but *sisters* do not always make confidants of each other. That's *very* true, said she, and seemed collected in herself, and as it were lost in thought for a minute. Falkland, who had remained silent all this while, now asked Cecilia what she purposed to do? Saying it was a miserable situation to be daily exposed to the addresses of an unacceptable lover; and at the same time to the importunate solicitations of perhaps *indelicate* relations. Since Mrs. B—, answered Cecilia, does not think it prudent to intercede for me, I will write to my mama myself to implore her protection; if she will receive me, I shall be very happy to remain as I am; if not—She stopp'd herself short. What then, my Cecilia, said Falkland. God knows what will become of me, said she, rising briskly from her chair; but indeed I never will be the wife of lord V—. She then bid me good-morning, and Falkland taking his leave at the same time, he handed her down stairs, when, having put her into her chariot, I observed from my window that he talked with her for some time, learning on the door of it, after which he kissed her hand, and she drove away.

I am utterly at a loss, my dear Sidney, what advice to give you, because I am really quite bewildered in my conjectures. If Cecilia's heart *be* prepossessed, 'tis a secret that she has guarded with the utmost caution, since even her sister is ignorant of it. But what if it should turn out that the affection which you encouraged between them and Falkland in their childhood should with regard to this poor young creature have stepped beyond the bounds which your maternal care would have prescribed? My dear, there is nothing improbable in this; yet if it be so, I am certain that Falkland is as much a stranger to it as the rest of the world. The manner in which he asked her the question with relation to her marriage with lord V—, convinced me he looked upon that match as on a thing which was likely to take place. If the case stands thus, I should think it would be better never to question

Cecilia on the subject. When we extort from another a secret which we should be very unwilling to learn, and which perhaps but for our own importunity we never should have known; it, in my opinion, in some degree binds up our hands, and prevents us from acting, in consequence of this acknowlegement, with that freedom which we should otherwise have a right to do, whilst acting under an apparent ignorance of the person's secret wishes. On the contrary, if your daughter should have courage enough voluntarily to disclose her mind to you, she lays you under no obligation of shewing the least indulgence in favour of a rash and imprudent prepossession; nor ought it to wound either your delicacy or your tenderness to exert yourself in doing your utmost to turn her from it. I have just here thrown out to you my sentiments at large upon the subject, though perhaps I might have spared them, as possibly my surmises (for they are nothing more) may be without foundation.

Upon the whole, I do not *recommend* it to you to recall your daughter home; yet I cannot help believing that it is more in *your* power than in that of any other person to bend her little wayward heart to that submission which her friends require. By all that I have been able to observe of Cecilia's temper, it is not one that will patiently submit to controul. You, my dear, have never had the opportunity of making any experiments of this kind. You who are meekness itself have always tempered your authority with so much sweetness, that your children, I believe, never once in their lives had the smallest merit in their obedience. Is it not natural then to expect that a young girl full of vivacity, of a high spirit, and not *unconscious* of her own worth, brought up with uncommon indulgence, should revolt against any act of violence done to her inclinations? More especially by those whose authority she cannot hold as sacred as that of a mother's. I am not to inform you that Sir George is rather apt to overdo every thing, and that he would exert as much force to remove a feather, as to lift an anchor. As for poor lady Sarah, as she never had the happy knack of conciliating any one's affections to her, so were she even mistress of a larger stock of prudence than Heaven has favoured her with, she could not expect to have any great influence. Cecilia has extremely good sense, and as much good nature, but she has a *will*, Sidney, a will which must be gently led, and not furiously driven; and I am satisfied she would do more to spare you an hour's uneasiness than she would to purchase a crown for herself.

I suppose you will receive a pressing letter from her, in order to obtain her recal to Woodberry. I have been minute in laying before you every circumstance that I could gather, and have given my thoughts to you freely upon the whole, that you may be the better able to form your own conclusions. If you judge it proper to send for her, remember you have measures to observe with Sir George Bidulph, and that it will be incumbent on you to convince him by your conduct, that you took this step, in order by your own immediate influence to promote the general wishes of the family, rather than to gratify Cecilia in the indulgence of (I cannot help, my dear, calling it) her perverseness.—

[The letter Miss Cecilia Arnold writ to her mama, begging to be recalled home, is omitted.]

Letter XXXVIII.
Mrs. Arnold to Sir George Bidulph.
Woodberry, Feb. 6th.

I cannot express to you, dear brother, how extremely mortified I am at Cecilia's childish ill-judged obstinacy. I was in hopes my lord V—'s merit, joined to the duty she owes to the will of her parents, would by this time have determined her in his favour; but I find I am disappointed in my expectations, and deceived in the opinion I had too partially entertained of my daughter's discretion. I have received a letter from her in which she has entreated my permission to return to Oxfordshire. I know not whether 'tis with your knowledge she has written it, nor indeed whether it will be prudent in me to yield to a request, which whim rather than judgment seems to dictate. If you don't disapprove of it, however, I should be pleased that she were sent home. Do not imagine, brother, I mean this as an indulgence to her caprice; so far from it, I have no other motive to urge my compliance than a belief that it may be in my power to bow her mind more effectually by such means as I can use when she is with me, than by all the arguments to which I could have recourse by letter, and which I have already vainly applied. There are a thousand little avenues to the heart which are shut up, and almost imperceptible to every one but those who have traced them from infancy. I think Cecilia loves me, and could not bear to be a witness to that uneasiness which she herself caused to so affectionate a mother.

If my lord V— is not already tired with the pursuit, my doors shall be always open to receive him, and he may depend upon having in me a warm and sincere advocate. A little time may work a favourable change; and Cecilia (who, I am sorry to say, has discovered on this occasion more wilfulness than I thought was in her nature) may perhaps, when less urged, open her eyes voluntarily to her own interest and happiness, as well as that of her friends.

As for my daughter Dolly, I flatter myself her behaviour will continue to be such as will give lady Sarah and you reason to be satisfied with her. I have no account of her health; she complains not; but I have my fears, yet I check them, as I am sure she is in the hands of very tender relations. I hope lady Sarah will continue her friendly care of her so long as it will be convenient to her to retain my daughter in London.

I shall next week (if nothing intervenes which may give me cause to change my design) send my chariot for Cecilia. Mrs. Askham is so kind as to promise she will go to town for her, in order to bear her company down. Be so good as to tell my daughter this, as I do not mean to answer her letter. Mean while pray inform her that she has, for the first time in her life, much displeased me by her conduct.

I am, &c.

Letter XXXIX.
Mrs. Askham to Mrs. Arnold.
London, Feb. 12th.

My dearest Madam,

As you expected that I should set out on my return to Woodberry with Miss Cecilia as on to-morrow, and will no doubt be surprized at my delay, I must beg leave to tell you that I fear I shall be detained in town a few days longer; but I am sure you will excuse me when you know the reason, which is, that my sister Main has just lost her favourite child; and as she expects every hour to lie-in, my brother has begg'd of me earnestly not to leave her in her present distress. As I could not refuse this request, I hope I shall have your permission to stay with her till the painful minute is over. I believe this account will make you easy with regard to our return; I shall therefore now inform you about your family.

I drove directly to Sir George's on my arrival in town yesterday, and having sent in my name, was asked up stairs to lady Sarah's dressing-room. It was about two o'clock. I found her ladyship at her toilet; Miss Arnold was at work by her, and Sir George was reading a news paper. He tossed it down when I came in, and I thought looked a little coldly at me; he rose, however, and bowed to me very civilly. My lady, who saw me as she sat opposite the looking-glass, asked me how I did, though without turning her head about; my dear Miss Arnold ran and embraced me. (I know, madam, you like I should be particular.) I suppose, Madam, said Sir George, Mrs. Arnold has sent you for her *prudent* and *obedient* daughter; he laid a great stress upon those two last words. I am come for Miss Cecilia, Sir, said I, if she has yours and my lady's permission to return. Lady Sarah only said Umph! In her scornful manner, though still without taking her eyes off the glass. I am sorry, said Sir George, that I ever had any thing to do with her, she has vexed me heartily; but it shall be the better for *you* Dolly. Is Miss at home, Sir? Said I. You may suppose, answered lady Sarah, that we should hardly suffer a young lady so willful as she is, to have the liberty of going abroad without some of us with her; for my part I would not take the charge of her, for there is really no knowing—She stopped there; I was very much concerned, on hearing that Miss Cecilia was in the house, not to find her in company with her sister and the rest of the family, and was afraid they did not admit her into their presence. May I be allowed to see her, Madam? Said I; for as I have directions to carry her out of town to-morrow, I believe Miss would like to be apprized of it as long before as possible. Oh, answered Sir George, for that matter you may assure yourself she is in readiness; however, if you chuse it, Mrs Askham, you may go up stairs to her; I fancy you will find her in her own chamber. Be sure now don't be *severe* on the poor child, nor repeat any of the *harsh* things her *mother* says on this occasion. Sir George spoke this in his biting, ironical way; but I would not seem to understand him; and rising up, I believe, Sir, said I, she will find her mama very angry with her; though I shall not take the liberty of saying any thing on the subject. Miss Arnold rose at the same time, with a design, I believe, of shewing me to her sister's chamber; but Sir George stopped her, Where now, Dolly? Said he; Mrs. Askham and your sister may have secrets; pray, my dear, don't interrupt them. Miss Arnold sat down again immediately; Upon my life, said Sir George, if you were not the best girl in the world, that little vixen would be enough to spoil you. At the same time he bid my lady's woman wait on me to Miss Cecilia's chamber.

I found the dear creature by herself, very busy in packing up some of her little nicer things in band-boxes[1] for her expected journey. She sprung to me the moment I entered the room, and throwing her arms round my neck, after having enquired about her mama's health and that of Mr. Price, When are we to go out of town? Said she. To-morrow, my dear, answered I, (for as I had not at that time called on my brother, I knew not that I should be delayed). Thank God! Thank God! Answered she, I hope my mama is not *very* much displeased with me? My dear madam, you can't suppose she is much satisfied with your behaviour; but I am not commissioned to say any thing on this head from her. I had rather you *were*, answered she, and that my mama had sent me a great scolding by you, for I dread the mild correction of *her* eye more than all my uncle's violence, and lady Sarah's ill-nature. I wish, continued she, poor Dolly were going out of town along with me; for I am sure she as little likes staying here as I do, only she has not spirit enough to say so. I hope, my dear, said I, you won't put it into her head to desire it, for that would be making an entire breach between your mama and Sir George! By no means, answered she, smiling; he intends to make my sister his heir if she does not disoblige him as I have done. I would not for the world interpose; but besides, it is not in my power, for do you know that for this week past they won't let my sister converse with me, for fear, as my uncle says, of my perverting her? Bless me, Miss Cecilia, cried I, is it possible that things have gone so far? Oh yes, said she, you see I am grown a sad girl since I left Oxfordshire, and all this because I won't marry a man I don't like! As I resolved not to enter on that topic with her, I replied, But how can you be deprived of your sister's conversation; I thought you had slept together? No, answered she, we always have had separate apartments here as well as at home; but we used, notwithstanding, to have our hours for a little private chat; but now we never speak but in the presence of my uncle and aunt, which confines our conversation to meal time; for I take as little of their company as I can, and my poor sister is always pinn'd to lady Sarah's sleeve: 'Tis a dreadful life, added she, sighing; do they think to bend my mind to their purpose by such severity? No, no, Mrs. Askham, my heart revolts against such tyranny; yet I am glad they have made use of it, because—Because what, my dear? Because I shall return with double fascination to a parent from whose tenderness I have every thing to hope.

---

1 Lightweight storage boxes used for hats or accessories.

I made no reply to Miss Cecilia, but here, will you forgive me, my ever respected and dearest madam, if I take the liberty to say that I am afraid our young lady's reliance on the mildness of your disposition, has encouraged her to stand out so positively against the will of her friends. Perhaps, Madam, if you were a little less indulgent, miss might be more tractable. She likes not to be controuled; and, I can't help saying, that I believe Sir George has been rather too strict with her. She flies from him to you; possibly if your countenance were to be a little changed towards her, she would fly from you to lord V—, who she knows idolizes her, and who to be sure would be a noble and happy match for her. Excuse me, Madam, for thus hinting my thoughts; but as you have sometimes condescended to ask my opinion, and even to take my advice, I hope you will pardon me.

I did not think it proper to stay any longer with Miss; but telling her I should be ready to attend her the next day, I went down stairs again to know at what hour Sir George should think it convenient for me to call for her. He told me, at what hour I pleased. I said, At eight o'clock in the morning; Sir George replied carelessly, With all my heart. Poor Miss Arnold looked wistfully at me, as if she were desirous that I should not go away so soon; for I had not sate down when I returned again into Lady Sarah's room. Sir George observed it; Come, said he, to Miss, I know you long to have a little conversation with your old friend: lady Sarah, do you dine at home? You will excuse my observation here, Madam; but I thought Sir George gave this hint to my lady, in order to put her in mind of asking me to dinner, though he would not venture himself to invite a person whom my lady remembered to have been his sister's servant; but I shall always be proud of the title, and so I should be, even if I had not owed to you, Madam, the prosperity I now enjoy. My lady replied, Yes sure, Sir George, we have company you know. Miss Arnold then took courage to say, Mrs. Askham, can you oblige me with your company this afternoon? For I have scarce had time to enquire after my mama and I should be glad to ask after all our neighbours in the country. I hardly knew what answer to make; for though I wished as much as my dear Miss to see her again, yet I did not know whether my visit would be agreeable to lady Sarah; but before I had time to reply, her ladyship said, Do come if you can, Mrs. Askham, I am sure my niece will be glad to see you. I told Miss Arnold I would wait on her, and took my leave.

Having found my brother's family in the distress I have already mentioned, I thought it still more necessary to go, in order to tell

Miss Cecilia that her journey must be deferred for a day or two; accordingly about five o'clock I went to Sir George's; I enquired for Miss Arnold; the servant said she had not yet left the parlour where they dined; but that Miss Cecilia was gone up to her own chamber; and if I pleased he would call her to me. I desired he would do so; and she presently flew down to me. I am sorry, said I, Madam, to see you absent yourself thus from your friends, especially as you are so soon to leave them. I do not like to be brow-beaten, replied she; formerly every thing I said and did was admired; but times are sadly altered with poor Cecilia; besides, I do not like the company they have with them, they are formal old people, and I was glad to slip away. I have received a letter to day from my lord V—, added she, all in the same breath, a very decent one it is; the man seems to have some sense and some delicacy; I hate him for it; because it will make me appear the more inexcusable. I wish I could like him, but—I am a perverse fool, and there's an end on't. She gave me the letter to read, telling me at the same time that my lord V— had not been to visit Sir George for two or three days past, which her uncle and aunt laying to her account, had teized her to death on the occasion. After I had read the letter, having told Miss that I could not possibly leave town the next day, (at which she seemed sadly vexed) I informed her I should write to you, to let you know the cause of our delay, and that I should be very glad if she would allow me to inclose to you, my lord's letter. Dear Mrs. Askham, said she, how can you desire such a thing? I have not shewn it to a mortal but yourself, and would not have my mama see it for the world. I should appear so giddy, so obstinate, so unaccountable! I am sorry then, Madam, said I, that you have shewn it to me, for I shall certainly think it my duty to acquaint your mama with every thing I know concerning you, therefore you may as well let her have the letter, for I shall assuredly give her the contents of it. Well, put it in your pocket then, said she, with some displeasure in her looks, and don't let any one here see it; for we just then heard Miss Arnold at the door, who, having enquired if I was come, ran to receive me. She asked me over and over again after her dear mama, then enquired for all her friends in the country, one by one, and demanded when you had heard from Mr. Falkland, whom she said she had not seen since the night that some little dispute had happened between him and Sir George. Both the ladies expressed themselves much concerned at this affair, and said they hoped it had not given you any ill impression of Mr. Falkland, as you knew Sir George had never been well inclined towards him.

I think poor Miss Arnold does not look very well; she is rather thinner than she was, and her spirits seem but low, which I attribute chiefly to the thoughts of parting with her sister. I hope, however, Mrs. B—'s fears for her health have less grounds than she apprehends; for Miss herself says that if she were to return to the country to her former quiet life, she is sure she should be perfectly well. I believe so too, yet as I am certain your recalling her would highly disoblige Sir George, with whom she is a very great favourite, I believe, Madam, you will think it advisable to let her stay in town at least till the latter end of spring.

I here inclose lord V—'s letter, which as I thought it would be acceptable, I would not defer the shewing it to you till Miss Cecilia's return, though I am in hopes that will not be retarded above a day or two.

I am, & c.

Letter XL
Lord V— to Miss Cecilia Arnold
Grosvenor Square, Feb. 12.

Madam,

I do not give the name of an apology to the reasons I am going to offer for having taken the resolution of absenting myself from you. An excuse implies, at least, a supposed offence; but where there is an utter indifference on one side, assiduity or inattention on the other, must pass equally unregarded and unobserved, and an apology must consequently appear impertinent. Yet, madam, if in your disengaged moments you should casually bestow a thought on me, I must beseech you not to imagine that I can either resent or blame your coldness towards me, or that I can ever cease to admire and respect you; and while I lament my misfortune in not having been able to gain your affection, I would fain flatter myself that this has not proceeded so much from aversion, as from a sentiment of delicacy. Conscious beauty and worth are ever tenacious of their own privileges, and should not be approached by the ordinary avenues. I ought to have considered that as my happiness depended only on *you*, I should, at least, have tried to obtain an assurance from yourself, that your heart was not intirely averse to me, before I ventured to expose you to the solicitations of your friends in my favour. I acknowledge my error, madam, and ask your pardon for it; yet it was an error into which I was led by the partiality of Sir George Bidulph and my lady V—, who gave birth to my secret wishes almost as soon as I had conceived them, and flattered me with certainty before I durst flatter myself with hope. But though I have been sufficiently punished for my presumption, I think I owe you a reparation for the trouble I have given you. I am highly bound to Sir George for the zeal with which he has endeavoured to serve me; but as I cannot bear to see you, for whom I would sacrifice my life, made uneasy, I know of no way to rid you of the importunity of your friends on my account, than that of remitting my unacceptable addresses. Yet do not think, madam, I am so temperate a lover as intirely to yield up all pretension to your favour: if your heart is not already engaged, I will dispute it with any future pretender; but I will owe it to no one but yourself. Sir George Bidulph mentioned to me a design you had of returning into the country: if it be to avoid me, madam, let me conjure you not to deprive your friends of the pleasure they enjoy in your society, nor yourself of any satisfaction you can receive in theirs. My happiness is too immaterial to be put in the balance with yours: and I promise you, whatever it may cost me, that I will not enter Sir George Bidulph's house whilst you continue there, unless I have expressly your permission to do so; and with regard to Sir George himself, as good-breeding must oblige me to excuse this part of my conduct towards him, I shall do it in such a manner as not to leave you open to the slightest reproach. Time and your own generosity, madam, are the only advocates on which I shall henceforth rely; if Mrs. Arnold would be so good as to second their operations, I should not despair of success. I know her character too well to fear your suffering any thing from the rigour of authority; and should my heart impel me to carry my vows down to Oxfordshire, tho' I should still be wretched enough to have them rejected, I should not have the additional grief of seeing you persecuted for what cannot be attributed to you as a fault.

I am, &c.

Letter XLI
Mrs. Arnold to Lord V—.

Woodberry, Feb. 15.

My Lord,

I have seen your letter to my daughter; though I must tell you honestly I am not indebted to her candor for this participation.

She shewed it but to one single person, who insisted upon communicating the contents to me, and accordingly sent it to me.

I thank you, my lord, for the frankness as well as the tenderness of your behavior to a girl, who, I am afraid, is too thoughtless to be sensible of your value. I expect my daughter home every hour, as, at her own earnest request, I sent a friend to London for her four days ago. As you possibly may be ignorant of her motions, I give your lordship this notice, on purpose that you may not unnecessarily absent yourself from my brother, who, I am sure, esteems and honours you sincerely.

With regard to Cecilia, all I can say is, that as she is not ungrateful, I hope that, after a little time and reflection shall have brought her to a due sense of your merit, her heart will dictate to her a proper acknowledgement of it; in the mean while, you may depend on all my good offices. I will advise as a friend, and admonish as a parent; but, as your lordship observes, I *can*not exercise the rigours of authority. Your lordship will always be an acceptable guest to me, let the motive of your visits be what it will; and be assured, I should receive you with a double satisfaction, if I could give myself a nearer title than that of

Your lordship's most obedient, &c.

Letter XLII
Miss Cecilia Arnold to Miss Arnold.
Woodberry, Feb. 20th.

Dolly, my dear Dolly, do not be angry with your sister for leaving you. Angry, did I say? No, that, I am sure, you cannot be. I never saw your face clouded with a frown since I was born; let me then rather beg of you not to be grieved at my absence. Indeed, my dear, if I could have supported the very uneasy life I led in town, I would, for your sake, have endeavoured to have submitted to it. But you know it was impossible; besieged daily by the importunities of a man whom I could not bring myself to like, at the same time that I was conscious of his worth; urged to a painful degree by the friends I so much respect, and reproached with ingratitude and disobedience, at the time when my heart was filled with acknowlegement and duty. My dear, it is a miserable situation for a girl, who is not a fool, to have nothing but *will* to oppose to *reason*, and that was the situation of your poor sister; for now he is out of my sight, I am ready to allow that my lord V——deserves a much better wife than Cecilia. I would to heaven he had one tomorrow a thousand times richer, handsomer, wiser, better: and now, I think, I am out of his debt; for he never wished me any husband but himself.

Well, but now I must tell you, that though I am rejoiced to find myself at home, I am very far from being as happy as I used to be. My mama, Oh, sister, my mama is intirely in my lord V—'s interests, and condemns me exceedingly; Mr. Price does the same: good old man! I love him, though he chides me from morning to night. Mrs. Askham, who is of the cabinet-council here, has taken up the same tone, and I am tossed like a shuttle-cock from one to t'other; but then they do not give me such hard blows as my uncle and lady Sarah used to do; besides I have longer recesses; for I make frequent escapes into the garden, and tho' the weather is not very inviting, the gravel-path in the wood is always dry.—Ah, Dolly, I would fain tell you something; but the time is not yet arrived, perhaps it never may—Yet, if I have any skill in the stars, it will not be long before I shall unveil my mystery.

As I hate to be confined in *any* thing, so do I particularly hate to be confined in my writing; therefore, if you have a mind to give my rambling imagination full play (which, for your own enter-tainment, you ought to desire) you must allow me to direct to you under cover to Mr. Main, whose scrupulous exactness, I presume, will not object to the conveying a letter privately from one sister to another, for if my uncle is to inspect all my letters, you will never get any thing more from me than four stiff lines written in my best hand, such as schoolmasters receive once a year from the children they teach to write; in which they beg pardon for past faults, and promise amendment for the time to come.

I have begun by sending this to Main, with a charge to give it into your own hands; and this same post brings a fine flourishing letter of thanks to lady Sarah for all civilities to me. I had as lief[1] have let it alone, but my mama insisted on it; and to say the truth, lady Sarah was kind enough to me at first, and, I believe, would have continued so, if lord V— had not unluckily thrust in his nose to disturb our union. Do you know that my mama has written to him, and hinted that she would be glad to see him here? 'Tis very true, I assure you; she shewed me a copy of her letter. If he should come down, let them beware of driving me to extremities—From whom do I inherit this stubborn spirit of mine? I do not remem-

1   As well, preferably.

ber my papa, but I have often heard he was a mild-tempered man; and for my mother, has she not been a prodigy of suffering patience! Ah, Dolly, why am not *I* more like her?—Adieu, dear dear Dolly.

Your own CECILIA.

LETTER XLIII
Extract of Miss Arnold's Answer to the foregoing.
London, Feb. 23.

——Lady Sarah received your letter in good part, as you know she loves to have civil things said to her; but my uncle called you a little hypocrite.

Lord V—was here the other day; he told us he had been indisposed for some days past, which prevented our seeing him. He expressed himself much concerned for having been the occasion of driving you from town; blamed himself for having been too precipitate in urging his suit, till a longer proof of his affection had a little better intitled him to solicit your favour. He said he had received a very obliging letter from my mama, which had given him new life, as she had assured him in it of her warmest concurrence in promoting his wishes; he added, that with this encouragement he purposed renewing his attack in Oxfordshire; but that he would first give Miss Cecilia time to recover herself from the fatigue she had undergone in town from his importunities. My uncle seems much pleased with this step of my mama's; for I believe he was afraid my lord would intirely have given up the pursuit. He said, (speaking of you) after his lordship was gone, That girl is the veriest little tyrant in nature; she has different ways of subjecting every one to her will; she awes lord V— with her saucy looks, and subdues her mother with her sly caresses. *I* am the only person who can deal with her. My sister *pretends*, added he, to be angry with her; but we shall see whether she has resolution enough to exert a proper authority on this occasion; for I am determined to be at Woodberry at the same time that my lord V— is there, or I am sure his journey will be to very little purpose. How I tremble for you, my poor Cecilia! Yet indeed, my dear, I think my lord V— worthy of you, if you were even more amiable than you are. He is an admirable man; he has every thing in his favour; every heart loves him, but that perverse one for which he sighs; but perhaps my Cecilia has not one to bestow on him. Ah, my dear, there is a secret locked up in that little close bosom of yours, that you would fain let out; give it vent, my love; I promise you to keep it inviolably, if you require it of me. If you have given your affections to a deserving object, I pray heaven you may meet with a return: for would it not be a dreadful thing to love without being beloved again? yet still more dreadful to lose the heart you think you have a right to possess! I don't know why these melancholy thoughts have occurred to me; but my spirits are exceedingly depressed. Mr. Falkland, I hear, went out of town today. I am glad he is returned to Oxford, and wish he had never seen London. I am afraid he has been too much dissipated here; but he is good, and will recollect himself: tell him I say so. Mr. Main has promised to deliver all your letters carefully to me; therefore do not restrain your pen.——

Letter XLIV
Mr Falkland to Sir Edward Audley.
Oxford, Feb. 27.

Tell me, Sir Edward, it is the tenure by which man holds his scanty pittance of happiness, to pay with remorse every pleasure that he tastes? What a day of exultation, of rapture, has this been to me! Such as thou, in thy wild excesses, couldst never have an idea of. But when I have told you the cause, you must assure me, nay, you must swear to me, that I am honest; for spite of my transports, something knocks at my breast, and whispers, 'Falkland, thou art a traitor!' Busy spright, thou liest; dare not to interrupt my joy with thy cursed croaking.

Having stopped to make a visit on my way hither, I arrived here late last night, and set out this morning, about ten o'clock, to pay my respects at Woodberry. Mrs. Arnold and Mr. Price, I was told at the gate, were gone to assist at the wedding of the two of their friends, who lived about a mile off, and were not expected home till evening. Mr. Price, it seems, was to marry them; and Mrs. Arnold, who had bestowed a fortune on the young girl, was to give her away. I enquired for Miss Cecilia, and was answered that she was at home. I entered the doors with a palpitation of heart. She flew down stairs to meet me; my arms involuntarily clasped her. My dearest Cecilia! Dear Orlando, how I rejoice to see you here again! We entered the parlour together. How beautiful she appeared to me! I thought there was a tenderness mixed with pleasure in her looks, that I had never observed before.

After forty inquiries, on her side, relative to the Audley family, and as many on mine with regard to her own, we both, for some time, remained silent, each looking as if they wished the other would speak. At length, How comes it, said she, that you have left London so soon? Because, said I, there was nothing there that had any charms to retain me. Then you have brought back your heart, she replied, with a look that fascinated me.——Ah, Cecilia, I brought it not hither! This answer escaped me; I knew not what I said; yet my words were accompanied with such a expression of countenance as required not an explanation; a deep vermillion covered her white skin, even to her neck—She was silent for a little while, then assuming an air of sober command, Falkland, said she, tell me *truly*, have you bestowed your affections? An important reason makes it necessary that you answer me with sincerity.

What a temptation was this, Audley, to be a villain! Dazzled as I was with hope, my head was almost giddy. I seized her hand, and pressing it to my lips, Yes, cried I, I *do* love; you have a right to know the secrets of my heart; a heart that was your *own* before I knew I had one to give! I am satisfied, said she, restraint and dissimulation are at an end. I wanted but this assurance; and now I will give my reason why I refused my lord V—. What a noble frankness was here! how unlike a *woman*! no affected confusion, no pretty coyness, after such a declaration! Amazed, overwhelmed, and penetrated to the soul, I fell at her feet, and grasping her knees with the action of a madman, Oh, Cecilia, cried I, dare I believe my senses? Is it possible that the poor ill-fated wretch you see before you, the neglected, the despised Falkland, should be the object of my Cecilia's secret love! Oh, could I have divined what passed in your heart!——And here, Audley, recollecting myself at once, I was upon the point of declaring—but fear, or love, or falsehood, call it what you will, checked my tongue.—I always thought you loved me, said she; yet, Falkland, you should have spoke first, and spared me the pain of extorting a confession from you; had you made it sooner, it might have saved me from the difficulties with which I am now embarrassed. And from what would it have saved *me*? whispered I to myself, and muttering an imprecation on thy head, Audley. Taught from my infancy, replied I, to look upon you as something sacred, I never dared to let a sigh transpire before you. 'Twas that, said she, that modest diffidence, that distrust of your own worth, that won me, and long since determined me in your favour; and if I have till now concealed my sentiments for you from all the world, 'twas from an impulse of pride; or perhaps I should give it a contrary name, and call it humility. I knew not whether a youthful inclination (however lively) without encouragement, without even hope, would not be extinguished by absence, or perhaps turned to another object; but since I find I am still beloved, what reason have I to hide an honest and well-grounded affection? Orlando, added she, collecting her sweet features into a grave and even solemn look, I have as little levity and as much true honor in my soul as any of my sex; but I will not be a slave to false delicacy, nor sacrifice my own happiness to the vanity of my proud relations. Do you know, pursued she, with her usual quickness, that my uncle and my lord V— are coming down hither? I will throw myself at my mama's feet, you shall do the same; I know she loves you. If we obtain her consent, I shall give myself but little pain about the displeasure of the rest of my family. Trembling with apprehension at what I heard her say, my thoughts were all confusion—'Twas now too late to make the hateful confession—I hung down my head, without being able to answer her. Are you afraid, said she, to acknowledge the truth to my mama? The question suggested a reply. I *am*, said I. Mrs. Arnold will not, I *know* she will not consent to my happiness; and a mother's *prohibition* deprives me, for ever, of my Cecilia. I cannot consent to risque my life (for no less is at stake) upon the fiat[1] of Mrs. Arnold's lips. Her tenderness for you may lead her to forgive a step, when irrecoverably, to which she dare not yield her assent before-hand. Mrs. Arnold lives not to herself, she has ever been a slave to the capricous will of others. True, replied Cecilia; yet I think she *might* be prevailed on. Oh, never, never, said I. Has she not as good as given her promise to lord V—? invited his visits down hither? Your uncle Bidulph comes with him, to arm his sister's heart, by his own example, with severity against her child. *I* am banished your presence, forbid even to think of you, insulted perhaps by the man against whom, for your sake, I would not lift my arm; you exposed to the reproaches of your family, and probably to new persecutions, and all this without resource.—Ah, my Cecilia, what consolation would it be to a wretched lover to think that for his sake, his beloved devoted her youth to a single life, and suffered thus for her virtuous constancy? I had seized her hand while I spoke. She snatched it from me, to dash off a tear that started into her eye. If my uncle

---

1 Sanction.

and my lord V— come down hither, said she, and my persecution is again renewed, Falkland, I am afraid, I am afraid I shall o'erleap the bounds of duty; for force will make me desperate. Call it not desperation, said I, to fly for shelter to the man that worships you. Our hands once joined, who can untie the knot? Let me only conjure you, for the present, to keep your secret with the same caution that you have hitherto done. Our mutual affection once known, the consequence would be an eternal separation. Let us then conceal it, till it will not be in human power to disjoin us. Though I will never submit, replied she, to have a choice forced on me, yet should I be very unwilling to marry without my mama's approbation; against her *express command* I certainly never would. There is but this alternative then, cried I; either to banish me from your thoughts for ever, or *venture* to make me happy, without hazarding an express command to the contrary; for such be assured, my Cecilia, you would receive from your mama, who, bigotted to the tyranny of duty, would think herself bound, on this occasion, to act conformably to the desire of her family, though her own heart, perhaps, would dictate to her much milder measures. Hear my resolution, Falkland, said she, laying her hand on mine. My mother's repose is as dear to me as my own. If I can avoid this match with lord V—, I will wait patiently till the resentment of my friends is a little subsided, when I am determined at all events, to open my heart to my mama, and I think she will not sacrifice her daughter's peace of mind to an idle prejudice. But if, on the contrary, I am to be *compelled* to marry (for my uncle, I can tell you, is capable of going such lengths) this hand, without farther consideration, is yours.—Think you not, Audley, that I kissed a hundred times that beautiful hand, the pledge of my future felicity?

Would to heaven my lord V— and Sir George Bidulph would come immediately down to Woodberry, that my little chased fawn might fly for refuge to my arms! She has hitherto kept her own counsel; I have conjured her to do so still. Her sister is too timid to venture on divulging *her* secret, unless it were to prevent what she will not know till it is too late for prevention; and then to what purpose disturb a peaceful union by a useless discovery? Have I then any reason to dread consequences? I would fain be happy; yet there is something which will not let me, something that tells me I have done *wrong*. Yet how? which way? I have made some slight promises to another, extorted from me in a thoughtless hour of spleen and disappointment. What is there in that? Would it not be a greater crime to fulfil than to break those promises? In one case, I bind an unhappy girl for ever to a man that cannot love her, and therefore does not deserve her; in the other, I cost her a few tears, perhaps, make her fret for a month or so; she calls me perfidious, dismisses me from her heart, and there's an end on't. Prithee, Audley, is not this the fair ways of stating the account?

'Tis very late, so I'll e'en to bed, and dream, if I can, of my beloved.——

Friday morning.

I broke off here last night, and threw myself into bed in hopes of enjoying over again in sleep the pleasures of the preceding day; but no such thing; I have had a wretched night, and have now started up again at five o'clock in the morning, and struck a light, for I cannot rest. Oh, may my Cecilia's slumbers be softer! I said I would dream of her, and so I did; but it was some demon, not the god of Love, who presided over my visions.—I know you will laugh at me, yet I am exceedingly shocked, and long for day-light, that I may go out and shake the folly off.

Write to me, Sir Edward, encourage me, rouze me, or, spite of my efforts, I shall droop again before I reach my promised goal of happiness.——

Letter XLV
Sir Edward Audley to Mr. Falkland
London, March 1st.

Out upon thee for a visionary coxcomb! why thou wilt dwindle into a mere old woman at last. Thou art frightened with a dream! the scarecrows of thy own sickly imagination pursue thee in thy sleep, and thou very manfully criest out for help, *rouze me, encourage me!* Oh, thou chicken hearted Falkland, must thou be spurred on in the road to happiness? Is there not a green sward all the way before thee? not a single impediment but what thy own folly creates! Why, under what a triumphant star wert thou born! Oh, the sweet shepherd of Ida that holds commerce only with divinities![1] Whilst poor I must be content

---

1 Paris, prince of Troy, was in exile at Ida when he was asked to judge who was the most beautiful of the goddesses Hera, Athena, and Aphrodite. Paris chose Aphrodite, and his reward and punishment was the love of Helen of Sparta, thus sparking the Trojan War.

with grizettes.[1] Well, I envy you not your success with Cecilia; *I* but fooled with her, for I do really love her sister, and would not have yielded her to any one but yourself. Things are now in their right channel again; you have secured *your* love, help me to do the same by *mine*, and I will allow thou *art* a man.

I am entirely of your opinion that it would be downright cruelty to keep a poor girl to a silly promise, as she herself declared to my sister that she did not know what she was doing when she made it; and of which, spite of her affection to you, she has a hundred times repented since. Sophy who you know is much in her confidence, has told me that Miss Arnold had often declared to her she would give the world to recall the hasty step she had taken; Not, added she, but I love Falkland, and would prefer him to all mankind; but then the disobedience of the act! the grief it would be to my mama, the resentment I shall draw on myself from all my family! I cannot bear the thoughts of it. Then would she burst into tears, and wish she had never known you. why, what a flegmatic[2] love is this, Falkland! How unlike the aetherial fire of thy Cecilia! I do verily believe, and I speak to you now without either raillery or prejudice, that after the first shock which her pride might receive at finding herself deserted, she would at the bottom of her heart be glad that she was absolved from a promise which terrifies her every time she thinks of it; and which, you may take it on my word, you would find it almost impracticable to make her fulfil. She would do mighty well to be the mistress of a Don Bellianis, or a Sir Launcelet, who could afford to waste seven years in strolling up and down the world, without either meat or drink, in order to prove his constancy;[3] and after that would think himself fully paid, if he were allowed to brush his beard (which he had vowed never to shave till he saw her again) on her lilly white hand through the grated window of some inchanted tower. She would suit to a hair, I say, a fellow who would be content thus to love in

---

1 "A French girl or young woman of the working class, esp. one employed as a shop assistant or a seamstress" (*OED*).

2 Sluggish.

3 Sir Edward refers to the *The Honour of Chivalry: or The Famous and Delectable History of Don Bellianis of Greece* by Jerónimo Fernández, the first English edition of which was published in 1671–73 by Francis Kirkman (1632–80). See John Hardy, "Johnson and Don Bellianis," *Review of English Studies* 17.67 (1966): 297–99. Sir Lancelot is a legendary knight of the round table and lover of Queen Guinevere.

buskins;[1] but for us modern gallants, who have not so much time to throw away on sighing, give me a girl who has spirit enough to spring out of a window into our arms; such a girl as Cecilia, who, above disguise, avows her love, and spite of the stern brow of parental authority, bestows her person and her fortune where she has given her heart. As for Dolly, 'tis such a frigid soul that I am amazed how a spark could be kindled in such an ice-house as her bosom; much puffing and blowing must it have cost the little demon Love to light the flame, and after all 'tis but a sickly blaze, you see, which like a dying lamp pops up and down, whilst Duty waits with his extinguisher in his hand, to flop down on it the first moment he catches the little urchin napping.

Depend upon it, Falkland, this fearful girl would never have courage enough to fulfil her engagement, till after she had made you serve as long an apprenticeship as old father what's-his-name did for his wife. Things indeed were better managed in those days than they are at present; for a man was then at liberty to marry two sisters, which was the case of the aforesaid patriarch;[2] and if one could do so still, the affair might be made very easy; for you might take Cecilia now, and I'll engage Dolly would keep cold very well for about fourteen years.

After all, Falkland, I think the best thing you can do, is to make over to me your *imaginary* right (for a real one you have not) in this girl. I'll take her with all my soul, and shall not think the worse of her, for her having formerly liked a handsomer fellow than myself. I'll trust to her religion to keep her faithful to me, once I am vested with the awful name of husband. By the way, those prejudices are not without their use amongst the women, they often keep the poor things out of mischief when nothing else would. Give it me therefore in black and white (that we may have no after reckonings) that you yield up all pretensions to Dorothea Arnold, and I'll take her off your hands.

Sir George Bidulph goes down to Woodberry.——Good! matters must then be soon brought to a crisis. His peevish wife is not so vigilant as himself; and if I knew the day, the hour, the

---

1 Half-boots worn by actors in ancient Athenian drama.
2 Sir Edward makes reference to the biblical story of Jacob. That patriarch served Laban, his mother's brother, for seven years for the right to marry Laban's daughter Rachel. Upon his wedding, he realized that he had been tricked and married to the eldest daughter, Leah, instead. Jacob was permitted to marry Rachel as well, but had to serve an additional seven years for her (see Genesis 29).

minute that united you to Cecilia; on the same day, hour, and minute, would I possess myself of the elder hope of the family. I have conceived my plan; but 'tis your hand, Falkland, must help me to execute it; and when our uncle Bidulph has turned his back, you shall hear from me to some purpose.

Letter XLVI
Mr. Falkland to Sir Edward Audley
Oxford, March 4th.

My good genius is at work for me; blessings on lord V— for taking the resolution of coming down to Woodberry! He arrived there yesterday; little did the fool imagine that he was coming on the spur to the destruction of his own hopes. What a *gracious* reception did he meet with from Mrs. Arnold! What a delightfully cold one from my adorable! Things are, I hope, as you say, drawing to a crisis; but this lord V— is too temperate, and the elements too equally mixed in his composition; his breath alone is not sufficient to raise the storm that is to drive my Cecilia from the harbour of her mother's arms; his sighs like gentle breezes do but lift, and give a livelier motion to the waves. 'Tis Sir George Bidulph, who like the boisterous north wind, will blow a storm, work all into foam about him, and force my little pinnace from her moorings. Would he were come! But what can his absence from London do for *you*? Do you think it will make your access to Miss Arnold less difficult? Be assured, Audley, I do most sincerely wish her yours, and do hereby renounce all right and title to her. I am certain that you would make her a much better husband than I should, and therefore shall be ready to concur with you in any measures to obtain her; but to tell you the truth, the thing appears so impracticable to me, that till I know your plan, I must consider your hopes as almost desperate, and cannot help being sorry for you in the midst of the tide of joy that flows in upon my heart.

As for my own part, I begin to be quite reconciled to myself; and if my solitary hours are sometimes clouded with a little remorse, the rays of my Cecilia's eyes disperses it as sunshine does a vapour.

End of the Fourth Volume

CONCLUSION

OF THE

MEMOIRS

OF

Mifs Sidney Bidulph,

As prepared for the Prefs

By the LATE EDITOR of the
FORMER PART.

VOLUME V.

LONDON:

Printed for J. Dodsley, in Pall-mall.
M DCC LXVII.

Continuation of the Memoirs of Miss Sidney Bidulph

Letter XLVII
Mrs. Arnold to Mrs. Cecilia B—.
[The letter to which this is an answer is omitted.]
Woodberry, March 9th.

I wish, my dear, I could give you a satisfactory answer to your enquiries; but I really now think matters wear a much worse face than ever they did. You know I already told you, that having urged every thing I could in favour of my lord V—, I thought it prudent to drop the subject for some time, in hopes Cecilia's gratitude for such a condescension, would have more weight with her when left to the workings of her own heart, than all my brother's boisterous proceedings, joined to the teizing of lady Sarah, which my daughter declared had only served to heighten her dislike to lord V—, who had been the innocent cause of the uneasiness she was made to suffer.

Things were in this suspended situation, when I received a polite letter from my lord V—, begging my permission to pay me a visit. It was accompanied with another for Cecilia, full of tenderness and respect; but without any of the impatient flights of a lover. Cecilia said upon reading it, I wished my lord V— would allow me to enjoy myself in quiet; he knows I quitted London to avoid him, why will he pursue me down hither? I was offended at the peevish manner in which she spoke, and told her she must not presume on my indulgence, to treat with contempt, or even indifference, the man I so much respected, and to whose family I had such strong obligations. She seemed abashed at my rebuke, and said she should always behave to lord V— with that deference and esteem which she thought due to him. I answered his lordship's letter directly, which he had sent express; and the next evening I had the pleasure to receive him in person. With what satisfaction did I embrace the amiable son of my dear lady V—, and of her worthy lord! I had not the least recollection of his features, for it is thirteen years since I have seen him. His noble stature, and military air, give a dignity to his person that recommends him at first sight; and I could not help giving a look of astonishment at Cecilia, who was in the room with me when he entered. She received him with great civility; but a coldness which seemed to mortify him. My son Falkland happened to be with us; my lord politely saluted, but spoke not to him. Orlando reddened like fire; I saw he had not forgotten the resentment you formerly told me he had conceived against him. I was vexed he happened to be present, and should for the boy's sake have taken care to have prevented this abrupt interview, if I had thought my lord V— would have been so expeditious in making his visit after the receipt of my letter.

I was desirous my son and he should be on more sociable terms; I asked my lord if he did not think Mr. Falkland had a strong resemblance to his father? He replied, he had but an imperfect remembrance of the elder Mr. Falkland's face, having seen him but a few times in his life; whence he took occasion to address my son, and asked him some questions relative to the course of his studies; (my lord himself was bred at the same university). Mr. Price had now got upon his favourite topic, and entered with vivacity into the conversation. In the course of which, he took occasion to mention his pupil's design of going into the army. My lord V— highly commended his choice. Orlando received his civilities with coldness, and very soon took his leave. After he was gone, his lordship told me, he should very soon have a cornetcy vacant in his regiment, as the officer who now had the post, had, on account of very ill health, desired leave to quit the army, and meant to return to England as soon as he was able to endure the fatigue of the journey. 'Tis at Mr. Falkland's service, added he, and I should have offered it to the young gentleman himself, had you, Madam, delivered your sentiments with regard to the course of life of which he has made choice; but if you approve of it, I shall think myself happy in his acceptance of this mark of my respect for him. I acknowleged, as it deserved, this instance of his lordship's goodness and consideration for a youth, who I told him had always been regarded by me as a son. Mr. Price expressed himself as warmly as if the favour had been conferred immediately on himself; and said he considered his young friend as singularly happy in being under the patronage and protection of lord V—.

I indeed thought myself much obliged to his lordship, yet I know to whose account I ought in reality to place this mark of his bounty: he thought to please Cecilia by shewing such a distinction to her brother; but she seemed not sensible of his intention, and her behaviour was constrained for the rest of the evening.

You know I am an early riser, yet my lord V— prevented me the next morning, for I found him in the parlour when I came down stairs; neither Mr. Price nor Cecilia were yet stirring.

After our first salutations, Well, my dear Madam, said he, may I yet flatter myself with any thing like hope? I told him frankly, that I could not say he had made the smallest progress in my daughter's affections; expressing at the same time my surprize and my concern, and assuring him nothing could give me greater pleasure than an alliance with his family. I am at present, said he, under the most disagreeable dilemma in the world; I came not down hither to importune Miss Cecilia; the principal motive of my visit was to pay my respects to you, and I meant not to remind your daughter of my love by any other marks of it than my submission and my assiduity to please; but Sir George Bidulph told me on the eve of my departure from London, that he meant soon to follow me down hither. Now as I am very much afraid that his interfering too warmly will rather destroy than promote my interests, I ventured to hint this tenderly to Sir George, insinuating at the same time that I should have better hopes of succeeding, if he would permit me to pursue my own method in endeavouring to gain his niece's affections, who, I said, I thought had already been too much urged. He laughed, and told me, I did not know her; but I dare not repeat to you all Sir George said on the occasion.

I answered his lordship, that I knew my brother's manner, and therefore begged he would speak freely. You must not then be angry, replied lord V—, but these were Sir George's words: 'Cecilia is vain, and loves to be admired. She has had her little brain turned with flattery, and fancies she ought not to give up her power under a romantic courtship of seven years. Her mother' (remember, Madam, you are not to be angry with me) 'has spoiled her by too great an indulgence; and an absurd old relation of ours has made her still more untractable, by leaving her a fortune in her own power. Though I have a perfect good opinion of her, yet I think a girl thus circumstanced, as she has it in her power, so she may have it a *little* in her inclination to chuse for herself, and who can answer for the choice of inexperienced youth? I believe as yet her heart has received no impressions. She had three adorers whilst she was with me, besides your lordship; but she shewed not the least liking to any of them; and her sister, on whose word I am sure I can rely, declared she believed her inclinations entirely disengaged. 'Tis upon this assurance, therefore, that I have been the more peremptory with her, as I consider her declining your hand merely as the result of obstinacy and caprice; and if we give way to her in this instance, relying perhaps on the fond partiality of her friends, her next step may be to give us a relation, who possibly may have no other merit, but what her fancy discovers in him. Lady Sarah and myself, added Sir George, desire ardently to see her yours. My sister and Miss

Arnold both profess to do the same; my lady V—'s sentiments, you know, agree with ours, so do those of all our friends.——' I interrupted Sir George here; But if the sentiments of the lady herself, said I, are averse to me, I am not a lover so void of delicacy as to seize an unwilling hand, joined to mine merely by the authority of parents. Psha, cried Sir George, 'tis such lovers as you who make the women so insolent; do you think it absolutely necessary that the lady whom you marry should be as much in love with you as you are with her? I told him, No; but that I thought it absolutely necessary that there should be at least no *dislike* on the part of the lady. Sir George was here pleased to pay me some unmerited compliments, and bid me at the same time recollect that you, Madam, who had not only married without inclination, but, as he believed, with strong prepossessions in favour of another, had made a most exemplary wife even in the most trying circumstances; and he was convinced you had had as sincere an affection for Mr. Arnold as if he had been the man of your choice. I stopped my lord here, to assure him that my brother had spoken the truth. All this I own then, Madam, pursued he, has encouraged me to persevere; but what at present distresses me is, that I am apprehensive, when Sir George comes down to Woodberry, he will be for pushing matters to an extremity; for he declared, if his niece continued obstinate, that he would renounce her! What shall we do, dear Madam? added he, for I solemnly aver to you, that passionately as I love Miss Cecilia Arnold, I would desist from my pursuit sooner than draw on her the resentment of her friends, if I thought that would be a means of preserving her from it; but matters have already gone so far, that even that would be attributed to her by Sir George as a subject of complaint equal to a peremptory refusal on her side. I told his lordship he had formed a very just conclusion, as the blame must certainly light on Cecilia, let our disappointment in this union wear what face it would: I know of no means then to be pursued, added I, but to suffer my brother to be decisive on this occasion. If my daughter's reluctance does not amount to aversion, (which I have not the least reason to think it does) she will certainly yield rather than forfeit her uncle's regard; and, in that case, you may depend on the goodness of her heart for a suitable return to your tenderness. On the other hand, if her caprice is insurmountable, I know she has spirit enough to be resolute in her refusal, let the consequences be what they will. If this should be the issue, Madam, replied lord V—, I must conjure you not to let Cecilia feel a *mother*'s resentment, as well as that of her other relations; remember the *heart* is not at our own disposal.—How I admire the generosity of this worthy young nobleman!

I shall pass over the four or five intermediate days till my brother's arrival, in all which time Orlando never came near us, though Mr. Price writ to him to let him know my lord V—'s kind intentions towards him, and recommended it to him to come and thank his lordship. I am afraid this youth is of a proud and vindictive spirit!

Lord V— all this while never entertained Cecilia on the subject of his love. She seemed to listen to him with pleasure on every topic, and the poor man appeared to me to be afraid of forfeiting this satisfaction, by touching on the only string which he knew would make discord.

Having had no previous notice of my brother's intended visit but what I received from lord V—, who did not himself know the precise time of his coming, he came upon us a little abruptly last night just as we were sitting down to supper. Cecilia turned pale on his entering the room; and I thought Sir George seemed at a loss what face to wear towards her, as he had resolved to deport himself accordingly as he should find her disposed towards lord V—.

How amiable was my lord V—'s conduct on this occasion! He affected an appearance of satisfaction, which I knew he was very far from feeling at his heart; he even assumed an ease in his behaviour towards his mistress, which gave him the air of a lover who was far from being discouraged.

Cecilia's uneasiness was too visible not to be observed by my brother. He only waited till the servants were withdrawn to ask her too roughly, I thought, whether she still retained the same *pretty inflexibility* which she had carried with her out of town? She made no reply. Softly, my dear Sir George, said my lord, we must not have our happiness disturbed by harsh interrogations; I never enjoyed so perfect a satisfaction as I have done for these last five days. You then are come to the use of your reason, niece, rejoined my brother, looking at Cecilia with a sort of pleasure mixed with distrust. I tell you again, said my lord, smiling, we won't be interrogated; Miss Cecilia is all goodness, all condescension. I am extremely glad to hear it, cried my brother.—Sister! Mr. Price! what say you? for a lover's word is not always to be depended on with regard to his mistress. Mr. Price was silent, only by a little nod of his head indicated that he had no great hopes of the business. I can't tell how to answer you, brother, said I. Ha, I thought so, cried my brother. Pray, my lord, to what may Miss's *conde-*

scension have amounted? To sit in the same room with you, perhaps, or suffer you to take up her glove if she happened to drop it? Cecilia sat biting her lips, her looks full of vexation. Mr. Price began to pat softly under the table with his foot, which is a habit he has given himself when he is discontented with anything. I have no reason to complain, Sir George, said my lord V—, with that assured tone which hope inspires. I'll be sacrificed, cried my brother, if you have gained an inch of ground since you came down hither! I flatter myself I have lost none, answered lord V—, and I am perfectly satisfied with my prospect of happiness, however distant it may be. I honour your lordship's patience extremely, said Sir George, though it is a virtue of which I never had the good fortune to be possessed. I have not the least objection, continued he, to a man's going through all the ceremonials of a lover for a few months, provided he is sure not to be disappointed in the end; but (excuse me, ladies) I would not sacrifice my time to any of you, unless I had an absolute certainty of obtaining my wishes; which I own, my lord, does not seem to be your case. I am, nevertheless, satisfied to wait, Sir George; the experiment is well worth the trial; and I am resolved to be indebted to no one but the lady herself for a happiness, which, from that circumstance, would come with redoubled value. Mighty well, said my brother, I see we are likely to advance wonderfully: your lordship, however, must take your own way. I thank you, Sir George, said my lord V—. What news is there in London? This question gave the conversation another turn, and we chatted on indifferent things till my usual hour of retiring, when my lord V— rose and wished us a good-night. Mr. Price, who had, in complaisance to my brother, already exceeded his customary hour of going to bed, followed him immediately. Cecilia was now going to withdraw, when my brother requested she would stay a few minutes; she sat down again in her place. I see, said he, from what has passed this evening, that my lord V— is just where he set out at first. I was in hopes, Cecilia, that your mother's personal influence would by this time have been able to subdue that unpardonable obstinacy, which has already so much disgusted all your friends; but as I find it has had no effect, I shall desire no other favour of you than to answer me one plain question, which I wish to have resolved as well for your own credit, as for the peace of mind of my lord V—. He thinks you have been too much pressed by your friends; perhaps you think so too; and that you should have had more time allowed you to cultivate such an esteem for him as would voluntarily induce you to make him your choice. He is willing to leave this desirable issue to time; tell me truly, then, if your friends are satisfied to indulge you in this, if you think you can then bring yourself to accept of lord V— for a husband? Beware of playing the coquet, child, (seeing she answered not directly) my lord V— is not a man to fool with; answer me without evasion; I have an opinion of your frankness; if you require the foppery of a few months dangling, why, be it so, I shall leave his lordship to pursue his love-process according to his own method. Cecilia, who had kept her eyes fixed on the table whilst her uncle spoke, now raised them to his face, You will not, I hope, Sir, said she, be offended if I answer you with that sincerity you require of me: I cannot think of lord V— for a husband. She withdrew her eyes again from Sir George's face, in which I saw indignation beginning to kindle. You prefer Sir Edward Audley, perhaps? Believe me, Sir, I never entertained a thought of him.—Mr. Hyndford possibly, or Mr. Gage? (you know they were both her admirers) Indeed, Sir, I like neither of them.—Was there ever such an unaccountable little wretch! said Sir George, angrily. Only I can't think you so void of pride, and so regardless of the honour of your family, I should think you had set your heart on some one you are ashamed to name! And apropos, sister, what is your charge, Mr. Falkland, doing at present? The manner in which my brother spoke this, and the indignant eye he fixed on Cecilia, shewed too plainly where his suspicions pointed. I thought just then of what you, my dear, formerly hinted to me, and felt myself exceedingly shocked. However blind Cecilia may be with regard to my lord V—, replied I, I am satisfied neither her prudence nor her duty would suffer her to engage her affections, contrary to the interests as well as happiness of her family. You forget, cried Sir George, that young ladies brought up in shady groves, by murmuring rills, always consult the inclinations of their own hearts, before they do that of the interests of their family; 'For what are titles, wealth, or fame, to love!'

The sarcastic air with which my brother accompanied this, seemed to cut Cecilia to the quick. She turned towards me, and with a spirited action catching me by the hand, If I am permitted, Madam, said she, to decline my lord V—'s alliance, you will find I shall justify the opinion you are so good as to have of me; for I here promise you, that however I may be impelled by inclination, (for I will not pretend to answer for my own heart) I will never transgress the duty I owe you. And so your friends are to sit down contented, ma'am, on the strength of this equivocation, said my brother, to wait till your capricious ladyship shall find yourself in the humour to obey them! May not the same speech serve your turn for any other match that may be proposed to you? If you have taken the resolution to live single, you had best say so at once? Sir, I have made no such resolution.—Very well, Miss, you may retire; we'll talk to you farther on this subject to-morrow.

I know not what to make of this girl, said Sir George, (after she was gone out of the room) but this much I am sure of, there must be something more at the bottom of all this than dislike of my lord V—: if her heart be engaged, it is, (I am almost ashamed to say it) but it is, it must be to Falkland; for be assured, Sidney, that young fellow inherits all the art of his d—n'd mother.—Dear brother, how can you be so implacable? You have already, said he, been a martyr to your own credulity, and that of other people; for Heaven's sake, sister, at length learn a little worldly wisdom. I know Falkland hates lord V—, and without insisting on his being himself the favourite of Cecilia, I am certain he secretly puts her against him, for she was more decisive in her rejection of him to-night than ever I heard her before. I could not help agreeing with him in this observation. I think then, said he, the seldomer you admit of his visits the better; and I shall take it as a favour, if you will at least prevent them whilst I continue here; for I would by no means chuse to see him after what passed between us, the par-ticulars of which I suppose your daughter may have informed you. I told him Mr. Falkland had never come to my house since the first night of my lord's arrival, when they happened to meet; and at the same time I let him know the obliging offer my lord V— had made him. 'Tis more than he deserves at his hands, said my brother, and had I thought it worth while to inform lord V— of his audacious behaviour, I believe the young man would have received a compliment of a very different nature from him; but I am glad that I had caution enough not to trouble him with the petulance of a forward boy, and am now extremely pleased that Falkland is likely to be sent out of the way.

I intended sending off this letter to you to-day; but as it is already of an unconscionable size for the post, I will defer sending it till to-morrow, when I shall have the opportunity of a private hand; for I am just this minute told, that one of lord V—'s ser-vants is arrived from London with some dispatches to him, and that he is to return again to town to-morrow. I have not yet quitted my chamber this morning; but I am now summoned to breakfast, so here will I lay down my pen.

Monday night.

Nothing, my Cecilia, nothing but fresh embarrassments; where they will end Heaven only knows! My lord V— received a packet of letters from London this morning, and amongst others, one which brought him an account of the death of that officer, whose commission he had promised to Orlando. My lord V— lamented him as a very worthy man and a good officer; but declared his satisfaction at the same time, at having it in his power to fulfil his promise to Mr. Falkland sooner than he expected. My brother immediately laid hold on the hint, and said he thought Mr. Falkland should be very glad to embrace such an opportunity of entering immediately into service, as the campaign would probably soon open; and that, in his mind, he could not do better than set out immediately for the regiment. My lord V— was of the same opinion, saying, as the military life was altogether new to the young man, it might be of advantage to him to be a little acquainted with it before he was called into the field. What's your opinion, sister? Said Sir George. My lord and you are such good judges of the question, answered I, that I cannot hesitate a minute in agreeing with you. What say you, my good Sir? (to Mr. Price). I am entirely of your mind, said Mr. Price, and think the army itself the properest school to fit him for his profession. And you, Miss Cecilia, (rivetting his eyes on my daughter's face) what do *you* think? She lifted not her's from off her work, but with a deep blush, replied, I think as you do, Sir. I wish you did so in *other* respects, answered my brother, coldly. I observed my lord V—'s eyes had been turned towards Cecilia from the time Sir George had put the question to her. Her too apparent confusion had a visible effect on him; he turned pale, and rising off his chair, went out of the room. Sir George said it would be proper to apprize Falkland of the affair, that he might get himself in readiness with all convenient speed; a line from you, sister, will be sufficient on this occasion. I suppose he will not require much time for preparation. I said I would go and write to him directly. I had but just got into my closet, when my brother tapped at the door, and telling me he wanted to speak with me, begg'd I would allow him a few minutes' conversation. Having let him in, Do you think, said he, with his usual abruptness, that your daughter has bestowed her affections on Falkland, or not? for I am satisfied *you*, as well as I, observed the agitation into which she was thrown on the mention of his departure. I did, answered I, and am exceedingly alarmed at it. A mean-spirited little d—l, said he, stamping with his foot! is the curse of worthless husbands to be entailed on the family![1] Softly, dear Sir George. ——Softly! cried he, I have not patience to think of such a depravity of mind: admirable fruits of her education indeed we are to expect, when we see her prefer to such a man as lord V— a little insignificant wretch, without family, fortune, or even name! Oh, Sidney, see what your imprudent charity has done! Spare your reproaches, dear brother; if the thing be as you suspect—*If* it be! interrupted he, why can you have any doubt about it? One thing, however, let me warn you against; do not examine your daughter on the subject; I know the ascendancy she has over you, and how easily your heart is to be melted; the secret once declared, the young lady will have no more measures to observe; 'tis from her pride only that I entertain the least hopes of turning her from this scandalous attachment. Whilst she believes us ignorant of it, perhaps she be may ashamed to acknowledge it; and if we can get Falkland fairly out of the way, a little time may probably bring her to herself. The opportunity which now offers to send him out of the kingdom must by no means be let slip. My coldness towards him (which he very well knows) will be a sufficient excuse for your not asking him here whilst I remain with you, which I purpose doing till he leaves England: this you see will cut off all communication between him and Cecilia; after he is gone, I fancy we shall have less difficulty to manage her. This was what I wanted chiefly to say to you, what do you think of it?

I have not the least objection to your design, answered I; only I think it would be proper that both my lord V— and I should see Mr. Falkland before he goes away; and it would appear very particular even to my lord himself, if Orlando were not permitted to take his leave of Cecilia. I hate those *takings of leave*, answered Sir George; however, when he is in readiness to depart, that may be contrived; but let me of all things advise you not to suffer it to be done in the presence of lord V—, lest Cecilia's emotions should betray her folly; and lord V— knows the world too well to be imposed on by the pretence of *sisterly* affection. My brother left me at these words, and I sat down directly to my escruitore to write a few lines to Orlando, wherein I informed him of the news my lord V— had received this morning, and that in consequence

---

1 Sir George thoroughly disliked Mr. Arnold for his treatment of Sidney, whom Arnold had cast off so he could squander his fortune on the perfidious Mrs. Gerrarde.

of it, it was thought expedient by his friends (I named myself, lord V—, and Mr. Price) that he should repair immediately to the regiment. I desired him to bespeak every thing that was necessary for this expedition, telling him that Mr. Price should call on him in a day or two with whatever sum of money he should want; and that as I found my brother still retained a strong resentment against him, I must deprive myself of the pleasure of seeing him whilst Sir George continued at Woodberry, hinting at the same time we would contrive to meet before he left the country. I sent my letter off directly, and in return received a note from Orlando, promising he would obey my instructions. He writ a letter at the same time to lord V— politely thanking him for the honour he had conferred on him.

I can add nothing more to this very long letter but my own disagreeable reflections. Indeed, my dear, I am now exceedingly afraid that my poor unhappy girl loves—Oh, Cecilia, my hand shakes when I add the name of Falkland! Your surmises on the occasion I thought not well founded; for I concluded I myself must have been the first to discover this fatal inclination. Is it not amazing that a creature, who has never been from under my own eye, should have been able with so much art to conceal a secret of this nature? Yet I hope it has proceeded no farther than a secret preference of Falkland in her own heart; but if their love should be mutual and acknowledged! Good God, in what a dreadful situation are we all! Yet I cannot inform myself as to this; *you* first advised me against examining Cecilia on the subject, and I followed your advice, yet more in compliance to a judgment which I think superior to my own, than a persuasion in that particular instance of its being rightly formed. My brother entering pretty much into the same sentiments with you, has laid on me the same injunction; I now see the necessity of it, and have promised to observe it. Perhaps the absence of Orlando may work a favourable change for lord V—; I should be exceedingly grieved at parting with him if I had not this desirable point in view, for I would fain flatter myself that Cecilia's attachment may be at bottom but a childish inclination which will dye of itself when the object is removed from her sight. I observed when she sat down to dinner, that her eyes looked as if she had been weeping, yet she affected to be as chearful as usual; my brother seemed pleased with this effort of hers; it justified his sagacity in supposing she would be *ashamed* to give way to a weakness of which she did not suppose her friends suspected her. My lord V— was melancholy and frequently absent, yet abated not of his tender attention to

Cecilia; I believe our thoughts all centered in the same point, however differently we were affected.

Heaven send a favourable issue to an event which now hangs in such suspence!—

Letter XLVIII
Miss Cecilia Arnold to Miss Arnold
Woodberry, March 10th.

The time is come, the hour is at length arrived, when it is permitted Cecilia to unlock her bosom and pour out the secrets of it into that of her dear Dolly; yet do not look down upon me, my sweet philosophic sister, because perhaps your loftier mind is incapable of a weakness to which my feebler reason has yielded. You know I am a proud little hussy, and cannot bear contempt.

[She then proceeds to give her sister an account of the mutual affection between her and Mr. Falkland, with the manner of their disclosing it to each other, pretty nearly as Mr. Falkland has already related it in his letter to Sir Edward Audley; after which, she tells her of the particulars that occurred from the time of Sir George Bidulph's arrival at Woodberry down to the period where Mrs. Arnold concludes her last letter and then continues:]

I judged from everything I observed that my uncle suspected Mr. Falkland to be the man whom in the bottom of my heart I favoured; and that this more than any thing else had determined him to hasten his departure out of the kingdom. I saw too plainly that my mama, in regard to my marriage with lord V—, meant to yield up her natural right in the disposal of me, and to delegate her power to Sir George; and I had reason to believe that my lord V—'s passion for me was strong enough to surmount the scruples which his delicacy might otherwise have thrown in his way, with respect to a woman who he was convinced entertained not any inclination for him, provided he thought her indifference proceeded not from any prior engagement of her affections, and this was a point of which I judged both my mama and my uncle would labour to persuade him. The former, from really entertaining no suspicions of the truth; the latter, from a belief that I dared not acknowlege it. All these conclusions I drew from several little observations I had made at different times, upon their different conduct. What part could I chuse in such a dilemma? I had promised Falkland to be his at once, in case I saw no means of escaping the other match. He pressed me to the accomplishment of this promise; yet my love for *him* could not so far extinguish that which I bear my mama, as to think of this without shuddering. I resolved therefore on an expedient which you, I believe, will think a strange one, yet the event justified my prudence in making choice of it. This was no other than opening my heart to lord V. himself, and imploring even his assistance against his own interests, the interests of his love!

After forming my design, I was not slow in executing it. I writ two lines to my lord V— wherein I told him I had something important to say to him, and begg'd he would meet me next morning at seven o'clock in the cedar parlour. This room, you know, as we hardly ever make use of it, secured me against the fear of interruption, even from the servants. I ventured to leave my little note myself on my lord's dressing-table, where I knew he must find it when he retired to his chamber to go to bed.

I was so agitated the whole night at the thoughts of what I had to say to *him*, and what he might surmise of *me* in the interim, that I slept not a wink, and as soon as I saw broad day-light, I arose, dressed myself, and softly crept down stairs.

It was but three quarters past six; but my lord had prevented me, and was already in the parlour. I said I hoped I had not made him wait, and referred him to his watch to shew that it was not yet the appointed hour. In matters of mere business, Madam, said he, a man may satisfy himself with being barely punctual; but where the concerns of the heart are at stake, he must be a fleg-matic lover indeed who is not a little before his time.

I felt myself exceedingly embarrassed; I scarce knew how to begin the conversation. My lord V— has a manly steadiness in his deportment that inspires one with a kind of awe; I almost wished myself in my own chamber again, but it was now too late. I made a motion for him to sit down, he did so, and I took my place opposite to him. He remained silent, though with an impatience in his looks mingled with love and respect. I collected myself as well as I could, and addressing him, If I had not, said I, the highest opinion in the world of your lordship's generosity, as well as of your prudence and the goodness of your heart, I had not dared to take the step I have now done. I must believe your curiosity is excited to know what I have to say; my lord, I mean to open my whole heart to you. He bowed to me, and I thought seemed to tremble from head to foot, which, little coward as I am, encouraged me to proceed. I should be both insensible and ungrateful, continued I, if I were not full of acknowlegements for the kind sentiments with which you honour me, and for the extreme delicacy you have observed towards me; but, my lord, when I say I acknowlege both, I must add that I can only do it with gratitude and esteem; the return you desire is not in my power to make. I own you deserve my heart; but that was bestowed long before you favoured me with your affection, otherwise I should allow myself to be unjust in not giving you the preference of which I think you so worthy. My lord bowed again. I *owed* you this explanation, my lord, continued I, and should (exclusive of any other reasons) have thought myself bound to make it, as well in justification of my own conduct, (which must otherwise appear very capricious) as to shew you the entire confidence I have in you. Having gone thus far, my lord, I mean not to stop here, I will not confide in you by halves; Mr. Falkland is the person who has had long possession of my affections; and to deal plainly with you, I never can think of making any other man my husband.

I thank you, Madam, answered my lord V— and admire your sincerity, though it has confirmed my despair.—I know, proceeded I, what my uncle's designs are; from some hints he dropt, I am satisfied that he suspects I love Mr. Falkland; he is earnest to get him out of the way; I see well the measures he intends to pursue after that; he is extremely persevering in every thing he wishes to accomplish; he has your lordship's alliance much at heart—He interrupted me here with some vivacity, And can you think so meanly of me, Madam, said he, as to believe that after the declaration you have just now made, I would like a ravisher seize your reluctant hand? No, Madam, precious as I should esteem the gift were it voluntarily bestowed, I would not accept it when forced on me by the authority of a parent. Pardon me, my lord, answered I; I entertain not the least doubt of the generosity of your way of thinking; but every man is not so delicate. There may be some who would not scruple to take me even circumstanced as you know me to be; and my uncle's prejudices are so strong against Mr. Falkland, that once he is gone, though your lordship were even out of the question—My lord again interrupted me; How grieved am I, Madam, said he, that you are so soon to be separated from the object of your love; but do you wish that I should contrive to postpone Mr. Falkland's journey till I go myself to join to army, which will not be for some time? I cannot now recall the charge I have bestowed on him; had I sooner known the interest you have in him, I would not have been the means of exposing to the chance of war a life so precious to you; but be assured, dearest Miss Arnold, I shall have the warmest attention to his preservation, his interest, and his honour. I will forget that he is my rival while I consider him only as one that is dear to you. I could not refrain from tears. Oh, my lord, you oppress me, said I: sentiments so noble! –So virtuous! why have not I a heart to give you! Yet do not think so slightly of me as to believe I have any reluctance to Mr. Falkland's pursuing the paths of honour which you have chalked out for him; I rely stedfastly on the promise you have given me, and if he should happen to fall, I think I have strength of mind enough to console myself by reflecting on the cause. A manly tear sprung into my lord V—'s eye, which dashing off with a smile, Charming heroine! he called me. Then after a short silence, Do you wish, Madam, said he, that I should leave the house, and at least free you from the sight of a man whose presence serves only to embarrass you? I will, if you please, endeavour also to draw Sir George with me to town, that you may be freed from the restraint which now debars you of the sight of your happy lover. You are too, too good, my lord, said I, and I am almost afraid to put your generosity to any farther proof. Ah, do not spare me, Madam, answered lord V—; after having lost all hopes of your heart, my situation cannot be rendered more unhappy by any additional mortification; tell me what can I do, to shew you how much I am devoted to your service? I premised to your lordship, said I, that if I had not the highest opinion imaginable of you, I had not dared to proceed as I have done; but I confide wholly in you, and am now going to demand an important proof of that regard which you profess for me.

Mr. Falkland, despairing of the consent of my friends, urges me to marry him privately before his departure. I received a letter from him yesterday to this effect, wherein he says, 'tis the only means to secure his future happiness, and make him easy under our separation. I have promised to be his; yet cannot persuade myself to take such a step without first endeavouring, if possible, to move my mama, at least, in his favour. She loves him dearly, and is of so tender and yielding a disposition, that, were it not through fear of my uncle's resentment, I should, before this time, have not the courage to do so. Will you, my lord, be my advocate on this occasion? Your example, your influence, must have great weight both with her and my uncle. I believe your lordship knows that I have a fortune not inconsiderable in my own power: 'tis not then with any interested view that I would wish to obtain their consent, but to spare my family the pain they must feel for having driven me to an act of disobedience, and myself the grief of being divided from relations I love so tenderly. Do you then, madam, said my lord, rising off his chair with some emotions, mean to go abroad with Mr. Falkland? Oh, by no means, answered I; I desire no more than to quiet Mr. Falkland's fears, who dreads the thoughts of leaving me in my uncle's disposal. May I, my lord, may I expect the favour I have demanded of you? You have imposed a hard task on me, madam, answered lord V—. Is it that you think I have but a feeble passion for you? or that you believe I am void of sensibility? Neither the one nor the other, said I; I believe you love me sincerely, and I am sure there exists not a more noble or feeling heart! Those are the very reasons which determined me to make the request to you. I would not have asked a man of an ordinary soul; such are not for common minds: but you, my lord, I know, are equal to them. Will you then, will you give me this last generous proof of your love? Madam, I *will*, said my lord; you shall see, by this effort to oblige you, what I am capable of doing for your happiness—What, indeed, would I *not* do! he pronounced these last words in a tone that made me think he was almost moved to tears. I felt my eyes moist—I will not thank you, my lord: where a favour is *above* acknowlegement, words are of no use. I do not despair, said he, (recovering himself) of working on the ductile heart of Mrs. Arnold; but for Sir George Bidulph, I scarce know how to make the attempt; yet I will venture on it for your service.—What is *his* interest, what are *his* feelings, what *his* loss, in comparison to *mine*! My lord clasped his hands together in uttering this last word, fixing his eyes on me at the same time with such an expression of sadness as wounded me to the very heart. I was obliged to turn from him to hide my tears. I beg your pardon, Madam, said he, I meant not to move your pity, or to inspire you with any regret for *my* fate; forgive the last transports of a passion which has already caused you but too much uneasiness.—Ah, my dear, is not this an exalted man? Why were we not born for each other!

I have a thought come into my head, said my lord, which I beg you will let me pursue my own way. Sir George Bidulph and I are engaged to dine to-day with Doctor T. one of the heads of the university; but I will make some pretence for not attending him, because I should like to take this opportunity of having some conversation with Mr. Falkland. Will you, Madam, send him a line to request his company here at five o'clock this afternoon? you may say I wish to talk to him; but I beseech you not to hint any thing more—Ask me not, added he, how I mean to proceed; I will not tell you my plot, though you yourself shall be an actor in the drama. I told him I should leave the conduct of the scene entirely to his lordship, and should not make any enquiries into his design. I then said I believed it was almost my mama's hour of rising, and would therefore detain him no longer. He immediately withdrew, and I slipped up to my chamber by the back stairs, and writ a few lines to Mr. Falkland just in the terms my lord prescribed.

Orlando had sent me word in his letter of yesterday, that he would see me this very morning: for though he has not made his appearance at our house since my lord V— has been our guest; we nevertheless sometimes steal half an hour's conversation in my ivy-bower, as I call it: you know he can enter it without being seen, by means of the little door that leads into the field, to which he has got a key. I expected him therefore, I say, this morning; but I was desirous of preventing his visit, that I might not be under a necessity of making any previous explanations, as my lord had requested that I should not. Having dispatched my note, I sat myself down to give you this account. I shall break off here, and shall re-assume my pen in the evening, to tell you the result of my lord's intended measures.—*What* will they produce! I have a thousand worlds at stake! Oh, sister, sister, how my heart beats with apprehension!—

* * * * * *

Ten o'clock at night

Oh, day the fairest sure that ever rose,

————— : : —————

Go, wing'd with pleasure take thy happy flight,
And give each future morn a tincture of thy white![1]

Ha, said I not well, my dear, that my lord V— was the noblest of men? Oh, Dolly, what transports would it give me to see *you* the happy wife of that worthy lord! You think me mad, and, to say the truth, I am a little beside myself, things have taken so strange, so unexpected, so charming a turn! To put an end to your suspence at once, and to give you a satisfaction equal almost to my own, know that Falkland, *yours* and *my* beloved Falkland, is at length

---

1 From a poem by Matthew Prior (1664–1721), "Henry and Emma" (1708): "O Day the fairest sure that ever rose! / Period and End of anxious Emma's Woes! / Sire of her Joy, and Source of her Delight; / O! wing'd with Pleasure take thy happy Flight, / And give each future Morn a Tincture of thy White."

permitted to call me *his*! But take, according to my mama's method, every thing in order as it happened; there is not a circumstance but what is worthy to be writ in letters of gold.

My uncle, agreeable to his engagement, went to dine with Doctor T. My lord V— feigned himself a little indisposed, and sent an apology. Mr. Falkland, in consequence of my summons, came precisely at five o'clock. My lord V— had ordered one of the servants to wait his arrival at the gate, and to conduct him directly to my dressing-room, where he had previously desired me to be in readiness to receive him. I resolved implicitly to follow his instructions, and was there accordingly when Mr. Falkland was shewn into the room. He supposed this was done by my private directions; and as there was nothing extraordinary in my lord V—'s desiring to see him at this particular juncture, he was not surprized at it. He had been informed by my note that my uncle was not to be at home, and concluded we had taken that opportunity to send for him. He naturally imagined that lord V. would not think of entertaining him in my apartment, and expecting to be called away into another as soon as his lordship should hear of his being come, he resolved to spend the few minutes he supposed he had to be alone with me on the subject which was nearest to his heart; so that entering at once into it, without asking any questions relative to lord V—, he began to urge me with extreme earnestness to consent to the having our hands joined before his departure; but finding me more reluctant than ever to his proposal, he fell on his knees before me, and was employing all the rhetoric of a lover to persuade me, when we were surprized by the sudden appearance of my mama and lord V— who entered the room together.

I will not speak of my *own* confusion at this sight; great as it was, it was nothing in comparison to that of Falkland. As I had already paved the way of my mama's coming to the knowledge of our secret, I was prepared for the discovery, though I little expected my lord would have made it in this manner; but for poor Orlando it was a thunder-clap that he could not support. How I felt for him in that minute! and secretly reproached myself for not having given him some little notice of the step I had taken. My mama started back as she entered, for she saw him on his knees holding one of my hands. She leaned with her back against the wainscot, and without being able to speak look'd at us by turns; but with more, I thought, of sorrow than surprize in her countenance. Mr. Falkland, his face covered with a deep blush, hung down his head, and as if overwhelmed with a consciousness of some unpardonable crime, seemed afraid to lift up his eyes to my mama. How *I* looked I don't know, but I suppose very like a fool. My lord V— had the only unembarrassed face amongst us. He, however, kept silence, and, I thought, for a while appeared to enjoy the confusion into which he had thrown us all. At length approaching Mr. Falkland, he took him by the hand, and with an ingenuous freedom, Recover yourself, Sir, said he, and do not be ashamed to own a passion for an object so worthy of your love as Miss Cecilia Arnold; and you, Madam, (turning towards me) have no reason to blush for returning the tenderness of this amiable young man. I no longer complain of your indifference for me, the cause too well justifies your sentiments; and I should be the most unjust as well as unreasonable of men, if I did not at once yield up all pretensions to a heart, whose prior engagements, as they forbid all hope on my part, so do they deprive me of any pretence for complaining.

Mr. Falkland, encouraged by my lord's friendly and generous declaration, now ventured to look up. My lord, said he, I am too much confounded to return you the acknowlegements that I ought.—There is something in your conduct that amazes!—that almost dazzles me!—forgive me, my lord, my confusion will not suffer me to express what I feel.—Then drawing near my mama, he flung himself at her feet. But can *you*, Madam, said he, can *you* forgive the presumptuous wretch, who, forgetting the thousand obligations he has to you, and the distance that fortune has thrown between us, has dared to lift his eyes up to your Cecilia? I thought this was my time to speak, and following Mr. Falkland's example, I threw myself suddenly at my mama's knees, which I embraced; And can you, mama, said I, pardon the ungrateful girl, who, spite of her duty and the love she bears you, has ventured to bestow her heart without your knowledge? Good god! cried my mama, crossing her arms upon her breast, whilst we both hung upon her, *What* is this that you acknowlege! I *can* not punish you; and I *ought* not to pardon you—Pray, my lord, help me to disengage myself from these unfortunate children.—And why disengage yourself, Madam? answered my lord, why will you not rather suffer yourself to be touched with compassion? What recompence can you make your child for dividing her from the only man she can love? And what will avail all your maternal care of this young man's infancy, all your kind attention to his education, and your concern for his future welfare, if the same hand which has so long cherished and preserved him, now dashing with bitterness all your benefits, wounds him where the heart most sensibly feels, blasts all his hopes, and consigns, perhaps, his promising youth to despair? Ah, Madam, you cannot have the heart to do it—let your children's tears prevail; let my entreaties, who sacrifice an interest *much* dearer than a parent's; let your own tenderness, a mother's tenderness speak in their favour.—My lord might have continued his supplications, if his own emotions would have suffered him; for we were none of us in a condition to interrupt him. Mr. Falkland and I were drowned in tears; my dear mama's eyes ran like two fountains, yet she made an effort to break from us; but we both clung about her feet. Do not leave me, mama! I sobbed out.—Have pity on me, Madam! was all Mr. Falkland could utter.—Have pity on *me*, my poor mama cried out, and do not tear my heart thus between you!—Just as she spoke these words, my uncle Bidulph and Mr. Price presented themselves at the door.—(Their sudden appearance looked like enchantment; but I'll tell you by and by how it came about.) What can all this mean? cried my uncle, as he entered the room: then stopping short, My lord V—! has any misfortune happened in the family since I left you this morning? There has, said my mama; I leave it to my lord to explain to you what it is. I know of none, answered my lord V—, but what it is in your power, madam, and that of Sir George Bidulph to turn into a blessing. Then addressing my uncle, Look at this pair prostrate before you, Sir George, said he, look at them, and guess the rest. It should seem, replied my uncle, as if this young lady and gentleman were solliciting Mrs. Arnold's consent to their marriage; yet I cannot think it possible that my niece should be so lost to duty and discretion, or that Mr. Falkland has so far forgot himself—Mr. Falkland started up from his knees, piqued with resentment at the severity of my uncle's expression, and turning to him with a spirited air, though not without respect, No, Sir George, said he, Falkland has not forgot himself, he remembers the obligations *above* recompence that he has to that best of women, (pointing to my mama) he remembers that he is an unhappy orphan without a friend to own him, he remembers too well the misfortune of his birth, and he knows too that if it had not been for Mrs. Arnold's pious care, his mind might have been debased as low as his fortune, which now exposes him to the contempt with which he is treated. Yet conscious as he is of all this, he has dared to love your niece, nay, to own it, and is even bold enough to sollicit Mrs. Arnold for her consent to his happiness; for under all these mortifying disadvantages, he remembers that he owes his birth to a man whose son (had it not been for the fatal blow that robbed *you* of his valuable life) would have reflected honour, not disgrace, on the family to whom he should have allied himself.

My uncle seemed struck at Mr. Falkland's resolute reply; I see, said he, you have inherited at least some share of your father's *spirit*. I have addressed you, Sir, answered Mr. Falkland, as a man, as my equal, and one to whom I owe no obligation upon that score. I hope I have not transgressed the bounds which decency and good manners prescribe; but when I consider you as the uncle of Cecilia, the brother of Mrs. Arnold, and *once* the dear friend of my poor father, I again re-assume my suppliant posture (falling on his knees and seizing my uncle's hand): Oh, Sir George, *can* you treat with inhumanity the son of Falkland? My mama wept aloud, my lord V— seemed with difficulty to refrain from tears; for my part, I was quite dissolved, and the good old Price blew his nose two or three times; my uncle himself appeared a good deal moved. My lord V—, said he, it was not kind in you to lead me into so disagreeable a situation as this. I own I am quite at a loss to account for your lordship's conduct on this occasion. Account for it, answered my lord, from motives of compassion, from that pity which I see at this minute working in your own breast. I shall explain myself at large to you hereafter, mean while I must assure *you*, that you have been drawn into this affecting scene entirely without the participation either of Miss Cecilia or Mr. Falkland, and Mrs. Arnold has been equally surprized into it with yourself.

Let me beg of you, Sir, to rise, said my uncle, to Mr. Falkland. He did so. I am forced, continued Sir George, into a very disagreeable share in this eclaircissement; I am heartily sorry, I ever interfered in the disposal of Miss Cecilia; but I thought I was acquitting myself of a duty, and at the same time that I was not rendering an unacceptable service to your lordship. The happiness that you would have conferred on me, answered lord V—, I shall acknowlege with the highest gratitude whilst I live, and I call to witness him, who made and who knows the secrets of our hearts, that if I could have obtained that of your niece, I would not have given up my interest in her for anything this world contains; but, Sir George, the lady *herself* acknowleged to me her love for Mr. Falkland; and after that confession, what proof could I give her of the sincerity of my attachment to her, but to endeavour, as far as was in my power, to promote her happiness? It rests not on me, my lord, said my uncle, coldly, to facilitate or retard her happiness, as you are pleased to call it; I fancy the young lady is almost her own mistress, for I presume my sister has half consented already. You wrong me, Sir George, answered my mama; I appeal to my lord V—, and these children themselves; if I have in the least yielded. However I may be touched by this unhappy event, I owe you that deference, brother, that I here declare I never will give my consent to an union that has not your appropbation. My uncle was going to reply; I was afraid he would by a decisive negative put an end to all our hopes, and I was resolved to prevent him. Hold, dear uncle, said I, and before you determine our fate, suffer me at least to exculpate myself from the charge of disobedience. I own I love Mr. Falkland; *That*, if it *be* a fault, as it was an involuntary one, has not infringed the laws of duty. I was taught from my earliest childhood to consider him upon a footing of equality; I loved him from the example of those whom I thought it a merit to imitate. I knew my fortune entitled me to a richer match; yet I knew at the same time it gave me a privilege that I valued above riches. I need not here, Sir, repeat the words of Mr. Warner's will.*Yet I have not, I mean not to avail myself of the power that has given me; I will not abuse the good opinion Mr. Warner had of me, nor the confidence with which my mama has ever been pleased to favour me. I would fain owe my happiness to your indulgence, Sir, and that of the best of mothers. I have not bestowed my affections unworthily; Mr. Falkland's family is superior to my own, his education, his accomplishments, his mind, all are worthy of his birth. You *may* forbid me to be his; but I never will be the wife of any other man. For Heaven's sake, my dear Sir George, said my lord V—, consider a little of the merit of your niece's conduct; has she it not in her power to marry Mr. Falkland, and to bestow her fortune on him? where will you find a young creature tenderly attached as she acknowleges herself to be, who would forego such a privilege, and

---

* Mr. Warner had in a preamble to that part of his will which related to his two young kinswomen, made use of the following words: 'And forasmuch as parents, guardians, and relations, do sometimes from mere caprice, or a greediness of wealth, withhold their consents to marriages on which the happiness of their childrens lives depends; I do hereby give and bequeath to my two kinswomen Dorathea and Cecilia Arnold, the sum of twenty thousand pounds each, to be at their own full and free disposal at the age of eighteen years, relying on their prudence and the goodness of their dispositions; to the end that they may not (as their mother was) be compelled through fear to accept of a man they do not like.' This last act of Mr. Warner's was very consistent with the character of that whimsical, though very worthy man. [Frances Sheridan's note.]

sacrifice her own happiness to gratify a mere punctilio?—Her mother did so, interrupted my uncle—And how often, Sir, (as I have heard my mama say) did you reproach her for that?[1] answered I; and what pains did you not take to persuade her to stick to her first engagements? The cases are very different, said my uncle; Mr. Falkland was a match of which the first woman in the kingdom might have been proud to accept: I mean not to depreciate this young man; but I must say, the personal merit, the character, the fortune of his father—Oh, Sir, cried Mr. Falkland, I know how much he was superior to me in every thing; yet there was a time when you saw him stripped of his fortune, his character stained by a dreadful event, robbed almost of his reason, and obliged to abandon his family and the country; yet even then, under those circumstances of complicated misery, you thought him worthy of your sister,[2] the best and loveliest of women; how can you then, Sir, reject the unhappy son of him whom you once preferred to all mankind? I remember the day, said poor Mr. Price, (whose voice already faltering with age, was rendered still more unsteady from the emotions of his mind) I remember the day when I joined that lady's hand to Mr. Falkland's. He was then such a fine young man as my pupil is now, and Mrs. Arnold was such a beauty as her daughter Cecilia; you, Sir George, with your own hand gave the bride, and joyful you were to bestow her on your noble friend: I did not think I should have lived to see the hour, when a child of his would be despised and spurn'd from your family! The good old man melted into tears as he spoke.

So! said my uncle, I find you have got Mr. Price of your side as well as my lord V—; he affected to say this carelessly, but I saw he was moved. I ventured to clasp my arms round him, All the afflictions of my dear mama's life, said I, and the cruel misfortunes of poor Mr. Falkland's, were owing to the mistaken zeal of

---

1 Sir George was implacably angry with Sidney and Lady Bidulph for refusing the elder Orlando Faulkland. Readers will remember that Faulkland had fathered a child with a woman who had allegedly seduced him for money. He refused to marry this woman until Sidney insisted he do so; the marriage led directly to his ruin.

2 At the end of volume three of *The Memoirs of Miss Sidney Bidulph*, Faulkland returns to Sidney believing he has accidentally killed his wife in an altercation with her lover. Sir George and Mr. Warner convince Sidney to marry Faulkland and abscond with him to Holland. When it is discovered that Mrs. Faulkland is still alive, Faulkland dies, possibly by his own hand.

my grandmama Bidulph for her daughter's happiness; will *you*, Sir, pursue a conduct that you have often so justly censured? will *you*, imitate that stubborn authority that you have so often condemned? and will *you*, in the person of that friendless young man, perpetuate the miseries of his father whom you have so often deplored?

What is it that you would have me do? said my uncle, gently disengaging himself from my hold. You do not seem to consider *my* character: what a figure should I make in life, if after being known (for the thing can be no secret) that I was in treaty with lord V—, I should all of a sudden break off, and consent to a marriage where the disparity is so obvious? Methinks you should in the midst of your passion have some regard to your reputation; for matches of this kind are rarely concluded with the consent of parents, but where there are reasons to which, for the lady's sake, her friends are obliged to yield. That is by no means a necessary conclusion, Sir George, answered my lord V—, nor is the world so severe in its censures as not to suppose that parents may sometimes have tenderness enough to sacrifice their own wishes, however laudable, to the more immediate happiness of their children, nor will any one be in the least surprized, that two amiable young people, bred up together, should have a preference for each other, without drawing any inferences unfavourable to either side. Do you hear that, Madam? said my uncle to my mama. Oh, sister, you may blame yourself for all this! I do, I do, cried my mama, I acknowlege my error, I feel the punishment; but it is now past remedy. Brother, added she, I yield up Cecilia to your disposal; had you been able to accomplish an alliance with lord V—, my joyful consent would have gone along with it; since we are disappointed in that, I can only say, that let your determination be what it will, my concurrence shall go hand in hand with it. A very pretty way, said my uncle, smiling, of flipping your neck out of the collar: Ah, Sidney, I guess to which side of the question your approbation would willingly attach itself. And so do I too, said Mr. Price; I know Mrs. Arnold's love for her children would incline her to wish mutual happiness. What is there lost by the exchange, said lord V—, but a worthless title on which Miss Arnold would reflect more honour than she could receive from it? Mighty fine, mighty fine, said my uncle. Well, ladies and gentlemen, you may act as you think proper; but supposing *I* were to give up my interest in this affair, how do you think to answer it to lady Sarah? If you, Sir George, said my lord V—, will, by determining yourself in our favour, (how delicate was that little word *our*!) permit Mrs. Arnold to do so too, *I* will engage to reconcile lady Sarah to our proceedings. Will you? said my uncle: faith, my lord, then that is more than *I* would undertake to do; but I grant your lordship's eloquence is very much superior to mine.

My uncle walked about the room, and appeared irresolute and unwilling to speak. Let me conjure you, Sir, to pronounce my sentence, cried Mr. Falkland, for I stand here in the condition of a criminal, whose life or death depends on the lips of his judge. Mercy! mercy! in a tremulous voice, cried the venerable Price. And forgiveness, added I, again falling at my uncle's knees. Come, Sir George, said my lord V—, I know you will yield; lessen not the grace by deferring it too long. Well—since I *must* yield— Mrs. Arnold, you have my consent to act agreeably to your own inclinations.—You see, Sir George could not bring himself to yield with a good grace; but this was enough; my mama sprung to me, and raising me up, Cecilia, said she, I forgive you, and charge *myself* with the error of your conduct. She then led me to Mr. Falkland, and putting my hand into one of his, Take her, Orlando, said she, I give her to you for the love I bore your father; I pray Heaven make your marriage happier than—My mama could proceed no farther, her voice was choaked by tears. Mr. Falkland kissed her hands upon his knees; then approaching my uncle, he bent one knee to him in token of acknowlegement and duty. My uncle stooped down his body in a bowing posture; but without offering to raise him, only said, Sir, I sincerely wish your happiness. Mr. Falkland then thanked my lord V—, and Mr. Price in their turns, who both embraced and congratulated him.

This affair being now determined, said my uncle, I should be glad to know what Mr. Falkland means to do? I should suppose that what has now passed ought not to make any change in his resolutions with regard to the army. I know of no profession to which he can betake himself with so much honour; and as it is that to which he has been always destined, he would appear with a very ill grace at such a juncture as this, when all the young men in the kingdom are eager to express their zeal for the service of their country, if he should now decline the opportunity which my lord V— has given him to shew himself at least as forward as others. My lord V— was silent, yet it was very easy to see by his countenance that he was of my uncle's opinion, for my lord V—, my dear, is a soldier from head to foot. As for myself, though I secretly wished Mr. Falkland had not embraced so hazardous a way of life, and already began to tremble at the thoughts of his departure; yet after the bravery I had shewn in my conversation with lord V— on this subject, I was ashamed to make the least objection. Mr. Falkland, I believe, guessed what passed in my mind. There is nothing, replied he, which is capable of making me change my resolution, unless it be the will of Miss Cecilia; if she does not forbid it, I shall esteem myself happy, if under the auspices of my lord V— I am permitted to follow both my duty and my inclination. I know not whether Mr. Falkland was quite sincere in making use of the last expression; but the affair had been put to him in such a light by Sir George that he could not well make any other reply. What do *you* say, madam? said my lord V— I was vexed the question came from *him*; I thought myself doubly obliged to comply. Far be it from me, my lord, said I, (very stoutly) to obstruct Mr. Falkland's road to glory!

You do not intend then, I presume, said my uncle, to marry at this juncture? I suppose Cecilia would not chuse to make a campaign? and I think, Mr. Falkland, after the assurances he has just now received, may venture his mistress in the hands of his friends till his return, when he may appear in a sort of rank in life that will better justify our consenting to this marriage; for after all, what a strange appearance would it have for a match to be clapt up so suddenly for such a girl as Miss Arnold with a lad in the university? A little constrained smile which shewed itself at once on the face of lord V—, my mama, and even the serious good old Price, gave a kind of tacit assent to my uncle's observation. There is one method, said Mr. Falkland, to obviate this apparent impropriety; our marriage may be kept concealed.—My uncle objected to this, and offered reasons unnecessary to be repeated, and which I should have been much better pleased he had not offered at all. Mr. Falkland was earnest in having the affair concluded his own way, when my mama, afraid, I believe, of his offending my uncle, interposed; Let us consider of this another time, said she; it is a thing of too much consequence to be determined so hastily. Then, with a design to turn the discourse, she asked my lord V— how he had contrived matters so, as to assemble the whole family together at so critical a juncture? Lord V— related as much of the conversation I had had with him this morning as he thought necessary to his purpose; kindly suppressing that circumstance of my having asked his mediation; but acknowleging at the same time, that from the moment I had opened my heart to him, he had resolved to do his utmost to assist me. He said, that having desired Mr. Falkland's company that evening under colour of business, he had given private orders to one of the servants to conduct him to my dressing-room, and in about a quarter of an hour after his arrival to come into the room where he was sitting with my mama, to give him notice that Mr. Falkland was come. I concluded by that time, said my lord, that the lovers might be engaged in an interesting conversation; and not doubting but our sudden appearance would make an open for the scene I meditated, I very naturally requested Mrs. Arnold to step with me into the chamber, where I was told Mr. Falkland waited for me. I led you, madam, as you know (proceeded he, addressing himself to my mama) in a most favourable moment to your daughter's apartment. As for Sir George, I believe he must have been extremely surprized at receiving a note from me whilst he was at dinner at Doctor T.'s, to beg he would return home as early in the evening as possible, something of importance requiring his presence. I had before-hand engaged Mr. Price in his pupil's interests, and obtained from him a promise of assistance. By calculating hours, I was certain Sir George would arrive here a short time after Mr. Falkland, whom I had appointed to come at five o'clock; I begged of Mr. Price to be in the way to receive him, and without letting him know that Mr. Falkland was in the house, to conduct Sir George directly to us. This, madam, is the machinery of which I have made use to bring about this unexpected catastrophe, and I draw some consolation in having at least been instrumental to Miss Cecilia's happiness.

I now gave Mr. Falkland a hint to retire, lest he should renew those instances that I saw were so unacceptable to my uncle. He took his leave after reiterated acknowlegements to every one present.

My uncle was not in a very good humour for the remainder of the evenings, and often recurred to what lady Sarah would say to this *flagrant* event. He said he would write to her in order to prepare her for it, before he would *venture* to acquaint her with it as a thing on which we had concluded. So that, my dear, you are not to mention a syllable to her of what I have now written to you. My mama was rather thoughtful; yet I fancy at the bottom she is not much displeased. Our dear good old man seemed quite delighted; and as for my lord V—, he behaved like an angel; without arrogating to himself any merit for what he had done, or appearing even conscious of the generosity of his own conduct, he shewed only that modest and placid composure which a good mind feels on having acquitted itself of a duty.

My mama, with whom I had half an hour's conversation before she retired to bed, demanded many particulars of me relative to the attachment between Mr. Falkland and me; to all her questions I answered with great sincerity. She said, she had been rather too precipitate, and that she owed you that mark of respect as well as tenderness, to have made you acquainted with the affair before it was decided: but I ventured to answer for my dearest Dolly, that she would be perfectly satisfied with the determination. My mama said she supposed Mr. Falkland would be extremely urgent to have our marriage concluded before he left England; and that she was sure Sir George would be averse to it: For my part, added she, I shall be neutral; since I *have* consented, I desire not to yield my concession by halves. I assured her I would much rather the marriage were postponed till Mr. Falkland returned home again, which I hoped, if Heaven spared his life, would be in less than a year. It then rests upon you, child, said she, to determine the matter one way or other.

I am sorry my mama has in this instance given up her authority over me, because it is less in my power than it would be in hers to oppose Mr. Falkland's entreaties; yet I will on this occasion try what my influence over him will effect. I am sure it will be more grateful to all parties, to have the business deferred, even to the worthy lord V— himself; and I owe him at least this compliment.

After a day spent in so much anxiety, and concluded with so much agitation, I was very glad to get up into my own chamber, and sit down quietly to finish my letter to you, if such a volume can be called by that name. I have spent half the night in writing it, and am glad I shall have an opportunity of sending it off tomorrow. My mama tells me my uncle intends writing to lady Sarah to-night, just to make an opening, as he calls it, of this most *astonishing* affair! The messenger sets off by day-break, and is to return again in the afternoon, so that I shall hope for a line from you by him.

I expect some violent rubs from lady Sarah, but they will only grate the skin a little; and so long as I am out of her reach, the scratches will heal of themselves.

From you, my love, I look for congratulations; and can only in return wish you as happy a lot as that of

Your CECILIA

Letter XLIX.
Mr. Falkland to Sir Edward Audley.
Oxford, March 10th, eight o'clock in the evening

[In this letter he gives his friend a brief account of what had passed that evening at Mrs. Arnold's, and then proceeds:]

—Here's a revolution for you, Audley, beyond hope, beyond imagination! What would I now give to recall a few short months! But I will not spend my time in useless imprecations, either on your unlucky zeal, or my own folly. I have but one hope now left to remedy the past evil, and that is a reliance on the meek forgiving temper of Miss Arnold, joined to her fears of acknowleging a fault of which you say, and I believe she has, more than once, in secret repented. I know her gentle nature will not suffer her to think of revenge. To what purpose then, by an ill-timed avowal of her own weakness, destroy the happiness of others, without deriving from it any consolation to herself? You will see by the inclosed letter, which I have left open on purpose for your perusal, the arguments or rather the conjurations (for the case will not admit of many arguments) of which I have made use, to prevail with her to bury in eternal silence our ill-fated amour.

The favour I have to entreat of you, Sir Edward, is to get this letter put into her hands with the utmost privacy, and all possible speed. Her maid has been the medium through which all my letters have lately passed, and you may safely confide it to her care.

I shall, in order to be before-hand with the family of Woodberry, dispatch this by a special messenger, who has orders not to spare his horses; so that I presume this may kiss your hands about your ordinary hour of going to bed. I take it for granted, Cecilia will now give her sister a faithful narrative of this whole affair; and that lady Sarah will also receive advice of it from Sir George; but if you are punctual I must anticipate them all; for my letter may easily salute poor Dolly Arnold's uprising to-morrow, and the deuce is in it if any intelligence from them can reach her before mid-day at soonest, or perhaps not till Wednesday; for not having the same reasons to urge their expedition that I have, they may probably make use of the ordinary conveyance of the post.

My heart would fain deliver itself up to extacy, yet dare not do it. Oh, Audley, if Miss Arnold should forgive, as well as release me of my promise! in that case I should only desire you to pray (if you ever perform such a ceremony) that I might not run mad for joy. As for your schemes with regard to possessing yourself of this girl, I would recommend it to you to lay them aside, for I think it will be a vain attempt. If hereafter I should see the smallest open for your succeeding with her, be sure, Audley, you will find in me a zealous friend.

Letter L.
(Which was inclosed in the above.)
Mr. Falkland to Miss Arnold.

Oxford, March 10th.

I am unworthy of your smallest regard, madam.—I hate myself, and deserve to be abhorred by all the world; but more particularly by you whose confidence I have betrayed, and whose esteem I have repaid with ingratitude. You have long perceived, and sometimes (though I own but too tenderly) reproached me with my growing coldness. Conscious as I was of my guilt, I had not the courage to acknowlege it; but endeavoured by mean arts to palliate a crime, which I could not expiate. But let me tear off the treacherous veil, and expose at once to your eyes this vile offender! this *pretended* admirer of Miss Arnold; but the *real lover* of her sister. Yes, madam, I own I love Cecilia. My passion for her took root before my heart was capable of deceit; and the first treachery of which I was guilty was in offering those vows to you, which I had secretly dedicated to her. Our mutual misfortune has arisen from my coming at the knowledge (by means of my too officious friend Sir Edward Audley) of those favourable sentiments with which you honoured me, at a time when I was so far from indulging myself with a hope that I had touched Cecilia's heart, that I presumed not to entertain the most distant thought of being beloved either by you or her. And I call Heaven to witness that I did my utmost to guard my heart against a prospect so seducing, so full of charms.

You may remember, madam, it was long before I transgressed the bounds I had prescribed myself; that by a fatal concurrence of circumstances, my evil genius impelled me to offer you a heart which was not mine to give; but I soon found my error, and the discovery was followed by the deepest regrets for having deceived a woman whose merit rendered her so worthy of a better lot. Accuse me of falshood, of infidelity, and, if you please, of the blackest dissimulation; I merit it all; but charge me not with inconstancy, for light as that censure is in comparison of my other crimes, 'tis the only one of which I can exculpate myself. My love for Cecilia was but for a while suspended, it never was extinguished; and the first moment in which I saw her, after our fatal engagements, it blazed out again with redoubled force. I will leave it to her, madam, to tell you what has been its progress since; and will hasten to that point where every hope, and every wish, where, in one word, my soul is centered. Your sister has condescended to honour me with her hand; your mama (mine too let me call her) touched with compassion, has been prevailed on to yield it to me; and even Sir George Bidulph has at length suffered himself to grant a reluctant consent. Your friends will themselves soon inform you of every particular. But can I, dare I presume to urge the injured lady, whom I have so highly offended, to concur with her family in making happy the undeserving wretch, who so justly merits her utmost indignation? Yes, my amiable and respected friend, I *must* conjure you; the despairing Falkland throws himself at your feet covered with shame and remorse. His life is in your hand, the life of him you once loved, and who but for a fatality which he could not overrule, would have made it the study, the pride of that life to have deserved your love. Think that the peace of your whole family is interwoven with mine; think, should our unfortunate engagements be known, what might be the consequence of Sir George Bidulph's justly provoked indignation, of your revered mama's but too well founded sorrow, of your dear Cecilia's grief and disappointment; and if you don't yet hate me, think of my pangs, and remember my unhappy father's fate! Think what will it avail you to divulge a crime, of which, though I feel the horrors, I cannot repent?

You are too good, too compassionate to punish a weakness, to which I have been driven by an irresistible impulse; 'tis in your power to make me the happiest or the most miserable of men. Let me beseech you, madam, not to consult on this occasion the dictates of your resentment; but let the daughter of *Mrs. Arnold* imitate her mother's admirable example, who more than once yielded up her own dearest interests to promote the good of others, contenting herself with the silent applause of her own noble mind. Write to me, I conjure you, pour out your indignation on me; but conclude with a line of comfort and just say, 'Falkland, I bury your trespass in oblivion.'

The speed of your courier has answered the keenness of your wishes. I found the poor benumb'd devil waiting for me when I came in from the tavern where I had supped. And so you think I am to dispatch your letter to Miss Arnold, return you by the bearer an absolution signed by her in form, and congratulate you on your approaching felicity, and sit down contented with *your pity* on the loss of my hopes? Why, what a sot art thou, Falkland, to fancy I can look with patience at thy victory, and at the same time see all my own expectations blasted! A notable compliment you have paid me truly, in yielding up to me your pretensions to a woman whom you do not love; but without making one effort to promote the accomplishment of my wishes. Is this your friendship? this the zeal that I expected from you? Selfish as thou art, thou huggest thyself in thy own prosperity, and leavest thy friend to the gaping ruin that surrounds and is ready to swallow him up, without even stretching thy hand to draw him forth! But I will be plain with you at once, Falkland, I will not send your letter to Miss Arnold, an opportunity now offers to put me in possession of her, which at the same time that it redeems me from destruction, will more effectually secure you against a discovery than all the whining epistles you could scribble to her from this till dooms-day. You think the affair impracticable, brainless fellow as thou art; why 'tis as easy as lying; and thus will I effect it:

Write me a short billet to Miss Arnold, tell her that, 'having something of the last consequence to communicate to her, you are come to town on purpose to have a personal conference with her. That to avoid being seen in London for particular reasons, you have repaired privately to that house at Brumpton' (where you may remember my mother had lodgings the beginning of the winter when Harry had the chin cough[1]). Insist on her meeting you there; you may say, to give it a better colour, that you have no objection of my sister's being present at the conference, (by the bye, both my mother and sister are now on a visit to our cousin Bateman at Hampton-court): inclose this letter to me. Assure yourself she comes at all events, 'tis a matter of duty, putting love out of the question. The house you know stands along in the

---

1 The whooping cough, an epidemic that typically affects children, characterized by violent coughing and a noisy intake of breath.

middle of a garden; what a charming cage to enclose so pretty a singing-bird! The daughter of the woman who keeps it is a very good girl, and my particular friend; 'twas I who recommended the lodgings to my mother, as I now and then sleep there a night or so for the benefit of the air. And now, Falkland, that you may not have any qualms upon you, take my most solemn oath, which I never violate to *man*, that I will not injure the fair one. Miss Arnold is not a Theodora Williams, she was not born to be the mistress of any one; but I think she will make an admirable wife. You will see it will all end in that; for how can a young lady think of shewing her face again in the world, after passing two or three days privately with a young fellow, unless she appears in that character? Once I get her in my net, I shall give her no other cause of complaint than that of detaining her as my prisoner; for I mean to deport myself towards her with the sanctity due to a vestal; and when she is my wife, you know, I can command her lips, so that you will have nothing to fear from her. I dispatch your express off again without lots of time. Having made the dog half drunk, I wish he may not break his neck before he arrives at Oxford.

If Miss Arnold should receive an account of what is going forward at Woodberry, before you have time to return me the answer I expect, so much the better; she will be the less surprised at your desiring a meeting with her, and the more curious and impatient to have an explanation from you. But trust not to the slow conveyance of the post; leave that for such plodding souls as are content to send their dull conceptions the common dog-trot road; but fiery spirits, such as you and I, should always have their Mercuries[1] ready to dart forth in an instant and execute their high behests.—

Letter LII
Miss Arnold to Mr. Falkland.

[It appears that she inclosed in this, the letter which her sister Cecilia had written to her, which she received the day after its date; and writ to Mr. Falkland by the return of the same messenger, who left it for him as he passed through Oxford, in going home to Woodberry.]

---

1 Couriers. In the classical tradition, Mercury is the messenger of the gods.

First read the enclosed, and then form to yourself an idea of what she feels that writes to you! I will not answer my sister's letter, indeed I *can* not; for what could I say to her? Must I tell her, 'Cecilia, you cannot be the wife of Falkland, *his* faith's already plighted?'—but to whom?—Oh, Falkland, why did you deceive me? I do not ask your love, I know that is lost to me for ever; but I would beg you to have pity on poor Cecilia, on my mama, and, if you can, try to have a little on me. If you were torn from me by death, it would not be *quite* so terrible, for then I could follow you in silence and without shame; but to be disgraced thus, cast off, and for one's own sister too! that's very hard. Prithee, dear Orlando, wait till I am dead before you marry my sister; it will not be long before you shall see that day. A constitution naturally feeble, a long struggle against what at length bore me down, joined to sickness and inward grief, had already warned me that I had not long to live. Save yourself then, save yourself the remorse of seeing my days cut short by your own hand; save the tenderest of mothers the anguish of feeling her daughter fall a victim to despair; and save your dear Cecilia the horror of knowing you to be the cause of it. She is unwilling at this juncture to give you her hand; pray to not urge her to it.—You are going to leave England—before your return, I shall, in all human probability, be in my grave. You will then be at liberty to pursue your happiness; I love you too well to deprive you of it. I will not tell my sister that you ought to have been mine; let her become your wife, but let *me* not live to see it.

Letter LIII.
Mr. Falkland to Sir Edward Audley.
[In which he inclosed Miss Arnold's letter.]
Oxford, March 12th.

You have but half done your work, Audley, for I find I am not yet a finished traitor. The reading the inclosed letter, which I have just received from Miss Arnold, has thrown me into a cold sweat, and I almost repent of my injustice to her. There is something in her soft complaints that pierce my heart; yet I have gone too far to recede.—What will become of me!—I would give up every hope I have in life (except the possession of Cecilia) to restore this unfortunate girl to the peace of which I have robbed her. She bids me suspend my marriage—What may be the consequence of such a suspension? If she had asked me to send her a leg or an arm by way of expiation for my offence against her, I think I should have done it freely.

All the miseries she has foretold perhaps may come to pass, and my life may be rendered more wretched by the accomplishment, than it would be by the disappointment of my wishes. My infidelity conducts *one* child to the tomb, and the life of the *other* is imbittered from the same fatal source. Mrs. Arnold, that respectable woman who has been more than a parent to me, curses me as the cruel destroyer of her family.—Execrable, ungrateful Falkland! And thou, Love, inexorable fiend! will nothing satisfy thy vengeance but my life, or that of the unfortunate Miss Arnold?

I *will* not write that cursed letter to her which thou hast dictated; I will not add treachery to treachery. I could almost call this a sacrilege, for is it not giving up the sacred treasure of innocence to a wicked spoiler? Let the ruin that gapes for you swallow you up quick if it will; for my part, I am not fit to live.—Prithee, Audley, come down and shoot me through the head; for if someone does not do it for me————

Letter LIV.
Sir Edward Audley to Mr. Falkland.
London, March 12th.

Of all devils, I hate a penitent devil. What noble figure does Satan himself make, as he is described in the sixth book of Milton,[1] where he boldly defies the whole artillery of Heaven! And what a sneaking rascal does he appear in the fourth book, where, just like Falkland, he recapitulates his woes, and bemoans his lost estate! But do, go on, give up Cecilia, to oblige her sister, and leave thy name upon record for the arrantest poltroon that ever dared to call himself a man. But what then? You will have the consolation

---

1 *Paradise Lost*, the epic poem by John Milton (1608–74) depicts the fall of man as orchestrated by Satan. Book four features Satan's moment of doubt, wherein his face is contorted by conflicting emotions: "Thus while he spake, each passion dimm'd his face / Thrice chang'd with pale, ire, envie and despair, / Which marrd his borrow'd visage, and betraid / Him counterfet, if any eye beheld" (lines 114–17). Book six depicts the epic battle between the angels and the fallen. Significantly, Audley does not descant rightly on this or the following moral stories (see Appendix A).

of having done a good-natured thing, and then *consciousness of inward rectitude*, as old Price used to say, will at any time make amends for the loss of twenty or thirty thousand pounds, and the finest girl in Europe. But the mischief of it is, the substantial part of the evil won't be remedied by this either, for thou art so involved in treason, that take which side thou wilt, the matter *can't* be mended. Let's reason a little. Miss Arnold, you say, has cause to complain of your treachery. Granted: (for argument's sake only.) But will not Cecilia have the same cause to complain if you forsake *her*? She, being ignorant of the priority of her sister's claim, has certainly by the laws of equity as good a right to you as the other; nay, if one takes in the whole merits of the cause, a better; for she had secretly determined in your favour, before the other little trembling fool dared even to persuade herself that she loved you. The affair, however, is, I confess, somewhat nice, and I am inclined to think, that were Solomon now alive, and the case brought before him, your sweet person would be condemned to undergo the same sentence which he passed on the harlot's child.[1] We should then see which of the two girls deserved you best. I'll be hang'd if Dolly would not be content with half of you. Why, what a letter have you received from that pretty Automaton![2] The deuce take those milky dispositions, say I, that have not gall enough in them to rouze them to a little choler. Would not one, on such an occasion, have expected a noble burst of rage befitting the mouth of a princess in a tragedy? Or supposing the nymph to write in the elegiac strain, should not the paper have been blotted with her tears? ought she not to have called you *charming* though cruel betrayer, and conjured you by every thing that was tender to return to your first vows? And should not there have been some little insinuations of hanging on a willow, or drowning in a purling stream? But no such thing, Sir; this piece of living snow does not even strive to recall you; she renounces your love, she vouchsafes not even to upbraid you, and desires no other favour than that you would *postpone* your marriage till after her death, of which she talks as familiarly as she would do about a puppet show. Hang me, if I don't think she uses

---

1   The judgment of Solomon is in 1 Kings 3:16–28; when two women lay claim to the same infant, King Solomon offers to split the child in two. The real mother cries out against this judgment, thus revealing the other woman to be false.

2   "A human being resembling an automaton; a person who acts, or appears to act, in an inhuman, mechanical, or unemotional way" (*OED*).

you scurvily, and that she does not deserve the least pity at your hands.

And all this water-gruel stuff has thrown you into a cold sweat! How I blush for thee, Falkland! If thy body were as infirm as thy mind, thou wouldst not be fit to breathe out of an hospital. And how like a coward dost thou conclude thy letter! Thou dost not deserve so noble a death, as that thou wouldst receive if I were to take thee at thy word.

But to come at once to the material purpose of my letter. You say you *will not* deliver Miss Arnold into my hands, into the hands of a *wicked spoiler*. Falkland! I expected you would have believed my oath upon this occasion; but your own want of sincerity makes you suspect that of others; then hear me swear. [Sir Edward Audley here makes use of such imprecations as the editor would not transcribe.] By all this, I vow, if you do not deliver her into my hands, I renounce all farther communication with you, and will with my own proper tongue, divulge your folly, and what you *call* your crime, to all the Bidulph family, to all the world, till you are the ridicule and contempt of all that know you. You know I dare do what I say. Weak irresolute man, are these the hopes you gave me? Can the feeble complaints of a love-sick girl shake you thus? and make you cancel the bonds of a sworn friendship? And what would be the consequence of your dastardly compliance? If you leave England without making Cecilia yours, mark my words, you lose her for ever. Left in the hands of relations that contemn you, exposed to the conversation of a rival, who, though I like him not, let me do him the justice to say, has but too much to recommend him. And who can answer (though my vengeance were out of the question) who can answer for the generosity of a forsaken mistress? think you that Miss Arnold would not divulge the secret? Oh, you know but little of womankind; if *we* do not betray them, they are sure to betray themselves. In a word, you have no security but in the method I have proposed. Your own interest as well as mine should determine you at once. Put me in possession of my *prize*, and I'll answer for the accomplishments of *your* wishes; nay, I'll undertake to exculpate you from the imputation of this double treachery, at which you are so much scared, and that by the easiest turn imaginable. I will tell the lady that you had really come to town on purpose to prostrate yourself at her feet, and beg her forgiveness: That you had actually intended meeting her at the very place appointed; but that, as the hour of this dreaded interview drew near, you found you had not courage enough to support the sight of *her* you had so much injured;

wherefore calling for pen, ink, and paper, you had contented yourself with writing to her, and having left the letter in my hands to be put into hers, you immediately mounted your horse and again went out of town. Then will I faithfully deliver to her your petitionary scroll; in which if she finds any inconsistencies, it must be imputed to your troubled mind. And after having assured her of the sincerity of *your* intentions, I will take upon *myself* the blame of having turned them to the interest of my own love.

Things will not now admit of foolish delays; you know my ultimate resolution, so I leave you to think of it, and give you four and twenty hours to consider of my proposition, but not a minute beyond it.

Yours, E.A.

[Here follow in the order of the manuscript two letters; the one from Sir George Bidulph to lady Sarah, dated the same night with that of Miss Cecilia Arnold to her sister, in which Sir George gives some account of the unexpected event which is likely to take place at Woodberry; which letter is omitted to avoid repetitions. The other is from lady Sarah in answer to it, which, as her sentiments may be gathered from letter fifty-six, it is not thought necessary to transcribe.]

Letter LV.

Mr. Falkland to Sir Edward Audley.

[In which was inclosed a letter to Miss Arnold, written agreeably to the instructions sent to Mr. Falkland by his friend.]

Oxford, March 12th, ten o'clock at night.

Here, take it then, Sir Edward. I have written it whilst your menaces are fresh, and the dread of losing my Cecilia stares me in the face. I will not read the perfidious scroll a second time, lest I should relapse and tear it to a thousand shivers.—If Miss Arnold can be prevailed on to accept of you for her husband, take her, and my felicitations with her; but remember I tell you, Audley, if you break your faith with me, and abuse the power I have now entrusted to your hands, your life shall answer for it.—

Lady Sarah to Sir George Bidulph.
London, March 15th.

My Dear Sir George,

We are all here in the greatest confusion imaginable. I believe it is a very true observation, that evils never come alone. Miss Arnold, your grave, prudent, favourite niece, has thought proper to elope. She asked my leave yesterday morning to wait on Mrs. B—, who, she said, had sent to request her company to dinner. You know no one on earth can be more careful than I am of what company I let her keep; but as Mrs. B— is really an extremely good sort of a woman, and very well-bred, I never scrupled to let her go there. Mrs. B—'s family dine early, and Miss chose to go even sooner than their hour of dining. As she complained of not being very well, I sent her in my own chair: Robert attended her. I had an infinity of visits to pay in the evening, and when I went out, ordered my chair to go again for her at seven o'clock; but when I came home, which was at a little after ten, I found all the house in a bustle; the servants told me Miss Arnold was not yet come in, and that they could give no account of her at Mrs. B—'s. I immediately called up Robert, who said that having attended her in the forenoon to Mrs. B—, that he and the chair man had orders to wait a while; that Miss Arnold staid not longer than a quarter of an hour there, and then directed them to carry her to a milliner's shop[1] in the same street, where she went in and looked at some fans; after which she stepped to the door, and telling the servants, that as she had several things to buy which might detain her a good while, they need not wait, for being so near Mrs. B— with whom she was to dine, she would walk back to her house. The man says he begged she would let the chair carry her back, lest she should catch cold; but she insisted on her going home, telling Robert his lady might have occasion for him; upon which they went away, and left her there. I asked the fellow why he did not tell me this as soon as he returned; but his answer was, he thought nothing of it.

When they went for her in the evening to Mrs. B—'s, they were informed that she had not been there since noon. The brutes had not the sense to ask any more questions; but came away with this answer. I hurried away directly to Mrs. B—'s, and found the poor woman really under great uneasiness; for having been told by her

---

1 A milliner is a maker of hats and other women's apparel.

own servants that mine had been to look for Miss Arnold; she had it seems in the interim sent to my house to know if she were returned home. All the account she could give me of her was this. That she had in reality sent the evening before to request Miss Arnold's company to dine with her, as she was to be quite alone; that your niece had sent her word, she could not then give a positive answer, as lady Sarah was not home (which was indeed true): That when Miss Arnold had called upon her about one o'clock that same day, she told her she was only come to make her excuses to her for not having it in her power to dine with her, as we had company at home, (where were two or three *humble* friends) but that she would slip out to her for a couple of hours in the afternoon: she added, that Miss seemed in a good deal of haste, and took her leave in less than a quarter of an hour.

Finding I could learn no more from Mrs. B—, I drove, late as it was, to the milliner's, and took the pains of climbing up two pair of narrow dirty stairs to the woman's chamber. I asked her if such a young lady, describing Miss Arnold's dress and equipage, had not been at her shop that day? She told me there had; but that she had not the honour of knowing her; and that the lady, after having bought some little matters of her, had requested that she would let one of her shop maids call her a hackney-coach, which she did, and the young lady drove away in it, having pulled up both the coach windows; but she heard not to what place the coach-man was directed. I made her in my presence demand of her servant, whether she knew the number, or the coach-man? The wench said she knew neither one nor t'other, having met the coach by hazard in the street: And this was all the information I could get, notwithstanding the infinite trouble I took on the occasion. I am most exceedingly vexed that I took the charge of any young person, with whose disposition I was not better acquainted; yet I really thought Miss Arnold a modest good young body; but 'tis plain I was deceived, for be she where she will, 'tis certain she is gone with her own inclination, and had concerted her whole plan before-hand. 'Tis quite an ænigma[1] to me, *with* whom or *to* whom she can be gone; but I take it for granted, there is some intrigue in the case, and that following her sister's example, she means to introduce into the family some little obscure wretch. Mrs. Arnold may now see the consequence of breeding her daughters in the country. Yet I really pity the poor woman, for being so unfortunately in her children. As matters

---

1 Enigma.

now stand, I supposed neither you nor my lord V— will think it necessary to stay much longer at Woodberry. Pray present my humble service to his lordship, and believe me to be, &c.

Letter LVII.
Sir Edward Audley to Mr. Falkland.

Brumpton, March 14th.

All's safe; I have her, Falkland; the soft turtle[1] may beat her wings against her prison walls, but it will not be in her power to escape. Let me tell you how it was.—Having received your letter early yesterday morning, I dispatched that which was inclosed for her, by a porter with proper instructions. He brought back just two lines, to inform Mr. Falkland she would, if possible, see him the next day at the place appointed, and that she should bring Miss Audley with her. A note was by the same messenger brought to my sister, (whom you may suppose she did not know to be out of town) wherein Miss Arnold told her she had important business with her, and begged she would be at home the next day in the forenoon, when she would call on her.

Having secured my ground thus far, I drove out this morning to my lodge, leaving a strict charge with David to be on the watch at home, and when Miss Arnold called for my sister, if on not finding her in town she should ask whether a note had not been left for her the day before? David was to produce the identical note out of his pocket, (which having been only wafer'd, I had with ease opened and sealed up again) and to tell her he would be sure to give it to Miss Audley, when she came to town, which would not be for these five or six days. This you see reduced her friend to go to her rendezvous without her. I ordered my rogue, who you know has the finest simplicity of countenance imaginable, to tell her, if she should chance to enquire how I did, (which was natural enough) that I had drove out that morning to take the air, To *Brumpton*, as he thought he heard me direct the coachman, but he could not be positive for fear of telling a lye. This precaution was necessary, that she might not be surprized or alarmed at seeing me receive her at her first coming instead of you.

Every thing happened just as I had foreseen; and between two and three o'clock, I saw a hackney-coach driving up briskly up to

---

1 Turtle dove.

the house. I was ready at the door to present her my hand; she looked as pale as ashes, and trembled from head to foot. Oh, Sir Edward! was all she could utter. Compose yourself, dear madam, was all my reply. I supported her up stairs to the dining-room, for she was scarce able to walk, and placing her in an easy chair by the fire, took a turn about the room to give her time to recover herself.

Where is your friend, Sir? said she, at length. I now approached her, and with the voice and look of a suppliant, Prepare yourself, madam, said I, to hear a story, which though perhaps it may excite your resentment against me, yet must it turn your juster indignation against a perfidious man who has betrayed you. (You know I was not to mince the matter.) Where is he? cried she, where is Falkland? looking wildly about her. He is not now here, replied I. Not here? good God! and she started from her chair: I ventured (putting one knee to the ground) with a timid action, such as you have seen used by a poor spurn'd lover in a tragedy, to lay hold on the corner of her robe, and gently withheld her from going. Have patience, dearest madam, and hear what I have to say. Falkland is no longer worthy of you, he abandons you, and marries your sister—I could add no more; for, as if struck by a sudden flash of lightening, she fell senseless on the carpet. I endeavoured to recall her to life by the ordinary means of chafing her temples, and throwing water on her face, but to no purpose; and to own the truth, I thought her soft eyes were closed for ever. I hastily called up the matron and her daughter, and having with their assistance raised the lifeless beauty, we put her into the arm'd-chair, and I retired to another room, as the women proposed cutting her lace, at which operation my bashfulness would not suffer me to be present.

Having brought her to herself, I was summoned again into the chamber. She had a bottle of salts in her hand, which she held to her nose, her eyes were still shut; but on my asking tenderly how she did, she opened them, and looking earnestly at me, and then by turns at the two women, Did not some of you tell me, said she, that they were actually married? Well, who can help it! Cecilia has eyes and a heart as well as other people; but then one's own sister, there is something so mortifying in that! Would not you think it very hard, Miss? to the young damsel who stood by her. I perceived she was not perfectly come to herself, and making a motion to the women, they withdrew, and I placed myself on a chair beside her, though at a respectful distance. Endeavour to collect your spirits, dearest Miss Arnold. I could kill myself for having been (though unwillingly) the cause of throwing you into such disorder. But are you sure, said she, that you have told me truth? for men are so *very* deceitful—I have Falkland's own word for it, answered I.—Oh, then he *is* here after all? said she. He is not, I assure you, madam; he is now actually at Oxford.—But, I tell you, Sir Edward, I had a letter from him yesterday, and I promised to meet him here to-day, or else I dreamt so, for every-thing appears very strange to me. 'Tis very true, said I, he came to town yesterday in order to have a conference with you. And here, Falkland, did I faithfully acquit myself of my promise to you, describing you as a man overwhelmed with shame and remorse for your crime; and concluded with presenting her the letter, with which I told her you had charged me. An indignant blush kindled for a moment on her languid face, whilst she read; which fading away again into its former paleness; This is cruel, said she, it pierces deep; and she shrunk as if she had felt herself stung by something venomous.

He told me, said I, that you had requested of him to postpone his marriage—So, then, interrupted she, with a half smile, you know the whole of my disgrace! Say rather of your injuries, said I, and of Falkland's baseness, (it was meet that I should abuse you like a dog); but passionately as he adores your sister, he said he found it impossible to obey you; and as Miss Cecilia had already consented to be his, he was resolved to press her to the immediate accomplishment of her promise, depending on the gentleness of your nature, which he thinks will not suffer you to interpose your wrongs to divide them. He begged of me to say every thing that I could in extenuation of his fault; and without listening to the reproaches that I made him, left me in order to take the post immediately for Oxford. What could I do, pro-ceeded I, softening my voice, and preparing to breathe out some tender things, what, charming Miss Arnold, could I do?—Alas, she heard me not; a second fainting-fit had seized the mournful fair. During the time that I spoke, she sate with her head reclined on one of her arms, which rested on the elbow of the chair, her hand covering her eyes partly concealed her face from me; but the conclusion of my tale again deprived her of her senses, and it was the dropping of this white and lifeless arm that advertised me of it.

Again were the women called up, again had we recourse to all the female apparatus of hartshorn, hungary-water, and burnt feathers,[1] for this fit was longer and more obstinate than the former. At last she came to herself; but the women found her so extremely feeble, that without saying anything to me, (who had once more withdrawn; observe my punctilio, Falkland) or even consulting Miss Arnold herself, they immediately undressed her and put her to bed in an adjoining chamber, before she had sufficiently recovered her recollection to oppose their motions.

Having given the due praise to this their prudent conduct, I desired them both to attend on the lady with the utmost care and respect; and if when she was thoroughly come to herself, she should attempt to rise in order to go away, that they, through a tender care of her health, should by no means permit it; but to calm her uneasiness they were to tell her, that I (being in the utmost fright and anxiety about her) had gone to town in the coach which had brought her thither, in order to bring a physician, and had charged them not to let her stir, till I had his opinion whether she might be removed with safety.

Having thus disposed matters, I drove home in the aforesaid coach, (which she had retained in order to bring her back) and in about two hours returned again accompanied by an able doctor, whom I had brought to visit the sick lady. One of my trusty guardians met us in the hall, and taking me aside told me, that the young lady having recovered herself pretty well soon after I had gone away, had expressed the utmost surprize and terror and finding herself in a bed in a house she knew not, demanded where she was? and where Mr. Falkland and her sister were? to both which questions the women having answered her agreeably to the truth, she desired that her cloaths might be brought to her, that she might dress herself and go home. They then told her, according to my instructions, that she must not think of stirring till the arrival of the doctor, whom they expected every minute; and that they could not answer it to their consciences, to let her depart in the weak condition in which she then was, without his leave. She insisted nevertheless on going; but a fresh obstacle was represented to her, viz. that she had no method of conveyance to town. She was quite out of patience at this, and said she would walk; but this was treated as an impossibility; for had she even

---

1 These are methods to revive someone who has fainted. Hartshorn is ammonia obtained, sometimes, from hart's (deer) horns and made into smelling salts; Hungary water is a solution of wine and rosemary flowers; the smoke of burnt feathers was thought to help revive fainted patients.

been in a condition to undertake such a walk, the roads were so wet and dirty as to make it impracticable; she knew not a step of the way; they had no body they could send to conduct her; and they themselves, poor souls, could not leave the house; the mother was old and infirm, and the daughter could not be spared, as she had the care of every thing upon her. She still continued earnestly asking for her cloaths, that she might at least get up and dress herself, in order to be in readiness to return to town with the physician, whom they said they expected; but this request they also thought themselves obliged for the lady's good to refuse; so that partly by entreaties, partly by arguments, and partly by a little gentle compulsion, they had still detained her in bed, where she had continued to talk, and bewail herself without ceasing.

After having received this account, we proceeded to the chamber of the lady. I kept an aweful distance, not presuming to appear in sight. The doctor approached her bed-side, and desiring permission to feel her pulse, pronounced her in a fever, and that the consequence would be fatal, if she ventured to leave her bed.—He asked her if she felt any pain? She made him no answer, but pointed with her finger to her forehead. I thought so, said he, but I shall order something for you; then charging them that she should be kept extremely quiet, not suffered to speak a word, and be made to drink plentifully of balm-tea;[1] he called for pen, ink, and paper, and sate down to write his prescription. Whilst he was thus employed, I ventured to draw near the bed-side, and speaking in a low voice, I told Miss Arnold, I only waited her commands, to go to town again in order to acquaint her friends with her situation; and asked whether she would not chuse to have lady Sarah Bidulph come to her, since the doctor was of opinion it might endanger her life to be removed?

I do indeed find myself, said she, quite unable to rise; yet I should have made a shift to walk if they had let me gone at first; but now my strength is quite exhausted; my head too feels giddy, the chamber seems to turn round.—Lady Sarah will certainly attend you when she knows the condition in which you are; shall I wait on her madam, for that purpose? Oh, Sir, do you think she would shew any compassion to such a cast-away? No, no, she must not know a word of the matter. For God's sake, Sir, (joining her hands together, and speaking quite in a whisper) can't you

---

1 Medicinal tea made with balm, a resin derived from trees of the genus *Balsamodendron*.

contrive to have a chair sent to me here! I may be carried to Mrs. B—'s, I promised to go to her this evening.—I perceived she made this request in a low voice, that the doctor might not hear her and oppose it; but as it was my interest that he should, I answered her loud enough to reach his ears; I will send for a chair immediately, madam; I think you cannot run any great risque in being carried to town, provided you are wrapped up warmly.—The doctor, who had just then finished his prescription, turning hastily about, What is that you are pleased to say, Sir, said he, that the lady will run no risque in being carried to town? I should hope so, Doctor, replied I, as it is of the utmost importance to her to return thither this evening. If she has any thing that required her attention that is of more importance to her than her *life*, said he, 'tis another affair; and in that case, I don't see any occasion you had to consult me; but as I look upon her to be in a dangerous way, having one of those rapid fevers which increase hourly, you are to take the consequence of removing her upon yourselves; but I shall expect at least that *my* character will be cleared from any blame that may alight on it. He then threw his prescription on the table, which he had held in his hand while he spoke, and left the room croaking out presages of mortality in case of disobedience to his orders.

The two women who were present, and who seemed extremely frightened at what he said, now declared with one voice, that they would not suffer the lady to be stirred; to be sure the doctor knew better than we did, what was proper; and they were surprized that a gentleman of my sense would offer to act contrary to his advice. As for the poor lady herself, it was no wonder she did not know what she was saying, as sickness was so apt to put people out of their right minds; but for their own parts, they would not for all they were worth in the world have such a sin to answer for as the lady's death, which no doubt would be the consequence of her leaving her bed in the terrible condition in which she then was.

Miss Arnold, now finding all her hopes of getting away entirely frustrated, burst into tears; Then I am lost, said she, exposed, and ruined! I cannot out-live the shame of having the cause of this illness known. Have patience, dear madam; I will go to Mrs. B— to inform her of your situation; your *illness* cannot be kept a secret, though the *cause* of it may; you must confide in some one; Mrs. B— is a good woman, she is your friend.—Sir, I have no friends, no relations, I am a poor creature abandoned by every body.—Do not say so, madam; you see a man before you who would sacrifice his life to serve you.—Thank you, Sir, thank you;

I would be glad to see Mrs. B—, though I believe she will not come to me.—I will go to her directly, madam; there is no doubt but she will attend you. In the mean time be assured you are in the hands of very careful and very honest people. I hope in a day or two you will be able to venture out; In the interim, let me conjure you to compose your thoughts as much as possible; the re-establishment of your health depends chiefly on the tranquillity of your mind.

I took my leave on this, and making a sign to the antient matron, she followed me out of the room, leaving her daughter at the bed-side of the lady. I asked her what she thought of the real state of our patient's health. She said she was certain that the whole of her disorder arose from the violent agitation of her mind, and that she believed a good night's rest would set all to rights again, that she had felt her hand, and thought her not in the least feverish; on the contrary, she had found her extremely low; and as her strength and spirits had been so much exhausted by her fainting fits, she was of opinion that a glass or two of good wine would be of more service to her than all the drugs in the apothecary's shop. As I have an implicit faith in this good woman's skill, I remained perfectly satisfied with the judgment she had pronounced; and agreeing with her, that the sickness of the mind was beyond the power of medicine to reach, I contented myself with ordering the prudent dame to give the lady some of her own little innocent cordials, which she kept for her private drinking, and to pass them on her for the doctor's prescription.

You will already be surprized, perhaps, that after having already had the advice of an eminent physician, I thought it necessary to ask that of an old woman. To account for this part of my conduct, you must know that this same doctor, though exceedingly skilful in his way, is not remarkable for his veracity, and in the case before us had said neither more nor less than what I dictated to him; In short, it was no other than my villain David, on whom I had clap'd a large periwig, and given him a diploma to practise in the present emergency.

This imaginary indisposition (for there is more of fancy than reality in it) has been the luckiest thing in the world, as it has furnished me with a pretence for detaining her one night at least without having recourse to absolute force, which was my original intention; for my plan was to have set out with her at midnight, and carried her to my friend Bendish's house on Bagshot-heath,[1]

---

1 A heath in Surrey, England.

whom I have already apprized of my design. His mother is lately dead, and he is now king of the castle. Thither do I mean to convey my prisoner; but I think from the view of things which I now have, that I shall be able to effect this by stratagem, which I should much prefer to violence for more reasons than one.

The house in which we are at present, I do not look upon as a place of security for any long continuance; for besides its being too near London, there is more than a chance of her being discovered here by means of the coachman who drove her down hither; for though I have endeavoured, by virtue of a good bribe, to charm the dog's tongue to silence, yet 'tis natural to suppose the Bidulphs will leave nothing unattempted to find him out; and the same specific of which I made use to shut his mouth, will infallibly open it.

'Tis my wish to have it *blazed* abroad that the fair-one is in my hands; my only care is to secrete her till the insolent family shall think themselves happy in finding her no other than my wife.

Set thy mind at rest, Falkland, with regard to her health; for be assured her disorder is nothing more than the natural consequence of that flurry into which she has been thrown by this day's adventures. Somewhat, perhaps, may be attributed to the skill with which the doctor conducted himself: for let a person be but a little indisposed, and at the same time under a violent depression of spirits, (which was our case) and a judicious physician shall be able, at any time, to persuade them that they are in mortal danger.

To-morrow you shall know how I acquit myself of my pretended commission to Mrs. B—; but as I would not keep you in suspence, I shall send this off directly by Jerry, who is now cracking his whip in the yard, as I ordered him to attend on purpose for my dispatches. I suppose to-morrow, or next day, you will have lady Sarah's account of this affair come lagging in like a jaded horse that was thrown out of the course; and then we shall have the old house at Woodberry in such a commotion as you have sometimes seen an ant's nest. Probably it may retard your nuptials for a while: but if they wait till the stray'd lamb is recovered, it will require more patience than can be reasonably expected in a lover; for I tell thee, Falkland, that powers terrestrial nor infernal shall not snatch her from me.

'Tis now eight o'clock. I am supposed by Miss Arnold to be at London. She expects every minute the arrival of her friend Mrs. B—. I go to put an end to her expectations, at least for to-night.—

Letter LVIII.
Sir Edward Audley to Mr. Falkland.
Brumpton, March 15th.

Here have I been since last night, Falkland, like a spider spinning my toils, with no other materials than what my own proper brains furnish me withal. And my poor little fly, unconscious of the snare, is now so intangled, that, hopeless of escape, she has e'en left off struggling.

After I had left her yesterday evening, in order to wait on Mrs. B—, she remained pretty tranquil, in hopes of her friend's arrival. Not to keep her, however, too long in an uneasy state of uncertainty, I thought proper, after I had dispatched my letter to you, to send a note to her by one of the women, with orders to say she had received it from my servant; in which I told her, that Mrs. B— would attend her the next morning; and that, not thinking it prudent to allow myself the liberty of seeing her that night, I chose to write rather than be the bearer of this message. There was decorum for you! I can tell you, it had its weight; for she praised my discretion, at the same time that she expressed herself exceedingly grieved and disappointed that Mrs. B— did not come to her immediately. She remained very unquiet the whole night, without once closing her eyes. Sleep, barbarous sleep, forsakes the pillows of the unfortunate. Gladly would I have watched her restless couch—but decency forbid it; and I had this account only from the nymph who passed the night at her bedside. About eleven o'clock I thought it expedient to make my appearance; and having begged the favour of an audience, I was admitted into her chamber. (I must observe here, by the way, that she had again called for her cloaths, and had intreated for leave to rise in order to receive me, but was peremptorily refused by her careful nurses; one of them, however, was commanded to stay in the room.) Well, Sir, said she, with a look of impatience, where is Mrs. B—? I went to her house, madam, agreeably to your desire, as soon as I got to town—And won't she come, Sir? Unfortunately, madam, I could not see her last night; her maid told me she had been taken suddenly ill, and was obliged to be put to bed about an hour before. As I found it would be impossible for her to attend you that night, I did not care to disturb the poor lady's repose, by informing her of your situation. It was for the same reason, with regard to you, (pardon me, dear madam) that I ventured to deceive you, by writing you word she would wait on you this morning. I thought, indeed, I but anticipated the truth; that I could have answered for her intentions; and that her disorder, which I hoped was but some little temporary complaint, would not have hindered her from fulfilling the promise I had made in her name. God help me! then I am not to see her? Is she sick, Sir? or is it that she refuses to come to the succour of such a poor forlorn wretch? I made a long pause, then replied, She is *really* ill, madam.—I wish that was the only disagreeable circumstance I had to tell you—Another long pause, with a very troubled countenance—Pray, sir, speak; have you seen Mrs. B—? I have, madam, I was at her house again this morning; and having sent up word that I had important business with her, I was admitted to her chamber, where I found her in bed; for she still continued ill. I wait on you, madam, said I, at the request of Miss Arnold, who, relying on the friendship you have always had for her, requests to see you immediately on a very particular occasion—She cut me short before I had time to proceed—Good God, cried she, what has the rash girl done! You'll pardon me, Sir Edward, but I cannot help calling her so. I know she has not been at home all night. Lady Sarah Bidulph sent hither, both last night and this morning, in search of her—I little imagined she had put herself in your hands!—Then lifting up her eyes, Poor dear Mrs. Arnold, said she, how much are you to be pitied! Though I must acknowlege, sir, you are a more eligible choice than Mr. Falkland. I found Mrs. B— was possessed with a belief, which, had it been well founded, would have made me but too happy. I made haste to undeceive her, assuring her I was very far from being the fortunate man she supposed me, and was going to explain the reality of your situation, when by the most unlucky chance imaginable, we were interrupted by the arrival of lady Sarah Bidulph. She was ushered into the chamber by Mr. B— himself; so that we had not the least previous notice of her coming. It seems her anxiety, with regard to you, madam, had brought her in person to enquire if Mrs. B— had learned any news of you. Mr. B—, I suppose, had been told that I was with his lady, and his curiosity to know the occasion of this visit had induced him to lead in lady Sarah in that abrupt manner. We can get no tidings of this unfortunate girl, said lady Sarah, as soon as she entered the room; dear Mrs. B—, have you heard nothing of her since? Here is a gentleman, madam, said Mrs. B—, who can give you some account of her. Lady Sarah turned towards me, and, with a look of astonishment scarcely to be described, What! Sir *Edward Audley!* said she; and stopped, looking at Mrs. B—, as if her amazement had deprived her of the power of speech. Oh, oh, then I suppose, said Mr. B—, that the young ladies resolving to keep each other in countenance, Miss Arnold has given Sir Edward to your ladyship for a kinsman. I am very sorry to say, replied I, that the lady has not done me that honour. So much the worse, cried Mr. B—with an oath, (for the poor man swears sadly); for if a girl elopes from her friends, and spend the night Lord knows where, unless she can account for it by matrimony, she'll make but a devilish silly figure when she comes back. You'll forgive me, madam, for repeating his words; but you know Mr. B— has a coarse manner of expressing himself.

I now found myself under such an embarrassment that I scarce knew what to say. I saw the justification of your character (dearer to me than any other consideration) required my declaring the truth at large; yet the not having your permission to make any explanations to lady Sarah Bidulph, checked my tongue; and before I had time to frame any reply, Pray, where is the lady? said lady Sarah, if I may take the liberty of asking. As I thought in this particular any concealment would be highly improper, I hesitated not to tell her precisely where you were; adding, that as a sudden and violent attack of illness had detained you the whole night, and, as I feared, was still likely to confine you for some time to your bed, you had begged to see Mrs. B—, to whom you would make such explanations as you hoped through her mediation, would induce your friends to pardon a seeming failure of duty, into which an unexpected event had unwarily led you. I suppose, answered lady Sarah, that the young lady, seeing the good effects of her sister's fine-laid stratagem, intends to play the same farce over again at Brumpton that Miss Cecilia did at Woodberry; and hopes, under a pretence of illness, by getting her friends about her, to prevail with them as easily to consent to her whimsies as they have done to those of her sister. Faith, I am of your ladyship's opinion, said Mr. B— laughing; but if you would take my advice, you would e'en let Sir Edward keep her now he has her. Such a faux pas as cannot be mended, are always best overlooked: and when she appears as lady Audley, it will be nobody's business to enquire how it came about. Provoked as I was at the gross manner in which Mr. B—delivered himself, and still more at his daring suggestions, I yet endeavoured to preserve my temper; and too much flattered by the hint he had thrown out, pardon me, dearest Miss Arnold, if for a minute I presumed to entertain a hope upon which I dare not now enlarge. I contented myself, however, with replying, that I should think myself but too happy to give my name to Miss Arnold, let that even be brought about by what means it would. Then addressing myself to lady Sarah, I will not, madam, said I, take upon me to explain the motives of the lady's conduct, which, however strange it may appear, I dare venture to say, she will be able to justify. Riddle me, riddle me ree, cried Mr. B—; but how, in the name of wonder, came Miss Arnold to put herself under *your* care, Sir Edward? And how came it, sir, rejoined lady Sarah, that you did not acquaint her family last night with her situation? Perhaps, interposed Mrs. B—, Sir Edward knew not of it till this morning. Yes, madam, replied I, and your servants have been careless in not informing you that I was at your door last night; when being told that you were not to be seen, I was obliged to defer the account I had to give you till this morning. As for the two questions which lady Sarah and Mr. B—have demanded, I must leave it to Miss Arnold herself to satisfy them. It is a most unaccountable affair, said lady Sarah. I suppose, sir, that lady Audley and your sister are with her. Neither one nor the other, madam; unluckily they are both now out of town. Gracious! exclaimed lady Sarah, and has the girl passed the whole night in a lonely house, without any one in it but servants? You cannot think Sir Edward so inattentive as that comes to, replied Mr. B—, with a sneer, which indicated a meaning too injurious not to rouze my utmost resentment; but my tender regard to your reputation making me fearful of a quarrel, I seemed not to have attended to him, and only replied to lady Sarah, that you were in the hands of very worthy and sober people, who, I was sure, would not be wanting in the utmost care and respect. Then asking Mrs. B—if she thought her health would permit her to pay you the desired visit, as you were not in a condition to be removed, she replied, 'Tis impossible, Sir Edward; I have a fever on me the whole night, and find myself unable to lift my head from my pillow; otherwise you may assure yourself nothing should hinder me from seeing the poor child. But you, lady Sarah, I make no doubt, will think it absolutely necessary to go to her immediately. *By no means*, was her cold and preremptory reply. I expect Sir George in town tomorrow night; he is the properest person to enquire into this business.—Will you in the mean while, madam, send some one you can trust to visit her? said I; your own woman? I am so far of Mr. B—'s mind, answered she, that I think the less noise there is made about this wretched affair the better. There is no trusting to the discretion of servants; they very often betray secrets, only to let people see they are trusted. A pleasant entertainment it would be to the town to hear that *my* niece was found in a little lodging house at Brumpton! for there is not a living creature but knows of her having gone off somewhere in a hackney-coach. It seems, madam, that lady Sarah had discovered this circumstance by having traced you to a milliner's at whose shop you can been yesterday. (You must know, Falkland, that Miss Arnold herself had related this particular, when in endeavouring to prevail on my women to let her go, she had, by way of proving the necessity she was under of returning home, told them of the shifts she had been obliged to use in getting to Brumpton unknown to her family.) And my people, continued lady Sarah, have been to enquire for her at every house in London where I visit; so that it will be impossible for *me* ever to think of taking her home again, were she even inclined to return.

Poor Mrs. B— sighed, and, seemingly fatigued with the length of our conversation, I know not what to make of this unhappy affair, said she; but I will suspend all judgment till I hear what Miss Arnold has to say for herself. Mean while let me beg of you, Sir Edward, that lady Audley or your sister may be sent for to be with her. Poh, poh, said Mr. B—, the shortest way, Sir Edward, will be to trundle her down to Oxfordshire, and ask blessing of the good lady her mother. Mrs. Arnold is in a complying humour. Why not accept of you for a son-in-law as well as Falkland? I condescended not to answer Mr. B—'s ill-timed pleasantry; but applying myself to his lady, Then, madam, you do not give me any thing in commission to say to Miss Arnold? Tell her from me, said Mrs. B—, that nothing shall prevent my going to her the moment I am able to leave my bed. And tell her from *me*, rejoined lady Sarah, that she may expect a visit from her uncle as soon as he comes to town. If she can satisfy *him* with regard to her conduct, I fancy the rest of her friends will excuse her; mean while, I think her character cannot suffer more by passing *two* nights under the protection she has chosen, than it probably has done by staying one. That matter is settled then, said Mr. B—, rising off his chair, as if to put me in mind of retiring. I took the hint, and immediately withdrew, mortified to death at the unfortunate success of my embassy.

What think you of this little history, Falkland? Was it not well conceived? and have I not made the personages talk and act in character? Oh, I know them all; and you know I have a knack at entering into the sentiments and expressions of those I would represent.

I would not break the thread of my narration to tell you Miss Arnold's comments, which were many, during my recital. But when I came to that part of it, *Tell her she may expect a visit from her uncle as soon as he comes to town!* she clapped her hands together; Then I am undone! said she. Oh, Sir Edward, what have you brought on me! Had you suffered me to have gone home yesterday, all this might have been saved; it were better I had died a thousand times than live to be exposed to so much shame! Forgive me, dear madam, said I, I meant all for the best, tho' my zeal for you has unfortunately produced such ill effects. I am, upon your account, as much alarmed as you are at the thoughts of this threatened visit from Sir George Bidulph; yet how can we prevent it? He comes, said she, wringing her hands, armed with the terrors of a judge, to examine the poor little criminal! he finds her in an obscure house out of town—True, madam, (interrupting her) and under the immediate protection of a man whom, next to Falkland, he most hates; not a soul with you but people whom that very man has placed about you; how are we to account for all this? (Observe the *we*, Falkland; you see I made myself a party.) Must I undergo the mortification, said she, of disclosing all my disgrace, and that to a *man* too? a severe and vindictive relation, from whom I can expect nothing but reproaches! no kind friend to mediate or throw in a softening word in extenuation of my fault!—Oh, Sir Edward, I cannot stand this dreadful interview.

At all events, madam, said I, Sir George Bidulph must not see you. His impetuosity might be fatal to you in the weak condition in which you now are. Let *me* stand the brunt of his resentment. I care not for his anger; or at worst—I am ready to sacrifice my life for you. She knew too well the tendency of my words, the frightful image of a quarrel between her uncle and me, ending perhaps in a duel, rushed at once upon her imagination. Let me go, cried she, let me hide myself where I may never be heard of more! Oh, Sir Edward, what miseries have you brought on me! Why did not you let me go yesterday? What recompence can you make me for the loss of friends and of character? Was life to be put in competition with them? This was the very subject which I wished should get possession of her mind, and I was resolved to make it operate with its full force. Let me conjure you, madam, not to afflict yourself with needless apprehensions; your friends, I hope, will be in time appeased; and for your character, there *is* a way, if I durst presume to name it, by which it might be recured from the smallest shadow of reproach.—I stopped here, as if afraid to proceed—No, no, sir, nothing but the grave can screen *me* from reproach.—Dear Miss Arnold, permit me to tell you, that you *have* a resource, not, I hope, so desperate, so hateful to you, as that which you mention. What is it, sir? for I know of none. To give the man who has unfortunately been the cause of having your character called into question, a legal right to defend it as his own. (Was not this hinted with as much delicacy as lord V— himself could have done it?) Oh, Sir Edward, is *this* a time?— I interrupted her; I grant you, it is not, madam; and I should have too much respect for your well-founded grief to make such a proposal, if I did not think it the only means to obviate what I at least flatter myself is the principal cause of it. Your friends already suspect that I am particularly interested in the unfortunate step you have taken. The manner of your coming hither, of which they are apprized, has all the appearance of a premeditated flight on your side. How are you then to explain this part of your conduct? Do you think, madam, it will be considered as a greater crime by your friends to return *my* love than that of the ungrateful Falkland? Oh, Sir Edward, what have you let me into? you have completed my destruction!—Let me beseech you, madam, to consider a little how extremely critical your situation is. What will be the consequence of your confessing the truth? You doom to despair the unhappy man who implores your pity and forgiveness—Oh, not for the universe, she cried; I would die rather than see him unhappy! You plant a dagger in your poor Cecilia's heart, and ruin the peace of your whole family! She breathed a deep sigh, striking her hands gently on the counterpane of her bed. Then, madam, think how you are to excuse yourself. Will the intention be deemed less faulty than the act? It was to Falkland's infidelity, not to Miss Arnold's awakened duty, that her family are indebted for her late acknowlegement of her error. Sir, the thought is enough to turn one's brain! I am not able to support it. This is all your doing, Sir Edward; if you had suffered me to have gone—I acknowlege it, madam, and would die to repair my mistake, if that would do it—Let me go, sir, (looking on each side the bed, as if for her cloaths) let me fly to my mama; she'll advise me, she'll give me some comfort in my misery. Madam, I will not oppose your will, you shall have my chariot, when you please, to convey you home; but have you determined what conduct you are to hold with regard to Mr. Falkland and your sister, supposing even we should be able to form some pretence for your having come hither? I will not say a word, said she, which can prevent their marriage; no, no, I love them both too well to disturb their happiness. Charming generous creature! said I; then you will probably, in a few days, be a witness to the joyful nuptials of the happy Falkland. Oh, that's too much, said she, I did not think of it before. I cannot be a *witness* to them. Lord! what shall I do? I tell you again, Sir Edward, my head is almost turned, and I am sure I should not preserve my senses if I were to see my uncle. You shall not see him, madam; neither do I think it adviseable for you to trust to the strength of your own resolution in being present at your sister's marriage, which must unavoidably be the case if you go down to Oxfordshire. Suppose, instead of a journey thither; you were to retire to some friend's house, and wait there till after Mr. Falkland's departure from England, which will take place immediately after his marriage. You will, in the interim, have time to consider of what is best to be done to extricate yourself from the difficulties in which you are entangled. I am sorry, added I, that neither my mother nor my sister are in town, as it prevents me from offering you their house as an asylum. I thank you, sir, said she, but I will go to Mrs. B—'s; she is the woman in the world whom, next to my mama, I most revere. I am extremely mortified, my dear Miss Arnold, said I, that I am now under a necessity of telling you what, for fear of giving you pain, I chose before to conceal; but I doubt it will be impossible for you to be at Mrs. B—'s,—Mercy on me! why so, Sir Edward? I am sure Mrs. B— loves me, and would do any thing to serve me. I am satisfied of her kind intentions, replied I, but can you answer for those of her husband? I know he is a rough man, said Miss Arnold; yet I think he would not hinder his lady from giving shelter to a poor unfortunate creature, who has no other friend to whom she can fly. You judge too favourably of him, answered I; for when his lady was lamenting that it was not in her power to attend you on account of her illness, he replied, You need not make yourself uneasy about that, Mrs. B—; for were you even able to go, I should by no means approve of your interfering in a business of this nature. Leave the lady to the conduct of her own relations; and let me request it of you, not to interpose one way or other. You may judge by this, madam, whether Mr. B—'s doors are likely to be open to you. What will become of me! cried she. I have then no resource left—Oh, Sir Edward Audley, into what an abyss have you plagued me!—I will send for my mother and my sister directly, madam, they are only at Hampton Court; they can easily be in town to-night. I am sure they will joyfully receive you. Mrs. Arnold has a great regard for lady Audley; she can have no objection to your being with her—True, sir; but *why* am I to be with lady Audley? Why not go home to my mama? What reason can I offer for that? That your health would not permit you to take the journey; and finding Mr. B——'s doors shut against you, and that you had incurred the resentment of lady Sarah, you had no other alternative.—And here a thought has just struck me, by which you may very naturally account for your coming hither in the private manner that you did. You know your uncle Bidulph has thought proper to forbid any connection between you and my family, at the same time that neither he nor lady Sarah are stranger to the friendship that subsists between you and my sister. Now, madam, why may it not be supposed that you had been prevailed on, from the love you bear Miss Audley, at her earnest request, to meet her here? The fear of having a thing (interdicted by Sir George) discovered, is a sufficient reason for the precautions of which you made use; and the sudden and violent illness which attacked you here rendering it impossible to be concealed, obliged you to have recourse to Mrs. B——, as you had not the courage to apply to lady Sarah herself, after such a palpable breach of your uncle's commands. We may leave it to Sophy, continued I, smiling, to frame an excuse for her having desired to see you in this clandestine manner. Perhaps a stolen wedding was intended, to which you were to have been a witness; and which I happened to discover, prevented, and sent my sister directly into the country. I dare say she will not scruple at inventing an innocent tale for your service; and if you will, for once, condescend to give your suffrage to a slight deviation from fact, in order to prevent such complicated mischiefs as a discovery of the real state of the case would produce, I think there will be no difficulty in gaining credit to so plausible an account.

You see, Falkland, with what cautious terms I dressed the falshood that I was suggesting to her, and how much I avoided giving it the appearance of a lye, that terrible naughty thing, which being the single crime that little children can commit, the avoiding it is the first moral principle that is inculcated into them and which sometimes sticks by them their whole lives; as was the case with Miss Arnold; for, notwithstanding all my gilding and varnishing, she discovered the face of the ugly phantom.—Lord, said she, what a despicable creature have I made myself, to be reduced thus to such mean shifts! My dear madam, of two evils we must always chuse the least. True, said she, yet were *I* only to be the sufferer, I would not submit to the telling such a falshood; but when I think of—She stopped short, striking her forehead with one of her hands.—Oh, Lear, Lear, whispered I to myself, beat at this gate that let the folly in, &c.[1] Well, madam, I think we have at length found an harmless expedient, by which we may be delivered from our difficulties. I will immediately dispatch a messenger to Hampton court to request the presence of the two ladies in town to-night. Mean while let me conjure you to endeavour to take a little repose, I am sure you stand in need of it; you may depend on seeing my mother and sister by suppertime. I was going to leave the room. Hold, Sir! cried she: you may save yourself the trouble of writing to lady Audley, and her the inconvenience of hurrying to town, for I am now determined to go home to my mama. Since I am reduced so low as to be under an absolute necessity of telling a falshood, I may as well do it at once without aggravating my fault by absenting myself longer from my family, and exposing my character to any farther censures. I know the worst that can befall me at home, and will try to support it; there fore, if you would oblige me, furnish me with the means of getting immediately to Woodberry; I am able enough to undertake the journey; I would set out directly.—

This was just what I expected. I had for this very purpose furnished her with a plausible tale, of which, spite of her love of truth, I knew she would make use, rather than continue any longer in a situation which, it must be confessed, was not the most eligible. You will ask perhaps, why I did not take her at her word, and under pretence of sending her to Woodberry, lay hold of this opportunity of conveying her to Bagshot? I'll tell you, because I knew I could do it as well to-morrow, or even the next day. And you are to observe that as soon as she should find herself carried to a different place from that where she expected to go, I must drop the mask at once, and I think it more for my interest to wear it a little longer. I hope to make a sort of merit with her of my respectful and distant behaviour during the time I have had her so entirely in my power. A merit, let me tell you, not to be overlooked in a man so *desperately* in love as I am. And then my running away with her was not a premeditated scheme; no, no, it was suddenly suggested to me by the violence of my passion, on finding her determined to put herself into the hands of a family from whom I could expect no quarter. This you see softens the trespass down to a mere love transport, and will much sooner obtain forgiveness than could possibly be expected for a

---

1 Sir Edward quotes these lines from Shakespeare's *King Lear*: "O Lear, Lear, Lear! / Beat at this gate, that let thy folly in, / and thy dear judgment out!" (1.4.270–72).

concerted scheme. So that, in short, I now begin to think I shall have less difficulty to prevail with her than I at first apprehended. By the bye, she has been extremely courteous to me, and expresses herself very thankfully for all the trouble I have taken to serve her.

You are not to wonder then, that I endeavoured to turn her from her design of setting out directly, as she said she would, for Oxfordshire. I would not for the whole earth, madam, said I, dispute your pleasure in any thing; but let me conjure you to have a little more regard to your health than to think of undertaking such a journey, till you have at least, by one night's repose, in some measure recruited your strength. The women who attend you, tell me you slept not last night, you have taken no refreshment since you have been here, you must be extremely feeble; let me prevail with you—She interrupted me, Sir, I find myself much better than I was; I am not indeed quite well, yet I think I am strong enough to undertake such a little journey. You will much oblige me if you will furnish me with the means of setting out immediately—But, madam, consider, Sir George Bidulph is still at Woodberry; your sudden appearance there, as it must surprize him extremely, so must it put him upon enquiring into the motives of it, and force you into disagreeable explanations.—This seemed to startle her; I would not wish to meet my uncle, said she, yet he will hear the whole affair from lady Sarah as soon as he comes to town, and in how terrible a light must I appear till he has it explained! Leave it to your mama, said I, to explain it to him; Mrs. Arnold will hear you with indulgence, and represent the story in the tenderest manner to Sir George. I had much rather it were so, replied she. Yet the staying in this house another night, with absolute strangers—'tis so improper, so imprudent! better risque any thing.—I put her in mind of what lady Sarah had said, that her character would not receive any more injury (in case even of the affair's being known) by staying two than one night in the place where she then was.—She seemed half inclined, yet loath to yield; when lifting her modest eyes to my face, I shall be permitted then, Sir, said she, to remain here with no other company but the two gentlewomen of the house? I understood her meaning; Undoubtedly, madam, replied I, I shall return to town directly. I would not for the world alarm you by my presence. And to-morrow you will be so good as to let me have your chariot, Sir? Certainly, madam.—I retired immediately; but instead of going to London, only withdrew into another chamber, where I sate me down to give you this farther account of my proceedings. I mean not to leave the house to-night, for I would have it *published* that I have not lain at home, since the day of elopement.

I intended to have sent this off to you to-night, but upon second thoughts will defer it till to-morrow, when I may have something farther worth communicating to you. I am just now told that the lady is risen, and has requested a dish of tea, which is the first nourishment the perverse beauty would receive, as she has only been prevailed on since yesterday noon to wet her lips once or twice with a little wine and water.

March 16th.

We have just had the prettiest altercation imaginable, but it is all blown over, and we are now the best friends in the world. The lady rose at eight o'clock this morning, though as the damsel, who lay on a pallet by her, informed me, she slept very little more last night than she had done the night before. Her first enquiry was, whether the chariot was arrived? She was answered, No. She complained, was sullen, and would eat no breakfast; a common practice it is with ladies, when they are vexed, to fast out of spite. I heard her (for I was in the chamber adjoining to hers) traversing her room all the morning; then speaking to the women who were with her. 'Twas very hard, she said; sure Sir Edward Audley would not break his word with her! By no means, my dear creature, whispered I to myself; but you must nevertheless restrain your impatience, for it is not at all convenient that you should set out so early. About twelve o'clock I sent up to desire permission to ask her how she did; and was immediately admitted. Her countenance cleared up when she saw me. Oh, Sir Edward, I was afraid you had quite forgot me! I enquired after her health. She scarce allowed herself time to answer me—Is the chariot come, Sir? for I have been ready these three hours. I am rejoiced to see you so much better madam; but to tell you the truth, I so little expected to find you so well recovered, that I would not order the chariot till I first knew whether you were in a condition to travel.—Bless me, Sir, how can you disappoint one so! I am very well, extremely well. What carriage brought you down hither? I'll take *any* vehicle—I care not what it is. Madam, I rid; I generally take a ride every morning, (I was booted[1]). Well, Sir, let me beseech you, if you *mean* to favour me with your assistance, to let your servant go to town directly and order down your chariot or

1 Wearing boots for riding.

hire me another coach. I will go myself, madam; I am now returning home, I did not think it had been so late; but a circumstance
has occurred to my thoughts this morning, which makes me wish
you would defer your journey for to-day.—Indeed, Sir, I will not
defer it—(rather in a peevish tone for so gentle a creature)
Madam, I presume not to dictate to you; but I would just remind
you that as your uncle Bidulph is expected in town to-night,
should you set out for Oxfordshire, 'tis highly probable you may
meet him on the road; and how disagreeable such a reencounter
would be to you, is worth your consideration.—I would not meet
him on any account, said she; yet if the windows of my carriage
are drawn up, I think there will be no difficulty in concealing
myself. Do not trust to that, madam; you know you must stop on
the road, you may happen even at the same inn to pop on each
other. What would Sir George think of such a flight? for though
he may not yet be apprized of what has happened, yet the seeing
me with you—She took me up short; Sir, there is no necessity for
that; I shall think myself sufficiently obliged to you for one of
your servants to conduct me home. I found by this, the ungrateful little gipsey, notwithstanding all my kindness to her, had no
thoughts of making me any return; but I was prepared for this
refusal. I see, madam, said I, how unacceptable all my services are
to you; that shall not, however, prevent my doing my utmost to
oblige you. I go, madam, to fulfil your orders. My chariot shall
attend you; it probably cannot be with you in less than about a
couple of hours; but be under no anxiety. You must necessarily
sleep on the road to-night; I suppose it will be a matter of indifference to you whether you lie twenty or thirty miles out of town.
'Tis quite equal to me, said she; yet had you been so good as to
have let me depart early this morning, I might have slept at
Woodberry to-night. I begged pardon for my omission, and as a
farther precaution to hide herself from Sir George Bidulph's
sight, I recommended it to her not to alight out the chariot when
the horses came to be changed. She said she would not alight till
she came to the inn where she was to lie; and thanked me for the
hint, the intention of which I believe I need not explain to you.

Thus having restored tranquility to the breast of my fair, I
withdrew; but instead of going to town myself, I dispatched my
imp to order the chariot down at *three* o'clock, and not before;
this will cost us another hour of fretting, but no matter: Charmer,
thou must bear greater disappointments than that; I have
directed at the same time my sister's maid to make up a little
packet of her young lady's linen, and some other necessaries,

and put them into the coach-box; see how provident I am, Falkland.

You will desire to know perhaps how I meant to act in case Miss Arnold had consented to have gone to my mother's house? Why, just as I mean now to act. I did not lie awake spinning such flimsy toils as were to be brushed away by the white finger of a baby. My mother was to have been very ill, not able to come to town, and alarmed to the last degree at the thoughts of how much a young creature's character might suffer by being alone under the care of a giddy boy like me. She conjures her to come down directly to Hampton court, where her cousin Batemans would be rejoiced to receive her. She sets out for this purpose, and then the business is done, let me but get her out of London in a vehicle of which I govern the motions.

You are to observe, that never having but once gone the road from Oxford to London, she knows nothing of the geography of the country. Besides, the fear of meeting our uncle Bidulph will make her afraid to peep her nose out. The horses are to be changed at Hounslow; but as she sets out with mine, and a good coachman, you know, having too much regard to his master's cattle to drive them like post-horses, she must be content to go the first ten or dozen miles at a very moderate pace; after which, as ill luck would have it, one of the fore wheels failing, we are all of a sudden obliged to stop; by this time, by my calculation, it will be near dark; the footman, or coachman, no matter which, steps into a gentleman's house before whose door the accident happened, to get a hammer and nails, careless blockhead as he is to forget such necessary implements on a journey. This is the cue for Harry Bendish (at whose house David has arrived before this present writing) to make his appearance. He entreats the lady to step in whilst her chariot is repairing. The coachman having by this time dexterously applied the hammer, the wheel is in *reality* put out of a condition of rolling, and the lady reduced to the necessity of accepting of a bed at this hospitable gentleman's house. And where is Audley to be all this while? why, on horseback, close upon the track of the chariot; and as a soon as his pretty is housed, as if touched with the spear of Ithuriel,[1] he starts up in his own proper shape.———

---

1   In Milton's *Paradise Lost*, Ithuriel is an angel, the touch of whose spear reveals Satan, who has been disguised as a toad (See *Paradise Lost* IV: 808–11).

Bravissimo, the chariot is this minute arrived; I am supposed to have come down in it in order to bid Miss Arnold adieu.— Farewel, inexorable fair; but—I'll meet thee at Philippi.[1]—

Letter LIX
Sir George Bidulph to Mrs. Arnold.

London, March 17th.

Dear Sidney,

I have just discovered in what manner your daughter has disposed of herself, and suppose it will amaze you as much as it has done me, when I tell you she has thought proper to make choice of Sir Edward Audley. The gentleman, I presume, finding himself unacceptable to one sister, addressed himself with better success to the other. This, as lady Sarah observes, is the consequence of that weak indulgence which has been shewn to Cecilia. These events have overturned all my views, and I find I am to look for heirs *out* of my own family.

From the lights that had been got before my arrival in town, Mr. B— judged that the shortest way to come at the discovery of this affair, would be by advertisement to offer a reward to the coachman who carried a young lady on such a day and hour from such a place; and accordingly, at lady Sarah's desire, he put such an advertisement into all the papers yesterday. The fellow came to me this morning, and declared he had carried the lady so described to Spring garden passage,[2] where she alighted and walked toward the Park; and that he knew no more of her. With this unsatisfactory account, I own I should have been put off; when lord V—, who very luckily happened to be with me, and whose thoughts were more disengaged than mine, suspecting the fellow did not speak truth, proposed bringing him before a magistrate. The man seemed frightened and unwilling to go; which confirming my lord in his suspicions, we threatened sending him to prison. Upon which he acknowleged that he had carried the lady to a house at Brumpton, which he said he was ready to shew us; where, after having set her down, a gentleman whom he did not then know, but whom he found afterwards to be Sir Edward

---

1 Site of the battle between, on one side, Marc Antony and Octavian and, on the other, the assassins of Julius Caesar.

2 Spring Gardens, now a street in London, was a public park named after Sir William Spring.

Audley, came in his coach to town; that he drove him to his house in Bond-street, where he gave him five guineas, with a strict charge, in case of enquiry, not to own that he had carried such a lady, threatening to be the death of him if he disobeyed him. Having secured the man till farther enquiry, I went immediately to lady Audley's house, where I was informed that she and her daughter had been at Hampton-Court for these ten days past. As for Sir Edward, the servants could give no account of him, but that he had been out of town since Thursday; but where they knew not. Not being able to obtain any farther information from them, I drove to Brumpton; here I had the mystery explained by the old beldam who keeps the house. She said Sir Edward Audley had lodgings in her house, which he kept the year round; and where, being but a *puny* gentleman, he sometimes lay for his health. That on Thursday a young lady had met him, that she supposed was either his wife or his *sweetheart*; but that it was none of her business to enquire. That they passed the whole day together; and that the lady had lain there that night. I asked if Sir Edward had slept with her; she assured me that he did not, the lady having been so much indisposed that her daughter had been obliged to sit up with her all night, and that Sir Edward had lain in another chamber; but that the next day they both went away together in Sir Edward's chariot; but to what place she could not say. I asked her several questions to try if I could entrap her in her answers; but she replied readily, and with seeming truth, to all my interrogations; and concluded with declaring solemnly she knew not who the lady was; but that she made no doubt but that she either was, or would be married to his *honour*. This is the sum of what I have been able to gather; and as I conclude with my land-lady of Brumpton, that the lady *is* by this time married to his honour, I do not mean to give myself any farther pain about her. As for your daughter Cecilia, I have nothing more to say, than as you are entirely at liberty with regard to the *time* of her nuptials, I am only commissioned from lady Sarah to tell you, that she begs to be excused from being present at them; and I must request the same favour with regard to myself.

I am, &c.

P.S. Though such disagreeable news as this letter contains would reach you full soon enough by the post, yet to put an end to so uncomfortable a state as that of suspence, I shall send it by an express.

I have not been composed enough to write to you, Audley, till this day. My thoughts have been all tumult. Your exploit, as you may well imagine, threw all the family into the utmost consternations. Lady Sarah's account reached them but twelve hours later than yours did me; for though she writ not till the day after Miss Arnold's departure, she trusted not to the conveyance of the post. My Cecilia was drowned in tears; Mrs. Arnold almost stupefied with grief; the good old Price lifting up his hand and eyes in astonishment; Sir George Bidulph execrating the art and dissimulation of women, and muttering ungrateful hints to poor Cecilia. I, traitor as I am, seeming—no, Audley, not *seeming*; but really taking part in the general uneasiness; and lord V— (What a slave am I in comparison of that man!) endeavouring to console us all. Sir George and his lordship set out for London the next morning, in order, if possible, to discover the bottom of this dark affair, not one of them being able to form a single conjecture which could throw the least light on it. What a dreadful interval have I endured from the time of Sir George's quitting us till now! I would not for millions pass eight and forty hours more in the same manner. You are to know, that since my last to you I had pleaded my cause so successfully, that I had prevailed on Cecilia to consent to our marriage before my departure. Mr. Price, who is ever on his pupil's side, had worked on Mrs. Arnold. Lord V— was so generous as to join them both, and they had all together so wrought on Sir George Bidulph, that he at last consented, provided we were married privately, and the affair kept secret till my return; when it was proposed to procure for me such a rank in the army, as would somewhat better intitle me to the honour of this alliance. Oh, the pomp of Bidulph blood! In short, the wedding day was fixed for the twenty-second of this month, and I was to depart for Germany on the thirtieth, for so it had been originally determined by lord V—; and Sir George made this a preliminary to his hard wrung concession. He agreed; however, to be present at the ceremony, on condition that lady Sarah could be persuaded to come down. Lord V— and he were to go to town in order to prevail on her if *possible* to condescend so far; but at all events Miss Arnold was to be sent for on the occasion.

Thus were matters determined, when this heavy unexpected blow fell upon us, and seemed to overwhelm the whole family, even the very servants, with affliction. One would have thought that Love himself had been scared from this mansion of sorrow. Cecilia could not listen to his soothing voice, while her mind continued under such terrible apprehensions for her sister's fate; and shall I own it to you, Sir Edward, I felt such pangs of remorse, that had it not been too late, I would have given up all and dared to have been honest.

There were some passages in both your letters that plucked my very heart-strings. Oh, Audley, do I deserve to be beloved as Miss Arnold loves me! *She would not say a word to hinder my marriage, she would die rather than see me unhappy!* How I could curse thee, thou barbarian, who couldst be proof against the tears, the swooning, the tender complaints of this amiable unfortunate girl! But why should I blame thee? am not I myself the cause, the wicked cause of all her distress? Yet take heed, take heed how you treat her; if she yields herself to your wishes, I will endeavour to be as happy as my guilt will let me; but if you have recourse to violence, remember how I closed my last letter—that's all.—

I am just now returned from Woodberry, where I read a letter that Mrs. Arnold received from Sir George this evening, wherein he tells her the following particulars: [Mr. Falkland here gives his friend the substance of Sir George Bidulph's last letter.] This eclaircissement has given quite a new face to our affairs. Mrs. Arnold, though by no means charmed with her son-in-law, yet being relieved from a state of the utmost uncertainty, and the most alarming fears, is become much more tranquil. When one apprehends the very worst that *can* happen, one is even happy to find it not *quite* so bad, though still bad enough in conscience; wherefore Mrs. Arnold, after having expressed her admiration at Dolly's *amazing* conduct, comforted herself with the hope, that possibly Sir Edward Audley might turn out a soberer man than he now promised to be, as he was the son of so *very* good a woman.

She then tenderly reproached Cecilia, telling her she had made a precedent which she (Mrs. Arnold) could not tell how to defend herself from following; viz. that of granting forgiveness to one sister as well as the other. There's comfort for you, Audley! As for Cecilia, after a thousand pretty exclamations of wonder, she concluded with saying, her sister was very sly, for she had never the least suspicion of her liking Sir Edward. I whispered to her, Your sister may retort the same reproach on you, my sweet Cecilia. She gave me a little pat on the cheek, then said, she had indeed often observed that her sister was particularly fond of

Miss Audley; that she sometime fancied there were secrets between them; that she even *lately* had suspected that Dolly's heart was touched; but by whom she could not conceive. I breathed a conscious sigh! Mr. Price said he was glad the affair was cleared up, though it was by no means in so desirable a manner as was to be wished.

Mrs. Arnold then demanded of me, if I were not in the secret of your love for her daughter? This was a home push; but I parried it as well as I could, by telling her I had looked upon you to be so general a lover that I did not believe there had been any thing serious in your attachment to Miss Arnold, though I had often heard you declare yourself her admirer. Cecilia laughed, Then he only *pretended* to admire me, said she. I'll assure you, if I had thought that I was addressed only for a blind, I would have used Sir Edward a thousand times worse than I did.

Having canvassed over the first part of Sir George's letter, the conclusion, in which *I* was most interested, came next on the tapis; and here you may be sure I did not fail to lay hold on that paragraph wherein he says, '*You are intirely at liberty with regard to the time of Cecilia's nuptials.*' I hope then, madam, said I, addressing Mrs. Arnold, that this event will not make any change with regard to my happy day? I don't see why it should, said Mr. Price; you find, madam, Sir George does not seem to expect it should; and since neither he nor lady Sarah intend to favour you with their company, and this affair has deprived you of that of Miss Arnold, the marriage may be conducted with still more privacy, for I suppose, unless it be Mrs. Askham, you will not think it necessary to invite any one. I mean to have no one else present, replied Mrs. Arnold, except one or two of our own people. The day then stands as it did, Audley, the day for my translation to the skies; for I think I shall look down on those poor mortals called kings and emperors, when I can call Cecilia *mine*. Mr. Price is to join our hands, by favour of a special licence,[1] in Mrs. Arnold's own house. Happy Woodberry! what a different aspect dost thou now wear to what thou didst when I first quitted thy hospitable roof, uncertain, fearful, almost hopeless of my Cecilia's love! Yet I cannot be perfectly at ease till I hear that you are happy in the possession of Miss Arnold, with her *own consent*. Your wishes once accomplished, I shall have nothing to fear, and I think in her present entangled situation it would be madness in her to refuse you.—

---

1 Couples could avoid the public spectacles of declaring banns and the church ceremony by obtaining a marriage license (Stone 30).

Letter LXI.

Sir Edward Audley to Miss Audley.

[The letter to which this is an answer does not appear; and a former letter from Sir Edward to his sister, in which he gives her a brief account of his adventure with Miss Arnold to the morning of that day on which he carried her off, is omitted.]

Bagshot, March 17th.

Why, what a barbarous little termagant art thou, Sophy, to rate thy poor brother so unmercifully for a harmless piece of knight-errantry? I looked for commendation and applause, and instead of that you stop my mouth with, *"Tis downright villainy in you, brother!"* Why, 'tis downright cruelty in you, sister, to say so. Where is the villainy of seizing the pretty for which I have been so long spreading my toils? watching with a patience which exceeded that of Job[1] himself; rising up early and going to bed late; passing whole nights without sleep; dispatching couriers from day to day; wearing my poor pens to the stumps; and killing all the post-horses between this and Oxford: and now that I have fairly hunted the little shy animal into my net, I am to be called names, and that by you too, recreant varlet as you are, who originally helped to lime the twigs[2] which we spread to catch the timorous bird! Oh, fy, fy, Sophy! I did not expect this from you. Yet after all I forgive you, child; your indignation on this occasion is natural, and not only pardonable but even commendable; for, libertine as I am, I should hate the woman who allowed herself to think as freely as I do; and should despise even you if you did not feel on the present occasion precisely as you do.

You thank your stars, you say, that you had no hand in this last stroke of my mischievous politics. You may thank you stars as much as you please; but you are nevertheless more obliged to me than you are to them, who might, if I had pleased, have led you into the scrape in spite of all the stars in the hemisphere: but I avoided it on purpose; for though I am an extravagant fellow, I would not have my *sister* so far unsex herself as to have been aiding and assisting in so bold an enterprise as this is. As far as a simple love-plot goes, I know you are excellent; but a stroke of

---

1 Patriarch of the land of Uz and eponymous protagonist of the biblical Book of Job, his name is synonymous with extended and undeserved suffering.

2 "To smear ... with bird-lime, for the purpose of catching birds" (*OED*).

this nature exceeds thy feeble abilities, and is worthy only of myself. I commend your prudence, and the reasons that you give for not informing my mother of the affair. Let her be innocent at least of *this* offence; for however pleased she might be at the bottom with my success, it will be for her credit to be ignorant of the means I have used to accomplish it.

As for yourself, my Sophy, though I am *sure* you are very angry with me, yet am I sure also your curiosity is such that you would give one of your white teeth to know what is now passing here. I will gratify you therefore at less expence; and to be as minute as you can desire, I will take up the thread of my narration just where I broke it off in my last. [*Sir Edward here tells his sister the manner in which Miss Arnold was carried to the house of Mr. Bendish, which as it had been preconcerted, was exactly as he had before described it to Mr. Falkland. He then proceeds:*] Miss Arnold could not be prevailed on to alight, till being assured by the servants that it would be impossible to repair the wheel without taking it off the chariot, and that even then it would require a considerable time to set it to rights; she at last vouchsafed to give her hand to Bendish, who led her out with wonderful ceremony. By the bye, I believe she was the first modest women (his own mother excepted) whom he had ever approached.

Just in that juncture (for I had fallen behind a little on purpose) did I ride up to the door in full gallop, calling out to know what was the matter? I immediately lit off my horse, and addressing Miss Arnold, who was in the utmost astonishment at seeing me, I told her in two words that as I could not think of trusting her only to the care of servants, I had, spite of her pro-hibition, ventured to follow the chariot on horseback; that my horse happening to have a shoe loose, I had stopped for a few minutes to get it fastened, which occasioned my not being with her when the accident of the wheel happened. I then gravely saluted Mr. Bendish as a gentleman with whom I was not acquainted, and thanking him for his obliging assistance, fol-lowed him and Miss Arnold into the house.

We were shewn into his best parlour, or as old dame Bendish used to call it, her drawing room; where the blockhead over-shooting the mark, had a tea-table set out with every thing ready to make tea and coffee. I could have buffeted him for this piece of ill-timed attention, which looked too premeditated; and I took it into my head at that minute to let my fair-one enjoy one night of undisturbed repose, before I opened to her the book of fate wherein her destiny was written.

As you know the character of Harry Bendish, though you have not the happiness to be personally acquainted with him, I believe you will think Miss Arnold was not under the most sanctified roof in England, and that the conversation and manners of her host would rather shock a woman of delicacy; but you are mistaken, for my friend Harry acquitted himself to a miracle, considering how little he had been accustomed to the company of, not *ladies*, but *gentlewomen*. The worst of it was, that being thrown out of his bias, he scarce knew what to say; and though he by no means wants parts, yet not daring to enter on his usual topics, he seemed rather deficient in common sense; and in avoiding to be thought a rake, he hardly escaped being considered as a fool. He told Miss Arnold, that having had the misfortune to bury his mother (the best old gentlewoman in the world) about three weeks ago, he was not so happy as to have any lady in the house; and therefore desired to know if she would permit his housekeeper to come in and make tea. Then turning to me, She is a devilish handsome wench, I can tell you, Au—I gave him a look that would have petrified Medusa herself, and arrested my own name, which was just popping out of his mouth. He turned it off with an Augh—and two or three coughs. By the greatest good luck imaginable, Miss Arnold did not distinctly hear what he said, as he was seated next to me, and she at the opposite side of the fire. I repeated; If she be as *handy* a wench as you say, sir, I believe she had best come in and do the honours of your tea-table. He rang the bell, though not recovered from his confusion, and ordered one of the servants to send in the housekeeper; but was answered that she was gone very ill to bed. I am sorry for it, said he; for she was such a favourite of my mother's, that since *her* death I have put the care of my house intirely into this good body's hands. Miss Arnold was then requested to take the trouble of making tea herself; which she did.

We were informed, in about half an hour, that the wheel was *unmendable*; it was made of unseasoned wood; the coach-maker was the greatest rogue in Christendom; and finally, there was no proceeding without a new wheel, which could not be procured that night. Miss Arnold looked mortified and dejected. Our friend said, he was very sorry he had not a carriage to offer her; if he were master of a coach-and-six, it should be at her service; but as the matter stood, he hoped she would accept of a bed as his house. I thought it proper here to close in with the proposal; and thanking the gentleman for his politeness, I told Miss Arnold she could not do otherwise than accept of his obliging offer, as we were six miles from an inn. She seemed not to relish the scheme; but having no other choice to make, she was obliged to acquiesce. She complained of being fatigued, and somewhat indisposed, and said she should beg leave to retire as soon as a chamber could be got ready for her. Upon which a chambermaid was called, and ordered to conduct her to the apartment which before had been allotted to her. You may be sure the servants had their lessons; so that she was not likely to discover that night into what part of the world she was got.

Poor Bendish, who had been under a cruel restraint in her presence, swore he never was so embarrassed in his life; but being now at liberty, we enjoyed ourselves over our bottle till midnight.

When I rose this morning, being informed the lady was already up, I went down to the parlour, where I found her. After the first civilities were over, she begged of me to enquire if the carriage was ready. She said she was impatient to be gone; for though she was much obliged to the gentleman of the house for his hospitality, yet as she thought herself in a very improper situation, she could not leave it too soon.

It was now time, Sophy, to confess my crime; and as I had nothing for it but to brazen it out, I approached her with an assured air, and requested of her to be seated till she heard what I had to say. She obeyed me but by halves; for without sitting down, Well, sir, said she, *what* have you to say? That I cannot think of parting with you, madam, now that chance has so luckily thrown you into my possession—Not think of parting with me! what do you mean, Sir Edward? 'Tis time, madam, to undeceive you; you are not on your road to Woodberry, but in another part of the country, and in the house of a particular friend of mine, whither I have led you, on purpose, to secure to myself the happiness of seeing and conversing with you; a liberty in which I knew I should not be indulged if I restored you to your family. You cannot be serious. Sir Edward, 'tis impossible. Am I not at Beaconsfield?[1] By no means, madam, you are on Bagshot-heath, and in the house of my most intimate acquaintance. Mercy on me, what *will* become of me! Be not alarmed, madam, I entertain not a thought with regard to you that is not dictated by the most respectful love. Respect! Oh, Sir Edward, do you call it *respect* to betray me in this cruel manner? You must blame yourself, madam; your own coldness, your own unkind diffidence of me,

---

1 A town in Buckinghamshire, about twenty-four miles northwest of London.

which has urged me to this extremity. I own I have deceived you, and have nothing to plead in my excuse but a desperate passion.—I offered to conduct you to my mother's, under whose care and protection you might have remained till it was more convenient for you to return home. You refused the asylum of her house. Cruel creature! I saw too plainly the cause of your refusal. 'Twas I, I was the object from whom you would have flown. I afterwards begged your permission to attend you home; but even this favour I was denied, and you chose to abandon yourself alone to the hazards of a journey, rather than allow me even this small mark of distinction. Then it was (and not before) that love inspired me with this stratagem to detain a perverse beauty, who I found preferred still in her heart the ungrateful, the perfidious man who so flagrantly had deceived her, to the tender, the *honest* lover, who adored her with a sincerity not easy to be met with in our sex. I gave this latter part of my speech that sort of tone which indignant truth assumes, when it would defend its own rights. I thought, replied my captive, that the inclination you once professed for me, had been quite subdued. I fairly owned the state of my heart to your sister, and you yourself were not ignorant of my unfortunate attachment to another person. True, madam, and it was on that account that I gave up my hopes; yet pardon me if I add, and I think I may without vanity say, that *my* pretensions would, in the eyes of the world, have appeared better founded than those of Falkland. Yet I sacrificed all to friendship: let Falkland himself bear me witness that the name of *rival* was lost in that of friend. Nay, I went farther, and by trying to acquire a relish for other charms, endeavoured to root yours out of my heart; but my struggles were in vain, and at the time when I offered incense to your sister's beauty, I found myself in the condition of those feigned apostates, who whilst they bow down to a false worship, in their hearts still adore the true divinity. Yes, madam, I have been faithful to you, from the moment I professed myself your lover; and though I ceased to importune, I ceased not to admire you. Yet had Falkland been just, you should never have known me for any other than your friend; his infidelity, I own, renewed my wishes, and the accident which has now put you into my hands, has even encouraged my hopes.—What hopes do you then entertain? said she, with a countenance on which was painted more of terror than of any other passion. That you will make me happy, said I, by giving me your hand.—What here, sir? Now! now in this strange house? I do not say that, madam; if you will promise me faithfully to be mine, I will conduct you home. I am sure I can rely upon your word. I have some little claim to your consideration. Will you, madam, make me the promise I demand? (I knew she would not.) I cannot, Sir Edward, indeed I cannot. I never will marry, assure yourself I never will marry. But, dear madam, why so strange, so cruel a resolution? A lady in the pride of youth and loveliness to devote herself to a single life! 'Tis doing injustice to mankind; if you find *one* lover false, are the rest of his sex to suffer for that? Oh, Sir, all men are alike, I believe; I will trust none of them. There are, indeed, but too many of us faulty, answered I; yet assuredly, dear Miss Arnold, your censure is too general. It may be so, sir; but the only two in whom I have confided, have betrayed me. The faults which *love* commits against the object beloved, merit not so harsh an epithet; 'tis the crimes only of cool infidelity which deserve the name of treason. She made me no answer, but springing lightly to the window which looked into the fore-court, I thought, said she, I heard a carriage, and was in hopes it was the chariot; for, after all, I believe you only want to terrify me. If that was your design, you have but too well succeeded; you *have* terrified me, sir, exceed-ingly terrified me. To say the truth, the poor girl shook like a leaf, and was obliged to sit down in the window to support herself.

The noise she heard in the court, and which she took for the chariot, was nothing more than a little market-cart, which was used to carry home provisions, and which now arrived filled with necessaries for the house; and on its entering the court, she observed one of the servants lock the gate and take the key out. This action seemed to deprive her almost of her reason. She cast a frantic look at me, What, sir, am I a prisoner then? Am I to be detained here by force? No, no, I must not suffer this, starting up from her seat. I drew near her, and ventured to lay hold of her hand. Let me go, sir; let me be gone from hence this minute. Whither would you go, madam? Home, home; whither should I go but home to my mama! Unkind, said I, 'tis to Falkland you would fly, not to your mama; but remember he is now perhaps the husband of Cecilia.—What have I done to you, cried she, that you treat me thus inhumanly? A flood of tears succeeded her words. 'Tis a trite observation, that nothing affects a man so much as weeping beauty. I now felt the truth of it, and was really so touched at her tears, that I fell on my knees before her, and said as many tenderly extravagant things as if I had been actually over head and ears in love; but the obdurate fair was not to be moved. Let me be gone, sir, let me go home to my mama, was the burden of her song. But think of the consequences, madam, think of your reputation; 'tis already known that you have passed two nights in my lodgings.—In *your* lodgings, sir! Yes, madam, those apartments in which you spent two nights at Brumpton are mine; it will be known that you left them in my chariot, and that I accompanied you out of town, and that at a time too when you expected to receive a visit from your uncle. It will be known that, instead of returning home, you retired to the house of my particular friend, a single man, no lady to bear you company, and that I attended you hither: what must the world think of all this, madam? Will it not naturally conclude me to be already possessed of that happy title to which I aspire? And will it not be more for your honour, permit me to say, for the honour of your family too, to give proof to this natural conclusion, than by undeceiving people, to leave them at liberty to judge (pardon me, if I presume to say) perhaps very unfavourably of your conduct? She wrung her hands with all the marks of the bitterest anguish. I endeavoured to sooth her. Sometimes I implored her pity, and in the humblest language beseeched her to grant me the return I desired; then again I represented to her the precipice on which she stood. This last idea seemed to strike her with horror, and I really thought, more than once, that she gave some indications of a situation of mind too alarming to name; yet I hope 'tis nothing but her extreme sensibility, and that after those first violent struggles are over, reason and discretion will reassume their empire; and that finding she has no other party to choose, she will condescend to be lady Audley, with no other stain than what matrimony will wipe out, that of running away with her lover, rather than continue Miss Arnold with an indelible blot on her reputation.

Bendish entered the parlour during our conversation, or rather during my harangue; for I could obtain no answer from her. She just cast her eyes at him as he entered, and withdrew them again without speaking, or even returning his salute. He seemed abashed, and as if at a loss how to address her; when, after hoping she rested well, and saying it was very cold weather, he called for coffee, for we had not yet breakfasted. Miss Arnold remained in sullen silence, nor could be prevailed on to touch any thing. How wilful are you women, Sophy! I'll be hanged, if this pretty stubborn creature would scruple, with all her piety, to starve herself, rather than yield to the virtuous passion of an honest fellow like me. You would have smiled had you seen Bendish's aukward attempts to put the lady in good humour; for he, who only understood the affected coyness of a sempstress, was in hopes that at least half of Miss Arnold's reserve was grimace.[1] He told her, if she loved fox-hunting, he could mount her as well as any woman in England. She made him no reply. I am sorry to see you so grave, madam; I hope no part of my behavior has offended you. Sir, I am a stranger to *you*, I have no right to your friendship; yet it is cruel in you to enter into a conspiracy against a poor young person that never injured you. I am a helpless creature myself; but I have some friends that—She stopped herself short at this word, and hung down her head, as if stung with the bitter recollection of having lost her protectors; then added, I *thought* I had some friends; but now I remember I have lost them. You have a friend in Sir Edward, replied Bendish, that will make you amends for them all; take my word for it, madam, he will make you the best husband in the world—But, sir, I do not mean to be his wife. Was not this provoking, Sophy? And she spoke it with as cool a composure as if she had been her own mistress. You will think better of it, I hope, madam; I flattered myself that I should have found less difficulty in persuading you to a step, which I think the only one that can save your reputation. Ay, madam, think of that, said my friend Bendish; a lady's reputation is all in all: and, by my—I gave him a horrible frown, to stop the oath that I saw ready to slip out; for I had already forbid him to swear before her. He swallowed it, and hemming two or three times; And, upon my word, said he, considering the bad hands—I was afraid he was going again to blunder, in exposing, perhaps, his own character as well as mine; —Ay, said I, interrupting him, considering the bad hands into which a young lady may fall in this wicked world, once she has forfeited the esteem of her family, she cannot too soon put herself under the protection of a husband. I hope Miss Arnold will consider this. I shall give you, madam, all the reasonable time you can desire for reflection; but be assured I will not part with the blessing which my lucky stars have so unexpectedly thrown into my possession. You *must* be mine, madam; I would rather owe my felicity to your own voluntary condescension; yet once we are united, I will trust to you gratitude for a return to my tenderness. Miss Arnold made no reply. She seemed absorbed in her own thoughts. Ay, ay, said Bendish, love will come after; you cannot choose a worthier fellow than Sir Edward Audley. What say you, madam? when shall we send for the parson? I long, of all things, to dance at a wedding. I do not find myself in a condition

---

1 A sempstress is a seamstress. Grimace in this case is an affected air of displeasure.

to argue with you, replied the lady. May I be allowed to retire into another room? You command here, madam, said I; you are at liberty to do as you please *within* these walls; and from the moment that you confer on me the happiest of titles, you may dispose of *me* too as you think proper.

She rose off her seat, and, without vouchsafing me an answer, left the parlour, and ran up stairs; and we heard her bolt the door of the chamber wherein she had slept the night before.

Bendish said he would go and order his housekeeper to attend her; adding, it would be for my interest that she should converse with her; for she was a very sensible woman, and would try to persuade her to reason. In hopes, therefore, of some good effects from this conversation, I intruded not on her for the rest of the morning.

We heard no more of her till dinnertime; when she was humbly intreated to honour us with her company. She sent her compliments to Mr. Bendish, and said, she would take it as a favour if he would excuse her coming down, as she did not find herself very well. Determined as I was to give her as little room as possible to complain of my behavior, I sent her word she might consider herself as at home; for that she should be obeyed in every thing: and we sent her up three or four plates of the nicest things that were at table. The chamber-maid who attended her said, that she scarce touched any thing, and seemed very melancholy. Sweet obstinacy! but I hope to find her in better humour to-morrow. I asked my friend Harry, why his house-keeper did not stay to keep her company, and endeavour to divert her? he said she had been with her for some time in the morning; but he believed the lady did not much like her company: for it seems the blockhead had been so imprudent as to desire this woman to hint something to Miss Arnold (in case of her persisting in her refusal to marry me) which, I assure you, was very far from my thoughts, and which none but such a graceless dog as Bendish would have insinuated. I swore at him heartily for it; but he called me a dolt, and said I should see better effects from this little threat than all my cringing would prudence in a twelve-month. And faith, I begin to believe him; for in the afternoon, to my great astonishment, the goddess, of her own accord, descended to the parlour, neatly dressed with some of the spoils of your wardrobe, which had been left for her in her chamber. Her vouchsafing to put them on is a good sign, you will say. She made a cold apology for not coming to dinner; but said she now found herself something better. I see there is nothing like making you women afraid of us; for a man who is feared, is surer of *civil* treatment, at least, than he who is beloved: it is the nature of the little ungrateful sex!

Bendish gave me an intelligent nod and a wink when she entered the room, as much as to say, Who's in the right, you or I? She sat down, at our humble request; but it was visible that she put a violent constraint on herself in granting us this favour. I thought it not advisable to urge my suit at that juncture. I have gained some ground, and hope a few days prudent reflection on the lady's part, and a little wise management on ours, will induce her, *without* compulsion, to consent to my wishes. The conversation, for half an hour, was extremely stupid. Bendish talked of the improvements he intended to make in his great old-fashioned house, not one of which had either any meaning in themselves, or any reality in the intention. I affected to sigh often, gazed at the fair, and now and then threw in a word, such as, Ay, that will indeed be pretty—Oh, it will be much better so.—Miss Arnold seemed to give little heed to either of us, but appeared still buried in her own gloomy reflections. How childish was all this! Would it not be better, since she knows she *must* yield, to do it frankly, lest I should hereafter retaliate her coldness, and she should, in her turn, find herself obliged to become a wooer?

At last, in a pause of silence, I ventured gently to lay hold of her hand, and, with a soft voice, whispered to her, I hope the result of my dear Miss Arnold's deep meditations will not turn out unfavourably for me. She started, as if awakened from a reverie, whilst her lilly hand, like the sensitive plant, shrunk from my touch; and with a look of terror, mingled with an apparent fear of disobliging me, she as it were stole the hand from me that I had still followed and held. Then rising from her chair, Sir Edward, said she, excuse me for the present, my thoughts are too much disordered to talk with you; to-morrow, perhaps, I may be better able to speak. I bowed down to her shoe-tie, kissing at the same time, whether she would or no, the pretty little coy hand that she had withdrawn from me. She made Bendish a low curtsie; but this curtsie was not of the right breed: it proceeded from the same motive that makes the Indians worship the d—l. She immediately quitted the room, and tripped up stairs again to her own apartment. Sweet soul! I really am fond of her; and were she but grateful—But no matter for that, I'll make her a good husband; for I intend to reform after I am married. Bendish did not fail to exult on his superior address in having frightened her into good behavior, as he called it.

To-morrow then, Sophy, I may probably know my fate; that is to say, as far as it depends on a woman's *will*. Good creature! I hope, for her own sake, she will not oblige me to make use of my authority. I shall have a parson ready, an ancient friend and ally, who has lately taken orders. Falkland is to be joined to his Cecilia on Friday the 22d, and, on that same auspicious day, will I, like a sober and discreet gentleman, enter into the honourable state of wedlock. I love these little snug marriages, where Hymen comes as it were incog. without his tawdry saffron-coloured robe to sleer in people's eyes; and for his torch, he may clap it into a dark lantern.[1]

I have written you such a volume, that I question whether I shall be time enough for the post; so you must content yourself without knowing any farther particulars of to-night: and for the day of days, I shall be too much elated to descend to minute-nesses; therefore you are to look for nothing more from me than an IO,[2] which I will write you in huge capitals, without adding a single word more.

Letter LXII

Sir Edward Audley to Miss Audley

Bagshot, March 18th.

Now blasts upon her! She is gone, fled, vanished, out of sight, hearing, and reach! Talk of man's art! man's dissimulation! Why, we are lambs, doves, or if there be such things, sucking cheru-bims, to vile deceitful woman! The smooth little traitoress, to lull my vigilance to sleep, and even to sooth my hopes, at a time when she was meditating such a wicked escape! Yet *she* was not the con-triver of it herself; another *she* imp, who is gone off with her, was at the bottom of the plot. The house-keeper, she of whose discre-tion and honesty that fool Bendish vaunted so much, has been the instrument of mischief. Dull idiot that I was, to trust her with a tete à tete[3] to one of her own sex, of whose integrity I was not sure. I suppose she told a pitiful tale, and this officious gossip, thinking to be better rewarded by the lady's friends for a breach

---

1 Hymen, the Roman god of marriage, traditionally wore a saffron-colored robe and carried a torch. To sleer is "to look askance" but the word meant might be "fleer," which means to look at one as if to mock. The 1767 edition says "sleer."

2 Io! In Greek and Latin, an exclamation of triumph.

3 A private conversation.

of trust, than she would be by her master for her fidelity, took the wise resolution to assist and accompany her in her flight.

All we can learn is, that Mrs. Spillman (that is the name of this cursed woman) sent a note late yesterday evening by a peasant in the neighbourhood to the master of the post house at Bagshot, desiring him to send two of his best horses with a guide to Mr. Bendish's at four o'clock the next morning, two ladies being to depart at that hour on an affair of the utmost consequence. One of the horses was to be furnished with a side-saddle, the other, on which the guide rid, was to carry double. The man did as he was directed; and this witch having all the keys of the house in her possession, had nothing to do but to unlock the doors, and fly with my prey. The outer gate was found open this morning, and the housekeeper not appearing at her usual hour, the servants thought she had gone out early on some business. Miss Arnold (the sorceress, I cannot name her with patience) was not missed till nine o'clock, when a maid going to her chamber, to attend her as she had done the morning before, knocked at her door, but receiving no answer after repeated trials, she came to inform her master, for the door was locked. I ran, from a sort of foreboding of my misfortune, like a fury to her chamber, and burst the door open. What a legion of anathemas[1] did I then pour out on Bendish and every soul in this house! But to what purpose was my idle rage? No one could give any account of the lady nor of Mrs. Spillman. All we could gather is the account I have already given you, which I had from the innkeeper himself. Neither his servant nor horses are yet returned; I suppose they are detained to prevent our knowing what road they took. A needless precaution, for at the time we discovered their flight, was there a possibility of overtaking them?

Sophy, this blow has shook me like an earthquake, and will be fatal in its consequences. Falkland must be involved in my ruin, for assuredly *all* will come to light. As for the vengeance of the Bidulphs, I despise it; the *worst* that can result from it is light to the prospect I have before me.—This is the IO I promised you. Oh, my cursed stars!—Pen, get thee hence, I shall have no farther use for thee; Othello's occupation's gone![2]—

---

1 Curses.
2 From Shakespeare's *Othello* (3.3.49). The lines occur at the moment that Othello begins to believe that Desdemona has cheated on him, which leads him to imagine the end of his military career as well as his marriage. Sir Edward, in losing hopes of the Arnold fortune, is financially ruined and therefore his career as a gamester and a libertine is also at an end.

Letter LXIII.
Mrs. Arnold to Mrs. Cecilia B——.
Woodberry, March 19th.

Join with me in prayer, Cecilia, add your petitions to mine, that that patience and resignation to the Supreme Will, which has sustained my youth through a series of afflictions, forsake me not now in this hour of new and bitter calamity. My child!—my poor Dolly————

There—I have wept, and now I'll try to tell you; yet I fear it will shock you too much.—The poor child is—indeed, I believe, my dear, her reason is impaired. She is returned home to me; what a piteous spectacle! yet I bless Heaven that she has escaped the dreadful snare that was laid for her.

This day about noon my daughter Cecilia and I were sitting together in the parlour, when we saw a plain kind of a chaise, such as some of our farmers have, drive up to the door. Two women step'd out of it. We heard Miss Arnold's name pronounced by one of the servants, as if in an exclamation of surprise and joy; the parlour door was suddenly thrown open, and my poor dear girl ran in, followed by a pretty looking young woman, plainly, but neatly dressed. My child flew to me, and clasping her arms round my neck, let herself sink on my bosom; where she remained without speaking a word. The abruptness of her entry, accompanied as she was by a stranger, joined to the idea of her conduct which then appeared to me so faulty, equally shocked and offended me. I had not, however, the immediate power to recollect myself; but quickly recovering from my surprise, I disengaged myself from her embrace, and putting her from me with my hand, I was going to speak, harshly, I believe it would have been; but she prevented me, —Will you not receive me, mama? said she. Whither then must I fly for refuge! Nor you, Cecilia? (looking eagerly at her sister, who, checked by my example, had not ventured to approach her) do *you* cast me off too? Perhaps you do not know me; I think indeed I am sadly altered with the terrors I have undergone for I don't know how long; yet indeed I am your sister. This gentlewoman here can tell you what I have suffered; if it had not been for her, I don't know what they would have done to me—killed me, I suppose; for I never, never would have married Sir Edward Audley.

You may judge, my dear, how I was alarmed at hearing her talk thus. The young woman, who had hitherto stood silent, but who appeared extremely affected, now addressed herself to me, and with great modesty apologized for having so rudely broke in upon me. My design, madam, said she, was to have requested the honour of speaking a few words to you in private, in order to prepare you for seeing Miss Arnold; but the servant who let us in was so surprised and overjoyed at the sight of his young lady, that without giving me time to speak, his impatience to introduce her made him abruptly throw open the parlour door, and Miss Arnold entered before it was in my power to prevent her. Indeed, madam, she has been cruelly used; yet I bless God for having been the means of delivering her from the vilest of men.

My poor girl stood motionless, with her eyes fixed on me whilst this young person spoke; Cecilia melted into tears; for my part, I was so overwhelmed with dreadful apprehensions from what I had just heard, that without daring to demand an explanation, I could only express the terror of my mind by broken exclamations. The stranger easily comprehended which way my fears pointed.—Do not terrify yourself, good madam, said she; Miss Arnold received no other injury than that of being detained against her will, and brutally urged to marry a wicked man whom she hates. Had she not escaped his hands, I know not indeed whether her ruin would not have been by this time effected.

This declaration having calmed my thoughts a little, I turned towards my unhappy child; she was now locked in her sister's arms. Cecilia's face was wet with tears; she tenderly embraced Dolly, who, without seeming much affected with her caresses, asked her why she wept? Are you not happy, my sister? said she; has your lover forsaken you? No, replied Cecilia, sobbing, (who then perceived that the poor creature's thoughts were wandering) no, my dear, so far the contrary, that the day is appointed for uniting us for ever. We all thought you had been married to Sir Edward Audley, which made us give up the hope of having you present at our nuptials.—Fy, fy! how could you think so? said Dolly; I never loved Sir Edward, *He* never had my promise. How came you then to put yourself into his hands, my love? said I. Oh, mama, do not ask me, she replied, my recollection does not carry me so far back; but I believe that lady (pointing to the stranger) can tell you. The young woman shook her head; I'll tell you all I know of the matter, madam, said she, in a low voice, if you will allow me the permission of speaking to you alone. Lead your sister up to your own chamber, my dear, said I to Cecilia, and try to make her take a little rest; she seems fatigued, and to stand in great need of repose. She does indeed, madam, replied the young person, for she has scarce closed her eyes these three nights. My poor child, what have been thy sufferings! Her sister took her by the hand, Come, my love, will you come up stairs with me? Whither would you carry me? cried she, drawing back her hand; ah, Cecilia, will *you* betray me too? You would send me back to that vile Sir Audley; but you need not, I will not disturb your happiness, assure yourself I will not say a word to grieve you. I could not bear to listen to her: Take her from me, said I to Cecilia, it kills me to hear her talk thus. Go, my dearest, endeavour to get a little sleep; I will come to you in half an hour. You will not then turn me out of your house, mama? By no means, my beloved, I am not angry with you, I want you but to retire to your sister's or your own apartment to lie down for a little while. Is not there one Orlando, somewhere hereabouts? looking at her sister with a melancholy smile. Yes, yes, and you shall see him presently.—Nay, I do not want to see him, I am only glad to hear that he is alive.—And poor Mr. Price, is the good man in being yet, for he was very old the last time I saw him? Cecilia could not answer her; she again took her by the hand, and Dolly suffered her to lead her out of the room.

I gave a loose to my tears the moment she was gone; the young woman wept with me: Oh, madam, what a mournful sight to see so fine a young creature disordered in her mind! I have been apprehensive of some such thing these two days; but was not certain of it till now: what pity! but I hope in God she will come to herself, now she has got back to her friends.

After having dried my eyes, I desired her to relate to me what she knew with regard to my daughter.

She then told me that she herself was house-keeper to a Mr. Bendish, who has a house on Bagshot-heath; that she had been originally hired as a servant to his mother; a very worthy woman, who having died within this month, the son, on coming to the possession of her jointure, of which this seat is a part; had retained her in the same capacity in which he had found her; but perceiving he was a young man of very loose morals, she had determined to quit him.—I was obliged to listen to these and a few other unnecessary preliminaries relative to herself, before she came to that part of her story which concerned my daughter. I am entirely ignorant, madam, said she, by what means Miss Arnold first came into Sir Edward Audley's hands. She only told me it was by a strange unfortunate accident; all I know is, that four days ago she arrived at my master's house in the evening. She was alone, in Sir Edward's chariot, which broke (and as I have since learned, by a contrivance of his) just before our door.

Sir Edward himself followed her on horseback. The young lady was quite ignorant of his design; but Mr. Bendish, I am sure, expected them, for he had ordered two bed-chambers to be got ready, and a very handsome supper prepared. I knew not who the expected guests were till after their arrival, when I heard amongst the servants that the gentleman was Sir Edward Audley; but they knew not the lady. I was no sooner told this, continued she, than I was perfectly convinced there was some base design going on, for I was not a stranger to Sir Edward's principles. The poor creature stopped and wiped her eyes, into which the tears sprung fast. Are you then acquainted with Sir Edward, madam? said I. Yes, to my great sorrow, madam, she replied. I will tell you my unhappy story another time. I would not then ask her any questions, and she proceeded. It was my master's custom to call me into the parlour sometimes to make tea for his company, when any of them chose to drink it; but as I was resolved Sir Edward should not see me, I pretended to be sick that night, and shut myself up in my own room to avoid appearing.

The next morning my master called me aside, and ordered me to go into the young lady's room; She is a perverse silly girl, said he, that Sir Edward Audley has run away with, and is determined to make her his wife. If she consents quietly, well and good; if not, (swearing a vile oath) she may chance to repent her obstinacy. I know, added he, you women understand best how to deal with each other; and as I think you are a discreet sensible girl, I would have you represent to her the risque she runs of *more* than reputation, if she refuses to accept of him for a husband. He added to this many other things, and some promises in Sir Edward's name, to engage me in their unworthy design; and I engaged to do as I was directed. I own, madam, pursued she, that though pity would have induced me to assist one of my own sex, I had still a nearer reason for wishing to deliver the young lady out of her tyrant's hands.

I went immediately to Miss Arnold's chamber; she unlocked the door on my telling her I was the house-keeper, who came to offer her my service. I cannot express to you, madam, the compassion I felt on seeing so young and handsome a lady fallen in to the hands of such a profligate. I asked her whether I could be of any assistance to her in dressing? Alas! said she, I have nothing wherewith to dress myself; I have no cloaths but what you see on me; I am a poor unfortunately creature that have been trepanned hither I know not how. I replied, (by way of founding her disposition) I understood, madam, that Sir Edward Audley was so happy as to have your affections, and that you mean to make him your husband. They deceived you, said she eagerly; he never had my affections, nor whilst I have breath (clasping together her hands) will I ever be his wife. But, madam, you are in his power; how can you resist, if he should make use of that power to compel you? He cannot compel me to *speak*, answered she; nor can I resist if he and the horrid master of the house are determined on my death, for that will be the consequence of violence; but remember I tell you, I am a young person of fortune and condition, and some people may revenge my death, though they have forsaken me whilst living.

I saw by this, proceeded the young woman, that the poor lady had been cruelly betrayed, and I wanted to know no more, to resolve on delivering her from her persecutor. I took, however, the liberty of asking her her name, if she had no particular reason for keeping it secret. She informed me of it very readily, with some other circumstances relative to her family. Take comfort, madam, said I; I promise to deliver you safe into your mama's hands before two days are at an end. She looked at me as if doubtful of my sincerity. I do not wonder, madam, added I, that you should mistrust the honesty of every one in this house; you will find, nevertheless, that I will keep my word with you. As the keys of the outer doors are committed to my trust every night, I can with the greatest ease set you at liberty; it will not be difficult to provide horses, if you can venture to ride; and what is more, I will accompany you myself, and see you safe home.

You look, said she, like an honest young person, yet you *may* deceive me; but it would be a double crime in *you* to join with *men* against a poor unhappy creature of your own sex. I assured her she might depend on the truth of what I said. God bless you, said she, my good young woman. Your virtue shall not be unrewarded *here*, no more than it will be hereafter. She even embraced me, and seemed in an extacy of joy. To tell you the truth, said she, I had resolved to try if I could prevail on the chamber-maid, who attended me last night, to let me steal out to-night, when all the family were in bed. I intended to have offered her all the money I have in my pocket, and this ring in to the bargain (to a handsome diamond she had on her finger). I was afraid to make the proposal to you; your appearance, and the station you hold here, made me think you were not to be corrupted; but I imagined an ordinary body might be tempted by such a bribe; and once I got out, I would have ran till I came to the first house that would have given me shelter. I told the lady I was very glad she had no occasion to make the experiment, for besides the impossibility of any of the servants having it in their power to let her out of the house at night, she would have hazarded a discovery of her design, in having made the proposal of escaping. I then counseled her to behave less scornfully to Sir Edward, lest it should provoke him to take any measures that might frustrate our attempt. I cannot shew him any kindness, said she, but I will endeavour not to exasperate him. Perceiving a bundle lying on her table, I opened it, and found it full of fine linen of all sorts; the chamber-maid had before told me, she had received such a parcel out of the chariot which had brought the lady. I again asked Miss Arnold, would she not chuse to dress? I know not, said she, to whom these things belong, yet I should like to change my linen, and since they are here will put them on. I assisted her; she talked to me all the while, and seemed in extraordinary spirits; yet I thought now and then she spoke a little out of the way; but I was at that time far from suspecting that her head was disordered. I advised her not to let her joy appear, for fear it should give suspicions; she promised me she would not, and having informed her that at four o'clock the next morning, I should be in readiness to give her her liberty and attend her flight, I left her; taking care for the rest of the day, (by feigning still not to be well) to prevent my master from calling me on any pretence into the parlour.

It was lucky, said I, interrupting her in this place, that Mr. Bendish did not name you in Sir Edward's presence; people usually call their house-keepers by their sur-names and Sir Edward Audley might probably have been alarmed at hearing your's. I had for a certain reason, madam, said she, changed my name, when I first hired with old Mrs. Bendish; I called myself Mrs. Spillman, but my maiden name is Williams. You are then married? said I. Her having said her *maiden* name, suggested this question to me. The poor thing blushed exceedingly, and answered in a faltering kind of manner, Yes, madam; but it would have been happy for me if I never had. Again I perceived a tear start into her eye; but wiping it off, she proceeded: I know not what passed between Miss Arnold and the gentlemen for the remainder of the day, I was only told, that she excused herself from dining with them, but that in the evening she went down to the parlour for half an hour, then retired again to her chamber, where she was suffered to remain undisturbed for the rest of the night.

I took care in the interim to be provided with horses against the appointed hour; and when all the family were in bed, I stole softly to Miss Arnold's chamber. I found her up and dressed. She had even her hood and gloves on. She ran to me as soon as I entered, Are we ready to go, my good friend? said she. I told her it was but little more than midnight; and that as my master often sat up much later, I had not dared to order the horses so soon. I could have wished, madam, said I, that you had continued in bed, that you might have got a little rest, in order the better to enable you to undertake your journey. She told me she had not been in bed at all, having dismissed the maid who came to wait on her, and made her leave a candle burning in her chamber. I had no inclination to sleep, said she, though I do not remember that I closed my eyes last night.

Her impatience was extreme till the hour of our departure arrived; and I no sooner told her that the horses were at the gate (whither she had sent me at least twenty times before) than clinging to my arm she rather flew than walked down stairs. We immediately mounted; Miss Arnold chusing to ride behind the man, I took the single horse, and cold and dark as it was, set off joyfully on our journey; but the poor lady could not divest herself of her fears; she was every minute apprehensive of being pursued; and judging Sir Edward Audley would follow her on the track to Woodberry, she prevailed on our guide, by the promise of a handsome reward, to strike out of the high road, and by bye ways make out his journey to Oxford. I could not persuade her out of this whim. The fellow undertook it; but not being well enough acquainted with the country, he missed his way, so that after having rid thirty miles without having it in our power to change horses, we found ourselves still at the same distance from our journey's end. Miss Arnold was by this time so extremely fatigued that she was unable to proceed; her eagerness to get home was not however abated, and it was with the utmost difficulty that I persuaded her to stay at the inn where we then were till this morning, when the people undertook to procure for us a chaise, and I promised to set out with her as early as she pleased. She continued exceedingly pensive and silent all day; and as I lay in the same room with her, I am sure she scarcely slept the whole night. She rose, however, at five o'clock this morning; and notwithstanding the earnestness she expressed to pursue her journey, she seemed seized with a deep melancholy, and hardly spoke during the whole time we travelled.

I thanked Mrs. Spillman as she deserved for the timely succours she had afforded my dear unhappy child. It should seem to me, that this is some poor young person whom that most abandoned of men Sir Edward Audley has seduced; and probably some little jealousy, or even remains of love for her betrayer, may have mixed themselves with the more charitable motives of her conduct. Be that as it will, my obligations to her are not the less. Gracious God, what would have been my state if my daughter had fallen a victim to the villain's profligacy! But my mind is easy as to that particular, for she told Mrs. Spillman, that Sir Edward Audley had never in his whole behaviour towards her exceeded the bounds of respect. The wretch's views seem rather to have been on her fortune than her person; for I cannot suffer myself to believe that either virtue or honour had any share in restraining his licentiousness. By what wicked contrivance he first got her into his power, is the inexplicable part of the story, for the poor child seems not now in a condition to inform us. It appears from all I have learnt, that her first unfortunate step was a voluntary one; yet who knows what base arts might have been made use of to ensnare her into it? It is plain, she had no design of putting herself into this man's hands; but I must be content to remain in the dark till she is herself able and willing to clear up the mystery to me. I dare believe we shall find it a scene of treachery; at present I will not, by urging her to an explanation, exasperate the fatal malady which has laid hold of her, and which this enquiry when I first made it seemed to aggravate.

I am not of a suspicious nature; yet some things which my brother threw out when he was here with regard to lady Audley, joined to this event, has a little shook the good opinion I had of her. How shocked should I be to find that either she or her daughter had any share in this wicked scheme! Yet 'tis not *impossible*; for I know Dolly was very fond of Miss Audley.

My daughter Cecilia came in to us again in about an hour. She said she had persuaded her sister to lie down, and she was in hopes she had left her in a slumber; for that she had sat the whole time by her bed-side, and had not heard her either speak or stir. Sleep, perhaps, may contribute to settle her poor disturbed mind. God grant it! yet I dare not indulge myself in hope; I who now feel the bitterness of being plunged again into sorrow, at a time when I thought all the storms of my life were past, must not suffer my heart to be seduced from its present state of mournful submission, by the flattery of my own imagination. I have left Cecilia to entertain our new guest, who, though I know her not, has rendered us services too important not to merit every mark of friendship and distinction which 'tis in our power to bestow on her. She would fain have taken her leave of us; but I begged of her, if no particular business called her away, to make my house her own, till her affairs were in a more settled way, than it was probable from the nature of her situation they could be in at present. She thanked me with strong expressions of gratitude; said she had no other prospect but that of going to service again; and if I would allow her to remain in my house till she should find a place to suit her, she should think herself very happy.

You know, my dear, I am apt to be prepossessed at first sight; I have taken a liking to this young person, and if I find no material objection to her character, should like to take her to supply the place of Nelson, who is growing so indolent and unwieldy, that she can but ill discharge the duties of her employment. I do not mean to part with the poor woman, but I think 'tis time to let her lie by. See how composedly, my Cecilia, I talk of common matters, whilst I have that at my heart which weights me down to the ground.

Mr. Falkland went on a visit this morning to a particular friend of his, in order to take his leave, as he sets out the latter end of next week for Germany. Friday is the day appointed for his marriage, as I told you in my last, and he would not after that be willing to spare so much time from his Cecilia; for the gentleman whom he is gone to see, lives twelve miles off, so that we do not expect him home till to-morrow.

What a dreadful shock will it be to him, to find his poor sister in so deplorable a state! Mr. Price thinks it would be most prudent to conceal, if possible, her melancholy situation from him, lest he should embroil himself with that wretched man Sir Edward Audley. I am entirely of his mind; for who knows what fatal consequences might follow from Falkland's warmth, if he should resent as it deserves, and as he certainly would, this unhappy affair. Yet it will be difficult to keep from his knowlege that Miss Arnold is returned. If my poor girl were in a condition to be reasoned with on the occasion, I am sure she would readily agree to conceal herself in the house till after his departure. The family will then be at liberty to take such measures as may be expedient. The laws, I think, on those occasions are the properest instruments of chastisement; for I approve not of individuals taking the rod of vengeance into their own proper hands.

Be so good as to communicate this letter to my brother, and to lady Sarah. I hope Sir George's sentiments on this subject will agree with those of Mr. Price and mine. Tell him I would have written to him, but that I have scarcely strength or spirits to finish this my long letter to you.

I know, my Cecilia, you will be anxious to learn every circumstance which passes at this juncture, under the melancholy roof of your friend; I shall therefore inform you of them as they occur, and as I find myself able to write. I conclude as I began; join your prayers with mine, my dear, that it may please Heaven to restore peace to your disconsolate, &c.

Letter LXIV.
Mrs. Arnold to Mrs. Cecilia B—.
Woodberry, March 20th.

I told you in my letter of yesterday that Mr. Price and I were of opinion that it would be most advisable to conceal from Mr. Falkland the knowledge of my poor daughter's return. Upon consulting Cecilia on the occasion, we found her exactly of our mind; it is natural to suppose her tenderness for the man whom she already looks upon as her husband, would alarm her fears; yet she is so deeply affected with her sister's situation, that she expressed the greatest repugnance at the thoughts of giving him her hand at so unhappy a juncture, and urged Mr. Price and me to endeavour to prevail on Mr. Falkland to postpone his marriage till after his return to England. We both entered into her sentiments so far as to agree that this was not a house for Hymen to revel in; and that it would be impossible, with so mournful an object in our thoughts, for any of us to enjoy the satisfaction which would otherwise result from her nuptials; yet how to account for the deferring them was the difficulty. What pretence could we make to Falkland for so sudden, so seemingly unreasonable a change in our determinations? He left us with the certain assurance of seeing his wishes crowned in three days. What a cruel disappointment must it then be to him to find all his hopes overturned; and how could we answer to him such a flagrant breach of promise? In short, after long canvassing the subject, we found it impossible to acquit ourselves to Mr. Falkland, without letting him into the true motives of our conduct; and as that was the thing of all others we most wished to avoid, we were obliged to let matters rest as they were, so that to-morrow remains the day fixed for the wedding.

After having dispatched my letter to you yesterday, I returned to the parlour, where I had left Cecilia and Mrs. Spillman. I found Mr. Price with my daughter; but the good young woman has begged leave to be admitted to Miss Arnold's room, that she might watch by her bed-side till she awoke for the poor dear girl was happily then in a profound sleep. And it was in this interval that we had the conversation that I have related to you.

The tranquil slumber that the sweet child had now enjoyed for more than two hours, began to flatter me with some hope that we might find her in a more settled state of mind; and in that case we resolved to let her into our design with regard to concealing her adventure from Falkland, on which account she would herself see the necessity of our hiding her from his sight. But if, on the contrary, we found that her thoughts continued in the same unhappy frame, we determined to keep her in her chamber, under pretence that her uncle Bidulph was come down to look for her; for Mrs. Spillman had told me that Miss Arnold had expressed great terrors (she knew not why) at the thoughts of seeing him, and said she was flying to me in order to avoid him when she was ensnared to Mr. Bendish's house. We agreed also to say that Mr. Falkland was already departed for the army; and we resolved that Cecilia, Mr. Price, Mrs. Spillman, and myself, should sit with her alternately till such time as we should all be at liberty to change our proceedings.

Having thus, in the best manner we could, settled our measures, and given the necessary orders to the servants, I desired Mrs. Spillman might be called down to dine with us. She sent me word that Miss Arnold was just awakened, and had asked for a dish of chocolate; but that if I would allow her to dine in the young lady's room, she might persuade her to take something more substantial, as she had eaten very little for the three last days. I ordered something to be immediately carried up stairs, and flew myself to the poor creature's chamber. I found her awake, but still lying on her bed. She stretched out her hand as soon as she saw me. I gave her mine. She drew it to her lips, kissed it several times—but did not speak. How did you find yourself, my dear? Not quite so ill as I was, madam, yet I feel myself very feeble. No wonder, my child, you have neither slept nor eat for some days past. I pressed her to take something of what had been brought up to Mrs. Spillman. She tasted a little bit; but it seemed in mere complaisance to me, for she said she had no appetite.

She enquired for her sister. She is below stairs, said I; she and Mr. Price are at dinner together. She begged I would go to them; said she was very sorry I had disturbed myself to come to her; and that Mrs. Spillman would be so kind as to sit with her till we had done dinner, when she should be glad to join us in the parlour. I was delighted to hear her talk so composedly. I will go down to them, my dear, said I; and by-and-by we will all attend you in your chamber: for your spirits seem fatigued, and I would not have you quit it to-day. As you please for that, madam; but am I not to see Mr. Falkland? He is not present, my love—Ah, mama! I am afraid all is not right—Why did poor Cecilia weep to-day? I believe Falkland has left her. He has not, indeed, Dolly; if your sister wept it was only at the thoughts of your sufferings— The dear girl! said she, how kind that is of her! but I know she loves me. We will not then, mama, talk of my sufferings, since it gives her so much uneasiness; pray let them not be mentioned to her or Mr. Falkland; I would not for the world make them unhappy. How pleased was I to hear my poor child express herself thus! It was, as you see, half way meeting our intentions, and spared me the pain of deceiving her. You judge very rightly, my dear, said I; it would afflict Mr. Falkland beyond measure, if he were to know how you have been distressed; and perhaps engage him in a quarrel. Ah, mama, that would be terrible! for God's sake, let him not know it.—Poor Orlando! I would not hurt a hair of his head.—Then wringing my hand tenderly, Pray leave me, mama; you have not dined yet; you give yourself too much trouble about me. I dropped a tear of pity, mingled with satisfaction, at finding her, as I thought, though not recovered, yet much more calm in her mind, and, to all appearance, much more reasonable. I left her, and went down stairs; where I rejoiced the affectionate hearts of Mr. Price and my Cecilia with the account I gave them of her.

After dinner we all went up again to her chamber. She was still lying on her bed; but on Mr. Price's entering, whom she had not yet seen, she sprung up to receive him. With what tenderness did the good man accost her! and how affectionately did she return his caresses! Mrs. Spillman whispered me, that she had not spoke a word from the time I left her, but seemed to be buried in sadness. I told Mr. Price softly that we must endeavour to divert her, without mentioning any subject which could make her recur to her own melancholy thoughts.

I believe, my dear, you may remember to have heard me say that this kind old man has a peculiar knack at introducing a conversation. Few people have the art to enter suddenly into any regular series of discourse without a forced and abrupt, or, at best, an aukward appearance; yet he is so extremely happy in his manner, that he can at once engage and interest you in his subject, without your perceiving how you had been led into it. He exercised this talent very successfully on the present occasion, and soon caught Dolly's attention, who seemed to listen to him with pleasure. As for Cecilia, she was all ear. I took this opportunity of beckoning Mrs. Spillman out of the room, in order to have a little conversation with her. As it was necessary to conceal *her* from Mr. Falkland's sight, as well as my daughter, lest the appearance of a stranger should put him on making any enquiries, I thought it was proper to apprize her of our design. After having done this, I told her I hoped she would excuse my making a prisoner of her in Miss Arnold's chamber while Mr. Falkland was in the house. She said nothing could give her greater pleasure than the being allowed to attend on the young lady. I observed she coloured at the first mention of Mr. Falkland's name, and seemed very much disconcerted. After I had communicated to her what I had to say with regard to him, I asked her if she knew him? She answered, I believe I have seen him, madam; at least I remember to have seen a gentleman of that name with Sir Edward Audley, though I did not then know who he was. 'Tis very likely, replied I; Sir Edward and he were intimately acquainted. Ah, madam, had Mr. Falkland known Sir Edward's character, said she, I think he would have been cautious in forming any connection with him.

I perceived that her heart was open, and that she seemed inclined to communicate her own story, which she had promised to relate to me. I expressed some curiosity to know it, and she told me what follows.

[Mrs. Arnold here briefly gives the substance of this young woman's unhappy story, with which the reader is already acquainted in Mr. Main's letters to his sister Askham. She then proceeds:]

I have given you the purport of this unfortunate girl's narrative, though in much fewer words than she employed to relate it. Why, what an accomplished villain is this Sir Edward Audley! I do not doubt the truth of what this poor young creature has told me. The air of candor and simplicity with which she spoke, and the tears she shed during her recital, convince me of her veracity. She appealed to Mr. Main (whose integrity we both know) for the truth of many particulars; and added, she was sure he was thoroughly satisfied of her innocence, and the wrongs she had suffered. What an escape has my poor child had from this execrable man! and how naturally can Mrs. Spillman's conduct be now accounted for! She said, she had no hopes of Sir Edward's ever acknowledging her; yet she owned she could not bear the thoughts of his marrying another. The account she gave me of herself, has increased my compassion and esteem for her; yet I cannot think of retaining *lady Audley* (for such she certainly is) as a servant in my house. I must find out a more suitable way of shewing her my gratitude. I asked her, if she thought Mr. Falkland had been any way privy to the treachery which had been practiced against her? She assured me, that she did not believe he was; adding, that she supposed Mr. Falkland considered her in no other light than that of a woman kept by Sir Edward Audley. I was very glad to hear her make this declaration, as it would have given me a dreadful impression of Falkland, could I have thought him capable of being an accomplice in so black an affair. I am not, however, pleased to find that he was even so far in his wicked companion's confidence as to be acquainted with any of his loose secrets. I bless God that he has not been corrupted by the contagion of bad example, against which it is so impossible to guard a young man, once he launches out into the world. Orlando has been carefully brought up; and I hope a natural good disposition, co-operating with a virtuous education, will always prove an antidote against the poison of vice. I have now double cause to pray for his continuance in the paths of uprightness he has hitherto trodden.

On my return to my daughter's chamber, I found my two children still together. Mr. Price had just retired to take, as is his custom, his evening's nap. Dolly was helping Cecilia to sprig some fine muslin[1] that she is now working for an apron. On my entering the room, she ran to me, and whispered me in the ear, I have not said a word of the matter since, mama, said she, for fear of making poor Cecilia cry; I cannot bear to see her tears. I replied, You did well, my dear; and I have been telling Mrs. Spillman the precautions we intend to use to keep the whole affair from Mr. Falkland's knowledge. He leaves us next week, in order to set out for his regiment; and if, for the few days that he remains here, you will consent to keep yourself concealed in your chamber, he need not know of your being in the house. Oh, with all my heart, madam, said she, it will be better so; the sight of me might affect him too much.—Poor Falkland! I would not shock him upon any account. But when do you expect him here? for I have a notion he will steal away to the army without seeing any of you. By no means, my dear, we expect him home to-morrow;

---

1   To sprig is to fasten, for instance to a frame; muslin is a light cotton fabric.

for Friday is the day fixed for his marriage with your sister. Indeed! starting, and looking at Cecilia: then turning to me, and speaking very low, Do not believe it, mama, said she: I am certain he does not mean to marry her till he returns again to England; for by that time the whole affair will be forgotten.

I saw my poor child's imagination, filled with the idea of her own sufferings, was straying wide from the purpose of our discourse, and at the same time confounding together circumstances, which were in no-wise connected. I was too much affected to be able to make her any answer; and she added, still speaking so low as that her sister should not hear her, Oh, you do not know, mama, what dissemblers men are! As near as you have brought the wedding-day, you will see Falkland will give you the slip: and she smiled a little; then added, But I am sure he will have my sister when he comes back, because he loves her as he does his life, and there will be nothing then to hinder him.—Poor dear creature! the villainy of that vile Sir Edward has made her distrustful of his whole sex, and possesses her with a belief that Falkland will deceive her sister.

We were interrupted just here by the arrival of a neighbouring lady and her daughter, who came to pass the evening with us. Cecilia and I were obliged to go down to receive them, and we left Mrs. Spillman with Dolly.

The ladies stayed so late, that I saw my poor daughter but for a few minutes the rest of the evening. Mrs. Spillman persuaded her to go to bed early, as she had had so little sleep for some preceding nights. We have put a little tent-bed into her chamber, in which this good young body lies. We all breakfasted in her room this morning. She seems composed, but overwhelmed with sadness; and her charming face is so altered! it almost breaks my heart to look at her. Cecilia can scarce refrain from tears, even in her presence.—

They tell me Mr. Falkland is this minute returned. I will just see him, and then finish my letter. I am glad of a little relaxation; for I am quite tired with writing.—

I found him with his Cecilia. What joy at meeting again! If a single day's absence has appeared so grievous, how much are they to be pitied who are so soon to feel a separation, which may last many, many tedious months! Nay, heaven knows—but I will not forebode: 'tis nothing but my own gloomy thoughts which suggest to me apprehensions, I hope, without foundation; for does Falkland run any greater risque than hundreds of other gallant men who accompany him?

I shall be able to dedicate but little of my time to my poor girl to-day. Falkland's presence will be a restraint on Cecilia and me; and we can only see her by starts.

I intended here to have closed my letter; but upon second thoughts, I will leave it open till to-morrow, when I shall have the important article of my daughter's marriage to conclude with. It is not the thing of my choice; yet I hope my children will be happy. They are both worthy; and for the goods of fortune, they will have more than sufficient.

I endeavour to be cheerful, that Falkland may not have any room to imagine that I repent of having given a consent, which was indeed wrung from me; yet my spirits are sadly depressed; and, God knows, ill disposed to celebrate a festivity so joyous as that of matrimony *ought* to be.

We are to have no one present at the ceremony but Mrs. Askham, Nelson, and the butler: for poor Frederick Hildy would be miserable, if he were not allowed to see his young master, as he has always called Mr. Falkland, married to *Madam* Cecilia; for that is the title which he gives to both my daughters. These two, therefore, have begged to be admitted into the chamber, as Mr. Price, you know, is to perform the office in my house. Adieu then, my dear, till to-morrow.—

Friday evening, March 22nd.

I am writing to you on my knees, Cecilia; for that posture best becomes one on whom the Almighty pours out his wrath like a deluge! Yet I will not ask of Providence why, in the evening of an unhappy life, not, I think, stained with any peculiar guilt, I am thus overwhelmed with such tempestuous sorrows! I thought the storm was past; but it redoubles on my head, and I *must* sink under it.— Yet be comforted, my dear, there is *another* world. There, there do I look for recompence for my almost unprecedented sufferings here.

You will tremble when I tell you, Cecilia, that Falkland—Oh, God! that boy, whom I have so tenderly educated, and so dearly loved, that very Falkland is the viper who now stings me to death! You cannot credit it, I am sure; but I'll try to recal my distracted thoughts, so as to enable me to relate to you what this dreadful day has unravelled.

Dolly had been informed yesterday that Mr. Falkland was returned. She expressed not any desire to see him; but seemed to have her thoughts extremely agitated the whole day. Mrs. Spillman asked her the cause of it, (for Cecilia and I were but little with her). Her replies were broken and imperfect; yet Mrs. Spillman imagined they implied a suspicion that Falkland would not marry her sister: for she said she pitied poor Cecilia—yet she must bear her disappointment for a while—for after the death of a certain person, there would be nothing to hinder her nuptials. We attributed this merely to the disorder of her poor head; little imagining that she had a fatal reason for talking thus, which she kept concealed in her heart.

Cecilia thought it would make her easy, if she were convinced the marriage was really going to be solemnized. I was of the same opinion: in consequence of which, this morning, when Cecilia was dressed in her wedding-cloaths, I led her into her sister's chamber. You look very pretty, my dear, said Dolly; white becomes you extremely. Are you going abroad? (observing her more ornamented than usual.) You see your sister in her bridal habit, said I: take her by the hand, my love; for she is just now going to give it away for ever to Mr. Falkland. Ah, 'tis impossible, mama! said she. I am sure he does not mean it; though perhaps you have imposed on him, and he thinks that somebody is already in their grave. We knew not what to conjecture from her incoherent words; yet fancied by that *somebody* she meant Sir Edward Audley, against whom Falkland, believing him dead, no longer entertained any thoughts of vengeance. This was the idea which, without having time to reflect, struck me, and, I believe, entered at the same time into Cecilia's mind. Oh, how far were we from guessing the true object at whom the dear unhappy creature pointed! Cecilia embraced her, to hide her own emotion. Compose your thoughts, my dear, said she; all your friends interest themselves equally to make you easy. She knew not what to say to her. I with difficulty restrained my tears, and thought it best to break away before I melted quite, lest my disorder should be observed by Falkland, who was waiting for us in Mr. Price's study. Come, my Cecilia, said I, we are expected below stairs; we will return again to Dolly, after Mr. Price has given you the nuptial blessing. I took her by the hand; My dear (to Dolly) you will congratulate your sister presently by the name of Mrs. Falkland. Dolly made me no reply; but throwing herself into an armchair, seemed for a minute lost in thought: then lifting up her eyes to heaven, Poor wretch, said she, what will become of him!— We referred every thing she said to her own unhappy adventure; the particular circumstances of which being ignorant of, we knew not what turn it would be best to give our replies. Shall I send Mrs. Spillman to you, my dear? said I. She had slipped out of the room just as we entered, after having spoken a few words to

Dolly, which I did not hear. You need not, madam, she replied; she said she would return immediately: she is gone but to put on clean linen. Poor thing! she confines herself sadly to me. I had indeed observed that Mrs. Spillman was in extreme dishabille, being just as she had risen out of bed. I had given her a closet above stairs to dress and keep her things in; for she had brought some cloaths with her. I stepped up to her directly, and found her combing her hair. Let me beg of you, my good friend, said I, to hasten down to Miss Arnold. The poor child must not be left alone: her own reflections are but mournful companions. I did not think, madam, said she, that you would have made her so short a visit, or I should not have quitted the room; but I took the opportunity of your being with her just to slip out for a few minutes, in order to make myself a little decent: for I judged that neither you nor Miss Cecilia could have much time to spend with her to day; but I will get my things on as quick as possible, and attend her. I begged she would; and was returning again to Dolly's chamber, where I had left Cecilia, when I met Mrs. Askham in the lobby. She had just come up stairs. Mr. Falkland is impatient, madam, said she smiling, and has sent me to hasten the bride: and Mr. Price says he will chide her for making them wait so long. I did not dare to venture my own firmness again with the sight of my poor child; and fearful that Falkland himself might take the liberty of coming to seek her, if she staid any longer, I sent Mrs. Askham in to lead out Cecilia, and went downstairs myself: they followed me directly.

We found the good old man in his canonical habit; Falkland, elegantly dressed, standing by his side. The agitations of his mind were strongly painted on his face: I thought then his emotions proceeded from no other cause but what his present situation might naturally inspire. Oh, I knew not that a conscience stained with guilt upbraided him in that moment of approaching happiness.

Nelson and the butler were the only two servants that were admitted. I believe, said Mr. Price, rising and looking at his watch as we entered the room, that we do not wait for any more company; with your good leave, madam, we will not delay the ceremony. I bowed, and all present ranging themselves in the proper order, Mr. Price began the office; when coming to that part of the exhortation which says, *I require and charge you both, as you shall answer it at the dreadful day of judgment when the secrets of all heart shall be disclosed, that if either of you know of any impediment,* &c. which words he pronounced with that energy which accompanies him in all acts of devotion, having, by I know now what chance, cast my eyes at Falkland, I observed he shook from head to foot; his face was pale as death, and I saw he could scarcely support himself on his legs. I thought he was seized with some sudden illness, and in my fright was going to interrupt the ceremony, to ask him how he did, when it was indeed interrupted in a manner that makes my blood still run cold with horror! We heard a little bustle at the chamber door, as if two persons were struggling; it lasted not an instant, for the door was violently burst open, and in rushed my dear unfortunate distracted child, whom Mrs. Spillman in vain had been endeavouring to hold back. Mr. Price was just then making that solemn demand of *Wilt thou have this woman to thy wedded wife?* She gave a piercing shriek, and flying to Falkland, seized his hand, This hand is *mine,* said she: Oh, Falkland, you cannot till my eyes are closed give it to another!—Falkland dropped senseless at her feet.

A general consternation now spread itself through the little assembled congregation; the servants ran to the succour of the unhappy wretch who lay extended on the floor. Dolly still grasping his hand dropped on her knees by him, then seating herself on the floor, she laid his head gently on her lap, bathing his face with her tears. Cecilia stood aghast by their side; and Mr. Price, with grief and amazement in his looks, in silence fixed his eyes on this mournful picture. What were *my* feelings in this dreadful interval? No, Cecilia, they cannot be described; my sensations were strange! they were terrible! and unfelt before! The fatal truth rushed on my imagination at once, and all my poor child's disjointed words occurring to my memory, appeared now but too well explained. She continued weeping over him, while Mrs. Askham and the servants were using vain endeavours to recover him. He is dead, she said, he returns to me no more!—Look, mama, I have killed your poor Orlando!—Indeed I did not mean to do so, God knows I would have given my own life to have preserved his—I thought but to have saved him from a crime.—I perceived that Falkland was now coming to himself—He begins to recover, said I to Mr. Price; perhaps the sight of these injured faces may make him again relapse into a fit; let us retire, and leave him to the care of the servants. Mr. Price, without answering me, took Cecilia by the hand, and led her out of the room. Mrs. Spillman and I raised Dolly almost by force, for she would fain have staid by Falkland, who now opening his eyes, stared wildly about him like one awakened from the dead; but we hurried her out of the room, and almost choaked as she was with sobs, conducted her to that where Mr. Price and Cecilia were together.

We let her give a free course to her tears for some time, in hopes that might lighten her burden of woe under which her mind had labored. I was even pleased to see her weep, it was the first instance she had shewn since her grievous malady had seized her of that tender sensibility which was always her characteristic; and I was in hopes was an indication of returning reason, as in effect she soon after appeared more collected. She had disclosed an important secret, the concealment of which had so long hung upon her heart. She had given vent to her sorrow; and these two circumstances, added to the sudden fright she had received from the apprehension that Falkland was dead, had, if not restored her reason, yet at least called back her recollection.

Having a little composed her by assurances that Falkland was perfectly come to himself, I thought I might venture to question her tenderly on the subject of this amazing event. It seems to me, my dear, said I, that Falkland has deceived you; was he then a lover of yours? Ah, mama, I dare not look at you, (clapping both her hands before her eyes) I have been a rebel—I have been a disobedient wretch, and deserved in my turn to be punished by ingratitude; yet Falkland ought not to have imposed on me. I should not have blamed him for loving Cecilia; I know she is handsomer and more amiable than I am.—Did he make love to you before he addressed your sister? Oh, yes, yes, and gave me his promise, and had mine in return; I have been a sad undutiful creature;—but I am heavily chastised for it.—And did Falkland assign no cause of thus cruelly forsaking you? Ah, that is the hardest thing of all. I thought the shame of it would have killed me. Indeed it *had* like to have disturbed my reason.—What was it, my dear? Why, he said he had always been in love with Cecilia, and that his pretended love to me was but the returns of gratitude—He had found then that *you* loved *him* before he declared himself to you? The dear creature again covered her innocent face to hide her blushes. Ah, mama, 'tis a disgraceful story; do not urge me on that head—yet Falkland should never have known it, if it had not been for Miss Audley. She told it to her brother, and he assured *her* that Falkland loved me. So you see each was informed of the other's mind before we came to any explanations.

I asked her several more questions, and though she was not very precise in her answers, I could easily gather that the two Audleys had been the instruments to encourage and carry on this fatal connection. Will you inform me, my dear, said I, (since we know the most material part of your secret) to what end you went to that house at Brumpton, since it was owing to that unfortunate step that you fell into the hands of Sir Edward Audley? She was silent for a little while, and seemed as if endeavouring to recollect something that had slipped her memory. At length, I do not remember, said she, *all* the circumstances of that affair; but I think I went to that house to meet Mr. Falkland.—He writ to me to come to him there; I have his letter still in my pocket. She immediately produced a letter in Falkland's hand to that effect. We all examined it by turns. I thought Cecilia would have expired at the reading of it. It was plain this miserable wretch had betrayed her into the hands of his horrid associate! Good God, what a scene of iniquity was here disclosed! The whole mystery was now unravelled. I think, proceeded my poor child, that I was very ill whilst I was at Brumpton; but I could get no body to come near me, though Sir Edward Audley told all my friends the melancholy condition I was in. False, false man! you see in every instance how the poor creature was deceived! Lady Sarah, indeed, added she, threatened to send my uncle to me; and it was to avoid his terrible anger that I desired to be sent to my mama; but they catched me in a trap by the way.—Mrs. Spillman can tell you how cruelly I was treated, 'twas a mercy they did not turn my brain amongst them. Make yourself easy, my beloved, said I, you are now out of the reach of all harm.—Do you call me your *beloved*! said she: Oh, mama, I do not deserve so much tenderness. She dropped her head on my shoulder, kissing my neck through my handkerchief. Mrs. Askham entered the room, and whispered Mr. Price, who immediately went out. I asked her softly the occasion of it; she told me that Mr. Falkland had desired to speak with him alone.

Dolly rose up; she approached her sister, and clasping her arms about her neck—Ah, my poor Cecilia, said she, I am afraid I have broken her heart! but pray do not die, my love; *I* am the victim who must fall; and then you may be happy; a promise does not reach beyond the grave.—What an ill-fated wretch I am, to have disturbed the happiness of the two creatures in the world whom I love best!—Say rather, my dear, said Cecilia, that you have been the instrument of providence to prevent the greatest misfortune that could have befallen me; for how miserable should I have been, had I married Falkland! You *could* not, whilst I lived, said Dolly, without making him commit a great sin;[1] but when I am gone, indeed, my sister, you must marry poor Orlando; must she not, mama?

---

1 The exchange of promise between Orlando and Dorothea constitutes a vow legally and ethically between the two that they will marry and is almost as binding as a marriage itself (see Introduction, 30).

It was not a subject to be argued upon; I thought it better to change the discourse: We will talk of this another time, my dear, said I; mean while I think it will be best that Falkland should absent himself from us for a while; I suppose you will neither of you think it prudent to see him before he goes. I do not desire to see him, said Dolly; the sight of me perhaps might make him swoon away again, and I would not willingly distress him. Nor I, said Cecilia. She saw I wanted to get rid of the conversation.

Mrs. Askham took the hint, and requesting of Cecilia to shew her some pretty drawings of which she had lately made a purchase; my daughter asked her to come up to her closet, and they took Dolly with them. I begged of Mrs. Askham, as she went out, to stay and pass the day with us, and to prevent as much as possible the conversation's turning on the recent miserable event.

Poor Mrs. Spillman was almost afraid to see me, lest I should blame her negligence, which had occasioned so much disorder; but I told her the hand of Heaven had directed the whole. She said, that after I had left her, having huddled on her cloaths with all the expedition in her power, she had immediately gone down to Miss Arnold's room, when not finding her there, she ran, in the utmost fright, down stairs, and overtook the unhappy child, just as she had reached the door of the chamber where we were, and from whence all her efforts could not draw her; she had even pretty severely hurt Mrs. Spillman's hand, whilst she was endeavouring to hinder her from turning the bolt of the lock.

I was impatient to see Mr. Price, to know what had passed between him and his wretched pupil. He returned into the parlour to me in about an hour; his venerable countenance clouded with shame and disappointment.

He told me that Falkland, on his entering the room, appeared to him like a despairing wretch, surrounded with the horror of his own guilt. Do not think, sir, said he, that I have sent for you, to enter into a justification of myself; so far from it, I acknowledge myself the criminal, which I suppose you now know me to be. I shall reserve to another time the full explanation of my whole crime; I would only for the present entreat the favour of you to answer me a few questions.

He then asked when, and by what means, Miss Arnold had returned home? Mr. Price informed him minutely, and failed not to enlarge in a manner the most affecting on the poor creature's frenzy. He said, Falkland at this recital started off his chair, and, in an agony of passion, cursed himself as the author of such dreadful evils as he had brought upon my house. His tutor then repeated to him word for word the conversation I had had with Dolly after we had left him just recovered from his swoon. He listened to him in a gloomy silence, till Mr. Price relating to him that passage wherein Dolly had said, that she was *assured by Sir Edward Audley that Falkland loved her*; he cried out, The villain! the arch-fiend! 'twas he then was the builder of this vast fabric of iniquity, whose weight now crushes all beneath it! Mr. Price then told him of the letter which Miss Arnold had shewn us, and by which she was betrayed into that viper's hands. 'Tis true, said Falkland, 'tis all true; I have not an extenuation to offer which a hair would not outweigh in the balance. Mr. Price hinted, that as he thought his presence must be very distressing in house wherein he had caused so much affliction, he would advise him to retired to his college, till the time of his departure arrived.

I mean, said Falkland, to quit this house immediately; I would not present such a monster even to the eyes of the menial servants: but what does Cecilia say to this event? She bears it, said Mr. Price, with a firmness that does honour to her sex. That's some consolation, answered Falkland:—And Mrs. Arnold? He faltered in pronouncing my name. Mrs. Arnold, answered his preceptor, has been long inured to sorrows; yet this seems to press hard on her. Falkland burst into tears, and breaking abruptly from Mr. Price, ran out of the room; he heard him call his man in the hall, to whom he gave orders to saddle his horses; then stepping to his own chamber, he changed his cloaths, and in a few minutes after, attended by his servant, rode away from the house without attempting to see or speak to any one in the family. To what place the most unfortunate ill-fated wretch will retire to hide his shame, Heaven knows!

What a wedding-day has this been for poor Cecilia! My dear, the strength of mind of that young creature amazes me, and exceedingly lowers the opinion I had of my own constancy and resolution. For is not this a trial, equal, if not superior to any of those with which my youth was visited? yet with what a becoming, what a charming fortitude does she support it! She complains not of her own fate; but wholly attaching herself to the care of her poor sister, she seems even more solicitous than any of us to calm and divert her troubled mind.

Dolly appears rather more composed than she had been; yet whenever she recurs (as she often does in spite of our efforts to prevent it) to the fatal subject of all our griefs, she shews too plainly that her reason is far from having re-assumed its seat. What a painful constraint have I put upon myself since morning! I have not shed a tear; yet I think there is sufficient cause for tears; but the burden is too great to be relieved by such slight succours; and nature refuses to offer a resource so trivial and inadequate to the evil.

Adieu, my friend.

C.S.A.

Letter LXV.
Mr. Falkland to Sir Edward Audley.
Friday at midnight.

I have a long account to settle with you, Sir Edward, and there is but one way of closing it. Let me know when and where you will meet me.

O.F.

Letter LXVI.
Sir Edward Audley to Mr. Falkland.
Bagshot, March 23rd.

I am equally disposed at present to kill or be killed. You will find me at my friend Bendish's house, and if you call here to-morrow any time between seven and nine in the morning, we will take a turn on the heath together.

E.A.

Letter LXVII.
Mr. Bendish to Miss Audley.
Bagshot, March 24th.

Madam,
    I think myself very unfortunate in being obliged to communicate to you a piece of very afflicting news; but as it is impossible it could be kept long a secret from you, I thought it my duty to advise you of it the first. Your poor brother and my worthy friend, Sir Edward, was killed this morning in a duel, which he fought with Mr. Falkland, a gentleman whom I suppose you know. I was ignorant of the whole affair till it was too late to prevent it.

Mr. Falkland came to my house about eight o'clock this morning; I was in bed, and knew not of his arrival. He had half an hour's conversation in private with your brother; after which they both went into the garden together, and from thence by a back door into a retired part of the heath. Sir Edward's man, who it seems had some suspicion of the business, on seeing them go out, ran to my chamber, and alarming me with the danger, begged I would follow them, as he said he durst not.

I did so immediately, having only thrown on my night-gown and slippers. Just as I came within sight of them, Sir Edward discharged his pistol and wounded Mr. Falkland in the arm; but before I could reach them, Falkland fired his, and I saw Sir Edward drop. I ran up to him, and found the ball had passed through his throat close by the windpipe. He was not dead; but said, Bendish, you have just overtaken me; Falkland has killed me fairly, you may tell my friends so; and let my mother and sister know that I am married. If any female should come to claim my name after my death, let her take it; for it is all I have to leave her. He seemed to speak in great agony, holding his hand over the wound. He attempted to say something else; but his words were inarticulate, and he died in about two hours after he was carried into the house. I am most heartily sorry for his death, for he was as honest a fellow as ever lived; but we must all die.

Falkland is now confined to his bed in my house, and under the care of a surgeon, who says his wound is a very bad one. I find their quarrel was about a young lady that poor Audley had ran away with, and who, it seems, is now out of her senses.

Any commands that you or my lady Audley shall be pleased to honour me with, in regard to my dear deceased friend, shall be punctually obeyed by,

Madam,
Your most obedient, &c.
HENRY BENDISH.

Letter LXVIII.
Mr. Falkland to the Rev. Mr. Price.
Bagshot, March 28th.

Sir,

I suppose you may by this time have heard of the tragic event, which is likely to detain me for some time in a kingdom, to which as soon as it is in my power I shall bid an eternal adieu. But before I banish myself for ever from your sight, (Oh, that I could as easily banish the memory of my crimes!) suffer me, most revered of men, suffer me with that humility with which such a wretch as I am, should approach a sanctity like yours to pour out before you the effusions of a heart pierced with the deepest sense of its own guilt.

Do not think that my penitence proceeds from the languors of a sick bed; the dreaded vengeance of an injured family; or the keen disappointment of all my hopes in life. No, my venerable friend, (let me for this *once* call you so) degraded as I am by the vice and shame, my contrition does not arise from motives so mean, so base as these. My soul still retains unextinguished a little spark of that virtue which your pious cares first kindled, and which, had it not been for my own fatal perverseness, might have lit me to happiness and honour.

The torture of a painful and dangerous wound has never been able to force a groan from me; the impending resentment of those whom I have justly made my enemies has not robbed me of a minute's repose; and the total overthrow of all my worldly expectations, passed through my imagination like an empty vision. But when I think of Mrs. Arnold! of her children! and of you, my good old man, guide and instructor of my thankless youth, whose reverend age blushes to own the degenerate wretch who so disgracefully has baffled all his flattering hopes, I wish for death, and in the bitterness of my heart curse the hour that gave me being!

I would not extenuate by a single grain the weight of my offence. That suits not with a repentance so sincere as I hope mine is: yet I cannot help observing, that as the unfortunate man, whose life I have to answer for, was the primary cause of my departure from right, and led me as it were step by step to the gulph in which I am now swallowed up, 'twas just that Heaven should in its instrument of punishment make use of the hand of him whose mind he had perverted.

I purpose standing my trial for the death of Sir Edward Audley, and afterwards (as I have no apprehensions on that score) I shall throw myself as a volunteer into the army; for I cannot think of availing myself of my lord V—'s bounty to me, nor could I bear to look him in the face. I have now not a wish left but to be forgotten (for I dare not hope to be forgiven) by those to whom I was once so dear.

P.S. The unhappy deceased owned in his last minutes that he was married. I believe it was to the young woman who you told me had declared herself to Mrs. Arnold to be his wife. I had not supposed her such in his life-time; but it may be some consolation to her to know that he acknowleged her in the hour of death.

Letter LXIX.
Miss Cecilia Arnold to Mrs. Cecilia B—.
Woodberry, March 28th.

I am ordered by my mama to thank you, my dear madam, for your kind and consoling letter. She would have answered it herself but for an indisposition, which, though but a slight one, makes writing a painful task to her. She would not, however, as you had desired to hear from us, delay acknowleging your favour.

These are my mama's own words, which she charged me to make use of: but oh, my dear Mrs. B—, we are all dying with apprehensions! her disorder, I am afraid, is worse, much worse than she will own it to be. There has been a visible change in her from day to day, since that dreadful one of which she gave you an account in her last letter. She has entirely lost her rest and her appetite. A slow fever seems to consume her, attended with a constant thirst; yet she retains not a minute in her stomach the lightest liquids which she takes. She endeavours as much as possible to hide from us every symptom of her illness. Doctor Key attends her, and flatters us with the hope of her soon getting the better of it; yet I cannot rid myself of my fears. God preserve her dear and most precious life! If she should be taken from us, think, ah think, my good Mrs. B—, what would be the condition of two poor desolate creatures like my sister and me! The cause too! so mournful! 'tis not to be thought of without almost dying of grief.

We have had a letter from my uncle Bidulph, in which he writes word that it was reported, Sir Edward Audley had been killed in a duel, and his antagonist wounded. I suppose you have heard the account, and therefore I need not name to you his antagonist. Sir George says he knows not particulars, nor is certain even of the fact; but I believe he threw this in only to soften the shock which he knew this account must give us; and he adds, *if the news be true, 'twas pity the two associate fiends* (those were his terrible words) *did not perish by each other's hand!*

My poor mama was exceedingly shocked at this account, for it appears but too probable. Mrs. Spillman cried the whole day, though I think Sir Edward Audley ill deserves to be regretted by her.

We mentioned not the story to my sister; we are afraid of aggravating her malady, by any thing that would alarm her tender spirits. She appears pretty tranquil, yet we are in hourly fears of a relapse, for it is easy to perceive her poor head is not yet as it should be. We see no company, and therefore have not had this frightful news confirmed; but Mrs. Askham says she has heard of it from several people.

I divide my cares between my mama and my sister. My own particular griefs are absorbed in theirs; yet indeed, my dear madam, your little friend Cecilia has met with a heavy blow, and she feels it too at the very bottom of her heart.

We all join in most sincere respects to Mr. B—.

I am, madam, &c.

P.S. My mama received a letter yesterday from my lord V—. I know not the contents; but she says it is full of tenderness and friendship for her and her family. I doubt it not; he is a most excellent man.

Letter LXX.
Mr. Price to Mr. Falkland.
Woodberry, April 2d.

Sir,

Your letter of the twenty-eight past confirmed the account which before reached us of your tragic adventure. The unfortunate deceased, I fear, but too well merited his fate; yet I tremble to think that you have by this daring action so swelled the grievous account of your offences. I pray God continue to you that lively compunction with which, from a just sense of your errors, you seem at present to be filled. Great indeed has been your falling off from virtue! and terrible have been the consequences! yet the path is not irrecoverable: let that thought sustain your hope; but take care that it does not extinguish your repentance. You shall not want my exhortations and advice; I wish I could add a word of comfort; but I am afraid there is a woeful event approaching, which will greatly aggravate yours, and mine, and all our sufferings.

Mrs. Arnold is dangerously ill; her fortitude is at length vanquished; and she is now meekly sinking under that stroke, which as from a two-edged sword has at one blow clef in twain so many hearts!

She is desirous of seeing you, that she may with her own lips acquit herself of that great duty of our religion, namely to forgive those who have sinned against us. If you are in any wise in a condition to be removed, I beg you will cause yourself forthwith to be conveyed to Woodberry. Sorry am I to say, that this probably may be one of the last acts of piety, which my excellent friend and patroness may have it in her power to perform. Do not therefore let ill-timed and false shame, deprive you of so great a benefit.

I am, with ardent prayers for your amendment in this life, and salvation in the next,

Your sincere well-wisher and servant,

SAMUEL PRICE.

Letter LXXI.
Mrs. Askham to Mrs. Cecilia B—.
Woodberry, April 7th.

Madam,

I am desired by the mournful family to acquaint you with a piece of news the most afflicting that ever you received. I hope you have been prepared for it, and that the black seal on this letter will make you guess at its sorrowful contents.

Oh, madam,——my mistress! my benefactress! my friend! for such she *was!*——but *she* is happy, and it is the poor survivors who are to be pitied.

Miss Cecilia writ you word how fast her mama's health was declining. We all saw it, yet the admirable lady herself struggled against her disorder as long as she was able; but last Tuesday, finding herself much worse than ordinary, she was obliged to be put again to bed after she had risen and dressed herself.

I was with her, as I constantly passed every day at the house since Miss Arnold's return. Mrs. Askham, said she, smiling, and taking me by the hand, as I sat at her bed-side, I'll tell you a secret; then lowering her voice (for her waiting-maid was in the room) I am going very fast, said she; this last blow has struck home and effectually done its work. I was obliged to whip out my handkerchief, and could only answer, God forbid, madam! Do you then begrudge me my repose, my dear Patty? said she; I thought you would have congratulated me.—Do not say any thing to the poor children, added she; they will have time enough to lament me when all is over. There are two points which I would wish to accomplish before I die. One of them I shall not mention to you at present; the other is to see and be reconciled to Falkland; for indeed, Patty, Falkland is as much the author of my death, as if he had dispatched me with a pistol ball, as he has done Sir Edward Audley. Poor forlorn wretch! I *know* he will accuse himself of it when I shall not have it in my power to grant him pardon; 'tis for this reason I would willingly accord it to him now, as the last gift I have to bequeath him, for I have already taken care of his fortune. You have seen, continued she, the letter he has written to Mr. Price. I *think* his repentance is sincere; and in that belief, I would not wish to leave the world without affording him the single consolation he can now receive, that of knowing from my own mouth that I forgive him.

She then desired me to call Mr. Price to her, which I did; and after having given him her reasons for desiring it, she begged he would write a few lines to Mr. Falkland requesting his presence at Woodberry as soon as possible.

The poor lady complained of a pain in her chest, and a dizziness in her head. I entreated her to suffer another physician to be called in to the assistance of Doctor Key. My good friend, said she, if I thought I could be relieved by human means, I should think myself bound to follow your advice; but indeed, my dear, my case is out of the reach of medicine, and though I permit a physician to attend me for form sake, I *feel* that it is all over with me. Believe me, Patty, 'tis what I have longed for; and if I had not thought it a crime, 'tis that for which I should most earnestly have prayed.

She desired that Miss Arnold might be let to stay with her as little as possible; lest it should affect her spirits too much; but Miss Cecilia was almost constantly at her bed-side. The sweet young lady, what a dismal time she has had for this fortnight past! but she takes after her excellent mother in courage, as well as in every other perfection. Mr. Price, Mrs. Spillman, and myself, did all we could to entertain Miss Arnold, and divert her from going into her mama's room. We had a hard task to prevent her, she *would* attend her mama, was she not as capable as Cecilia? True, my dear miss; but the doctor has ordered your mama to be kept extremely quiet. She is forbid to speak, and one person is sufficient to be with her at a time. And why cannot *I* be that one person? for I would sit by her all day without opening my lips. Ah, Mrs. Askham, I see I am not thoroughly forgiven.—We were obliged now and then to let her go into her chamber. She would enter softly, peep in at the bed's feet, and after looking for about a minute sorrowfully at her mama, retire again without speaking.

The day passed over in this manner. Mrs. Arnold could not be prevailed on to touch any thing but a little weak chicken-broth; she said she had a loathing at the thoughts of eating; indeed her stomach had not been able to bear any thing solid for several days before. I would fain have passed the night by her, but she would not suffer me: You need not fear my *escaping* to-night, said she; I shall not accomplish my journey so soon.

When I attended her next morning, I found her, as I thought, much better. She told me the pain in her chest was intirely gone, the giddiness, which she had complained of the day before, was greatly diminished, and that she felt nothing but an universal feebleness, which, without being painful, had reduced her to a state weaker than that of a new-born infancy.

Never was any thing so calm, so tranquil as she continued the whole day. Mr. Price came in to sit with her. I have been thinking this morning, said she, of a circumstance, about which (though I look upon it as too trivial to mention in my will) I should nevertheless chuse to leave a memorandum. What is it, my good madam? said Mr. Price. It was always my wish, replied she, to live with as much privacy as possible, and to go out of the world with as little pomp as I came into it; and for this reason, it has ever been my intention to be laid, without any noise, and as little ceremony as may be, in the church of whatever parish I should happen to die in. I therefore just mention this to you, Mr. Price, as I think you the properest person to receive such an injunction. I hope, said the good gentleman, the fulfilling this injunction is a duty which will never be paid by me. My dear sir, replied Mrs. Arnold, do you say that by way of encouraging me with the hopes of *life*? Ah, I thought you knew me better; and that I had at least the credit with you of not being supposed afraid to die. That I am sure you are not, madam; you are a good woman; your life has been uniformly pious; and I think, as far as humanity will admit of the eulogium, you are *blameless*. I would not be guilty of arrogance, answered Mrs. Arnold; yet have I the inexpressible satisfaction to declare, that, upon taking a survey of my past life, I do not recollect ever to have been *wilfully* guilty of an action contrary to the duty I owe my Maker. Mr. Price lifted up his hands and eyes, as if in thankfulness to Heaven. I know, pursued Mrs. Arnold, it is more customary, and perhaps more becoming too, even for good people, when they find their end is drawing near, to accuse themselves as very sinful persons: but how easy is it to put on the robe of humiliation, and to assume the look and tone of penitence! whilst, perhaps, their heart does not, *can* not feel compunction for trespasses, which in their health and strength they thought too trivial for atonement, and which now, without making any real impression on them, they acknowledge more from supposition than recollection. Let those whose consciences are really oppressed, seek for consolation in an humble confession of their faults: but if the soul, retiring to search into herself, finds in those solemn hours, when nothing within can divert her from the awful scrutiny, nor from without can seduce her to pervert the truth, if then she finds that she is self-acquitted, let her boldly stand up, and, like righteous Samuel,[1] declare her own innocence; not presumptuously to vaunt a superior virtue, but to give our repining friends, who perhaps may too tenderly lament us, the greatest and best founded consolation they can receive: and this, my good sir, is my only reason for telling you that I am not afraid to die. I know it, madam, answered Mr. Price; and am as well convinced of your reasons as I am of the fact itself: yet you are still in the prime of life, and it is natural for your friends to wish that you should— What, my dear sir? drag on a few more miserable years? and have, in all likelihood, the infirmities of age super added to my misfortunes! No, no, my worthy friend, they love me not wisely who would wish to see my days prolonged. This is a fit season for my departure, when I look upon the summons to quit life as a greater blessing than any which could now be bestowed upon me in it. You know I have suffered a variety of sorrows; and though I may have (when my impatience got the better of my submission) in some unguarded minute wished for a release, yet still, in my calmer hours, I found some call that drew me back to life; some tie, that I could not see without regret about to be dissolved; and I found, upon reflection, that I should have died but half resigned. But my fate *now* seems to be consummated. Disappointed in my *lost* hopes, what is there to attach me to this world? Let me quit it then, whilst my longings after another are alive and warm; whilst the recent smart of my sufferings makes me consider my dismission as the tenderest mercy that my Creator (without reversing his own decrees) could vouchsafe me. This is

---

1   See 1 Samuel 12:3–5: "Behold, here I am: witness against me before the Lord, and before his anointed: whose ox have I taken? or whose ass have I taken? or whom have I defrauded? whom have I oppressed? or of whose hand have I received any bribe to blind mine eyes therewith? and I will restore it to you. And they said, Thou hast not defrauded us, nor oppressed us, neither hast thou taken ought of any man's hand. And he said unto them, The Lord is witness against you, and his anointed is witness this day, that ye have not found ought in my hand. And they answered, He is witness" (King James Version).

the use, my good Mr. Price, that I would fain make of my afflictions: 'tis the use I would have my friends make of them; and instead of murmuring that my years were so soon cut off, to return thanks to God that he did not lengthen them.

I have been enabled, madam, to give you the conversation of this blessed lady by Mr. Price's means, who having, after he had left her chamber, writ down every word she had said to him, suffered me to take a copy of it.

She continued the remainder of that and all the next day without any visible alteration. We would fain have flattered ourselves with hope; but we dared not even to hint it to Mrs. Arnold: *Her* hope and ours, Mr. Price said, had different centers.

She retained her usual sweet composure; and without affecting to be cheerful, shewed not the least appearance of gloominess or impatience. What a happiness is it, said she, thus to glide so smoothly from one shore to another! I feel neither pain nor sickness; and if it were not for certain sensations I have within, and which I cannot describe, joined to a feebleness which increases hourly, I should almost doubt whether my deliverance were so near at hand: yet I am sure my task will be accomplished in a day or two. Whenever the event happens, I would have Mrs. B— apprized of it tenderly. I have already desired Cecilia to prepare her for it by a second letter; for when she writ the first I knew not how long the combat might have lasted.

She mentioned Mr. Falkland several times; expressing some uneasiness lest he should not come, or, what would be worse, should not arrive time enough. For it is for his own sake chiefly, said she, I wish to see him.

Mr. Falkland, however, did arrive on Friday night. He was obliged to be brought in a litter: he had had a violent fever. His wound, it seems, was so dangerous a one, that the surgeons were for some time in doubt whether they must not have been forced to take off his arm. He was reduced extremely low, and could not bear the motion of any other conveyance than that by which he was carried.

Mrs. Arnold was told he was come. I am glad of it, said she; for I think to-morrow it would have been too late. The two Miss Arnolds happened both to be in the room, when notice was given that Mr. Falkland was below stairs. Their mama had before told them that she expected him; and now asked them, if they chose to see him, or would rather retire? They begged their mama's permission to stay. She requested Mr. Price to go and conduct Mr. Falkland up stairs, in order, I suppose, to give him an opportunity of preparing the unfortunate young man for such an interview; for probably he did not expect to see either of the young ladies.

Miss Arnold withdrew into a corner of the room, which being darkened by a screen, it was not easy to distinguish her. She sat down, covering her face with her white handkerchief. Miss Cecilia kept her place by her mama's bed-side; but I could perceive her colour came and went.—We all waited in silent expectation. I thought the time appeared long before Mr. Falkland came up stairs; yet I dreaded to see him: and when I heard the chamber-door open, I felt as if my flesh as it were crept. Mr. Price entered first, Mr. Falkland followed him with a slow pace; his left arm was slung in a black scarf, and he looked like one risen from his grave. Miss Cecilia rose up, making him a kind of salute, but did not speak. She was the first object that struck his eyes on entering the room; but he turned them quickly from her, as if the sight of her were insupportable to him. Oh, madam, had you seen him, you would, in spite of his faults, have pitied the unhappy youth! His countenance so abashed! so mortified! so afflicted! He approached Mrs. Arnold's bed-side with trembling steps, where, throwing himself on his knees, he hid his face on the coverlet, and burst into tears. The poor lady herself seemed exceedingly moved. She laid one of her hands on his head, and was for some time without being able to utter a word. Miss Cecilia could not constrain herself any longer, she wept bitterly; and poor Miss Arnold, who from her corner had observed what was passing, sobbed so loud, that I was afraid she would have been suffocated, and ran to her assistance. She put me from her gently; then rising up she stepped softly behind the curtain of her mama's bed, and bending down, with her arms half stretched out, hung over Mr. Falkland, as if she were inclined, but afraid to raise him up. His tears were still gushing abundantly. Mrs. Arnold at length broke her affecting silence; but the tone of her voice had something still more touching in it. It was interrupted and unequal; it was the voice of tenderness mixed with grief. I did not send for you, Orlando, to distress you thus—I believe you are sorry for the misfortunes that you have brought upon my family—I forgive you from my soul—This is not a time for reproaches; I would willingly comfort you, if I could.—Which *way*, madam? said Falkland, lifting up his head; do you think with such objects as *these* before my eyes (looking round him) that I can be comforted? Oh! no, no, though I have lost my virtue, I have not lost my feelings.—You must deprive me of memory, of reason, of humanity, before you talk of comfort! It becomes you, said Mrs. Arnold, to have a just sorrow for your misconduct; but do not let a too lively sense of it transport you into wild excesses. I would fain attribute your fault to youth, to passion; but above all, to wicked counsel and example. Do not, therefore, look upon yourself as abandoned to evil; but endeavour rather, in your future conduct, to make what atonement you can for the past. I speak this only with regard to what concerns your own welfare; for as to me and these two children, you have no reparation in your power—The evil is past remedy; and the only consolation that I have to offer you, is to tell you that you are *forgiven*. It was for this purpose only that I desired to see you, as I thought it might a little lighten the burden of a wounded conscience. I do therefore again repeat it to you, that I quit life with the same sentiments of compassion and maternal love for you that I felt when your helpless infancy was by your dear father first committed to my charge.—I think, added she, after pausing, as if to recover from the emotion which this last recollection had occasioned, I think I can venture to promise that my two daughters grant you as free a pardon as I do. What say you, my children?

Miss Cecilia was the first to reply; and stepping up to the bed-side, *I*, madam, am least injured of all, said she; yet were his offences against me even greater than they are, *your* example would teach me to blot them all from my mind; therefore, from henceforward, Falkland, you may again look upon me as your sister; but for any other tie, though you were to-morrow at liberty, and all my friends consenting to the union, I should for ever renounce it. Nor should I dare to think of it, replied Mr. Falkland. And you, my dear, said the excellent woman to Miss Arnold, do not you forgive this poor youth? Ah, mama, I have no resentment against him—I never had—'Tis *I* who should demand forgiveness of him; if it had not been for me he might have been happy, so might poor Cecilia, so might you: but I have broke all your hearts! yet indeed, Orlando, I did not mean to divide you from your love—I had made a resolution to die in silence—I know not what tempted me to break it, unless it be (which I suspect to be the truth) that I was that day seized with a strange distraction. Forgive me, sir, pray forgive me! And she held up both her hands, fixing her sweet eyes with a supplicating look on Mr. Falkland's face. Oh, God! cried he, wringing his hands, 'tis just that my punishment should be proportioned to my crimes! yet I cannot bear this! He turned from her in an agony of grief. She followed him—He will not speak to me, mama! I do not wonder he should be angry, yet I wish he would not hate me! Speak to her, said Mrs. Arnold, her voice broken with sobs— Indulge her; you see how it is with her. Mr. Falkland threw himself at her feet; No, dearest Miss Arnold, said he, Falkland is not altogether such a monstrous prodigy as to hate you! He esteems, he respects, he reveres you more than ever; and if he shuns your sight, 'tis shame, and not resentment, that bids him hide his face. Miss Arnold just lightly pressed with her fingers one of his hands. I am satisfied then, said she; and, with a pleased look, quitted him, and retired again behind the curtain.

We were all deeply moved at this scene. You may judge, madam, how the poor dying lady was affected. I drew near to the bedside. Her spirits seemed quite exhausted, and her face was in a cold sweat. I begged of her to take something to refresh her; and she suffered me to give her a little wine and water with a few drops in it.

I have now, said she, accomplished one half of my work; if I can complete the other, I shall die in peace. Cecilia, my dear, come hither. The young lady approached her; and Mrs. Arnold drew from under her pillow a letter. I received this some time ago, said she, from my lord V—. Let Mr. Price read it aloud, that you may all hear the contents of it. Mr. Price did so; and here inclosed, madam I send you a copy of it.

I did not choose, said Mrs. Arnold to Miss Cecilia, to communicate this letter to you, till I knew how your heart stood affected to Falkland. I therefore only told my lord V—, in answer to what he had written, that I should take a time to recal the subject to you. This is the time, Cecilia, that I have chosen. I have just now heard you declare that you renounced all union with Falkland. He is here present; here is your sister; and here our two worthy friends. Will you, my dear Cecilia, will you give your dying mother the consolation to think that she leaves her child under the protection of that worthy lord? If you heart is still repugnant to him, I do not mean by a *last* request to constrain it; but if you think you can be happy with lord V—, say you will be his wife. Miss Cecilia kneeled down, and taking one of her mama's hands, which she tenderly kissed, wetting it with her tears, yes, my beloved mama, I make you the promise you require, in presence of all these witnesses. I respect my lord V—, I honour him above all men; and if he is still willing to offer me his hand, I will receive it with gratitude. I thank you, my love, said Mrs. Arnold; my work is now finished.

She then desired her will might be brought to her, saying she had a few words to add. She directed me to a drawer in a little cabinet by her bed-side, where I found it folded up. I gave it to her, together with a pen and ink; and having raised her up in bed with her pillows at her back, she wrote a few lines. Then folding up the paper again, she put it into Mr. Price's hands, with these words, Let my brother Bidulph know that this was the last action of my life; and tell him—She stopped short, as if interrupted by some sudden and extraordinary emotion; a fine colour flushed at once into her face, and her eyes, which were before sunk and languishing, seemed in an instant to have recovered all their fire. I never saw so animated a figure! She sprung forward with energy, her arms extended, her eyes lifted up with rapture, and, with an elevated voice, she cried out—*I come*! Then sinking down softly on her pillow, she closed her eyes, and expired without a sigh.—Oh, madam, this was not the exit of a dying woman; this was the ascension of a blessed spirit to heaven! We were all surrounding her bed, our looks turned as it were mechanically towards the place where hers had been fixed; when turning them again towards her, The saint is at length fallen asleep, said Mr. Price; and quits life with the same dignity which accompanied her throughout all her actions!

I thought not at first that she was dead. Poor Miss Arnold was in the same error; and seeing her mama lie so still, What a sweet slumber this is, said she, and how suddenly it has fallen upon her! My poor mama! we have fatigued her with our discourse; but I hope this sleep will do her good. We must not disturb her. Come, Cecilia, let us leave her to her repose; Mrs. Askham will be so kind as to stay by her.

Miss Cecilia answered her not; but throwing one arm round her sister's waist, while with the other she covered her eyes with her handkerchief, she let herself be led out of the room; Miss Arnold, with a smiling countenance, looking back at her mama.

Mr. Falkland stood motionless at the bed's-feet, his eyes fixed in mute sorrow on the lifeless corse[1] of her, who had been more than a mother to him; for her whose days *he* shortened, by a conduct of which he now felt all the shame and all the guilt. The suddenness of her departure (for a few minutes before we saw no symptoms of approaching death) had amazed and terrified him. He beheld her some time in silence; then bursting into a passion of grief, little short of frenzy, he smote his breast, and tearing his fine curled hair out by the roots, And is this, said he, the comfort I was bid to hope in coming hither! to be a witness to the ruin and desolation that I myself have made! Look at the handy-work,

---

1 Corpse.

Falkland; behold the fruit of thy horrid perfidy! Was it not enough to drive our child to madness, to see that accomplished mind quite overturned and lost? Must I have the aggravated crime to answer for of making her an orphan too! Then throwing himself down by the body of Mrs. Arnold, 'Tis mine, said he, my accursed head that should have been laid low, and not this of the most respectable of women!

Mr. Price took him by the hand, and intreating him to rise, Have more respect, said he, for these pious remains, and do not prophane them by useless and outrageous expressions of passion. Let me beseech you, sir, to withdraw with me. This chamber must be left unmolested to Mrs. Askham and the women servants; we must now take our leave of it. Then by a motion, which appeared almost involuntary, he bowed to the honoured corse; and laying hold on Mr. Falkland's arm, drew him, not without difficulty, out of the chamber.

Thus, madam, have I given you an account of the last hours of Mrs. Arnold. I believe you know she was scarce eight and thirty; and she still retained a large portion of that exquisite beauty, which had been so much admired in her youth. We did not let Miss Arnold know of her death till this morning. It has quite overwhelmed her. Words cannot express the sorrow that is spread throughout the whole house. I shall do myself the honour to write to you again in a few days, as it cannot be expected that poor Miss Cecilia will be in a condition to do it. Mr. Price writes this day to inform Sir George Bidulph of our great loss; and I take the opportunity of sending this by the servant who carries his letter. May God preserve you, madam, to Mr. B— and your dear family. I am, with the utmost respect,

Madam, your, &c.

MARTHA ASKHAM

Letter LXXII.
Copy of Lord V—'s Letter to Mrs. Arnold, which was inclosed
in the above.
London, March 26th.

Madam,

I have, with unspeakable concern, received from Sir George Bidulph an account of the fatal event which has lately happened in your family; and take the privilege of a man honoured with your friendship, of mingling my sincere sorrow with yours on so affecting an occasion. Believe me, madam, whatever flattering suggestions my heart might whisper to me at another time, pity, at this juncture, forbids me to listen to them; and without triumphing over Mr. Falkland as a rival, or condemning him as a man, I cannot withhold from him that compassion to which his sufferings intitle him.

You are sensible, madam, that I did my utmost to promote a union, on which I thought the happiness of the most amiable of women depended. You will, therefore, but do me justice in believing that I lament with her the disappointment of her hopes. I aspired to her heart; that was denied me; yet she favoured me with her friendship, her esteem, her confidence. I shall endeavour to retain those as the corner-stones on which to build my future hopes.—I dare not at present enlarge on this subject; and shall, therefore, only beg of you, that if I can, in any respect whatsoever, be serviceable either to you or Mr. Falkland, you will command me to the utmost of my power.

I am, madam, &c.

V—.

Letter LXXIII.
Mrs. Askham to Mrs. Cecilia B—.
Woodberry, April 12th.

Madam,

I shall begin with telling you that the two young ladies are at present in as tolerable health as can be expected, considering the cruel blow they have just received. They neither of them, however, stir out of their chamber; nor have they seen Mr. Falkland since the night of their mama's death, though he is still in the house: for he was seized the next day with a return of his fever, and has been confined to his bed ever since; though I hope he is not in any danger.

Sir George Bidulph arrived here the day after he received Mr. Price's letter. He was deeply affected at entering the house; and when he saw the two young ladies, he wept bitterly, and with great kindness endeavoured to console them.

He desired to have a sight of his sister; and I conducted him into her chamber, where Mrs. Spillman, the house-keeper, and her own maid were sitting. He fixed his eyes on her, for some time, with great tenderness. Look, Mrs. Askham, said he, at that poor little pale piece of clay! We both remember her once the boast and ornament of her sex. She sacrificed the happiness of her whole life to a too rigid duty, and at length her life itself is sacrificed to ingratitude! Oh, Sidney, thou must be greatly recompensed, or—he stopped at this word; and desiring I would preserve for him a lock of her hair, he retired, the tears in his eyes.

Mr. Price said he had not yet opened Mrs. Arnold's will: as she had named Sir George Bidulph one of her executors, he told him he had waited for his arrival. Sir George requested it might be read. I was present with the two young ladies. She has bequeathed her real estate, which is considerable, equally between them, and has left to Mr. Falkland a legacy of ten thousand pounds. She has left to every one of her friends a token of remembrance; and has not forgot any one of her servants, even down to the lowest of them. In a little codicil, dated four days before her death, she bequeaths Mrs. Spillman three thousand pounds, charged on her daughters' estate, as she had already disposed of all her personal fortune in a variety of legacies. This, she says, she leaves her as a token of her gratitude for the eminent service she rendered Miss Arnold.

Mr. Price having read through the whole will, which was duly executed; came to those lines which the admirable lady had written a few minutes before her death. Here is something added, said he to Sir George, which Mrs. Arnold desired me to tell you was the last act of her life; and so indeed it was. These madam, were her words.

'My daughter Cecilia has given me her promise to become the wife of lord V—. 'Tis therefore my desire, that she give her hand to that worthy nobleman, as soon after my decease as decency will permit; and that she take her sister Arnold home to her own house, there to remain under her tender care, till it shall please Almighty God to restore her (of which I am not without hope) to the perfect use of her reason, and thereby enable her to conduct herself.'

Sir George Bidulph listened with pleasure to this article, looking affectionately at Miss Cecilia, who, together with her sister, was drowned in tears from the moment Mr. Price had begun to read. You have then consented, niece, said he, to marry my lord V—? I have, sir, replied the young lady. That's well! answered Sir George; *one* of you, at least, will be happy. He spoke not to Miss Arnold, but turned the conversation to some other subject. Mr. Price told me afterwards, that upon Sir George's being informed that Mr. Falkland was in the house, and very ill, he replied, 'What a mercy it would be to us all if he were to die! I cannot bear the thoughts of him, and hope we may never meet.'

When Mr. Price acquainted Mr. Falkland with what Mrs. Arnold had done for him in her will, it drew from him the most passionate exclamations of his own unworthiness, mixed with the tenderest acknowledgements of gratitude for her memory. He purposes retiring from hence as soon as he is able to go abroad, and to remain concealed at some friend's house, till he is ready to depart from England.

As Mrs. Arnold had desired to be buried privately in her parish church, she is to be interred to-night agreeably to her request. Sir George Bidulph intends returning to town to-morrow. The two young ladies continue here, neither of them choosing to accompany him to London; neither indeed does Sir George desire it, as it is expected the marriage of Miss Cecilia with my lord V— will very soon take place.

Thus you see, madam, things are in a more favourable train than could be reasonably hoped after so many disastrous events.

I am, madam, &c.

     ★ ★ ★ ★ ★

This is the last letter which appears in this collection. The remainder of Mrs. Arnold's history, or rather that of her daughters, is drawn up by Mrs. Askham herself; but as her style is somewhat diffuse, and the narrative contains many minute and some immaterial circumstances, I shall endeavour to compress it in as narrow a compass as I can; giving the readers only such events as they may naturally be supposed curious to know. I have taken the like liberty with some of Mrs. Askham's letters, for which I hope her daughter will pardon me; as, without altering the sense, I have only here and there changed the phrase.

The Conclusion of Mrs. Arnold's History

Mr. Falkland withdrew from Woodberry a few days after the interment of Mrs. Arnold, and retired to the house of a gentleman a few miles from Oxford. The two Miss Arnolds requested of Mrs. Askham not to leave them in their present melancholy situation; and they invited Mrs. Spillman to stay with them till her affairs were settled. Nothing could be more amiable than the behavior of Miss Cecilia to her sister; her whole time was employed in soothing and consoling her.

She mentioned not Mr. Falkland's name; or, if she did, it was but to return thanks to Heaven who had preserved her from the misfortune of being his wife. She spoke of lord V— with the highest veneration, and of her intended marriage with him as of an event which would make her happy. This was the only topic from whence poor Miss Arnold seemed to draw any consolation, for her tears perpetually flowed for the loss of her excellent mother.

Lord V— writ a letter of condolence to Miss Cecilia immediately after Sir George Bidulph's return to town. He touched with great delicacy, yet with the warmest acknowlegements, on the concession she had made in his favour, and hinted his intention of attending her at Woodberry as soon as her grief would permit her to receive his visit.

Things were in this situation, when the two young ladies were surprised one day by a very unexpected guest. It was Miss Audley, who, having come down to Oxford on some family affairs which her brother's death made it necessary to settle, took this opportunity of paying them a visit. She was in deep mourning, and her looks well corresponded with her habit. The two Miss Arnolds melted at the sight of a companion whom they had known in their happier days. Miss Audley mixed her tears with theirs, not from sympathy, for her heart was pierced with real grief for the loss of a brother whom (however unworthy) she had passionately loved. The sight of her two young friends revived her afflicting remembrance of him. The melancholy appearance of a house wherein she had passed so many cheerful hours, just deprived of its admirable mistress; the recollection of poor Miss Arnold's frenzy; of Falkland's despair (of which Mr. Bendish had given her an account); all these mournful ideas presenting themselves to her mind at once, joined to the inward consciousness of having herself but too fatally contributed to so many dreadful mischiefs, stung her with remorse, and probably for the first time in her life, made her reflect seriously on her own guilty conduct.

Miss Audley's education had been ill calculated to inspire her with the principles of virtue. Her early childhood had, in that respect, been totally neglected; having been, by the indolence of a mother, too fond of pleasure, turned over to the care of an ignorant governess of a boarding-school. Her more advanced years, under the conduct of that same mother, had been spent in idleness and dissipation: always used to expence, and brought up with the expectations of a fortune, she found herself now by Sir Edward's death, whose affairs were irretrievably involved, cut off from all her flattering prospects, and reduced to a mortifying dependence on her mother's small jointure. She was not able to sustain this change; and in proportion as she had been intoxicated by vanity, was she now abased by despondence.

She told the two Miss Arnolds, that she was come to take her leave of them; that her mama and she not being able to endure the living in England after the tragic event which had so lately happened in their family, were determined to withdraw into France, in order to pass there the remainder of their days. She expressed herself deeply affected at the miseries which had been brought upon Mrs. Arnold's house by her brother's means; acknowleged that *he* had been even more to blame than Falkland, and in the hurry of her spirits between confusion and remorse, accused herself bitterly for the part she had acted.

Mrs. Askham, who was present at this conversation, seeing the young lady's heart so open, and (as she hoped) so penitent for her fault, took this opportunity of telling her, that since she had the happiness of to be sensible of her errors, was so good as to be sorry for them, and so generous as to acknowledge them, that she hoped she would still go farther; and as the only compensation she could make was to render all the justice in her power to Mr. Falkland, it would be very acceptable to the family to know by what means he and Miss Arnold had been led into engagements so contrary to their duty; so contrary to Miss Arnold's reserved and timid disposition; and so contrary even to Mr. Falkland's own inclinations. She added, that they had got but very imperfect lights from Miss Arnold, and as it was a subject they never wished to renew to her, and which indeed she might not be so well qualified to clear up as Miss Audley herself, they should think themselves obliged to that lady if she would gratify them with the explanation they desired. Miss Audley replied, it will be a very shameful confession for me, Mrs. Askham, and probably were I to continue here I should not have the courage to make it; but since I am going to leave England, *never,* I believe, to return to it, I will, before my departure, give up some letters, which, in a light however reproachful they may put me and my brother, will at least in some measure justify Falkland: and this is a duty which I think myself *bound* to fulfil.

Miss Cecilia begged Miss Audley's permission to introduce Mrs. Spillman to her, as the acknowleged wife of Sir Edward.

Miss Audley received her with great civility and embraced her. She told her politely, how greatly she was afflicted that so unfortunate an event had brought her to the knowledge of a person, whom she should have esteemed herself happy to have called sister. She expressed her sorrow that her brother had nothing to leave her but his name; and said that she and her mama should be extremely pleased to see her in London for the little time they had to stay there. Mrs. Spillman received her caresses with great modesty; she had put on deep mourning; but not weeds.[1] She said, with regard to the first article, it affected her but very little, as by Mrs. Arnold's goodness she was amply provided for; and as for the second, You see, madam, said she, pointing to her dress, that I meant not to assume a title after Sir Edward's decease, of which he did not think me worthy during his life.

Miss Audley took her leave of the two ladies with the warmest demonstrations of regard, begging of them to attribute her imprudent conduct to no worse a motive than the true one, her strong affection to a brother, whom she had suffered to influence her too far.

My lord V— and Sir George Bidulph came together to Woodberry a few days after this. Miss Cecilia had too much good sense, and too much acknowlegement for her deserving lover, to propose unnecessary delays. She had already yielded her consent, and Sir George Bidulph availing himself of Mrs. Arnold's last request, that the marriage should not be deferred, he prevailed on his niece to fix the time before he left her; and in a month afterwards my lord V— had the happiness to receive the *willing* hand of the most charming of women from her delighted friends. Lady Sarah and Sir George came down on purpose to assist at the ceremony, and Mr. Price had the satisfaction of joining a pair, formed for, and worthy of each other.

---

1   "A black garment worn in token of bereavement; mourning apparel. Also, a scarf or band of crape worn by a mourner" (*OED*). Mrs. Spillman is not dressed in the apparel of deep mourning signifying widowhood.

My lord V— set out with his lady the day after their marriage for V— hall in Kent, the antient seat of his family; the place where Mrs. Arnold's first acquaintance had commenced with the excellent parents of this worthy lord. Miss Arnold accompanied them, and seemed to quit with pleasure a placed which served only to remind her of her grief.

My lord and lady V— earnestly solicited Mr. Price to take this journey with them, and to continue to them what he had been to Mrs. Arnold, the friend, companion and instructor; but the good old man begged they would dispense with him, saying he wished to pass the short remains of his life with his beloved and only child Mrs. Main; from whom nothing but his gratitude and attachment to Mrs. Arnold could have drawn him. His noble friends were obliged to acquiesce. He staid but a few days at Woodberry after their departure, in order to regulate some of their domestic affairs, that they had left to his care. He then repaired to London to pass the evening of his days with a daughter and son-in-law, who are highly deserving of all his tenderness.

Mrs. Spillman, who would never take the name of Audley, retired about the same time to her friends in Buckinghamshire.

Mr. Falkland had during this interim stood his trial for the death of Sir Edward Audley, and was, on the evidence of Mr. Bendish, acquitted. He immediately withdrew privately from England without bidding adieu to one of his friends, and as he had before resolved, joined the army in quality of a volunteer. My lord V— himself was obliged soon to follow him, and to quit his amiable lady at a time when he found himself more than ever passionately devoted to her; for the title of husband had but served to make him discover that she deserved his friendship and his confidence, as well as his admiration.

Lady V—, who determined to remain at her seat in Kent till his lordship's return, which was at that time uncertain, recommended, with a sweet ingenuousness, Mr. Falkland to her lord's care. If it be in your power, said she, advance his fortune, and promote his glory; your generosity promised me this at a time when he possessed the heart that is now wholly yours; I hope you will not have less attention to him, now that I consider him only as a brother.

Lord V— returned to England after the close of the campaign, in which Mr. Falkland had distinguished himself so as to gain the reputation of singular bravery. An event had also happened in his own country during his absence, by which he saw himself very unexpectedly restored to the inheritance of his ancestors.

The person who had succeeded to the greatest part of his father's estate was but a distant relation; he was an old man and unmarried, and now dying without heirs, he from a principle of justice bequeathed to young Falkland, the fortune which he had possessed in consequence of his father's misfortunes.

Miss Arnold was not as yet perfectly recovered from her former malady; some traces of it still remained, which her friends, however, had hopes that time would dissipate. A gentleman of high rank and fortune in that country, who had casually seen her a few times, became passionately in love with her, and found means to acquaint lady V— with his sentiments: who thinking that an amiable and deserving lover would, sooner than any thing else, detach her sister's heart from its former unhappy ties, and consequently restore her mind to its right frame, received with satisfaction his declaration, and promised at her lord's return that he should be permitted to visit Miss Arnold. She spoke of him in the mean while to her sister in the most advantageous terms; but found her utterly averse to the thoughts of a new engagement. Lady V—, however, was not without hopes of overcoming by degrees a repugnance which she considered only as the result of disappointment; and on her lord's arrival she was in haste to communicate the affair to him. She enlarged in her sister's presence, on the merit, the passion, and the considerable proposals of Miss Arnold's lover; and added, smiling, she hoped he would have his lordship's interest to promote his suit.

I approve highly of the gentleman, said lord V—, and should think it a happiness to have a man of his worth and consideration united to our family; but before I engage in his cause, I must acquit myself of a commission which I promised Mr. Falkland I would faithfully fulfil.

He then informed the two ladies of the acquisition Mr. Falkland had just received to his fortune. It was an estate of four thousand pounds a year. Falkland, said he, though I had made it my business to seek him out, had always avoided me; nor do I believe we should ever have had any correspondence, had it not been for this event. He wrote to me a few days before my departure from Germany, and here is his letter. My lord V— read it aloud to both the ladies.

Mr. Falkland began with beseeching lord V— to blot from his memory his past ill conduct, for which he expressed the sincerest contrition; and acknowledging with the utmost gratitude his obligations to lord V—, owned that shame would not permit him to do it personally. He then informs him of the large fortune which was just fallen to him, and proceeds in these words: 'Were it not for this event, I should wish that my very name might be forgotten, and that Miss Arnold should never more call back to her recollection the man who deserves nothing from her but contempt and aversion. I acknowledge, my lord, I *deserve* nothing else from her, and must even applaud her justice, if the distinction with which she once honoured me is turned into disdain: but, if on the contrary, the same fatality which first impelled, should still persist in attaching her inclinations to so unworthy an object, tell her I lay myself at her feet, not to make her an atonement, it would be a prophanation of the word to use it on this occasion; but to deliver myself up to her justice, and to endue her with a power (pardon the boldness of the expression) like that of Omnipotence, either to pardon and reward the repenting sinner, or to condemn him to punishment.

'If she pronounces the latter sentence, I may complain; but cannot condemn her. If the former, tell her, my lord, she shall find that I am a man whose heart has been early impressed by principles of virtue, however he may by passions have been hurried into vice, and cannot remain long a slave to it; and that her mildness, her sweet patience, and unexampled tenderness are able to kindle an affection stronger and more lasting, than her beauty, captivating as it is, could ever inspire.

'I have mentioned to you, my lord, the fortune of which I am now possessed, not as a circumstance which can give me the least merit with Miss Arnold, or that I think can in the smallest degree intitle me to her consideration; but to obviate the lightest suspicion which her friends might entertain, that interest could have any share in the declaration I now make. I consider it indeed as the most precious advantage which I can derive from this unlooked for benefit, that it permits me to discover those secret wishes which would otherwise have remained for ever hid within my own breast.'

He concludes with most earnestly conjuring Lord V— to acquaint Miss Arnold with his sentiments, and to communicate to him hers on this important subject.

Lord V— having finished reading the letter, It rests on you, madam, said he to Miss Arnold, to give an answer to Mr. Falkland. I have acquitted myself of my duty; but I would have you take a little time to consider.—Consult your own heart, my dear, said lady V—; I believe *that* after all must determine you.

Miss Arnold turned towards her sister, and addressing her with a sober and even commanding air, No, Cecilia, said she, I *will* not consult my heart, *that* has already betrayed me. I will consult my reason, (since Heaven has been pleased to restore it to me) I will consult my honour; those are the guides that shall henceforward direct your sister's actions. My lord, the subject requires *no* consideration; you shall know my sentiments this moment.

I loved Falkland from my childhood; but conscious that we were never meant for each other, I endeavoured to stifle a fatal passion, the consequences of which I had so much reason to dread. I could not succeed in my attempt, and then I had no resource left, but to resolve without divulging it to die a martyr to my own imprudence. I was baffled in this design too, my secret was unhappily discovered, and cruelly betrayed. Yet at the same time was I deceived into a belief that I was tenderly beloved. This belief, as it mitigated the shame I suffered from my own acknowleged weakness, so did it serve to strengthen an affection already but too deeply rooted in my heart; and when from Falkland's own lips I received a confirmation of what I had before been flattered with from others, I had not resolution enough to defend myself from giving him (however contrary to my duty) the faith he desired. I knew not at the time I made it, by what means I should be enabled to perform my promise; but we were both very young. He was designed for the army. I was in hopes that time, and his good conduct, might influence my uncle Bidulph in his favour; and for my dear mama, whose natural softness, joined to her fondness for Mr. Falkland, left her heart as it were open to the assault, I thought to have engaged you my sister, Mr. Price, and Mrs. B— to have worked upon her tenderness; and when you, my good lord V—, first proposed to us the honour of your alliance, I thought in you too to have obtained a powerful advocate. These were my hopes, and upon the strength of these I ventured to swear I never would be the wife of any other man—Falkland, I never will! cried she, stretching out her arms as if he stood before her. Lord and lady V— were startled at her action, and looked at each other; when she proceeded as if still addressing herself to Falkland; yet observe I do not violate my oath, when I declare I never will be *yours*. I here (raising up solemnly her hands and eyes) devote myself in the sight of Heaven and these my friends to a single life. How truly I have loved you, let my whole conduct witness. My tenderness was proof against a thousand marks of coldness and neglect. Your infidelity, avowed even under your own hand, could not shake my constancy; nay, even madness itself did not dispossess you of my heart! But the first thing that my recovered reason dictates to me is, that I *ought* not to be your wife. I owe this sacrifice (for such I acknowledge it) to all my friends; but *above* all to the honoured memory of my mama. I cannot *atone* for my disobedience; 'tis fit I should punish myself for it. Yet 'tis a great consolation to me, that I have it in my power to refuse that reparation which you now offer to make me. Then recovering from the transport in which she appeared as it were to have been rapt, and addressing herself to my lord V—, You have now, my lord, heard my final determination, said she; I have only to add, that I beg you will let Mr. Falkland know what it is.

However lord and lady V— might in their hearts approve her resolution, they nevertheless said nothing to strengthen her in it. Lord V— thought he owed thus much to Mr. Falkland, who had requested his interposition.

As the declaration Miss Arnold had made on this occasion, was the first regular explanation she had ever entered into upon the subject, so was this the first time since her own misfortune that she had ever shewed herself thoroughly mistress of her faculties; but as the loss of the man she had so perfectly loved had at first deprived her of them, so it seemed as if the having him restored to her (for that he should be so, depended entirely on herself) had in a great measure recalled to her the full possession of them; for it was observed that from that time she every day appeared more and more to recover her former judgment and tranquility, and in a little while she was perfectly restored, though she ever retained a soft melancholy, which time itself could not subdue. She kept her word faithfully; for she afterwards refused several considerable matches, preserving in her heart an inviolable attachment to her first ill-fated choice.

Mr. Falkland, obliged to submit to this second, and more affecting disappointment, returned not to England for many years. He afterwards rose to a distinguished rank in the army; but ever tenderly regretting the loss of Miss Arnold, he, in imitation of her, declared his resolution of continuing single. They* are both so at the time these memoirs are written, and will probably remain so to the end of their lives.

Miss Audley and her mother made choice of a remote province in France for their retreat, to which they withdrew soon after the death of Mrs. Arnold; not, as Miss Audley had declared, from any disinclination to remain in England, but because the state of their affairs made a scheme of frugality absolutely necessary.

---

* Mrs Askham dates her memoir 1738 [Frances Sheridan's note]

Miss Audley, before her departure, left in the hands of a friend all those letters that had passed between her and her brother that have appeared in this collection, as well as those which Sir Edward had received from Mr. Falkland; and Mr. Falkland himself had, immediately after his leaving Woodberry for the last time, sent to Mr. Price those which Sir Edward Audley had written to him; and it was by this means that they have been collected together.

Lady Audley died after about three years residence in France. Her jointure reverting to her younger son, a youth whom she had left in England, Miss Audley found herself so straightened in her circumstances, that she thought it prudent to retire into a convent; where the religious in less than a year prevailed on her to turn Roman Catholic, and soon after to become one of their community. Mrs. Askham says she knew a gentleman who was present when this unhappy lady made her profession in a convent of Carthusian nuns, one of the most severe orders in the Romish Church.

She concludes her history with many serious reflections, which though extremely pious and rational, the editor chuses to omit, thinking it a compliment due to the judgment of his readers to leave them to make reflections for themselves.

THE END.

Appendix A: Essays on the Education, Responsibilities, and Friendships of Young Adults

1. From John Locke, *Some Thoughts Concerning Education* (London: A. and J. Churchill, 1693)[1]

[John Locke (1632–1704) studied medicine and natural and moral philosophy and was the author of numerous seminal works on science, education, and epistemology. His ideas helped form the basis of social, political, and educational theory throughout the long eighteenth century. As a tutor at Christ Church, Oxford, Locke was responsible for the education and welfare of many young pupils, and he was the private tutor of Anthony Ashley Cooper, Second Earl of Shaftesbury. *Some Thoughts Concerning Education* was compiled from letters sent to Edward Clarke, which Locke later added to; it has been published in countless editions.[2] According to Locke, an effective education leaves the pupil with a sincere love for virtue and an affectionate respect for his tutor or parent. To that end, Locke discouraged harsh (corporal) punishment as well as "cockering" or pampering. His theory of the child as a blank slate, or *tabula rasa*, is one of the theories of the child that Frances Sheridan interrogates in *Conclusion to the Memoirs of Miss Sidney Bidulph*. In sections 56 and 57, Locke explains what he believes to be the "great secret of education": that the father should "caress and commend his children when they do well, shew a cold and neglectful Countenance to them upon doing ill," thereby making them early accustomed to be careful of their "reputations." In the last section excerpted here, Locke compares the relative faults of at-home and public school educations, ultimately favoring the type of at-home education given to the Woodberry children in the *Conclusion*.]

Section 42.
Thus much for the settling your Authority over your Children in general. Fear and Awe ought to give you the first Power over their Minds, and Love and Friendship in riper Years to hold it: For the Time must come, when they will be past the Rod and Correction; and then, if the Love of you make them not obedient and dutiful, if the Love of

---

1 The source of this excerpt is the seventh edition of 1712.

2 J.R. Milton, "Locke, John (1632–1704)," *Oxford Dictionary of National Biography* (Oxford UP, 2004).

Virtue and Reputation keep them not in laudable Courses, I ask, what Hold will you have upon them to turn them to it? Indeed, Fear of having a scanty Portion if they displease you, may make them Slaves to your Estate, but they will be nevertheless ill and wicked in private; and that Restraint will not last always. Every Man must some Time or other be trusted to himself and his own Conduct; and he that is a good, a virtuous, and able Man, must be made so within. And therefore what he is to receive from Education, what is to sway and influence his Life, must be something put into him betimes; Habits woven into the very Principles of his Nature, and not a counterfeit Carriage, and dissembl'd Outside, put on by fear, only to avoid the present anger of a Father who perhaps may disinherit him....

Section 56.

Reputation.

The *Rewards and Punishments* then, whereby we should keep Children in order, *are* quite of another Kind, and of that Force, that when we can get them once to work, the Business, I think, is done, and the Difficulty is over. *Esteem and Disgrace* are, of all others, the most powerful incentives to the Mind, when once it is brought to relish them. If you can once get into Children a Love of Credit, and an Apprehension of Shame and Disgrace, you have put into 'em the true Principle, which will constantly work and incline them to the right. But it will be ask'd, How shall this be done?

I confess it does not at first Appearance want some Difficulty; but yet I think it worth our while to seek the Ways (and practise them when found) to attain this, which I look on as the great Secret of Education.

Section 57.

First, Children (earlier perhaps than we think) are very sensible of *Praise* and Commendation. They find a Pleasure in being esteem'd and valu'd, especially by their Parents and those whom they depend on. If therefore the Father *caress and commend them when they do well, shew a cold and neglectful Countenance to them upon doing ill*; and this accompany'd by a like carriage of the Mother and all others that are about them, it will, in a little time, make them sensible of the Difference; and this, if constantly observ'd, I doubt not but will of it self work more than Threats or Blows, which lose their Force when once grown common, and are of no Use when Shame does not attend them; and therefore are to be forborne, and never to be us'd, but in the Case hereafter-mention'd, when it is brought to Extremity.

Section 58.

But *secondly*, to make the sense of *Esteem* or *Disgrace* sink the deeper, and be of the more Weight, *other agreeable or disagreeable things should constantly accompany these different states*; not as particular Rewards and Punishments of this or that particular Action, but as necessarily belonging to, and constantly attending one, who by his Carriage has brought himself into a state of Disgrace or Commendation. By which Way of treating them, Children may as much as possible be brought to conceive, that those that are commended, and in Esteem for doing well, will necessarily be belov'd and cherish'd by every Body, and have all other good Things as a Consequence of it; and on the other Side, when any one by Miscarriage falls into Dis-esteem, and cares not to preserve his Credit, he will unavoidably fall under Neglect and Contempt; and in that state, the Want of whatever might satisfy or delight him will follow. In this Way the Objects of their desires are made assisting to virtue, when a settled experience from the beginning teaches children that the Things they delight in, belong to, and are to be enjoy'd by those only who are in a State of Reputation. If by these Means you can come once to shame them out of their Faults, (for besides that, I would willingly have no Punishment) and make them in Love with the Pleasure of being well thought on, you may turn them as you please, and they will be in Love with all the Ways of Virtue.

Section 61.

Reputation.

Concerning *Reputation*, I shall only remark this one Thing more of it, That though it be not the true Principle and Measure of Vertue, (for that is the Knowledge of a Man's Duty, and the Satisfaction it is to obey his Maker, in following the Dictates of that Light God has given him, with the Hopes of Acceptation and Reward) yet it is that which comes nearest to it: And being the Testimony and Applause that other People's Reason, as it were by a common Consent, gives to virtuous and well-order'd Actions, it is the proper Guide and Encouragement of Children, 'till they grow able to judge for themselves, and to find what is right by their own Reason....

Section 70.

Company.

Having nam'd *Company*, I am almost ready to throw away my Pen, and trouble you no farther on this Subject: For since that does more than all Precepts, Rules, and Instructions, methinks 'tis almost wholly in vain to make a long Discourse of other Things, and to talk of that almost to no Purpose. For you will be ready to say, what shall I do with my Son? If I keep him always at Home, he will be in Danger to be my young Master;[1] and if I send him Abroad, how is it possible to keep him from the Contagion of Rudeness and Vice, which is every where so in Fashion? In my House he will perhaps be more innocent, but more ignorant too of the World; wanting there Change of Company, and being us'd constantly to the same Faces, he will, when he comes Abroad, be a sheepish or conceited Creature. I confess both sides have their Inconveniences. Being Abroad, 'tis true, will make him bolder, and better able to bustle and shift among Boys of his own Age; and the Emulation of School-fellows often puts Life and Industry into young lads. But 'till you can find a School, wherein it is possible for the Master to look after the Manners of his Scholars, and can shew as great Effects of his Care of forming their Minds to virtue, and their Carriage to good Breeding, as of forming their Tongues to the learned Languages, you must confess, that you have a strange Value for Words, when preferring the Languages of the ancient *Greeks* and *Romans* to that which made 'em such brave Men, you think it worth while to hazard your son's innocence and virtue for a little *Greek* and *Latin*. For, as for that Boldness and Spirit which lads get amongst their Play-fellows at school, it has ordinarily such a Mixture of Rudeness and ill-turn'd Confidence, that those mis-becoming and dis-ingenuous Ways of shifting in the World must be unlearnt, and all the Tincture wash'd out again, to make Way for better Principles, and such Manners as make a truly worthy Man. He that considers how diametrically oppo-site the Skill of living well, and managing, as a Man should do, his Affairs in the world, is to that Malapertness,[2] Tricking, or Violence learnt amongst School-Boys, will think the Faults of a privater Educa-tion infinitely to be preferr'd to such Improvements, and will take Care to preserve his Child's Innocence and Modesty at Home, as being nearer of Kin, and more in the Way of those Qualities which make an useful and able Man. Nor does any one find, or so much as suspect, that that Retirement and Bashfulness which their Daughters are brought up in, makes them less knowing, or less able Women. Con-versation, when they come into the World, soon gives them a becom-ing Assurance; and whatsoever, beyond that, there is of rough and boisterous, may in Men be very well spar'd too; for Courage and Steadiness, as I take it, lie not in Roughness and ill Breeding.

Virtue is harder to be got than a Knowledge of the world; and if lost in a young Man, is seldom recover'd. Sheepishness and Ignorance of

---

1 In other words, he will be in danger of becoming spoiled and self-important and reign over the household as a young master.
2 The quality of being presumptuous, impudent, or saucy.

the World, the Faults imputed to a private Education, are neither the necessary Consequences of being bred at home, nor if they were, are they incurable Evils. Vice is the more stubborn, as well as the more dangerous Evil of the two; and therefore in the first Place to be fenced against. If that sheepish Softness which often enervates those who are bred like Fondlings[1] at Home, be carefully to be avoided, it is principally so for Vertue's Sake; for fear lest such a yielding Temper should be too susceptible of vicious Impressions, and expose the Novice too easily to be corrupted. A young Man before he leaves the Shelter of his Father's House, and the Guard of a Tutor, should be fortify'd with Resolution, and made acquainted with Men, to secure his Vertues, lest he should be led into some ruinous Course, or fatal Precipice, before he is sufficiently acquainted with the Dangers of Conversation, and has Steadiness enough not to yield to every Temptation. Were it not for this, a young Man's Bashfulness and Ignorance in the world, would not so much need an early Care. Conversation would cure it in a great Measure; or if that will not do it early enough, it is only a stronger Reason for a good Tutor at Home. For if pains be taken to give him a Manly air and Assurance betimes, it is chiefly as a Fence to his Vertue, when he goes into the World under his own Conduct.

2. From Anonymous, *The Common Errors in the Education of Children, and their Consequences; With The Methods to Remedy Them Consider'd* (London: M. Cooper, 1744)

[The following excerpt is from an anonymous conduct book for parents (primarily fathers) on the education of boys and young men. For authority, the author cites the history and discourse on childrearing and education compiled from classical authors such as Plato, Cicero, Xenophon, Livy, Pliny, and Quintilian; but the work takes its major points from John Locke's *Some Thoughts Concerning Education* (1693). Following Locke's idea that the child is a *tabula rasa*, a blank slate upon which to sketch a character by careful education, the author in this section expounds the importance of example and education in the moral development of young men. In it we can glimpse the potential effects of contradictory influences, such as those of Mr. Price and Sir Edward Audley on young Orlando Falkland. Audley's letter LIV is an object lesson in the effects of bad or insufficient moral education on reasoning.]

---

1 "One who is fondly loved; one who is much fondled or caressed; a pet" (*OED*).

A Parent should be particularly cautious, that his Child keeps no bad Company, and that he himself sets a good Example:[1] For, if the Company he keeps be bad, Vice will soon creep into his Soul, and there settle....

Virtue is the chief End we ought to aim at, and which as Children advance in Letters, they ought to improve in, and be taught to pursue, as the ultimate End of their Happiness. "Virtue is a Man's surest Defence, without which we can never expect our Endeavours to succeed well."[2] Whenever they read of the lives and Actions of great Men, they should be ask'd their Opinion of such an Action or Saying, and why they take it to be good or bad. The Youth should be taught to descant upon their Actions, and shew wherein they were excelling, and where defective. This will soon give him early Seasonings of Morality. And it is much in the Duty of a Master, to improve his Scholars in Virtue, as in Letters.——But particularly ought he to give the Pupil frequent lectures on Swearing and Lying, which are generally the Root of Mischief and Wickedness, and which are Accomplishments which Youth chiefly attain to before anything. He should therefore be taught how ungenteel and unchristian a Dialect Swearing is, how it clashes with the Rules of good Breeding and Religion; That Lying renders a Man unfit for Human Society, and unworthy the Care and Regard of Heaven. In a Word, Vice must be painted to him in its blackest and most hideous Colours, and Virtue set before him in the most amiable Light....

3. From Samuel Richardson, *Familiar Letters Written to and for Particular Friends on the Most Important Occasions* (London: Rivington, Osborne, and Leake, 1741)

[Samuel Richardson (1689–1761) was the "celebrated author of Clarissa and Sir Charles Grandison" to whom *The Memoirs of Miss Sidney Bidulph* are dedicated. He popularized the epistolary novel form in the 1740s and '50s with *Pamela, or Virtue Rewarded* (1740); *Pamela II* (1741); *Clarissa* (1748–49); and *Sir Charles Grandison* (1753). Many instances in Sheridan's *Conclusion* provide interesting counterpoints to the ideas of the role of filial duty in marriage arrangements that appear in *Clarissa*. The following letters are from a volume that Richardson

---

1 We are all sort of *Camelions*, which take a Tincture from Things near us. *Locke*. [Author's note.]

2 *Xenophon.* [Author's note. Xenophon (c.430–c.354 BC) was a Greek historian who wrote on military history, biography, Socratic philosophy, and commentary on contemporary Greece.]

composed as examples of the "manner and style" of letter writing on a variety of topics of concern to the family and household.]

Letter XII.
Against a sudden Intimacy, or Friendship, with one of a short Acquaintance.

Cousin Tom,

I am just setting out for *Windsor*,[1] and have not time to say so much as I would on the Occasion upon which I now write to you. I hear that Mr. *Douglas* and you have lately contracted such an Intimacy, that you are hardly ever asunder; and as I know his Morals are not the best, nor his Circumstances the most happy, I fear he will, if he has not already done it, let you see, that he better knows what he does in seeking *your* Acquaintance, than you do in cultivating *his*.

I am far from desiring to abridge you in any necessary or innocent Liberty, or to prescribe too much to your Choice of a Friend: Nor am I against your being complaisant to *Strangers*; for this Gentleman's Acquaintance is not yet a Month old with you; but you must not think every Man, whose Conversation is agreeable, fit to be immediately treated as a Friend: Of all Sorts, hastily-contracted Friendships promise the least Duration or Satisfaction; as they most commonly arise from Design on one Side, and Weakness on the other. *True Friendship* must be the Effect of long and mutual Esteem and Knowlege: It ought to have for its Cement, an Equality of Years, a Similitude of Manners, and, pretty much, a Parity in Circumstance and Degree. But, generally speaking, an Openness to a Stranger carries with it strong Marks of Indiscretion, and not seldom ends in Repentance.

For these Reasons, I would be glad you would be upon your Guard, and proceed cautiously in this new Alliance. Mr. *Douglas* has Vivacity and Humour enough to please any Man of a light Turn; but, were I to give my Judgment of him, I should pronounce him fitter for the Tea-table, than the Cabinet. He is smart, but very superficial; and treats all serious Subjects with a Contempt too natural to bad Minds; and I know more young Men than one, of whose good Opinion he has taken Advantage, and has made them wiser, though at their own Expence, than he found them.

The Caution I here give you, is the pure Effect of my Experience in Life, some Knowlege of your new Associate, and my Affection for you. The Use you make of it will determine, whether you merit this Concern from

Your affectionate Kinsman.

---

1 The town of Windsor is about twenty-two miles west of London on the banks of the Thames. Its castle is one of the residences of the British royal family.

Letter LXVI
From a Daughter to her Father, pleading for her Sister, who had married without his Consent.

Honour'd Sir,

The kind indulgence you have always shewn to your children, makes me presume to become an advocate for my *sister,* 'tho not for her *fault.* She is very sensible of *that,* and sorry she has offended you; but has great hopes, that Mr. Robinson will prove such a careful and loving husband to her, as may atone for his past wildness, and engage your forgiveness. For all your children are sensible of your paternal kindness, and that you wish their good more for *their* sakes, than *your own.*

This makes it the more wicked to offend so good a father: But, dear sir, be pleased to consider that it now cannot be helped, and that she may be made by your displeasure very miserable in her own choice; and as his faults are owing to the inconsideration of youth, or otherwise it would not have been a very discreditable match, had it had your approbation, I could humbly hope, for my poor sister's sake, that you will be pleased rather to encourage his present good resolutions by your kind favour, than make him despair of a reconciliation, and so perhaps treat her with a negligence, which hitherto she is not apprehensive of: For he is really very fond of her, and I hope will continue so. Yet is she dejected for her fault to you, and wishes, yet dreads, to have your leave to throw herself at your feet, to beg your forgiveness and blessing, which would make the poor dear offender quite happy.

Pardon, sir, my interposing in her favour, in which my husband also joins. She is *my* sister. She is *your* daughter; tho' she has not done so worthily as I wish, to become that character. Be pleased, sir, to forgive her, however; and also forgive me, pleading for her: Who am,

Your ever dutiful Daughter.

Letter LXVII
The Father's Answer.

My *dear* Nanny,

You must believe, that your sister's unadvised marriage, which she must know would be disagreeable to me, gives me no small concern; and yet, I will assure you, that it arises more from my affection for her, than any other consideration. In her education I took all the pains and care my circumstances would admit, and often flattered myself with the hope, that the happy fruits of it would be made appear in her prudent conduct. What she has now done is not *vicious,* but *indiscreet;* for, you must remember, that I have often declared in her hearing, that the wild assertion, of a rake making a good husband, was the most dangerous opinion a young woman could imbibe.

I will not, however, in pity to her, point out the many ills I am afraid will attend her rashness, because *it is done*, and cannot be *helped*; but wish she may be happier than I ever saw a woman who leap'd so fatal a precipice.

Her husband has this morning been with me for her fortune; and it was with much temper I told him, That as all she could hope for was wholly at my disposal, I should disburse it in such a manner as I thought would most contribute to her advantage; and that, as he was a stranger to me, I should choose to know he *deserved* it, before he had power over what I intended to do for her. He bit his lip, and with a hasty step was my humble servant.

Tell the rash girl, that I would not have her to be afflicted at this behaviour in me; for I know it will contribute to her advantage one way or other: If he married her for *her own sake*, she will find no alteration of behaviour from this disappointment: But if he married her only for her *money*, she will soon be glad to find it in my possession rather than his.

Your interposition in her behalf is very *sisterly*: And you see I have not the resentment she might expect. But would to God she had acted with your prudence! For her own sake I wish it. I am
Your loving Father.

Letter LXIX
From a Father to a Daughter, in Dislike of her Intentions to marry at too early an Age.

Dear Sally,

I was greatly surprised at the letter you sent me last week. I was willing to believe I saw in you, for your years, so much of your late dear mother's temper, prudence, and virtuous disposition, that I refused several advantageous offers of changing my own condition, purely for your sake: And will you now convince me so early, that I have no return to expect from you, but that the moment a young fellow throws himself in your way, you have nothing else to do, but to give me notice to provide a fortune for you? So that you intend to be of no further use and service to me. This, in plain English, is the meaning of your notification. For I suppose your young man does not intend to marry you, without a fortune. And can you then think, that a father has nothing to do, but to confer benefits on his children, without being intitled to expect any return from them?

To be sure, I had proposed, at a proper time, to find an husband for you; But I thought I had yet three or four years to come. For, consider,

Sally, you are not fully sixteen years of age: And a wife, believe me, ought to have some better qualifications, that an agreeable person, to *preserve an husband's esteem,* tho' it often is enough to *attract a lover's notice.*

Have you experience enough, think you, discreetly to conduct the affairs of a family? I thought you as yet not quite capable to manage *my* house; and I am sure, my judgment always took a byas in your favour.

Besides, let me tell you, I have great exception to the person, and think him by no means the man I would choose for your husband. For which, if it is not too late, I will give good reasons.

On the whole, you must expect, if you marry without my *consent,* to live without my *assistance.* Think it not hard: Your disappointment cannot be greater than mine, if you will proceed. I have never used violent measures to you on any occasion, and shall not on this. But yet I earnestly hope you will not hurry yourself to destruction, and me perhaps to the grave, by an action which a little consideration may so easily prevent. I am

Your afflicted Father.

4. From John Gregory, *A Father's Legacy to His Daughters* (London and Edinburgh: Strahan, Cadell, and Creech, 1774)

[John Gregory (1724–73) was a Scottish physician, writer, and professor of moral and natural philosophy and mathematics at King's College, Aberdeen. He wrote *A Father's Legacy to His Daughters* after the death of his wife, Elizabeth, in 1762. The manuscript, which ostensibly contains in part the advice of Elizabeth Gregory to her daughters, was published after John Gregory's death in 1774.[1] As Lawrence Stone points out, *A Father's Legacy* registers the changing attitudes toward women in matrimonial matters, showing that they were no longer considered domestic upper servants, but equal participants in a "companionate marriage."[2] In this excerpt, Gregory advises his daughters to contract friendships and reveal secrets with discretion, especially in matters of love. His discussion of female delicacy here resonates with the concealed affections of Sheridan's heroines for young Falkland.]

---

1 Paul Lawrence, "Gregory, John (1724–1773)," *DNB.*

2 Lawrence Stone, *The Family, Sex and Marriage In England 1500–1800,* abridged edition (London: Harper, 1979) 219.

FRIENDSHIP, LOVE, MARRIAGE.

THE luxury and dissipation that prevails in genteel life, as it corrupts the heart in many respects, so it renders it incapable of warm, sincere, and steady friendship. A happy choice of friends will be of the utmost consequence to you, as they may assist you by their advice and good offices. But the immediate gratification which friendship affords to a warm, open, and ingenuous heart, is of itself a sufficient motive to court it.

In the choice of your friends, have your principal regard to goodness of heart and fidelity. If they also possess taste and genius, that will still make them more agreeable and useful companions. You have particular reason to place confidence in those who have shewn affection for you in your early days, when you were incapable of making them any return. This is an obligation for which you cannot be too grateful.—When you read this, you will naturally think of your mother's friend, to whom you owe so much.

If you have the good fortune to meet with any who deserve the name of friends, unbosom yourself to them with the most unsuspicious confidence. It is one of the world's maxims, never to trust any person with a secret, the discovery of which could give you any pain; but it is the maxim of a little mind and a cold heart, unless where it is the effect of frequent disappointments and bad usage. An open temper, if restrained but by tolerable prudence, will make you, on the whole, much happier than a reserved suspicious one, although you may sometimes suffer by it. Coldness and distrust are but the too certain consequences of age and experience; but they are unpleasant feelings, and need not be anticipated before their time.

But however open you may be in talking of your own affairs, never disclose the secrets of one friend to another. These are sacred deposits, which do not belong to you, nor have you any right to make use of them.

There is another case, in which I suspect it is proper to be secret, not so much from motives of prudence, as delicacy; I mean in love matters. Though a woman has no reason to be ashamed of an attachment to a man of merit, yet nature, whose authority is superior to philosophy, has annexed a sense of shame to it. It is even long before a woman of delicacy dares avow to her own heart that she loves; and when all the subterfuges of ingenuity to conceal it from herself fail, she feels a violence done both to her pride and to her modesty. This, I should imagine, must always be the case where she is not sure of a return to her attachment.

In such a situation, to lay the heart open to any person whatever, does not appear to me consistent with the perfection of female delicacy. But perhaps I am in the wrong.—At the same time I must tell you, that, in point of prudence, it concerns you to attend well to the consequences of such a discovery. These secrets, however important in your own estimation, may appear very trifling to your friend, who possibly will not enter into your feelings, but may rather consider them as a subject of pleasantry. For this reason, love-secrets are of all others the worst kept. But the consequences to you may be very serious, as no man of spirit and delicacy ever valued a heart much hackneyed in the ways of love.

If, therefore, you must have a friend to pour out your heart to, be sure of her honour and secrecy. Let her not be a married woman, especially if she lives happily with her husband. There are certain unguarded moments, in which such a woman, though the best and worthiest of her sex, may let hints escape, which at other times, or to any other person than her husband, she would be incapable of; nor will a husband in this case feel himself under the same obligation of secrecy and honour, as if you had put your confidence originally in himself, especially on a subject which the world is apt to treat so lightly.

If all other circumstances are equal, there are obvious advantages in your making friends of one another. The ties of blood, and your being so much united in one common interest, form an additional bond of union to your friendship. If your brothers should have the good fortune to have hearts susceptible of friendship, to possess truth, honour, sense, and delicacy of sentiment, they are the fittest and most unexceptionable confidants. By placing confidence in them, you will receive every advantage which you could hope for from the friendship of men, without any of the inconveniencies that attend such connexions with our sex.

Beware of making confidants of your servants. Dignity not properly understood very readily degenerates into pride, which enters into no friendships, because it cannot bear an equal, and is so fond of flattery as to grasp at it even from servants and dependants. The most intimate confidants, therefore, of proud people are *valets-de-chambre*[1] and waiting-women. Shew the utmost humanity to your servants; make their situation as comfortable to them as possible: but if you make them your confidants, you spoil them, and debase yourselves.

Never allow any person, under the pretended sanction of friendship, to be so familiar as to lose a proper respect for you. Never allow them to teaze you on any subject that is disagreeable, or where you have once taken your resolution. Many will tell you, that this reserve is inconsistent with the freedom which friendship allows. But a certain respect is as necessary in friendship as in love.

1　A male servant who dresses and attends to the personal needs of a gentleman.

Without it, you may be liked as a child, but you will never be beloved as an equal.

The temper and dispositions of the heart in your sex make you enter more readily and warmly into friendships than men. Your natural propensity to it is so strong, that you often run into intimacies which you soon have sufficient cause to repent of; and this makes your friendships so very fluctuating.

Another great obstacle to the sincerity as well as steadiness of your friendships, is the great clashing of your interests in the pursuits of love, ambition, or vanity. For these reasons, it would appear at first view more eligible for you to contract your friendships with the men. Among other obvious advantages of an easy intercourse between the two sexes, it occasions an emulation and exertion in each to excel and be agreeable: hence their respective excellencies are mutually communicated and blended. As their interests in no degree interfere, there can be no foundation for jealousy or suspicion of rivalship. The friendship of a man for a woman is always blended with a tenderness, which he never feels for one of his own sex, even where love is in no degree concerned. Besides, we are conscious of a natural title you have to our protection and good offices, and therefore we feel an additional obligation of honour to serve you, and to observe an inviolable secrecy, whenever you confide in us.

But apply these observations with great caution. Thousands of women of the best hearts and finest parts have been ruined by men who approached them under the specious name of friendship. But supposing a man to have the most undoubted honour, yet his friendship to a woman is so near a-kin to love, that if she be very agreeable in her person, she will probably very soon find a lover, where she only wished to meet a friend.—Let me here, however, warn you against that weakness so common among vain women, the imagination that every man who takes particular notice of you is a lover. Nothing can expose you more to ridicule, than the taking up a man on the suspicion of being your lover, who perhaps never once thought of you in that view, and giving yourselves those airs so common among silly women on such occasions.

There is a kind of unmeaning gallantry much practised by some men, which, if you have any discernment, you will find really very harmless. Men of this sort will attend you to public places, and be useful to you by a number of little observances, which those of a superior class do not so well understand, or have not leisure to regard, or perhaps are too proud to submit to. Look on the compliments of such men as words of course, which they repeat to every agreeable woman of their acquaintance. There is a familiarity they are apt to assume, which a proper dignity in your behaviour will be easily able to check.

There is a different species of men whom you may like as agreeable companions, men of worth, taste, and genius, whose conversation, in some respects, may be superior to what you generally meet with among your own sex. It will be foolish in you to deprive yourselves of an useful and agreeable acquaintance, merely because idle people say he is your lover. Such a man may like your company, without having any design on your person.

People whose sentiments, and particularly whose tastes, correspond, naturally like to associate together, although neither of them have the most distant view of any further connection. But as this similarity of minds often gives rise to a more tender attachment than friendship, it will be prudent to keep a watchful eye over yourselves, lest your hearts become too far engaged before you are aware of it. At the same time, I do not think that your sex, at least in this part of the world, have much of that sensibility which disposes to such attachments. What is commonly called love among you is rather gratitude, and a partiality to the man who prefers you to the rest of your sex; and such a man you often marry, with little of either personal esteem or affection. Indeed, without an unusual share of natural sensibility, and very peculiar good fortune, a woman in this country has very little probability of marrying for love.

It is a maxim laid down among you, and a very prudent one it is, That love is not to begin on your part, but is entirely to be the consequence of our attachment to you. Now, supposing a woman to have sense and taste, she will not find many men to whom she can possibly be supposed to bear any considerable share of esteem. Among these few, it is a very great chance if any of them distinguishes her particularly. Love, at least with us, is exceedingly capricious, and will not always fix where reason says it should. But supposing one of them should become particularly attached to her, it is still extremely improbable that he should be the man in the world her heart most approved of.

As, therefore, Nature has not given you that unlimited range in your choice which we enjoy, she has wisely and benevolently assigned to you a greater flexibility of taste on this subject. Some agreeable qualities recommend a gentleman to your common good liking and friendship. In the course of his acquaintance, he contracts an attachment to you. When you perceive it, it excites your gratitude; this gratitude rises into a preference, and this preference perhaps at last advances to some degree of attachment, especially if it meets with crosses and difficulties; for these, and a state of suspense, are very great incitements to attachment, and are the food of love in both sexes. If attachment was not excited in your sex in this manner, there is not one of a million of you that could ever marry with any degree of love.

A man of taste and delicacy marries a woman because he loves her more than any other. A woman of equal taste and delicacy marries him because she esteems him, and because he gives her that preference. But if a man unfortunately becomes attached to a woman whose heart is secretly pre-engaged, his attachment, instead of obtaining a suitable return, is particularly offensive; and if he persists to teaze her, he makes himself equally the object of her scorn and aversion.

The effects of love among men are diversified by their different tempers. An artful man may counterfeit every one of them so as easily to impose on a young girl of an open, generous, and feeling heart, if she is not extremely on her guard. The finest parts in such a girl may not always prove sufficient for her security. The dark and crooked paths of cunning are unsearchable, and inconceivable to an honourable and elevated mind.

The following, I apprehend, are the most genuine effects of an honourable passion among the men, and the most difficult to counterfeit. A man of delicacy often betrays his passion by his too great anxiety to conceal it, especially if he has little hopes of success. True love, in all its stages, seeks concealment, and never expects success. It renders a man not only respectful, but timid to the highest degree in his behaviour to the woman he loves. To conceal the awe he stands in of her, he may sometimes affect pleasantry, but it sits aukwardly on him, and he quickly relapses into seriousness, if not into dulness. He magnifies all her real perfections in his imagination, and is either blind to her failings, or converts them into beauties. Like a person conscious of guilt, he is jealous that every eye observes him; and to avoid this, he shuns all the little observances of common gallantry.

His heart and his character will be improved in every respect by his attachment. His manners will become more gentle, and his conversation more agreeable; but diffidence and embarrassment will always make him appear to disadvantage in the company of his mistress. If the fascination continue long, it will totally depress his spirit, and extinguish every active, vigorous, and manly principle of his mind. You will find this subject beautifully and pathetically painted in Thomson's Spring.[1]

---

1   James Thomson (1700–48). "Spring" (1728) is the first of four poems collected in *The Seasons* (1730). Thomson describes the effects of several kinds of romantic love. Of unrequited love, he says, "Thus the warm youth / Whom love deludes into his thorny wilds / Through flowery-tempting paths, or leads a life / Of fevered rapture or of cruel care— / His brightest aims extinguished all, and all / His lively moments running down to waste" (lines 1107–12).

Appendix B: Reviews of Conclusion of the Memoirs of Miss Sidney Bidulph

1. *The Monthly Review* 37 (1767): 238

In our account of the three preceding volumes of this work, published in 1761, (see *Review*, Vol. xxiv. p.260) we observed that the chief design of the lady to whom it is supposed the public are obliged for this ingenious romance, seems to have been *to draw tears from the reader, by distressing innocence and virtue as much as possible.*[1] In this design Mrs. S. appears to have persisted to the final conclusion of her work; and, in the perusal of these additional volumes, we have *felt* that she wanted not power to effect her purpose: for, indeed, the catastrophe of the *Arnold family* is a tale so extremely affecting and tender, that the reader who can peruse it without plenteously shedding tears over the distressful pages, must, surely, possess an heart of iron. But, as we have intimated in the former account of these Memoirs, it is much to be questioned if such pictures of human life, however justly they may be copied from nature, are well adapted to serve the cause of virtue: but this is a remark which we shall leave to the sagacity of our Readers.

2. From Alicia Lefanu, *Memoirs of the Life and Writings of Mrs. Frances Sheridan: With Remarks Upon a Late Life of the Right Hon. R.B. Sheridan* (G. and W.B. Whittaker, 1824)

[Alicia Lefanu (1791–1844) was the daughter of Elizabeth "Betsey" Sheridan and Henry Lefanu. She is the principal biographer of her grandmother, Frances Sheridan, and a novelist and poet in her own right. Her biography of Sheridan, published in 1824, is an account of the Sheridan family history and contains letters, extracts, and analyses of Frances Sheridan's works. Lefanu's long summaries of the novel have been redacted here.]

Mrs. Sheridan availed herself of this interval of returning health to renew her literary occupations. In the space of two years she conceived and executed the beautiful oriental tale of Nourjahad, and added two

---

1   Compare this praise to the now famous comment of Samuel Johnson, "I know not, Madame! That you have a right, upon moral principles, to make your readers suffer so much" (qtd. in Lefanu 113).

additional volumes to the novel of Sidney Biddulph,[1] which were not published until after her decease. To the last two volumes of Sidney Biddulph may be applied much of the criticism which was made upon the first part.

We meet our old acquaintances Sidney and Sir George again; with only these differences which we should observe in different portraits taken of the same individuals in youth or middle life. The additional personages introduced chiefly consist of the younger Faulkland, son of Orlando, the Audleys, the venerable Price (who was only introduced in the preceding volumes), and the sweet characters of Mrs. Arnold's two daughters.

By many persons, the second part of Sidney Biddulph was preferred to the first; as the production of a person who had acquired more extensive views of life, and a greater insight into character. Her talent for portrait painting had certainly improved; and the following character of the younger Faulkland given by his friend Sir Edward Audley, would not disgrace the most celebrated models of the country in which that style of writing was brought to perfection[2]....

In this portrait, sketched in France, there are characteristic touches that might be compared for discrimination with those of a De Retz, or La Bruyere.[3] It is in the deathbed of the pious and suffering heroine, in the closing scene of Sidney's eventful life, that the author sets her seal upon the whole, and illustrates her finely expressed moral, that it is in a future state of retribution alone, we can hope for an explanation of the ways of Providence, and that there we shall see all apparently unequal dispensations justified, and all seeming inconsistencies reduced to rule. When every worldly comfort vanishes from the sufferer's view, we see Religion, like a distant star, shining to light the pure and unpretending saint, to receive the rich reward long laid up for her virtues in Heaven. Though the last moments of Sidney are accompanied by every circumstance of bitterness that the ingratitude of those she loved, and the disappointment of her fondest hopes could impart, yet we find her firm and collected, and at the same time divested of none of her wonted tenderness. After a scene of most

---

1 It is common to see the first and last names of Sheridan's heroine variously misspelled in reviews and discussions, and Lefanu's biography is no exception.

2 See Audley's description of Falkland (83).

3 Jean François Paul de Gondi, Cardinal de Retz, was a French cardinal and memoirist (1613–79); Jean de La Bruyère (1645–96) was a French philosopher, and writer of *Caractères* (1688), which indicted the morality of famous men and women.

affecting pathos, which it would be injuring to attempt to abridge, she is in the midst of some affectionate injunctions to her remaining family when the sudden and awful, yet blessed transition from life to death, or rather from a living death to life, is thus powerfully and impressively described....

Surely it rather increases than detracts from the interest with which this passage must be read by every pious mind, to learn that it was not the creation of fancy, but the actual deathbed of a lady whom Mr. Richard Chamberlaine attended in the Isle of Man in his medical capacity, and communicated the affecting particular to his sister.

Select Bibliography and Works Cited

Armstrong, Nancy. *Desire and Domestic Fiction: A Political History of the Novel.* New York: Oxford UP, 1987.

Astell, Mary. *Astell: Political Writings.* Ed. Patricia Springborg. Cambridge UP, 1996.

Ballaster, Rosalind. *Seductive Forms: Women's Amatory Fiction from 1684–1740.* Oxford; New York: Clarendon P; Oxford UP, 1992.

Bowers, Toni. *The Politics of Motherhood: British Writing and Culture, 1680–1760.* New York: Cambridge UP, 1996.

The Common Errors in the Education of Children and Their Consequences; With The Methods to Remedy Them Consider'd Under the Following Heads. London: M. Cooper, 1744. Eighteenth Century Collections Online <http://gale.cengage.co.uk/product-highlights/history/eighteenth-century-collections-online.aspx>.

Davidson, Jenny. *Breeding: A Partial History of the Eighteenth Century.* New York: Columbia UP, 2009.

Doody, Margaret Anne. "Frances Sheridan: Morality and Annihilated Time." *Fetter'd or Free? British Women Novelists, 1670–1815.* Ed. Mary Anne Schofield and Cecilia Macheski. Athens: Ohio UP, 1986. 324–58.

Fitzer, Anna M. "Relating a Life: Alicia LeFanu's Memoirs of the Life and Writings of Mrs. Frances Sheridan." *Women's Writing* 15.1 (May 2008): 32–54.

Flint, Christopher. *Family Fictions: Narrative and Domestic Relations in Britain, 1688-1798.* Stanford, Calif: Stanford UP, 1998.

Garret, Nicole. "Frances Sheridan." *The Encyclopedia of British Literature, 1660–1789.* Ed. Jack Lynch and Gary Day. Wiley-Blackwell, forthcoming 2014. <www.literatureencyclopedia.com>.

Gonda, Caroline. *Reading Daughters' Fictions, 1709–1834: Novels and Society from Manley to Edgeworth.* Cambridge; New York: Cambridge UP, 1996.

Greenfield, Susan. *Mothering Daughters: Novels and the Politics of Family Romance, Frances Burney to Jane Austen.* Detroit: Wayne State UP, 2002.

Gregory, John. *A Father's Legacy to His Daughters.* Edinburgh: W. Strahan, T. Cadell, J. Balfour, and W. Creech, 1774.

Halifax, George. *The Ladies New-Years-Gift or, Advice to a Daughter.* Edinburgh: James Glen and Walter Cunningham, 1688.

Hardy, John. "Johnson and Don Bellianis." *Review of English Studies* 17.67 (1966): 297–99.

Harris, Marla. "Strategies of Silence: Sentimental Heroinism and Narrative Authority in Novels by Frances Sheridan, Frances Burney, Elizabeth Inchbald, and Hannah More." Dissertation. Brandeis University, 1992.

Hogan, Robert Goode and Jerry C. Beasley. Introduction to *The Plays of Frances Sheridan*. Newark: U of Delaware P, 1984. 1–38.

Holloway, Laura. "The Mother of Sheridan." *Mothers of Great Men and Women*. Baltimore: Wharton, 1883. 360–73.

Jones, Vivien. *Women in the Eighteenth Century: Constructions of Femininity*. London; New York: Routledge, 1990.

Kowaleski-Wallace, Elizabeth. *Their Fathers' Daughters: Hannah More, Maria Edgeworth, and Patriarchal Complicity*. New York: Oxford UP, 1991.

Kuti, Elizabeth. "Rewriting Frances Sheridan," *Eighteenth-Century Ireland/Iris an dá chultúr* (1996): 120–28.

Lee, Anna Maria. *Eminent Female Writers of All Ages and Countries*. Philadelphia: John Grigg, 1827.

Lefanu, Alicia. *Memoirs of the Life and Writings of Mrs. Frances Sheridan*. London: G. and W.B. Whittaker, 1824.

Lemmings, David. "Marriage and the Law in the Eighteenth Century: Hardwicke's Marriage Act of 1753." *The Historical Journal* 39.2 (1996): 339–60.

Lewis, Judith Schneid. *In the Family Way: Childbearing in the British Aristocracy, 1760-1860*. New Brunswick: Rutgers UP, 1986.

Locke, John. *Some Thoughts Concerning Education: By John Locke, Esq.* London: A. and J. Churchill, 1693.

Nelson, T.G.A. *Children, Parents, and the Rise of the Novel*. Newark: U of Delaware P, 1995.

Nicoll, Allardyce. *The Garrick Stage: Theatres and Audience in the Eighteenth Century*. Athens, GA: U of Georgia P, 1980.

Oliver, Kathleen M. "Frances Sheridan's Faulkland, the Silenced, Emasculated, Ideal Male." *Studies in English Literature, 1500-1900* 43.3 (2003): 683–700.

Perry, Ruth. *Novel Relations: The Transformation of Kinship in English Literature and Culture, 1748-1818*. Cambridge; New York: Cambridge UP, 2004.

Reeve, Clara. *The Progress of Romance*, vol 2. Colchester: Keymer, 1785.

Richardson, Alan, ed. *Three Oriental Tales: Complete Texts with Introduction, Historical Contexts, Critical Essays*. Boston: Houghton Mifflin, 2002.

Richardson, Samuel. *Familiar Letters on Important Occasions*. London:

J. Osborne, J. Rivington, J. Leake, et al, 1741. Literature Online
<http://lion.chadwyck.com>.

Richardson, Samuel, and Anna Laetitia Barbauld. *The Correspondence of Samuel Richardson, Author of Pamela, Clarissa, and Sir Charles Grandison*. New York: AMS Press, 1966.

Roulston, Christine. *Narrating Marriage in Eighteenth-Century England and France*. Burlington, VT: Ashgate, 2010.

Sheridan, Frances. *Cibber and Sheridan: Or, The Dublin Miscellany* (Dublin: Peter Wilson, 1743).

———. *Conclusion of the Memoirs of Miss Sidney Bidulph, As Prepared for the Press By the Late Editor of the Former Part. Volume III*. Dublin: J. Dodsley, 1767.

———. *The Memoirs of Miss Sidney Bidulph*. Ed. Heidi Hutner & Nicole Garret. Peterborough, ON: Broadview P, 2011.

Spacks, Patricia Meyer. "Oscillations of Sensibility." *New Literary History* 25.3 (1994): 505–20.

———. *Novel Beginnings: Experiments in Eighteenth-Century English Fiction*. New Haven, CT: Yale UP, 2006.

Stone, Lawrence. *The Family, Sex and Marriage in England 1500–1800*. London: Penguin, 1990.

Todd, Janet M. *The Sign of Angellica: Women, Writing, and Fiction, 1660–1800*. New York: Columbia UP, 1989.

Traver, John C. "The Inconclusive Memoirs of Miss Sidney Bidulph: Problems of Poetic Justice, Closure, and Gender." *Eighteenth Century Fiction* 20.1 (2008): 35–60.

———. "The Sense of Amending: Closure, Justice, and the Eighteenth-Century Fictional Sequel." Dissertation. Notre Dame, 2007.

Turnbull, Gordon. "Boswell's London Journal, 1762–1763, and Frances Sheridan's *The Discovery*: Imagining the Maternal." *Imagining Selves: Essays in Honor of Patricia Meyer Spacks*. Ed. Rivka Swenson, Elise Lauterbach, & Patricia Ann Meyer Spacks. Newark: U of Delaware P, 2008.

Watkins, John. *Memoir of the Public and Private Life of ... Richard Brinsley Sheridan, with a Particular Account of His Family and Connexions*. London: John Watkins, 1818.

Whyte, S. *Miscellanea Nova*. Dublin: Robert Marchbank, 1800.

Wilkes, Wetenhall. *A Letter of Genteel and Moral Advice to a Young Lady*. 1740. London: C. Hitch and L. Hawes, 1760.

Wilson, Mona. *These Were Muses*. Port Washington, NY: Kennikat P, 1970.

Wollstonecraft, Mary. *A Vindication of the Rights of Woman* (1792). Mineola, NY: Courier Dover Publications, 1996.

from the publisher

A name never says it all, but the word "broadview" expresses a good deal of the philosophy behind our company. We are open to a broad range of academic approaches and political viewpoints. We pay attention to the broad impact book publishing and book printing has in the wider world; we began using recycled stock more than a decade ago, and for some years now we have used 100% recycled paper for most titles. As a Canadian-based company we naturally publish a number of titles with a Canadian emphasis, but our publishing program overall is internationally oriented and broad-ranging. Our individual titles often appeal to a broad readership too; many are of interest as much to general readers as to academics and students.

Founded in 1985, Broadview remains a fully independent company owned by its shareholders—not an imprint or subsidiary of a larger multinational.

If you would like to find out more about Broadview and about the books we publish, please visit us at **www.broadviewpress.com**. And if you'd like to place an order through the site, we'd like to show our appreciation by extending a special discount to you: by entering the code below you will receive a 20% discount on purchases made through the Broadview website.

Discount code: **broadview20%**

Thank you for choosing Broadview.

Please note: this offer applies only to sales of bound books within the United States or Canada.